*Donna —
Thanks so much
on-going support!
Miss seeing you!
All the best.
— Steve*

The Student
A GIDON ARONSON THRILLER

Also by Stephen J. Gordon
In the Name of God
Confluence

The Student
A GIDON ARONSON THRILLER

Stephen J. Gordon

Apprentice House Press
Loyola University Maryland

Copyright © 2022 by Stephen J. Gordon

All rights reserved. No part of this book may be reproduced or transmitted in any form or by any means, electronic or mechanical, including photocopy, recording, or any information storage and retrieval system, without prior permission from the publisher (except by reviewers who may quote brief passages).

This is a work of fiction. Characters, places, names, and incidents are either the product of the author's imagination or are used fictitiously to facilitate the story.

First Edition
Printed in the United States of America
Hardcover ISBN: 978-1-62720-354-8
Paperback ISBN: 978-1-62720-355-5
Ebook ISBN: 978-1-62720-356-2

Cover design by Paige Akins
Author photograph by Sophie Bitran

Published by Apprentice House

Apprentice House Press
Loyola University Maryland

Apprentice House
Loyola University Maryland
4501 N. Charles Street
Baltimore, MD 21210
410.617.5265 • 410.617.2198 (fax)
www.ApprenticeHouse.com
info@ApprenticeHouse.com

*To Becky and the "Kids,"
I couldn't have done this
or so many other things without you.*

1

I was late coming home. Four months late. And the tardiness, if that word even applied at this point, was definitely my fault. Katie and I had made a deal and I had broken it. Pure and simple. She was pissed, and rightly so.

As I drove down the coastal highway, halfway around the world from her with the Mediterranean to my right, I shook my head at my own shortcomings. After she had gone back to the States, I was only supposed to stay two more weeks in Israel, but something unforeseen had come up. My friend and former CO invited me to temporarily rejoin my old unit, the Israeli Special Operations group *Sayeret Matkal*, as they worked on counterterrorism training and more. I had just come off an intense operation with them, and he'd see that further training would be part of my reserve duty. That offer shot to hell my two-week extension with Katie.

In my own defense, I did speak to her about it, and she said it was okay. But that was before either of us knew it would stretch out for months.

My relationship with Katie was still relatively new by long-term standards – almost a year – though we had bonded at first sight. She was one of the most intuitive people I had ever known, plus she had a dazzling smile and thoughtful, intelligent eyes. Katie was my confidant and friend. My partner.

I looked into the azure sky to see a flock of birds descending to the water. Out beyond them, halfway to the horizon, was a white sailing sloop heading south, paralleling my own course.

The mid-October sky was completely clear. Even the normal inland humidity was gone. It would have been nice to be have been on that sailing sloop way offshore, thinking only of the wind and the sea, not reflecting on my broken word, or my recent op.

* * *

We had inserted into Syria along the beach just south of Tartus. It was 3 a.m. on a night with a crescent moon. Our two Zodiacs, each with a seven-man Israeli team, put ashore without a sound, thanks to the silent motors. Twelve men came onto the deserted beach, leaving behind a comrade who would take his small vessel back out to sea to wait for our return. The lights of Tartus could be seen five miles up the shore, but the twelve of us were alone, and we moved up onto the beach toward a small road that ran parallel to the beach.

With the sand crunching under my boots, I grabbed a quick look to each side. All save one of us were dressed as Islamic fighters in camouflage uniforms and black balaclavas with green headbands, emblazoned with white jihadist sayings. The single soldier not attired as the rest was Yakov. He was dressed as a very attractive young Arab woman – if you could tell, as one could only see his face since he was wearing a *hijab*. Thanks to some padding, though, Yakov had quite a figure. He carried a compact Tavor assault rifle under his clothing on his back, while nine of us, including me, openly carried suppressed M4s. The remaining two team members had AK47s, which was most authentic to the Islamic fighter dress code. All had night vision goggles.

No words were exchanged as our group made its way toward the darkened road. We waited by a small depression along the edge of the semi-paved, rock-strewn street. Within a minute, a filthy white Citroen van came to a stop twenty feet from us. I recognized the driver from a briefing a week ago. He had arrived two days previously to secure the transportation. We all climbed into the vehicle, front and back. For the next twenty minutes we drove over potholed Syrian streets, often swerving through roads, alleys really, and past immaculate homes that abutted slum housing. Virtually no one was outside at this time of night, neither driving nor walking the streets.

Finally, the van pulled to a stop as we approached a row of dilapidated apartment buildings. The twelve of us stowed our night vision equipment, emerged from the van and began walking. Around the corner and a few streets up was a building Israeli Intelligence had been watching for a number of weeks. It was a building made of a crumbling concrete exterior that took up a small city block. Inside was a school for young boys. In the basement was what we believed to be an immense collection of weapons brought in from Iran with a destination of Southern Lebanon or the Gaza Strip. Ordinarily, the Israeli Air Force would have flattened the building, but with a school inside, complete with living space for young students, an air strike was impossible. Typical terrorist tactic: hide among civilians, especially women and children. We needed to destroy the weapons without collateral damage.

We fanned out into predetermined groups. The street we had chosen was perhaps three car widths wide. Grocery stores, apartment buildings, even a bank or two lined the trash-strewn road. The smell of garbage and urine hung in the air. The only source of light was the occasional bare street light and the crescent moon. We had debated about using our night-vision goggles, but the sight of a unit of men – and one "woman" – peering through NVGs and carrying weapons would trigger an alarm.

Command had decided on the rules of engagement. If we came across unarmed civilians, they would be bound and gagged and rendered unconscious with an injection of drugs. If we came across anyone carrying a firearm or had a firearm within reach, they would be shot with our suppressed weapons. Fortunately, the ten-minute walk to our destination was without incident. We split into two units.

My team stayed put, while the other team went around the block to approach the building from the other end of the street. Their unit had a *kallah*, a sharpshooter.

I gave the other unit time to circle the block, and then as I had taken point, peered around the edge of a corner café to see the school entrance halfway up the block and across the street. The building appeared completely dark. Two armed terrorists, dressed not all that differently from us, stood in front, guarding the entrance. We knew more Islamic fighters were in various rooms on the first floor. The cache of arms, we guessed, was in the basement. Intelligence had told us that the children were on the second and third floors in their sleeping quarters, and that two sentries were on the roof every night, occasionally peering over the sides.

I nodded to our "femme fatale," Yakov, and to the man who would be his companion, Ori. The pair rounded the corner and slowly walked up the street holding hands. As they approached the target building, their religiously forbidden display of affection drew the expected reaction of the guards. Within ten seconds they stepped away from the door. And then two things happened simultaneously. The sharpshooter from the other unit fired his suppressed M4, taking out both guards, and a Sayeret Matkal sniper on a slightly higher building a quarter of a mile away shot both sentries on the roof.

The two teams converged at the door and went to work. The guards' bodies were pulled into shadows and covered with a black tarp. We all re-donned our night vision gear, and a new soldier at point tested the front door; it was open. Both teams filed in and spread out. My squad cleared the rooms to the right. Two Islamic soldiers were sleeping on the floor, Kalashnikovs besides them. Each was shot twice. We rounded a corner to come face-to-face with a bearded man stumbling, half asleep, pulling up his pants. He had a pistol holstered on his right side. He was shot in the head. These were all men who'd use the children upstairs as human shields. None of my men hesitated. We walked through two empty classrooms. A room in the back of the building had a light on – a single bare light bulb hung from the ceiling. Two men were sipping thick coffee. You could tell, for the syrupy, sweet smell filled the room. Rifles were within reach of each of them. The soldiers were shot as the coffee cups were still at their lips.

In twenty seconds the entire first floor was cleared of terrorists.

A team went downstairs to check on the weapons' hoard while the rest of us moved upstairs.

On the second floor there were two bedrooms filled with cots and sleeping boys. A man sleeping near the door must have sensed us, and his eyes popped open. He saw Yakov in his *hijab*. In the split second he took to perceive the image, Yakov shot him with a suppressed Sig Sauer. There was a similar cough from a suppressed pistol in the room to our right. Ten seconds later, the second floor was clear.

The third floor was a virtual repeat of the second floor: boys' sleeping quarters, male guards. The guards met the same fate as their second floor companions.

In our earpieces came the word from the team in the basement. They had found room after room filled with RPGs, crates of AK 47s, ammunition, explosives, and long crates of medium range Iranian missiles. There was also a room with computers, maps, and papers.

The team moved into the next phase. While two men rechecked each floor for hiding places – false walls and niches cut into flooring – two other men raised their night vision goggles and went about waking the children. They told them in perfect Arabic that they had to leave the building now, that Sunni fighters – the opposition – were coming this very moment to storm the building. After a moment, the team members began to motivate the boys by screaming at them. They all ran down the stairs. Some of the children began to cry, especially when catching sight of bodies at their feet. But they all left the building.

The final team members, including me, grabbed laptops, broke open computers for their hard drives, and scooped up all the documents we could. Three others set explosive charges among the ordinance. Once everyone checked in, we left the building the way we had come. The screams of the children who were now in the street had begun to wake neighbors. Lights appeared in various windows throughout the block. We weren't worried. All eyes were on them, not us. We went back down the narrow street to the café corner I had used as a vantage point less than twenty minutes ago. As we were climbing back into the filthy white van, the charges in the basement went off. The windows of the first floor lit up as if filled by flashes of lightning. Cascading explosions thundered across the neighborhood. Twin additional eruptions rocked the earth under our feet as more of the cache went up.

The night sky was no longer night. First there were streams of white phosphorus shooting heavenward, followed by flames, and then finally smoke, as the building collapsed upon itself, leaving neighboring structures virtually untouched.

Our driver had plotted a backroads route to our exfil point at the beach. Twice we had to stop and douse our headlights as emergency vehicles hollered past. Once at the shore, our driver merely slowed as we reached the edge of the beach, and then left once we had poured from the van. He, and the sniper who had protected us from on high, would make their way back to Israel on their own. We moved down the beach to the waiting Zodiacs. We climbed in, carrying the reinforced bags with our treasure of documents and computers. As we skipped over the water, away from the beach and further into the Mediterranean, I looked back at the glow in the sky we were responsible for. It was beginning to die, but the columns of dense, black smoke continued to rise to heaven. I turned back toward the bow to see the horizon above the Mediterranean. The sky was dark blue, but the water was even darker. In a few minutes we turned south to parallel the coast and rendezvous with a missile boat.

* * *

The road sign announcing the approaching coastal town of Netanya pushed away the image of the Mediterranean night sky. It brought me back to Highway 2, heading south in the late afternoon. I was on my way to the airport and home. With my promise to Katie of only a two week stay echoing in my head, I was worried about what waited for me on the other side of the Atlantic.

I had never done anything like this in a relationship before: take advantage. I hoped Katie and I could weather it. While our phone conversations over the past month had become strained, I needed to talk to her face-to-face to explain.

As I sped down the coast, my desire to get to the airport as quickly as possible was being delayed by a single stop. I grumbled aloud at the unwanted detour: a meeting with David Amit of Israel's General Security Services, the Shin Bet. Earlier in the day, while still on-base and changing out of my uniform, I had received a call from him.

"Gidon," Amit had said, "I need to speak with you."

"Okay."

"In person."

I folded my green army fatigue top, holding it up in front of me. "Sorry, David. I'm on my way to Ben Gurion." Israel's airport just south of Tel Aviv.

"Meet me for ten minutes at a café along the beach near the Crowne Plaza."

"Ten minutes in Tel Aviv will be an hour out of my way."

"Gidon, it's important. I'd consider it a *tova*." A favor. "And I'll make sure the plane doesn't leave without you."

My eyebrows went up. I shouldn't have been surprised at his holding the plane offer, or maybe it was just bullshit. But, always good to have the Shin Bet owe you.

So, about forty-five minutes after I had started out, I parked curbside not far from the Tel Aviv marina, and headed to a small café along the promenade that separated the pricey hotels from the Tel Aviv beaches. Amit and another man were sitting across from each other at a small square table outside a café-bistro. Lone cups of coffee sat untouched in front of them. I sat with the Mediterranean and the low-angled sun at my back. They'd both have to stare into the bright sky to look at me. Amit was to my left and the other man to my right. They wore open collar, dress shirts. Typical Israeli style. Amit had on his signature black wire-rimmed glasses and furrowed brow. He nodded to me. I looked from him to the other fellow. He was clean shaven, had a round face, thinning hair, and wrinkles around dark eyes that casually assessed me. His face was familiar, but I couldn't place it.

The Shin Bet man made the introductions: "Gidon, this is Idan Gelvar."

I smiled, hearing the name, but not in amusement. "No. *Ani mitzta'air*. I'm not interested." I slid my chair back and stood up.

"It's not what you think," Amit countered.

"Really?"

The Shin Bet man nodded, turned his right hand palm up to my vacated chair, "Please."

I retook my seat, but watched the third man. With the name now matching his face, I knew who he was. He was Deputy Director of the Mossad.

"I'm not here in an official capacity. It's personal," the man with the dark eyes said in a voice that had the tenor of an old singer. The Shin Bet and the Mossad. I didn't want to be here.

Amit sensed my uneasiness. "Please hear what Idan has to say."

I looked at the man who was tasked with overseeing a good deal of Israel's foreign intelligence operations.

Idan Gelvar began, "Amit told me..." I was waiting for him to say, "*All about you*," but instead said, "you'd be the man who could help me." He paused for a moment, looked down at his coffee cup, and rotated it as if considering what to say. I had no doubt he already knew what he wanted to ask. He turned back to me. "You live in Maryland, correct? Baltimore?"

"I do."

"You're familiar with Johns Hopkins University, not the hospital or the medical school."

"The undergraduate school. I know where it is." I knew the campus – beautiful, in a park-like setting near the Baltimore Museum of Art. It had a mixture of old and new buildings. Strong programs in computer science, biomedical engineering, math and physics. But, I wasn't giving the Deputy Director of the Mossad more information than I needed to, or what he probably already knew.

"There's been a rise of anti-Israel sentiment on U.S. college campuses," he went on. "You already know this, I'm sure. It's a concern. On some campuses there have even been violent clashes between pro-Israel and anti-Israel groups…"

Was checking on campus unrest part of his purview, watching for terrorist recruitment?

He continued: "Columbia, Berkeley, schools in Texas and the midwest. Duke, Northwestern."

I looked at Amit, uncertain where they were going with this. Did they want me to keep an eye on radical activists?

The Mossad man continued: "It really is a test for the U.S. First Amendment. Our Ambassador was speaking at University of California in Irvine and four students shouted him down. They were finally arrested for violating the Ambassador's freedom of speech."

"And you know of a conflict at Hopkins? Really? I can't be an asset there, reporting to you."

"No, no. I wouldn't ask you that," the Deputy Director of the Mossad said.

Of course he would.

He reached into his pocket and pulled out a photo. Without even looking at it, he handed it to me. It was a head and shoulders two-shot of the Mossad man and a young woman, perhaps twenty. In the shot, both were dressed casually: Gelvar in a maroon polo shirt, and the young woman in a teal tank top. The woman's dark hair had been pulled back in a pony-tail to reveal an angular jaw and bright, brown eyes. She was smiling right into the lens. Gelvar and the young woman shared the same jawline.

"That's Noa, my niece...my sister's daughter. She's a senior at Hopkins, and I want you to keep an eye on her."

"Keep an eye on her. What does that mean?" A second went by. "What's she into?"

"Nothing. As far as I know."

He probably already had an entire dossier on her.

"Nothing," I repeated his line. "So, you're asking me to…"

"Check in on her from time to time. Make sure she's okay."

I looked from Gelvar to Amit and back to Gelvar. "Really, that's it, just look in on her?" I had no relationship with this person. No pretext to establish a rapport. Did he want me to follow her around and check on whom she interacted with?

"Really?" I repeated, considering standing up again. "Just check in and be sure she's okay?"

"The United States is a *bal-a-gan*." He used the Hebrew word for mess or chaos. "Kids going into schools, shooting teachers and other students, crazy people shooting innocent people in shopping malls, military officers opening fire on soldiers on a base…"

It was an interesting perspective from an intelligence officer of a country that fights terrorism every day. But I understood. In a way he had a handle on Israel's enemies. At his disposal were the resources and effectiveness of his country's security agencies. This was different. It was beyond his official reach. Still, check in on his niece? That was it? I began to shake my head.

"I promise that's all it is," Gelvar said. "There's no operation here. I'd send a team if there were. This is personal. I'm her uncle. I worry."

I looked into the Mossad man's dark eyes and couldn't tell a thing. If that's all this was, a loving uncle wanting to be sure his niece is safe and sound, I could find a way to check in on her. But I still didn't buy it.

"Gidon," Amit, my Shin Bet friend to my left said, "really. That's all this is. It's a personal favor. Not business."

I looked at Amit. The two of us have had our moments of distrust during missions, mainly in how much I was told or not told. In the end, though, we were always square.

"Show him the other picture," the Shin Bet man said to Gelvar.

As Gelvar handed me a 5 by 7 photo, it was the Shin Bet man who remarked, "Making contact with Noa won't be as difficult as you might think."

I looked down at the picture, a group shot photographed during an outdoor nighttime party on a deck or a patio. Five young people were in the picture, a young man and a woman sitting at a table and three people behind them. In the back row, Noa, the Mossad man's niece, was on the right with that undeniable jawline, then a blonde woman with short hair and big eyes on the left, and a curly-haired, young man in his mid-twenties between them. The man in the middle had an arm around each girl. I knew the young man, and looked up at Amit.

"That's Jonathan, your student, isn't it?" Amit said.

I looked at the picture again. It was indeed Jon, my star student who was minding my shop while I was halfway around the world. Amit had met him more than a year ago for just a few minutes. It was impressive that he remembered my right-hand assistant.

"Your student seems to hang out with Hopkins kids," Gelvar commented.

"Jonathan's never met a young woman he didn't like, or who didn't like him." I looked at his picture again. It was true. When Jon broke up with a girl there were never hard feelings on either side. I was going to ask where Gelvar got this picture, but it didn't really matter. I completely believed my star student and friend would hang out with Hopkins students.

"So," the man from Mossad asked once again, "will you check in on my niece for me?"

"*Ulay.*" Perhaps. "I'll assess the situation and let you know." I didn't know why I was qualifying my answer. I knew I was going to do it.

2

The United flight from Tel Aviv arrived into Philadelphia International at 5:30 in the morning, but my connection didn't get into Baltimore until almost nine. It was a relief being off the plane, but an increasing sense of dread accompanied each step down the long concourse. There was no shaking it. It wasn't the conversation with the two security men in Israel – that was halfway around the world – but here, now, there was the imminent reality that I had made a horrible mistake with Katie that may be unfixable. Instead of walking into her arms beyond security, there'd just be emptiness, and echoes of other people being welcomed home. Of course, I had called with arrival information, but she couldn't pick me up, saying she needed to be at work. At that point the phone conversation dropped into a long pause, and the woeful feeling began to take root. Four months earlier, Katie would have made arrangements and would have been at the airport with her beautiful smile and a tight embrace. Now, it seemed, she didn't want to see me.

As I walked down the seemingly ever-expanding concourse, I followed a twenty-something couple wearing flip-flops, shorts, T-shirts, and matching maroon backpacks. On my left was the Chesapeake Café, where more than a few business-attired travelers were getting an early start to the day with drinks in hand. To the right, floor-to-ceiling windows showed several empty airplane parking slots. I angled over to a row of seats, dropped my own backpack onto one of black chairs, and stretched my back. Out on the tarmac, a sleek JetBlue E190 taxied toward a runway. I picked up my backpack and walked on.

I stayed to the right of center, keeping eyes on the people in front of me, as well as on folks approaching. In a short while, the grouping around me surged forward, like we were being pumped down an artery. I passed a pair of men in jackets and ties, walked past a fellow in a gray hoodie and Orioles ball cap, and then two female flight attendants, wheeling small overnight cases.

As I continued toward the terminal and baggage claim, a loudspeaker recording announced the now ubiquitous "For security reasons, baggage left unattended may be removed and destroyed." In Israel that was code for being blown up. Probably here, too. Still, I had to smile at the euphemism.

About halfway down the pier I caught sight of an electronics gadget shop on the left, and without breaking stride veered over to it. A handful of customers, mostly younger than me, were scanning the merchandise on the shelves, displays, and at the checkout counter. I got as far as a swivel rack of cell phone cases and ear buds in the entryway. I stood half in the store and half out, and rotated the rack, examining the offerings. Beyond the display was a clear view of people walking past.

A granny holding the hand of her granddaughter crossed my field of view, moving toward the exit. An electric cart with only a driver aboard passed by next. It had a rotating yellow light atop a post rising out of the rear bumper. Seemed to me the warning light should have been up front.

A moment later, a family of four walked by, the dad carrying a crying blond-haired boy who couldn't have been more than five.

I pulled a package of red earbuds from the rack, read the back of the box, and then looked out on the concourse again.

Across the way, a steady stream of outbound passengers moved toward their various gates. They seemed more determined, more focused in their strides than the people heading toward baggage claim.

Made sense. Probably more anxious or excited about getting to their waiting areas.

The man I had passed earlier in the gray hoodie and Orioles cap approached a Nature's Kitchen Café across from me and stopped in front of a refrigerated display of premade sandwiches. He picked up a shrink-wrapped sandwich, looked at it, then replaced it, to take another, only to put that one back. He did this several times.

A college-aged young man being pushed in a wheelchair crossed in front of me. He had a boot on his right leg.

The man in the Orioles cap at the café had moved on to the drink display and did his pick-up and put-back routine again.

Maybe he was looking for something in particular. Nothing wrong with that.

A TSA officer in a blue shirt and navy pants came into the gadget shop and stood on the other side of the display rack next to me. I nodded to him, and he nodded back, cordially.

Across the way there was something odd in the way the man in the Orioles cap was positioned. He was half facing the refrigerated case and half facing me: sort of doing to me what I was doing to him. Watching.

I returned the $100 dollar earbuds to their hook, and then headed back onto the concourse toward the terminal. After about ten steps, I stopped, felt my right breast pocket, shook my head, and pivoted back in the direction I had just come. The man in the Orioles cap had left the café and had started walking again toward the exit, essentially thirty feet behind me, but stopped when I did my 180. I looked past him, and continued hustling, retracing my steps, but now in the oncoming pedestrian flow. A group of businessmen and women split off to avoid walking into me. I moved out of the exiting stream, sidestepping a disheveled, swarthy complexioned man with a five o'clock shadow. He could have been Middle Eastern, but maybe not. He was dressed in a gray herringbone sport coat with an open-collared blue shirt and dark pants. His jet black hair was a bit tousled. The look worked well. He

The Student

could have been a young college professor. That projection vanished, though, as soon as I passed him. He had bent over to tie his shoe, and as he leaned over, something pressed out against the inside of his coat near the small of his back. It could have been a rolled-up magazine in a back pocket, but it wasn't. I had seen too many of those bulges. It was the butt of a handgun.

What the hell. Thoughts of Katie, dread, relationship screw-ups, and the day ahead were now long gone. The man in the herringbone sport coat had bent over to give the impression of doing something natural or casual. He had been behind me, and now that I had switched directions he had to do something to keep me in sight.

Maybe he was law enforcement, and really was just tying his shoe.

I walked a few more feet, suddenly stopped, felt my breast pocket again, and came out with my boarding envelope and baggage claim ticket. I smiled, shook my head to myself, and put the envelope away. I turned around once again, and began walking at a faster pace toward the main terminal and baggage claim, passing the young "professor." A few seconds later, I saw the man in the Orioles cap at a sunglasses hutch. He hadn't made much progress; he must have stopped at every shop, waiting for me.

This was crazy. There was no reason why anyone would have me under surveillance. I hadn't been in the States in months. Could it have been my recent work? The op in Syria? I also had worked in France, Italy, and Great Britain. Maybe someone had recognized me in one of those locations. Had terrorists taken up revenge killings? Were suppressors at the end of their gun barrels, and all they needed was a secluded spot? This team of two would be the minimum for this, but doable.

A few months in counterterrorism training and operations, and I was seeing things.

I stopped at a Hudson News store and bought a large chocolate candy bar with nuts. While handing the cashier a five-dollar bill, my peripheral vision registered the man in the Orioles cap stepping into a Starbucks across the way. Once again, he was half-turned to me. I pocketed the change from the purchase, thanked the cashier, and then unhesitatingly walked across to the coffee shop. The man in the hoodie and the Orioles cap was now waiting in line, alongside a display case, looking forward and holding a wrapped wedge of pound cake. I cut in front of him.

"Sorry," I apologized, not trying to make eye contact for more than a second, and reached across his torso for a bottle of orange juice. I caught a whiff of the man's body odor, as well as a glimpse of a gun over his left hip. I looked at the bottle in my hand, as if trying to decide something, put it back on the shelf, and walked away.

Who were these guys? They weren't airport security. Despite the undercover appearance, they just didn't have the look. This man's eyes were clear, but weren't particularly determined, and in fact, he seemed nervous. This guy also didn't have an earpiece, though that was far from definitive of anything. They weren't Mossad or Shin Bet keeping an eye on me. Not Slavic, Eastern European, or Russian. Two guys hired to follow me or to rob me? And now at least one of them knew that I knew.

The concourse angled sharply to the left, skirting the incoming security station, and in a matter of feet, intersected with the main terminal. In front of me, escalators and stairs disappeared down to the lower level. I scanned the waiting crowd in the off-chance Katie had changed her mind and had wanted to surprise me, but of course, she wasn't there. I inadvertently sighed and headed down the steps.

The lower level was much more stark than the upper deck. The walls were all painted white, and only had an occasional Baltimore sightseeing poster as decoration: Fort McHenry, Ravens Stadium, the National Aquarium, the Baltimore Symphony Orchestra. Except for baggage pick-up, there wasn't much to see. A monitor noted that my baggage carousel was two stations to the left, where the conveyer had already begun circulating luggage. In a matter of minutes I pulled off my medium-sized gunmetal gray suitcase, and headed back toward the stairs. The man with the tousled hair and sport coat, not surprisingly, was sitting on the steps; I couldn't spot his friend in the Orioles cap. Maybe he had gone outside to wait for me to cover my egress.

I passed the man who I knew had a gun tucked in the small of his back and kept walking. He didn't look at me, and I kept my eyes straight ahead. With my suitcase handle in my left hand, I continued walking. I ambled around the stairwell toward an alcove. Inside the recessed area the passage turned left, leading to a series of unmarked locked doors. I parked my suitcase and backpack off to the side and walked back to the first turn. This was just off the main hallway, so hopefully, the men wouldn't feel threatened and approach with weapons out. My breathing settled and I loosened my shoulders and rotated my head to relax. A moment or two passed.

After twenty seconds the two men came for me. They were wearing rubber-soled shoes, but I knew they were close.

They came around the corner next to each other and froze when they saw me. They were quite a pair: one dressed like a professor, the other ready to watch a ball game on his couch. Both needed a shave and both were younger than I had first noticed. Perhaps mid-twenties. The Orioles fan was to my left, the man with the tousled hair to my right.

"Hi, guys," I said. "What's up?"

Both men began reaching inside their jackets. The man with the sport coat and expensive haircut had his gun in the small of his back. It would take him a split second longer to draw. The man in the Orioles cap beside him was reaching for the weapon on his belt. I pounded him twice in rapid succession along the corner of his right eye. He went over and down. I probably had broken, or at least chipped, the edge of his eye socket.

I turned on his partner. His right hand was reaching behind him. I kicked him just above the groin, rolling my hip forward to send him crashing backwards and down. Both men were sprawled on the ground, but only the guy I kicked was moaning. His friend was unconscious.

The altercation was over in under three seconds.

A second passed, and then in a low voice, I asked mostly to myself, "So who are you guys?"

The "professor" in the sports coat man wasn't articulating anything coherent. His eyes were screwed shut in pain; he'd likely be urinating blood for a while. I walked over to his unconscious partner. This had to be quick before someone turned this way. Bending over the still figure, I spread open his navy hoodie to see the gun I had spotted earlier. I froze. It was a Sig Sauer in a molded carbon fiber holster. Not a typical street weapon and carry. Special Ops and law enforcement used Sigs.

I continued to go through his pockets. In a minute I had the man's ID in hand. It was a folded, two-part ID: photo ID on the top and badge on the bottom. The card read *Federal Bureau of Investigation. Paul L. Landers, Special Agent.*

I looked at the man's face, which had already started turning black and blue around his right eye and cheek. I turned to the other Fed who was supine and still moaning, and then back again to the ID in my hands.

"Oh, crap."

3

"The first charge will be 'Assaulting Federal Officers.'"

The man who made the statement was standing a few feet to my left, looking down at me. I was seated along the shorter length of a dark laminate-topped table in a windowless, almost bare room. The Special Agent who was speaking was about forty, tall, and had the sloping shoulders of an athlete. He looked pretty solid, and wasn't the attorney-law enforcement type I had expected from the FBI. He did, however, have piercing blue eyes. Despite the icy gaze, I didn't wither, nor did I challenge him by locking eyes. I stayed calm. I wasn't the bad guy here, even though I did take down his men.

"Are your men dead?" The question came from my right.

Nate, my close friend, was leaning forward slightly as he addressed the Federal officer. Nate was about fifty, with more salt than pepper hair growing out from an almost shaved head. His hairline, as much as you could see of it, was receding, and that quarter inch of hair must have been driving him crazy. My friend was in a gray blazer, with a paisley tie loosened at the neck. Nate was the one who had brought me into the Federal Building. We thought that since he was a Baltimore homicide captain, he had the gravitas and reputation to keep me from immediately being thrown into a Federal holding cell. It worked, but it also took his strong insistence that I had reasonable cause for my attack on the Federal agents.

"Are they dead?" Nate repeated, calmly.

Special Agent Edwin Conniker looked at my friend, the cop. "No, they're alive."

"Are they in critical condition?" Nate followed up, still calm, still softly.

The FBI man looked over his shoulder to the fourth person in the room, a slender woman in a cream blouse and a green skirt that was probably the bottom half of a suit. The woman had never been introduced, though by the way she was standing off to the side and remaining quiet, I guessed she was the Special Agent in Charge. She was letting her associate do the interrogation, but was watching me closely. Neither agent was armed. Conniker's pants were loose around the waist. No doubt he wore his holster inside his waistband. Without it, his pants drooped. His weapon – as well as his boss's – was probably just on the other side of the door. They were indeed taking me seriously.

While the male agent and Nate sparred about me across the table, I looked back at the woman who as of yet hadn't said anything. She was leaning against the rear wall, taking in everything. She was younger than I'd have expected for someone in charge – about my age, I'd guess – and if she were indeed the SAC, she had to be something special, for her partner likely had seniority. As I watched her, she observed me observing her. Her eyes held some intensity. Was it focus…emotion… both?

Nate's calm, measured voice repeated his question, asking if the agent's men were in the ICU.

"No," the agent said. "They're not."

The homicide cop looked at the Fed with an expression that said, "So what's the issue here?" implying their agents were in the wrong, so they should let it slide.

I remained quiet, and watched the two agents look at me.

Agent Conniker leaned forward. "Why did you assault two Federal Agents?"

Nate responded before I had a chance to. You'd never know he was losing his patience, but I knew. It was in his flat, I'm-done-with-this, very calm tone. "Gidon's not into anything. It was your men who didn't know what they were doing."

I spoke for the first time: "They didn't identify themselves," I said evenly. "I came off my plane and spotted two curious-looking men following me. Well, curious to me."

My eyes met the woman agent's, then I continued: "I walked around, and stopped from time to time to get a look at them. Both were carrying guns."

Conniker and his boss exchanged a look, then turned back to me.

I elaborated: "One was carrying a weapon under his sweatshirt on the left side, while the other had his gun hidden under his jacket in the small of his back."

This time the agents looked at Nate who shrugged.

I went on: "I didn't know who they were, except they were armed and had some rudimentary training. As I didn't know what was going on, I maneuvered them into a location where I could privately ask them why they were following me." I turned to my friend the homicide captain who just shook his head at me. Nate knew I could be less than peaceful when I made such inquiries.

I turned back to the Feds. "I asked what they wanted, and they both went for their weapons. I wasn't going to wait to see the barrels." After a pause, "I didn't hit them without provocation."

"Your men should have ID'ed themselves first," Nate said simply.

Conniker countered: "They were reaching for their credentials."

"No, they weren't. Different areas of their persons. They were going for their Sigs. They panicked."

"A rookie mistake." This from Nate. "There's no case here." He could have said, "*You* have no case," but Nate kept it impersonal.

I looked over at the woman at the other end of the room, the one with the serious eyes, and asked: "What's this really about?" I was thinking of Conniker's comment at the beginning, that my assault on his men would be the "first charge against me." What would be the second charge?

The Student

The two Feds didn't say anything.

I certainly had my share of altercations over the past few years with some bad people here in the U.S., but I didn't have a sense that was the problem. My Israeli army service, also, was not a crime. After moving there a number of years ago I had been drafted into the IDF. Not an issue for a U.S. citizen either; I had made sure of that. And my prior work in Israel was unofficial, and not a violation of any US laws. This had to be something else.

"You think I'm Mossad," I looked at the woman agent, whose silence confirmed the assumption.

Nate said flatly, "You guys are so messed up."

"The two agents were following you," the woman admitted, finally speaking up.

"Why? And why do you think I'm Mossad?"

The FBI agents didn't respond.

From Nate: "You guys can answer now, or after Gidon retains counsel, when he or she asks you the same question. But, by that point you know he'll win any lawsuit which, understandably, won't put the folks in DC in a good mood."

The SAC nodded to Conniker. The FBI man placed a photo in front of me. It was a photo of a meeting I easily recognized since it took place about sixteen hours ago. The photo, taken with a telephoto lens, was a shot of David Amit, Idan Gelvar, and me, sitting at the outdoor café in Tel Aviv.

I looked up at the two FBI agents and just slowly shook my head. "You guys," I shook my head. "Seriously?"

"That's the Deputy Director of the Mossad," Conniker said.

"And David Amit of the Shin Bet," I volunteered. "Israel's General Security Services."

"We know," the SAC said.

"You think I'm working for Gelvar. You were hoping I'd implicate myself or lead you to Mossad agents."

Both of the FBI agents looked at me without speaking.

Nate had a low threshold for people who didn't think things through, and it was beginning to show. "You Feds should get out into the real world more, and stop reading emails from pre-adolescents in cubicles at Fort Meade."

More silence.

"They were giving you an assignment," Conniker asserted, about the Israelis in the picture.

I turned from one agent to the other: "Really? They were giving me a clandestine assignment as we sat in a café along the beach in Tel Aviv. That's what you think?"

"How do you know these men?" the woman agent asked.

"Well, Agent…?"

"Jeffries," she finally introduced herself.

"I only know Amit. We've helped each other out over the past year or so. Personal matters. Stuff I was looking into." I let a moment pass. "As far as Deputy Director Gelvar, that was the first time we met. He wasn't recruiting me. He was asking me for a nonbusiness, personal favor."

Before they could follow up, Nate's lack of patience surfaced again. "*No sabes ni madres.* You understand what that means, right? You know nothing."

They both nodded ever so slightly, as if being schooled.

"You have no intel on Gidon at all." Nate continued, still calm: "So, here's my theory how this got started – knowing how intelligence agencies function."

He paused to be sure he had their attention.

"A stringer for the CIA, some poor asshole they recruited in Israel, was following Mossad Deputy Director Gelvar. Gelvar sits down to a coffee with David Amit of the Shin Bet, and then Gidon shows up. This CIA agent wannabe who needs to earn his stipend, takes this picture and sends it off to his bosses who run facial rec on it. They pull up Gidon's driver's license and passport information. Then they see from his passport that he's traveled to Israel multiple times over the past few years. So someone begins making inquiries to find out who Gidon is. Turns out he's been in the Israeli army. Your eyebrows go up. However, you can't find out what he did in the army, because that information isn't readily available."

The two FBI agents were listening without reaction.

"Fact of the matter is," Nate went on, "that specific information about which unit he was in may not be available for one specific reason, or so you think. What might that reason be? Well, it's either because no one can find it so quickly, or that Gidon was involved in ..." Nate trailed off.

"Special Operations," Jeffries said.

"And to the geniuses in DC or Langley, that's only a short step to the Mossad."

"I did work in Special Ops," I admitted.

Conniker, who had lost some of his bluster, asked: "Shayetet?" He named the Israeli equivalent to the Navy SEALs.

I shook my head, "Didn't like being wet so much."

"Sayeret Matkal," Jeffries declared.

She knew her stuff. Her accent on the Hebrew was pretty good, too. I shrugged. "Doesn't matter, does it? Mossad did approach me any number of times, but it's never been of interest."

"Really?" Conniker asked.

"Really," I said.

"So why *did* Gelvar approach you?" the woman agent asked, moving closer to me.

"As I said, Agent Jeffries, he wanted me to do him a favor." I then explained about how he wanted me to keep an eye on his niece at Hopkins.

"And you think that's all there is to it?"

"I do. He's a concerned uncle who wants to be sure his niece is safe and having a good college experience in an environment that's sometimes hostile to Israel. And that's it." I wasn't sure I believed it, but I thought I sounded genuine.

"That's all there is to this?" she pointed to telephoto shot.

I nodded.

"Why you?" Conniker asked.

"Because," Nate answered evenly, which only emphasized his growing impatience, "Gidon doesn't work for them. It's personal. And Gidon, conveniently, lives in town."

Jeffries, looked at Nate, not ready to let it go. "Captain, how do you two know each other?"

Nate turned to me and I nodded.

The energy went out of my friend just a little, and he turned from one Federal Agent to the other. "About two years ago my daughter Laurie was backpacking at night through the north of Israel with a friend. They were close to the Lebanese border."

He looked at me, but I didn't say anything.

"As they were making their way down a rural road, a small group of Hezbullah terrorists on their way to a kibbutz came across them. They killed Laurie's friend with a single burst from an AK-47, and then kidnapped my daughter. They took her back into Lebanon, probably for some sort of exchange." Nate stopped and looked at me again. "Gidon led the team that crossed the border to rescue her. He found her in a darkened room in some shithole where she had been beaten and tortured. He freed her and brought her back to Israel. Laurie later told me that Gidon visited her almost every day for six months. If she's in one piece, it's because of him."

After a silent moment I turned to both FBI agents. They were both just staring at me, differently than before. While Jeffries had tried to read me earlier, the look in her eyes had changed. The intensity was gone.

I continued the account: "Nate and his wife Rachel were waiting at an army base. We met for the first time when I brought Laurie back."

"You told me Laurie insisted we meet you," Nate smiled at me.

"She did." After another moment, I added, "I came back to the States soon after that." I let another second pass. "So, Special

The Student

Operations for me, not Mossad. Like I said, that work doesn't interest me. What Gelvar wanted in Tel Aviv was personal."

Nate straightened his posture. "Satisfied?"

Conniker looked at his SAC who nodded. "Yes."

Nate stood up and I followed suit.

"Okay," Nate said, "if you need the help of BPD, you know where we are."

Neither agent responded. Then Conniker said, "I'll show you out," and the three of us moved toward the door.

I turned back to Agent Jeffries. "Sorry about your men."

"Yeah, well, they won't make that mistake again, will they?"

I bet they wouldn't, I thought, and we headed out. I also knew that the FBI wasn't going to let all this drop.

4

By the time Nate dropped me off at my place, it was early afternoon. My modest two-story home was on a tree-lined block north of the Johns Hopkins campus, off Charles Street. When Idan Gelvar in Tel Aviv asked me if I knew about Hopkins, I neglected to tell him I lived within a few miles of campus. Though he probably already knew that.

Once inside, I left my suitcase at the foot of the stairs and walked around the first floor, opening windows. After more than four months, the air wasn't as stagnant as I expected, but it wasn't fresh either. On the docket for the next few hours was taking a shower, unpacking, checking messages, food shopping, and collecting my mail from a neighbor. But all that would have to wait, as a single phone call took precedence. I stepped into my office.

The inner sanctum felt like a museum. I hadn't been here for a while, but the Chinese scroll wall hangings and Hebrew calligraphic prints were a warm, familiar welcome. I sat on the edge of my desk and picked up the phone.

"You have reached the office of Katie Harris," Katie's voicemail began. I waited for the rest of the message and the familiar beep.

"Hi, it's Gidon. Hope your day is going well." Under less stressful circumstances, I'd have started with a *Hey, can't wait to see you* message, but what came out was, "I'm finally home, though I had an interesting detour this morning. I'd like to see you and tell you about it, so let me know when's a good time. Talk to you soon."

This was so bizarre. Normally, I'd have driven over to Katie's school and popped in on her, but not now. On the other hand, maybe I was projecting too much bad karma. Maybe we just needed to see each other and talk. I hated not knowing stuff.

My suitcase seemed suddenly heavy as I carried it up the steps. After throwing it on the bed, and retrieving toiletries and some clean clothes, I headed for the comfort of my familiar shower. After thirty seconds under the spray, I looked over at a bar of soap Katie particularly liked, then turned my head toward the showerhead letting the water drive onto my face. Before ending the shower, I dialed back the warm water until the temperature turned icy cold for a moment, and then shut it off.

So what were the odds that Katie had called while I was in here? I toweled dry and checked the phone. There was one new message. My heart rate did go up a bit – what was I, 18? – but it was from Jonathan, my student, the one in the photo with Gelvar's niece. He said he'd be by the studio later this afternoon to say hello. I let out a breath, and then dressed and headed out.

***

There was a lot to think about: there was the personal stuff, which was enough by itself, Gelvar's niece, and then all that crap with the FBI – which I knew wasn't over. The best place for me to rebalance was a few miles away: my studio. Ever since returning from full time active duty more than two years ago, my martial arts dojo provided me with a base and a purpose beyond various jobs and professional and personal relationships.

The studio was on North Charles Street above 25th Street, a one-way, northbound road, home to ground-level businesses and upper-story apartments. It was a terrific location with a great neighborhood feeling.

I parked behind the building in a tenant's-only parking lot, and then circled around to the front entrance. My studio was nestled between a natural foods restaurant and a radio station. I had no idea what sort of music or talk shows the station aired, if any, but I was on a first-name basis with the owners of the restaurant next door. I walked past the outdoor spread of tables and chairs and sprinted up the five cement steps to a glass door, lined on the inside with white butcher's block paper. No lettering or signs indicated what business lay on the other side; there were just address numbers above the entrance. I unlocked the door and stepped in.

Bare entryway walls led to a large, square, cavernous room that was the practice hall. Except for floor-to-ceiling mirrors off to the side, a few hanging heavy bags, and a bench and folding chairs, the space was completely empty. Basically, there was the wood floor, and little else. My office was diagonally across from where I had walked in, off a back corner.

The small but comfortable space was not as Spartan as I had remembered. It had my desk and chair, computer, file cabinet, and a folding chair or two. Everything was as it should be, with the exception of a second-hand sofa. It was gone. In its place was a new green-brown club chair. Jonathan's doing, no doubt. Well, he was running the studio while I was gone, and the sofa was not particularly cherished after all. We'd have to talk about remuneration. I made a mental note as I sat down behind the desk and examined an untouched pile of mail. I looked around the room again and then slid open the bottom right desk drawer. Inside was a gun lockbox. I dialed the combination and opened the front panel. The .40 caliber Glock 23 was where I had left it, next to a loaded magazine and appropriate permits and papers.

The Glock was a present from Nate, a thank-you for bringing his daughter back alive. Generally, I didn't carry the gun, but six months ago it came in handy when two guys came for me in the middle of the night while I was here. The memory of that evening ran across my brain and then it was gone. Without picking up the gun, I secured the lockbox and closed the drawer.

The Student

Now, time to work out. In the second drawer of the file cabinet I kept a T-shirt and a pair of medium weight black gi pants. I changed into them and headed into the practice hall. For the next 45 minutes, after stretching out muscle groups from neck to toes, I laid into the heavy bag with punches, elbows, knife hand strikes, backfists, backs of the hands, and straight-on finger stabs; every possible striking surface from the elbow to my fingers. Once through with all that, I moved into the center of the room to hone multiple circular, spiral fighting forms. Finally, with sweat rolling down my face, I sat cross-legged in the middle of the hall, closed my eyes, and worked on clearing my mind and settling my breathing. At first, I reran yesterday's meeting with the Shin Bet and Mossad officers, my actions at BWI airport, and my meeting with the FBI. My breathing soon calmed and all those images faded out.

Sometime later – it was impossible to tell how much time had passed – the door to the street opened. I didn't really hear it, but knew it was opening. Everything around me had been calm, and then something caused a ripple in the serenity. Someone was stepping into the foyer, being very careful not to make any sound. I didn't get up or open my eyes. I clearly felt myself in the center of the large room – with someone approaching.

The man moving toward me was tall, slender, and carrying something. He silently put whatever it was down against a wall, and continued forward.

"Hi, Jon," I said, eyes still closed. He was a good fifteen feet away.

"Holy shit, Sifu, how do you *do* that?"

I opened my eyes, but stayed seated on the floor. "I've led a pure life."

"No, it can't be that."

I stood up and gave my star student and right-hand assistant a hug.

"Welcome back, Sifu." Once again he used my martial arts title, which predated my move to Israel and army service.

"Good to be back, Jon boy."

I looked at Jonathan. He was tall, curly haired, in his mid-twenties, and dressed in black gi pants and a red T-shirt with a dragon image on it. Jon had a Brad Pitt jawline and smile that exuded both warmth and mischievousness at the same time.

"Didn't expect you to be here, boss. Thought you'd be at Katie's school behind closed doors, if you know what I mean."

"Not today, Number One."

He looked into my eyes and then said simply, "Oh? Okay."

I shrugged.

"Okay, forget the woman. Tell me about the last four months with the special operations group I'm not supposed to know about."

I laughed. "Standing on one foot?"

"If that's what it takes." He balanced on one leg and assumed a martial art crane position.

"I did not miss that sense of humor." After a moment, I sat back down on the floor. "You first. Come, sit. Tell me what's been going on here. And thanks for the new furniture in the office by the way. What do I owe you?"

"Nothing. We had it at one of our properties. You needed it and we didn't." He sat down on the floor in front of me.

"Thanks. It's perfect." Jon's family was into commercial real estate. His dad had always been generous with me for taking Jon under my care.

"And the chair is perfect to crash on, though your legs sort of hang over the arm if you sit sideways," he smiled.

"Thanks for breaking it in," I smiled back, picturing Jon sprawled out on the chair-and-a-half. "Okay, talk to me about business."

For the next fifteen minutes he brought me up to date on what he'd been doing with the classes. I nodded and decided that for my first class back I'd scare the crap out of the students by working their asses off and fighting with a few of the upper belts. Then I'd back off and take a more supervisory role until everyone either got acquainted,

The Student

or re-acquainted with my style.

At some point Jon veered off topic to talk about some of the "smokin' hot women" in the class, and I just shook my head. "Business and pleasure, Jon. Business and pleasure. Watch the overlap." It never seemed to be a problem for him.

"I know. And now that you're here, boss, what chance do I have?"

We both laughed, knowing there was a line I wouldn't cross.

"Any students from Hopkins?" I asked.

"Yeah, a few actually. Why?"

"Don't go away." I stood up and sprinted for my office to retrieve my cell phone. On the way back I pressed the home button, and saw a missed call from Katie, plus a voice mail. I ignored the prompt and went to my photo file. Sitting back on the floor I asked, "How about Noa Biran from Hopkins?"

"Yeah, how do you know her?"

"She's the niece of someone I met in Israel. He had this picture of her." I showed him the digital version of the photo Gelvar had shown me at the Tel Aviv café.

"Yup," Jon said. "That's her. That was a great party. We have a mutual friend near campus who was having other friends over. I met her there. Anything I should know?"

"So you're friends with her?"

"We've hung out a few times since then. What's going on?"

"Not sure. Her uncle is worried about her. He's concerned how any anti-Israel unrest on campus may affect her. Just wanted me to keep an eye on her."

"Hey, I'll be happy to do that. I'm doing it anyway," he smiled. "Your friend doesn't have anything to worry about. Hopkins is a pretty boring place in terms of demonstrations. Everyone's into their work."

Once again, the thought I had in Israel crossed my mind: did the Deputy Director of the Mossad know something about radical campus activities he wasn't sharing, or was there something else going on with his niece, something relating to Gelvar professionally?

"You know," Jon went on, "if you want to meet her, I can bring her by class. She's been here before with friends."

"That'll work. Just don't mention this uncle thing."

"No problem…on one condition. Tell me something about the last four months while you were in the army."

I smiled, and told him about some of our urban combat training, the live-fire rooms, mock-ups of buildings we had to clear, and the night training exercises.

"Sounds awesome."

I shrugged.

"Now tell me what you're not telling me, Sifu. You're leaving out the *really* good stuff."

I had to smile again, but shook my head. We chatted innocuously for a while longer, and then Jon's cell phone rang and off he went. While he was gone, I played the message Katie had left earlier.

"Hi, Gidon. Glad you're back safely. Why don't you come by my place at 7:00. I look forward to seeing you." And that was it. I decided not to read anything into her tone or what she said or didn't say. Whatever was going to be was going to be.

Once Jon returned, I asked if he wanted to work with me on fighting and breaking out of grabs.

"Let me see," he said. "You just returned from four months of Special Operations training, you may have girlfriend problems, and you've been meditating so your energy is flowing super well. Sure, what could the downside be for me?"

I smiled once more. "All good, right? Let's start with push-hands."

We approached each other and stood with the back of my right hand touching the back of his right hand. The idea was to maintain contact regardless of how the other shifted. We swayed and moved in a circular fashion, shifting our weight back and forth. The movement began slowly but soon picked up speed. We brought in our other hands and increased speed even more. Soon, we were trying to throw each other off balance. That segued into light fighting.

Afterward, I showed him various applications of grabs and choke holds. He almost passed out only once when I had my arm wrapped around his neck. We finished with some high-speed attack and defense techniques. By the time we were done, an hour and a half had gone by.

Finally, when we took our break, Jon checked his cell phone.

"Time for more?" I asked.

"Can't. Got things to do before dinner."

"Is it that late?"

Jon showed me the time.

"Whoa." I needed to clean up and do some shopping before heading to Katie's.

Jon bowed to me and then we hugged.

"Great to see you, Jon."

"You, too. Sifu. And I want to hear about the *other* stuff."

"See you tomorrow."

With that, my number one student left, and I headed over to a bathroom and the shower stall I had installed in its back corner. So, for the second time that day, I took a shower, and then changed back into my street clothes.

* * *

By the time 6:30 came around, I had grabbed a sandwich, completed some quick food shopping, and stopped off at home to refrigerate the perishables. I also scooped up a bottle of Sauvignon Blanc.

Katie lived in a sleepy neighborhood off York Road, just inside the northern city-county line. The streets in the area were tree-lined, and houses were typically on the older side, two or three stories each, and most typically with a wide front porch. As I drove through the neighborhood, often slowing for speed humps, I thought about what Katie meant to me. She was the first woman I had an extended relationship with since Tamar was killed in Israel two years ago. It had taken me a while to find an emotional center following all of that – I was definitely a mess for a while – and Katie had helped me with that. Other relationships came and went, but Katie really "got" me. She understood my past, what drove me, and was okay with all my craziness.

Her sky-blue Mustang was parked in her driveway about midway up her block. There was an empty space along the curb next to it, so I slid my Grand Cherokee into the spot, grabbed my backpack, and then headed up her walk. Katie's solid wood front door seemed more formidable than I remembered, but maybe that was just my state of mind. I rang the bell, which was a little weird since I had a set of keys, but as I hadn't walked right into her house in more than four months, I wasn't about to take that liberty. My mind replayed miscellaneous long-distance phone conversations, the most recent of which was stiff and awkward.

In a matter of moments, the door swung open. Katie stood there with a smile on her face and that's all I needed to see. I dropped my backpack to the floor and moved right over to her. My arms found their way around her waist, and her arms held me tight as well. We kissed, and I lost track of time. Katie's lips and mouth were unbelievably sweet. At some point, she dropped her arms from around me and backed away, though she held onto my hands.

"Hey there, stranger," she said smiling.

We stayed about a foot apart, but I could still get a good look at her. Her shoulder length blonde hair was pulled back, fastened up off her neck with a barrette. Her blue eyes were clear and wide, though the corners were slightly creased. Katie was dressed in blue jeans and a trim, white V-neck T-shirt that accented her curves. I missed those curves.

"You look great," I said.

"You don't look so bad yourself," she smiled. "You look more… solid than four months ago." Katie took a step forward and put her right hand on my chest. She could surely feel my heart pounding beneath her palm. Maybe I was worried about this relationship for nothing. Maybe I had projected the strained phone calls, misreading the long silences between Baltimore and Israel.

"Yeah, well," I shrugged. "Running around, jumping, climbing, carrying stuff, daily physical training. It was all I could do to keep up with those kids."

She let go of my hands and moved into the living room. "Somehow, I think they had to keep up with you."

"I don't know about that. Anyway…" From the backpack near the door I pulled out the bottle of white wine I had brought with me, "I thought we could share this tonight."

Instead of responding to that, Katie said, "I was hoping you'd come by school today." She sat on the arm of her couch.

"I wanted to, but the FBI had other ideas."

"The FBI? What happened?"

I moved into the living room to be a little closer to her. There was something in Katie's posture, the distance she had put between us. "Oh, we had a chat at the Federal Building."

"Because…"

"Because I beat the crap out of two agents trying to pull guns on me at BWI."

She looked into my eyes.

"They were following me when I came off the plane. They didn't identify themselves. I didn't know they were FBI."

"Why would…"

"You remember David Amit?"

"Your Shin Bet friend."

"Yup. He called before I left for the airport and insisted I meet him in Tel Aviv. So, I made the stop, only to discover he brought along a friend, the Deputy Director of the Mossad."

"Oh no." Katie let herself slide off the arm of the couch and onto a cushion. "The FBI thinks you're a Mossad agent."

"Well, that's what the conversation was about at the Federal Building."

"Gidon, you're not working for—"

"No, no. The guy has a niece who's a senior at Hopkins. He's just worried and wants me to look in on her. It's personal, not business."

I let out a breath and told her the whole story, from the photograph taken of me at the café, to the agents trailing me at the airport, to them pulling guns on me, to my conversation with the Special Agents.

"Thank God for Nate," Katie said.

"Thank God for Nate," I repeated. "Anyway, that's why I didn't come to school this morning. By the time I got out of there, it was the afternoon, and to be honest," I paused and looked at her, "I wasn't sure you wanted to see me."

After hearing that last line, all Katie did was sit and say nothing.

I hadn't read the vibes incorrectly.

Finally, she looked at me. "I *am* angry with you."

I sat on the couch and took her hand. "I'm sorry I didn't come back sooner. I didn't expect to stay that long."

"It wasn't fair to me." She pulled her hand away. "You said you'd be back in two weeks, and then it was a month, and then it just kept going."

"I know. I should have just come back, but I got involved with stuff."

"Maybe you didn't want to come back."

I wasn't sure how to answer that. I wanted to come back, but I wanted to be with Special Ops also. I had prioritized. Katie and I had a relationship I thought was stable enough to do that. "It was a singular opportunity, and I didn't think it would jeopardize us. I thought you'd understand."

"We never discussed it." A moment went by. "You're not in the IDF anymore."

"Well," I began to say *I am, sort of,* but didn't get the chance.

"And you made a choice."

"It was important work."

Katie just looked at me, and I saw anger build in her eyes, but then she let it go. "You obviously didn't want to be here…with me."

"Not true. I did…and do want to be with you. Obviously. And I thought you'd be okay with it."

"You said you'd be back."

"I *am* back. Look at me. *Listen* to me."

"You're not aware of what you did wrong."

I took a deep breath. "Maybe so, but two things. One: if we have a solid relationship, it should weather this. You forgive people you love. Secondly, there's another reason I couldn't come back sooner."

Katie just looked at me.

"I was involved in an operation." Even as I said the words, they seemed lame. I wanted to tell her about Syria, but couldn't.

She nodded, but her eyes lost some focus. "The entire time you were away I read and watched everything about Israel…wondering about you."

A moment passed, then Katie went back to her theme: "You made a choice to stay and not come back. You wanted to be there. Not here. Though, I'm not surprised."

"I'm not sure what that means."

"I'm not sure what it means either."

I took her hand again, and she let me.

After a moment, she elaborated: "Knowing you, I'm not surprised you stayed. But knowing us, I was hoping you'd come back sooner."

"Hold that thought."

I sprung up and walked over to my backpack that was still on the floor near the front door. I reached inside the main compartment and pulled out a long, blue jewelry gift box, the kind that held a necklace. I handed it to Katie.

She looked at me.

"You know the shop. It's on one of the side streets near Ben Yehudah."

Katie opened the box and her eyes widened for a second.

"Gidon…" she shook her head and took out the handcrafted

necklace of small colored stones interspersed with complementing metal swirls and squares. It was a distinctly Israeli design. "I can't accept this." She looked me at me.

"Really? You don't understand my reasons and can't forgive me?"

"I *do* understand." She looked at me and there was a hint of tears in her eyes. "And that's part of what I want – need – to think about. I want to take a break."

"What does that mean?"

"I don't know. I want some time to think," she repeated.

"You sure about this?"

"No," Katie smiled. The glistening in her eyes had passed. "I'm not sure. Part of me wants to pull your clothes off right now and jump on top of you, and get back to where we were."

"Is that a bad thing?" I smiled back.

"No, it's not a bad thing. But," she let a few seconds pass, "as much as I want to do that and be with you, my feelings about this won't change. I want time to think about us and where everything fits in."

"If we take a break," I said, "you never know what might happen in the meantime."

"It's a risk."

"How long?"

"I don't know."

"And you say, *I'm* not good with defining periods of time?"

Katie smiled again, but this time more sheepishly. "If we're meant to be, we'll be." She put the necklace I had given her back in the box and held out it for me.

I shook my head. Some anger was beginning to work its way up my back and into my head. I kept it in check. "No. It's for you," I said calmly.

I looked Katie in the eyes, turned slowly, and headed back to the front door. I scooped up my backpack, smiled weakly, and walked out the door.

5

Some people can relate to being so exhausted they fall asleep as soon as their head hits the pillow. I was so exhausted I fell asleep on the way down to the pillow. I didn't know if it was jet lag – my body was still on Israel time seven hours ahead – or if it was the emotional drain, or both. It didn't matter. Sleep came instantly and deeply.

Two minutes later – or what seemed like two minutes – the phone rang. I sat upright in bed, heart pounding. My eyes saw my bedroom – the dresser, the closet, the windows – but my brain told me I was on the base in Israel: bare quarters, low bed, single chest of drawers, heavy curtains over a window, and both a Tavor Assault Rifle and an M-4 leaning in a corner.

The phone continued to ring. Consciousness fought embedded memory, and the haze thinned. After another ring I was able to focus, and picked up the phone.

"Hi, Sifu, it's Jon."

The red LED clock beside the bed read an incomprehensible 2:05.

"Yeah, Jon, what's up? Everything okay?"

"I'm in Noa Biran's apartment. She's okay, but— "

"But what?" An image of my conversation at the café soared through my mind.

"Her apartment's been broken into. You gotta see this. It's intense. Can you come down?"

"Of course."

He gave me her address and apartment number. "It's a secure building. Call me and I'll come down and let you in."

"Right. Did you call the police?"

"Noa did. They're here now, and the campus cops."

I didn't know if that was good or not, considering I might want to look around and ask Noa questions.

"Sifu?"

"Yeah, Jon?"

"You wanted to keep an eye on Noa. How did you know something was going to happen?"

"I didn't." But someone else in Israel might have.

* * *

Noa's apartment was in the Homewood House, an apartment building on 33rd Street, just off Charles. While the undergraduate campus of Hopkins was north of the city center and among heavily traveled streets, the setting was almost suburban, with some surrounding neighborhoods wooded, and homes perched on large lawns and open spaces. Housing immediately around campus, though, was more college-utilitarian: mid-rise apartments and buildings that varied in ages from the recent to those dating back to the 1900s. All this didn't mean curbside parking was available. No spaces were open in these early morning hours, either on main streets or on secluded side streets.

I drove past Noa's building. Not unexpectedly, a blue and white city police car was parked immediately in front of the entrance in a no-parking zone. After a second go-round, two things became very clear: the first was that a dark gray Accord was following me. It had laid back almost a block behind but made the same turns I did, and on occasion had to speed up to keep me in sight. FBI, no doubt. What a surprise.

The second thought, which annoyed me more, was I had to surrender to not finding a space. There were openings probably further from campus, but I was too tired to walk unnecessarily. I found an illegal spot between an alley and a fire hydrant and pulled in. Without a second thought, I reached into my glove box and pulled out small placard that Nate had once given me. It said simply, "Official Baltimore Police Business," and had the BPD seal with some signatures in the bottom right corner. I positioned the paper on the dash in front of the steering wheel and headed out.

33rd Street was pretty broad: two lanes in each direction and a yellow outlined turn lane between them. I headed back to Noa's building. Despite my fatigue, the surroundings registered on me, almost subconsciously. The sidewalks, from curb to apartment buildings, were wide and well kept. They looked new, sparkling as if something reflective had been mixed into the concrete. Toward the curb, high pressure sodium street lights illuminated the entire area in an orange hue, no doubt part of the campus neighborhood security to cut down on shadows and to deter loitering. There were also surveillance cameras mounted high up on several lampposts in each block.

The Homewood House apartment building entrance came up on my left with the cop car still parked out front. Double parked next to it was an unmarked, medium blue Crown Vic. As I approached the entrance, I reached for my cell phone to call Jon so he could let me in, but a red-haired, twenty-something boy in kelly green shorts and a dark T-shirt was on his way out. He let the glass door go as he had exited, so I sprinted up to catch it. A secure building, huh.

Noa's apartment was on the fifth floor. This building was exclusively campus housing, and looked pretty upscale for student living. Up on Five, the hallway was brightly lit and painted a neutral tan. About halfway down on the right, a door was open halfway, with a city cop standing guard just inside. The officer, on the younger side of thirty, was a head taller than me, and while his face was on the thin side, it belied the rest of him. He stood broad and solid.

"Can I help you, sir?" His voice was deep.

"Friend of the family." I looked over at Noa who was standing beside the couch, talking to a guy in a sport coat. She didn't see me, but I recognized her from her photo.

The cop looked me up and down. I was dressed in a pair of black BDU pants – the military's version of cargo pants, or maybe it was the other way around – and a red IDF Airborne T-shirt. They had been the only clean clothes I could put my hands on in my sleep-induced stupor after Jon's phone call. I, too, stood straight and tall, but felt tiny next to the cop. His right hand rested on his wide belt, just an inch from a holstered Glock 22. This was the same caliber as mine, but his weapon was slightly longer and held more in the clip.

"Pete, it's okay," I heard Jon's voice. "He's with me."

"Go ahead, sir."

He nodded and I walked into the apartment. Immediately, this was not what I expected from campus housing, but it had been a while for me. The main room was large and square, and had two couches on either side of a central coffee table. A dining room table was positioned in the back. This must have been the common room with bedrooms off at either end of the main room. A small kitchenette was to my right, with Jon leaning over a Formica counter. He came around as I walked in.

"Pete?" I asked, approaching him and repeating the cop's name. "You know the officer?"

"No. We just became friends."

I shook my head at Jon's amazing ease with people. I turned to the room to see what was going on. The Mossad man's niece was still speaking with the guy in the sport coat. Had to be a detective. Noa was slim, with a complexion not quite Mediterranean olive. Her eyes looked dark as well. She wore a zip-up maroon Hopkins sweatshirt, white shorts, and a pair of flip-flops. The detective, almost a head taller, smiled reassuringly as he spoke to her.

The lawman fit right in on this Ivy League campus, wearing a navy blazer and khakis, a blue patterned shirt and a light blue polka-dot tie on a dark field. The tie was loosened at the neck. His dark hair was neatly trimmed, but had some length to it that added to his preppieness. He looked like he was 12, but more likely was in his mid-twenties.

Standing nearby was Noa's roommate, who I also recognized from Noa's photo. She was taller than Noa, with blonde hair, cut to jawline length. She was speaking with a middle-aged campus cop.

I looked around the apartment. For a break-in, which is what Jon had reported, the place looked incredibly neat and clean. And then I saw it. On the entryway wall. It had been behind me when I had walked in.

In big, black, spray-painted letters were the words *DEATH TO ISRAEL*. Below them someone had taped up a green and white Hamas flag.

6

"You must be Sensei Aronson, Jon's teacher," Noa said coming over to me.

"Gidon." I shook her hand, clarifying. "Sorry to meet you like this," I nodded toward the words on the wall. "Pretty upsetting."

The Ivy League-looking detective came over, and scanned my attire. He indicated the Paratroop T-shirt. "Israeli Army? Are you active duty?" It must have been my posture.

"Not as of yesterday," Jon said from the side.

"It's more complicated than that," I corrected. "I live here."

"He's a counterterrorism expert," Jon volunteered. I shot him a look – which was rare for me regarding Jon – and he became quiet very quickly.

The young detective offered his hand, "I'm Detective Ed Soper."

"Gidon Aronson." After shaking his hand, I turned to the *DEATH TO ISRAEL* wording and the Hamas flag. "What do you think?"

The young detective hesitated to say anything official.

"You can talk to him, Detective," Noa said.

Detective Soper nodded. "Well, there's no sign of forced entry, either here or at the building entrance."

Considering how easy it was to walk in the building, that didn't indicate anything.

The middle-aged campus cop and Noa's roommate came over and stood quietly, listening to the recap.

The detective continued: "To my knowledge, nothing like this has ever happened here before." He looked at the campus security man who just nodded his head in confirmation. "There are other Israeli students here, but this seems isolated to Ms. Biran."

"And you haven't been vocal or anything?" I asked Noa. "No involvement in anything political? Didn't piss anyone off at a rally?"

Noa shook her head. "There isn't anything political here to get involved in. Besides, I'm here to work. It's one of the reasons I chose Hopkins."

"Any other anti-Israel feelings pointed your way?"

Noa's roommate, the blonde with the jawline length hair and dark eyes, answered: "Just 'Free Palestine' fliers posted all over school and stuck in mailboxes." There was a trace of a Middle Eastern accent in her speech.

I turned to the campus cop: "Any Palestinian school groups that you know of?"

"The detective already asked me," he nodded to the preppie cop. "No. Nothing. I get a list of all the student groups. Very little about Israel, either for or against. There is an occasional speaker on each side, but that's all it's ever been. Just speakers. Kids here just aren't that active."

Noa added. "I'm an international studies major, so sometimes we or other groups bring in experts, but it's never resulted in something like this."

"The place looks undisturbed," I noted, looking around. The apartment seemed extraordinarily neat, with the exception of some jackets draped over furniture and books scattered on table tops.

"This is the only thing," Noa responded. "We checked our rooms. Nothing seems taken or moved or anything."

"We have another roommate, but she's not here," the blonde roommate offered. "She's spending the night with her boyfriend at Georgetown. We checked her room. It's fine, too."

"Fingerprints?" I asked the detective.

"The forensics person just left. Took samples."

"So what's your next move?"

"We'll treat this as a hate crime. With Officer Richburg's help," he looked at the campus cop, "we'll get a list of who swiped in at the entrance downstairs tonight. Begin there. Tomorrow, we'll start asking questions around campus. Speak with administration about on-campus politically active groups, see if anything, or anyone, stands out. BPD takes this sort of thing very seriously."

Noa's roommate spoke up again, and looked between the detective and me: "Do you think it's okay to stay here tonight?"

"It's up to you," the detective responded. "I don't think anything will happen, but if you're uncomfortable, can you go to a friend's place?"

Both girls nodded.

"Maybe cover this with a sheet for now until we get it cleaned up," the campus officer nodded toward the spray-painted wall.

Wrapping things up, the City detective pulled out some business cards and handed one each to Noa, Officer Richburg, and me. "If you need anything, or if you think of anything, call."

"We will," Noa said. "Thank you."

Detective Soper smiled and said goodnight. He and the uniformed officer who had been guarding the door headed out. In the moment the door swung open as they exited, I could see a number of students hanging around on the other side. The big uniformed cop said something to them as the door closed behind him.

Back in the room, the campus cop, Richburg, turned to me. "You have a martial arts studio on Charles Street, right?"

I nodded. "How do you know?"

"Recognized your name. You taught some of my guys, the law enforcement students."

I turned to Jon, not having any idea what he was talking about.

"Hopkins has a law enforcement major," he explained. "While you were gone, two of the students came by to learn some hand-to-hand techniques. I mentioned you a lot during class."

"Thanks for taking care of them," Officer Richburg added. "They're

The Student

learning a great deal, they tell me."

"Jon's the man," I said. "I look forward to meeting the students."

"If you need anything," he looked at me, handed me his card, and then he too left.

Noa and her roommate collapsed onto the couch. They were exhausted. It was after 3 a.m. "Okay," Noa said, looking at me, "should I be worried? Am I being targeted?" Her dark eyes were wide and looking out at me from her light olive complexion. Her roommate placed a hand on her arm, reassuringly.

"I don't know," I said. "This seems pretty sudden and aimed at you, considering nothing else anti-Israel is going on around here. But it may just be some idiot trying to scare you. We have to find out why and who."

"Why target Noa, though?" the roommate, her slight Middle Eastern accent coming through once again.

I turned to the roommate, ignoring the question for the moment. "We haven't been introduced."

"I'm sorry," Noa said. "This is Aminah Hadad."

"And you're not from Israel or the US," I offered.

"Jordan," Jon piped in.

"Amman, to be specific," Aminah continued.

"How did you two meet?"

"We were classmates at Bar Ilan University outside Tel Aviv."

My eyebrows must have gone up.

Aminah Hadad smiled. "My parents are both educators and they wanted me to study in Israel. We're Christian, originally from Lebanon. They've always been pretty forward thinking."

Noa continued: "We were in an international studies program together, and became friends. We decided to both come to Hopkins for our senior year."

"Wow. *Kol hakavod*," I said. "Good for you. But I bet not everyone in both your families were happy about this."

They shrugged in unison, and said simultaneously, "Not our problem," and both laughed.

"So, getting back to this," I motioned to the wall, "this may be about you, or it may not be about you at all." I paused. "I met your uncle Idan."

There was a long silence, and I could see Noa getting angry.

Aminah asked her friend, "Who's Uncle Idan?"

Before Noa could say "Mossad," or anything relating to Israel's security, I offered, "He's an official in the Israeli government." Another moment went by in silence. "I met him the other day. Nothing sinister. Told me you were here, and wanted me to meet you." Close enough to the truth.

When Noa finally spoke, she had already made the leap in logic, considering his line of work: "You think this may be about him? Someone found out he's my uncle and...what?"

I shrugged. "I have no idea. It may not be that at all. Really, anything is possible. We have to look at everything. What concerns me, is why now to do this?"

"Jon told me you're Sayeret Matkal."

I looked at Jon who gave me a sheepish expression.

"Once upon a time," I answered.

"So, knowing what you know about Hamas, tell me the truth," she asked me again. "Do I need to be worried?"

In response, the following thoughts went through my mind, though they were more instinctive flashes: Item 1: there was no forced entry into the apartment. Someone either had a key or knew how to gain access. Item 2: if the apartment invader did not live in this building, he or she had the knowledge to get past the electronic lock downstairs, though, as with me, the entry door really wasn't an obstacle. On the other hand, the invader couldn't rely on someone letting him or her in. Personally, I wouldn't have left it to chance. Timing was too important to be sure that no one was here. Item 3: the apartment invader had to have some sort of surveillance set up to be sure no one was here. Item 4: once inside this apartment, he or she only spray-painted this wall and didn't touch anything else that we knew about. The fact that whoever it was could get in here without a trace to spray-paint a message was terrifying, even without the political content.

So, if this *were* the work of Hamas for whatever reason, I'd be worried, but that's not what I said to the girls. "So let's talk some more. Anything out of the ordinary occur lately? Notice anyone following you?"

Noa looked at Aminah. "No. I don't think so."

Aminah shook her head as well.

Going back to the Deputy Director of Mossad angle, "Did you receive anything from your uncle Idan, a package or an email? Anything?"

"I haven't heard from him in months."

"What about your parents, Noa. Do they live in Israel?"

"They're both in Seattle. My *imma* is a doctor and *abba* is a scientist in bioengineering or something." She used the Hebrew terms for mother and father, respectively.

"And did they email you, or send you something out of the ordinary?"

"We email each other all the time. Nothing unusual."

Jon spoke up for the first time in a while: "So if they're living in Seattle, is that where you live when you're not in school?"

"No. We live in Israel. Dad's office in Seattle is a branch of his Tel Aviv main office. Mom just rotated there over the summer. She was invited, I think."

"So, Gidon," Aminah began to ask, "you didn't answer the question. Is there something to worry about?"

Again, I had to think. Hamas had a political wing and military wing. The political wing attacks Israel in the UN and in other international bodies. The military wing blows up innocent Israelis in restaurants and on busses. They kidnap soldiers and hold them hostage for a release of prisoners. They kidnap teenagers coming home from school and shoot them. They fire rockets into Israel from Gaza to kill as many Israelis as possible. They make no distinction between civilian and military targets. So, was this a threat worth worrying about?

"Yes," I finally answered. "I'd take it seriously until we found out what this is all about."

Both girls blanched.

"More than anything else, I think someone's trying to scare you. But let's err on the side of caution. You have a place to stay, right? Earlier you said you did."

"You can stay with me. Both of you," Jon spoke up. "I have plenty of room."

Part of Jon's invitation, I knew, came from the social part of his brain, but more so, he felt he could watch out for them.

"It's a good choice," I agreed. "So, for tonight, or what's left of it, grab some clothes, your books, your laptops, and crash at Jon's."

Both Noa and Aminah suddenly looked at each other.

"What?" I turned from one to the other.

"Laptop," Aminah started. "Mine was stolen earlier today. I was using it in the library. I walked around the corner to get a drink – it took about fifteen seconds – and when I came back, it was gone."

I turned to Noa. "Is yours still here?"

She nodded affirmatively. "I checked before the police came."

"Do you share classes or anything?" Jon asked. I was thinking the same thing.

"Yeah, we do," Noa said. "Plus we have several research papers we're working on together."

"Let's take a look at it," I suggested. "Maybe you can tell if it's been accessed."

Noa nodded and left to retrieve her laptop. "What are you thinking, boss?" Jonathan asked.

"Well," I sat on the couch, "two thoughts. There has to be a reason for this," I nodded to the spray-painted message on the wall, "and I don't think it's against Noa personally. The apartment break-in was fairly professional, right? Why? Just to leave this message? The fact that someone can do that and only leave a message, that's pretty intimidating."

Noa returned with her laptop and joined Aminah and me on the couch.

"You think it's aimed at Noa's parents," Aminah posited, "to show they can reach their daughter for some reason?"

"Maybe. Or other relatives of Noa's," like her uncle, the Deputy Director of Mossad. "Toward what end, though?" A moment passed. "The other possibility is that all this was just cover for something else, like getting into your laptops. Maybe there's something you share."

"Which is why mine was stolen?" Aminah asked.

"Perhaps. Noa, you said you hadn't received any packages from your parents or uncle."

"No," the young Israeli confirmed.

"So, you're thinking it's something someone emailed?" Jon suggested.

"Again, maybe. Maybe there's some other commonality between the two of you. Or, I may just be completely wrong."

"So why wasn't Noa's stolen?" my student asked.

"I don't know. He may have thought he had enough time to download whatever he was looking for."

"If you're right," Noa looked at me, "then whoever tried to access the computers would never get in."

"Why?"

Aminah responded with a single name: "Carl."

Noa explained: "Aminah's boyfriend."

"He's not my boyfriend. Just a friend."

Noa continued as if she hadn't heard the correction: "He's in the Computer Science program. We think he's working for the NSA in one of the secure buildings on-campus." Both girls laughed.

Aminah continued, "He put some sort of super security system on both our laptops. No one except us can get in. He said he also put in a program that could somehow track anyone who tried to access the computers without permission."

"Let's talk to Carl," I said.

Even before I had finished the thought, Aminah had her cell phone out and was sending a text.

7

Carl arrived at the apartment door in less than ten minutes, and was totally not what I expected from a computer geek. When Aminah opened the door I saw a young man who could have been a jock. He stood just over six feet with shoulder-length straight brown hair and a five o'clock shadow. He had the sloping shoulders of an athlete beneath a purple Raven's jersey, with black cargo shorts and the inevitable flip-flops rounding out his outfit. The other thing that impressed me was that at just after three in the morning, he was wide awake.

Aminah introduced Jon and me, showed him the wall with the graffiti and the Hamas flag, and explained what was going on. He looked at Aminah and said, "Why didn't you call me sooner?"

"I know you were busy in the computer lab."

Carl went over and gave Aminah and Noa each a hug. I instantly liked him.

"Thanks for coming," I said. "I understand you installed a security system on Noa's laptop?"

"And Aminah's."

Noa handed over her MacBook. "Do your thing. Make it so."

He took it from her. "God, I hate these things."

Jonathan and I looked at each other.

Carl grinned at us. "Doesn't mean I don't understand them." He examined the closed silver MacBook in his hands, noticing several dark smudges on the case.

"The police checked for fingerprints," Noa offered.

"What I put on here is better than finding fingerprints." He sat on the couch. Once the power was on and booted up, his fingers danced over the keyboard. I couldn't follow what he was typing or accessing.

I said simply, "So you've done this once or twice before."

Still looking at the screen he smiled, "And you've jumped out of planes before."

"Only because soldiers behind me pushed me out," I smiled back. Once again I was impressed. I had no idea he had even really looked at me, let alone noticed my Airborne T-shirt.

"Roger that," he said, still without looking at me. "Okay, I've got good news and bad news and good news."

We were all looking at the laptop's screen, which had turned blue, and was now filling with computer code as Carl typed.

"Whoever broke into the apartment definitely tried to access this laptop. I can see the keystrokes."

Glad he could. I had no idea what the alphanumeric lines on the screen meant.

"The security system is designed to let an unauthorized user into the system to a point in order to see what he, or she, is trying to access. So the good news is I can tell that the Finder directory was pulled up. The bad news is, well, I guess it's good and bad news, is that the security system stopped whoever it was right there. They didn't get any farther, so we don't know what he or she specifically wanted to look at."

"Any other good news?" Jon asked.

Keeping his right hand on the keyboard with fingers still moving over the keys, Carl ran his left hand through the hair above his forehead. "The best news. Once the intruder tried to access this computer, the security system activated the built-in camera. We now have video of whoever tried to get in."

After a few more keystrokes, the blue screen and computer code vanished to be replaced by a video of a thin-faced young man, about twenty-five, alternately staring at us and looking down at the keyboard.

The man was blonde and wore narrow glasses. Beads of sweat were on his upper lip. He seemed particularly intense as he typed. In a few moments, he began to curse, as he couldn't get the laptop to cooperate. He paused a moment to think, then frantically continued typing. After ten more seconds, the bespectacled, thin-faced man strung four or five curse words together as one long epithet, typed a few more commands, and finally powered down the system – leaving us with a black screen.

Carl reran the video and freeze-framed the image on a clear shot of the intruder.

"Anyone recognize him?" I turned to the college kids.

All three shook their heads.

"Not someone from this apartment building?" I asked both girls.

They replied as one: "No."

"We pretty much know everyone here," Noa offered.

Carl looked up at me. "I can access some facial recognition software and see if I can find a match."

"No. Thanks." I thought of the girls' earlier comment about Carl perhaps working with the NSA. "If this thing about Hamas has any validity, I don't want any of you going any further. Everyone needs to stay away…don't try to figure it out." After a moment I turned to Carl, "Can you send me an image capture of this guy? I'll check him out." I didn't know if Nate had recognition software, but I knew Mossad and the Shin Bet did. The FBI did, too, but I wasn't going there.

"Just give me your email."

I did, and Carl's fingers glided over the keyboard again, and in less than thirty seconds he had sent me an image capture.

And with that, we were all pretty much done for the night. Carl hugged Aminah and Noa, we shook hands, and then he took off. The girls disappeared to grab some stuff to take over Jon's, leaving Jon and me alone in the common room.

"I'll keep an eye on them," he vowed.

"Take all this seriously, Jon. Situational awareness, always. Be paranoid."

"Got it, Major," he used my IDF rank. "er...Boss."

"I'm serious."

"I know, and I will be." He paused. "What are you going to do?"

"I'll come back to campus tomorrow and ask around about this guy."

In a few more minutes both college girls reappeared with backpacks, and the four of us left. As we rode the elevator to the first floor, Jon and the girls began chatting, but I wasn't paying attention. I couldn't help but go back to my conversation with Idan Gelvar in Tel Aviv. The Deputy Director of the Mossad was worried about his niece, and about 48 hours later this happened. Thank God everyone was okay, but the threat could be real. What did Gelvar know? Maybe there *was* a Hamas connection, and he needed me to confirm it before he sent in his own team.

We exited the elevator into the lobby, and then walked out onto 33rd Street to pause beneath an awning that said "Homewood House." The streets had remained quiet, though across 33rd street, a café was still open. Through the windows I could see a group of college kids huddled around a table, eating.

I looked back at the trio next to me. "Where are you parked, Jon?"

He nodded to the left, toward Charles Street.

"You?"

I nodded to the right. After a "See you later" to the group, we peeled off in opposite directions. The walk back to my Jeep took only a few minutes beneath the orange streetlights and security cameras. As I approached the Grand Cherokee I looked up the block and spotted the dark gray Accord that had followed me here. For a second I toyed with going over to the driver who no doubt was FBI, to tell him I was heading home. It seemed juvenile, so I just climbed into my SUV, and drove home, watching the gray Accord in my mirror follow me.

8

"I didn't know anything was going to happen." Gelvar's voice was as calm as could be.

There was no way I was going to sleep when I arrived home; my body was seven hours ahead and there was too much on my mind. So, I had placed a call to the Deputy Director after finishing half a cold bottle of Goldstar beer, an import from Israel.

"Idan, really? You didn't know." Calling the Mossad master by his first name was not unusual etiquette. In Israel, by almost the entire population, superior officers, politicians, even teachers were generally referred to by first names. It was like everyone was family.

"Nothing has come across my desk," he said with that smooth voice, "and there has been no chatter about terrorist activity in the States. If there had been, I wouldn't have brought you in." That didn't mean he didn't trust me; it meant I just wasn't one of his men. If the FBI were listening, I hope they believed that.

"Okay, I'm going to email you a picture of the person who broke into Noa's room. Perhaps you can ID him." The thought just occurred to me that more than one person might have been in her room. The guy who tried to access her computer might have had a partner or partners. There was also the missing roommate I needed to check out. Gelvar gave me his non-secure email; he wouldn't reveal his secure one on an open line. "Oh, by the way," my voice began to build a slight edge, "the FBI thinks I'm one of your men. We had a little chat soon after I arrived in town."

"What? Why do they think that?"

I told him about our picture being taken when the two of us, plus our mutual Shin Bet friend, spoke at the beachside café. If Gelvar was surprised, he didn't appear so. But I didn't expect he'd reveal anything anyway.

"Do you want me to call the Hoover Building and straighten it out?" the Israeli asked.

"God no, Idan. I'll handle it."

"*B'seder.* If that's what you want. If you change your mind, let me know."

I didn't respond. There was no point.

Gelvar finished with a simple, "I'll call if something turns up."

I didn't thank him, just, "I'll let you know if I find anything here." And that was it. I hung up, put down my phone and just stayed where I was.

I took another few swallows of beer and quickly reviewed my evening: the conversation with Katie, my reaction – essentially walking out once she had made up her mind – as well as what had happened at Noa's. There had to be some breadcrumbs at the University, either with the Campus Police, or maybe with some of the professors. It occurred to me I didn't have Noa's schedule, so I texted Jon: *Ask Noa to send me her class schedule.* After a few moments he texted back: *She'll email it to you.* They were still up. I had to smile.

Since sleeping wasn't an option at this point, I spent the next few hours, doing laundry, checking email, and paying bills. It was weird getting back to normal. After the conversation with Katie, a big part of normal didn't exist. I'd just have to compartmentalize. *Good luck with that,* I smiled to myself. I believed she still had strong feelings for me, certainly physical ones and that she recognized there was a strong emotional connection as well. Otherwise, we wouldn't have had that whole talk. On the other hand, maybe, I should go back to Israel, once this thing with Noa was resolved. All the second-guessing was taking up too much brainpower.

As the sun rose higher in the sky, I found myself driving back over to Charles Street and to my karate studio. There were some business logistics I needed to figure out. Jon had been running my classes for at least four months, and it wasn't fair to the students who had signed on with me. I'd need to talk with all of them and compensate the group one way or the other. My first class back would be later tonight, so my thoughts needed to be in order by then.

For the moment, there was too much to think about, so I headed toward the middle of the practice floor and began to "Walk the Circle," literally walking around a center point to begin a series of *pa kua* forms. The phone rang.

It was Nate. "Heard about the incident at Hopkins last night."

"Yup."

"Heard you went over."

"Yup."

"So, do you believe Mossad Man knew something was up?"

"Mossad Man?"

"Yeah. It's easier to remember than Idan Gelvar."

Obviously Nate had remembered the Deputy Director's name. He just wanted to show some justified disrespect and skepticism. "I have no idea. I tend to believe him. If he thought there was serious shit happening, he'd have brought in his own men, not me."

"Maybe he's having you assess the situation first."

"Thought of that, too."

"So, heard you and Katie broke up."

"Slick transition there, Nate." I paused. I continued to pace in my circle, but with the phone in my hand. "Yeah, she wasn't happy I broke my word about coming home. And the way she put it, she wants to take a break to assess us."

"I know."

"You know?"

"Katie spoke with Rachel a couple of weeks ago, while you were doing God knows what in the Promised Land." Rachel was his wife. "I put in a good word for you, just so you know. So did Rachel. I wanted to tell you, but there was the FBI interview crap and you needed to hear it from Katie anyway."

"Yeah. All true. So, you're calling to cheer me up."

"Yup. Feeling better, right?" He let a moment pass, then, "So tell me what you think about the break-in last night."

I stated my thoughts about the *DEATH TO ISRAEL* graffiti, the Hamas flag, and my musings in general. "Hopefully Gelvar will find a match to the screen capture."

"Don't want to give it to the FBI?"

"First let's see if there's something to give. You're not going to say anything to them?"

"And the point of that would be…?"

I smiled. Nate knew I'd take it to the FBI, or to him, if it turned out to be something. I needed to know before the Feds what was going on. Besides, I couldn't trust them to share their findings with me.

"So, you okay with Katie?" Nate asked.

"Katie who?"

"You're compartmentalizing. How's that going for you?"

"Ask me tomorrow."

And with that we hung up. Sooner or later, I'd be over Nate and Rachel's house for dinner, and the Katie subject would come up again. We could leave it for then. Meanwhile, I got back to walking the circle. I had made two revolutions when Noa came in. She was wearing black leggings and a belted tunic, and somehow looked refreshed. All I felt was worn.

"Hi," I said as she approached. "*Boker tov.* Good morning."

"*Boker or.*"

"Did you sleep?"

"A little." She stopped speaking and just looked at me

"What's up?"

Noa hesitated. She looked away for a moment, and then back to me. "I just wanted to say thank you for helping me."

I smiled. "I haven't done anything yet."

"Yes, you have. You're looking out for me, and that makes me feel better."

"Again, I haven't done anything, but you're welcome."

"That's all I wanted to say." She smiled and turned to the door.

"Do you need a lift?" Her back was already to me.

"No. Jon's outside in his car."

Of course. After a moment, before she got too far, "Noa?"

The niece of the Deputy Director of the Mossad turned back to me.

"Don't talk to anyone about this outside of our group. And if anything else happens, talk to me first."

She nodded. "Okay." She continued to the door.

"Noa?" She turned to me again. "Have you spoken with your folks yet?"

"They're on the West Coast. I'll wait a little while longer."

"You can give them my number if you want."

"Okay." And with that she left.

I got back to exercising. That was very sweet of Noa, to come by.

A full minute passed and then two more visitors came in: Special Agent Edwin Conniker and Special Agent in Charge Jeffries. It was that kind of morning.

Conniker, with his broad shoulders was in a black suit, white shirt, and monochrome dark red tie. Jeffries, unlike yesterday, had on a full suit as well, though hers was gray.

"Good morning, Special Agents," I said. "Come in."

"Good morning, Mr. Aronson," Jeffries answered. Conniker didn't say anything.

"I'd offer you some coffee or something, but I don't have any. We can go next door."

"Won't be here that long," Conniker, apparently in his bully mode, responded, looking around at the punching bags and miscellaneous martial art weapons.

Jefffries took a softer approach. "I understand there was an incident at Hopkins last night: the break-in and the anti-Israel graffiti."

"And the Hamas flag."

"You were there," Conniker stated. It wasn't a question.

The image of the gray Accord following me came to mind. "I came by to lend support. Like I said yesterday, I'm looking out for Gelvar's niece."

"So, what do you think?" Jeffries asked.

"You first. Why is the FBI interested?"

"No," Conniker asserted, "you go ahead. If you don't mind."

"Are you sure we can't go next door where we can sit and talk?"

"No, thank you," Jeffries said. She repeated her partner's question: "What do you think about last night?"

I recapped virtually all the same thoughts I had mentioned to Nate, except for obtaining a screen capture of the home invader. "It was a professional job. No forced entry, and the timing showed there had been surveillance. Nothing taken. So, intimidation? Something to do with Noa's uncle or her parents? Something else? I have no idea." I half wanted to ask if that jibed with the police report they had no doubt reviewed – but there was no point in giving them attitude. Instead, I returned to: "Now, why is the FBI interested?"

"Possible Hamas connection," Jeffries answered. "Can't overlook that."

And the fact that students at Hopkins work with the NSA. Noa and Aminah had giggled about that last night, in talking about Carl. They probably didn't realize how accurate they were. Computers and, in select buildings, applied physics. Both areas of interest to terrorists.

I watched Jeffries. She kept her eyes on me, assessing. I did the same to her, and noticed the cut of her suit jacket. It was tailored to cover her Sig, but there was still a slight bulge over her right hip.

"If it *is* Hamas," Conniker acknowledged, "and they wanted to send a message, the young lady would probably be dead or have been kidnapped." The statement was the first non-belligerent thing he had said to me since we met.

"I agree. Though either of those would escalate whatever it is."

"Could still be a threat to someone," Jeffries added. " 'Look how easy it is for us to get to your loved ones.' "

As the agents were speaking, there was a moment of *Why were they discussing this with me?* "So, you guys came here just to say hi and review the case?"

Conniker nodded. "Yes."

"No you didn't." I smiled and let a full moment pass. "You came to apologize for yesterday…And you wanted to see me in my natural habitat."

Conniker looked confused, but Jeffries began to crack a smile. She looked down briefly when she saw I noticed. She knew that I knew why they were here.

I took a breath to serious up. "You wanted to see how much I knew about last night, and how much I'd reveal." A moment passed. "Listen, Agent Jeffries, Agent Conniker, really. I don't know how else to convince you. This is a personal favor for Idan Gelvar, looking after his niece. I didn't know anything was about to happen. And if last night does involve Hamas, and it's not a simple college student intimidation thing or revenge thing, I'll call you. Promise." *You wouldn't be my first call, but you'd get called,* I thought. "You're the FBI."

They still suspected me of working for the Mossad. I could see it in Conniker's eyes. I didn't want to look at Jeffries' eyes just yet.

"Next time you're here," I suggested, "we'll go next door for sandwiches."

Both agents just looked at me, and Conniker shook his head. They both headed out.

* * *

The Homewood Campus of the Johns Hopkins University is an

enclave unto itself. It's a universe of students, teachers, administrative assistants, clerks, maintenance crews, and other support staff, plus a hierarchy of a president, deans, advisors, directors, and more. Since the University is a mini-city in its own right, the non-university population passes it by generally without much thought, except perhaps for a glance at how beautiful the grounds look.

North Charles Street borders the eastern edge of campus, and while the main entrance is off to the right, the more commonly used visitor entrance is on the campus' southern side, around the corner from the Baltimore Museum of Art. I drove past the museum and followed the road to the right to an underground garage. On the first ramp level there was a cluster of open spaces, and soon enough I was climbing the steps up to ground level. When I emerged into the sunlight, I was greeted by an immense expanse of grass, bordered by stand-alone stately buildings.

Without really getting my bearings I just started walking along a wide brick walkway, past Federal and Georgian style buildings, beneath oak trees, and benches. The path intersected others, some leading to various lecture halls. At some point, I meandered down a flight of steps toward more contemporary buildings, and then up a flight, past a row of columns, until I finally stopped to admit I had no idea where I was going. Young men and women – some tall, some small, some with backpacks, others unencumbered – all walked past me without even a glance. Many had an ear to a phone or were listening to something through ear buds.

The mid-October morning was unseasonably warm, and the student population was taking full advantage of the bright sun: the girls were mostly in short shorts and tops of various configurations – halters, T-shirts, tube tops – while the boys were mainly in cargo shorts and polos. Virtually everyone had on flip-flops.

Officer Sam Richburg of campus security, the campus cop I had met at Noa's last night, was waiting for me outside a campus café called The Daily Grind. I just had no idea where it was. I stepped over to a campus map bolted to a nearby pedestal to locate the coffee shop. Fortunately, I wasn't too far off; just two buildings away, down another brick path. It didn't take long to get there.

The café was on the upper level of a study center, just inside a broad patio area. Officer Richburg was sitting in the shade at a patio table next to the building's glass wall. He stood when he saw me approach.

"Mr. Aronson," he held out his hand.

"Officer Richburg," I returned the handshake. " 'Gidon.' "

" 'Sam.' " He nodded to the café on the other side of the glass wall. "Let me buy you something."

We headed inside and over to the coffee stand. Two young baristas, one male and one female, stood behind the counter. Richburg ordered a tea. I ordered iced coffee.

In a matter of moments we were back outside, sitting at the patio table. We were positioned opposite each other, but could still watch the college kids passing by.

"This is such a fascinating campus," the officer said. "Just look around."

I did. The patio where we sat was a large expanse, populated with white tables and chairs. Some groupings had umbrellas for shade, while others were beneath leafy trees. Not far from where we sat was a young female student with blonde, spiky hair, huddled at a table, working over a laptop. A small black bird stood on the tabletop keeping her company. Neither seemed to notice the other, but after short while the bird opened its wings and flew off.

"So, Gidon, what can I do for you?" Richburg took a sip of his tea.

"I just wanted to review some stuff with you."

He nodded.

"In order to access Noa Biron's building you need a key card, right?"

"For students, it's their ID. The appropriate dorm is programmed into their cards."

"And only residents of a particular building have access to that housing?"

"Yes. Well, and maintenance staff."

"One step at a time. Can you get a list of who lives in her residence hall?"

"I can." He let a moment pass. "You investigating?"

I nodded. "Noa's uncle works for the Israeli government. I'm supposed to look after her."

" 'Israeli Government.' " He looked at me for a moment, and I let him draw whatever conclusions he wanted. "You're Israeli military or something, huh."

I remained silent.

After another moment, he nodded. "The Feds must love you." Then, "What d'ya need?"

"I have a copy of Noa's schedule. Is it possible to get a list of the students in her classes and see if any of them live in her dorm?"

"You're thinking an inside job. My thought, too. It'll take some time, but yeah, I can check that out."

"I don't know if there are any commonalities, but if there are, it may give us a lead."

I looked at Richburg and wondered what his background was. Maybe ex-city cop, maybe ex-military. He was closer to Nate's age than mine, but his hair was longer than Nate's – by two or three millimeters – and had touches of gray around his temples. He also looked pretty fit.

"Anyone else have access to that dorm?"

"Maintenance people, as I mentioned, some administrators. I'll see if I can get a list." He paused. "Then we'll have to find out if anyone had cause to do what they did last night."

"Maybe I can help narrow the field." I took out my cell phone and showed him the photo that Carl's software had captured last night. "This is the guy who broke in. Be nice to match a name to the face."

"Email it to me."

Before Richburg could ask where the photo came from, I explained, "Noa's anti-theft software activated the camera as soon her laptop was accessed without a password."

"Nice." He gave me his email address. "I'll ask around." He took another sip of his tea and watched the girl across the way working on the laptop. Without taking his eyes off the girl he asked, "So your only connection to Miss Biran is through her uncle?"

I nodded. "The request to watch her came just two days ago."

Still not looking at me: "Curious timing."

"Yup." I looked at the girl across the way as well. "Raises some interesting questions, doesn't it?"

"Know anyone over there who can follow up, outside of the uncle?"

I nodded. David Amit, my Shin Bet friend, might be able to help, if I wanted to pursue it behind Gelvar's back.

After another moment, the girl working on the computer across the way closed the top, stood, and headed past us toward the door of the building.

"Any activists on campus?" I asked, looking at Richburg.

"A few. It's a quiet university. The students are into studying. They have clubs and extra-curricular stuff, like science clubs. The most edgy is probably an a capella group, but I'll check around."

"Thanks." I stood up.

Richburg didn't stand. "Let me see that picture again, the one from the computer."

I showed him the screen capture.

"You may want to try Resident Life. They're in charge of housing and assignments. If this guy had legal access, maybe someone over there knows him." He told me where the office was. "I'll call and tell them you're coming, otherwise no one'll talk to you." He thought for a second. "Ask for Darlene. She's really tight with the students. If that guy's from campus, Darlene will know."

"Thanks." Richburg stood and I held out my hand: "I'll keep you posted." I turned to leave.

"Feds talk to you yet?" he asked before I had moved a step.

I smiled, turning back. "This morning. You know the importance of your campus."

He nodded. "Show them the picture?"

I just looked at him, deciding whether to be honest or not.

"I wouldn't have either."

I looked at the campus policeman, "Thanks for the coffee. Next time, I'll buy…and we'll go off campus."

He held my eyes for a second and nodded. "Next time."

* * *

The main Residential Life office of the Homewood Campus was across a large quad area, past more Georgian style buildings, along yet another brick walkway, and on the ground level of a modern-style building featuring a lot of glass. I took the four concrete steps two at a time and pulled open the right-hand side of a pair of double glass doors.

Almost immediately I was faced with a waist-high counter, where a young man and a young woman sat at computer terminals. A middle-aged woman of about fifty, with shoulder length dark curly hair woven with strands of gray stood between them. She was just standing there, scanning a printed list of some sort. Off to the right was a small lounge area with padded armchairs flanking a coffee table. No one was there.

The middle-aged woman with the curly salt-and-pepper hair looked up over her reading glasses. Her eyebrows arched, furrowing her forehead. "Can I help you?"

"Yes. Hi. My name is Gidon Aronson, and—"

"Sam just called about you."

She came over. She was my height and looked me right in the eye, though the gaze wasn't a challenge. Lines around her eyes made me think she smiled or laughed easily or often.

"You must be Darlene."

"I am." She shook her head. "Horrible, horrible what happened in that apartment last night. I heard about the graffiti."

"Scary stuff."

"The girls okay?"

"Yeah."

"Good. Now what can I do for you? Sam says you're investigating."

"I am." I pulled up the screen shot of the thin-faced guy who broke into Noa's room. "Recognize this man?"

She looked at it and said, "Seth Bruce."

"You're sure."

She nodded, and the red-headed young woman to my left at the computer station spoke up without taking her eyes from the screen, "She's freakish like that. She remembers *everyone*."

I turned from the redhead back to Darlene. "Seth Bruce? Who is he?"

She took the cell phone from my hand and looked at the man's photo. "Last year he was a graduate student who was an R.A."

"Resident Advisor?"

"Yes. Didn't come back this year."

Maybe he did. For a one-night visit. "Have an address for him on file?"

She handed the phone back to me and turned to the redhead. "Sheryl…"

"I'll check."

Darlene continued while Sheryl worked at her station: "R.A.s have different arrangements with the University. Some get paid straight out, sometimes they get free housing in exchange for being an R.A., or sometimes they get a deduction on tuition."

"And Seth?"

She shrugged. "I can recall their names and faces, but not much else." She gave me a big smile, and the lines around her eyes crinkled. "Besides. How he was paid wasn't through here. That happens across the quad in Admin. But we may have an address for him. If not, you'll have to go to the registrar and, well, no one wants to do that." Sheryl and the young man on the other side of us laughed.

"Got it," Sheryl said, and both of us walked over to the redhead. She turned the monitor so I could see. "His address is in Brewer's Hill." Darlene said. "Near the Natty Boh sign."

"You know this town," I smiled.

"Born and raised, hon," she smiled back. "I'll write down the address."

As she wrote, I asked, "Is this a problem, confidentiality and all that?"

She shrugged. "Anything I give you, you can find online." Darlene handed me Seth Bruce's address. "So you think he's involved with what happened?"

"Won't know until I speak with him." Yeah, I was pretty sure he was involved. "Do you remember where he was an R.A.? Which building?"

"Homewood House." No hesitation. Instant recall.

"I'm telling you, she's freakish," Sheryl said from the side.

I smiled not only at Darlene's memory, but at what she remembered. The Homewood House was Noa's residence hall.

* * *

East Baltimore, like many sections of most towns, is one neighborhood after another. In Baltimore's case, as you head east off the end of I-83 you soon come to Patterson Park, and then after some turns, Canton, and then Brewers Hill. Once home to the National Bohemian and Gunther Breweries, the area today was well on its way to becoming a trendy, urban area of renovated houses, office buildings, and retail spaces.

The Seth Bruce address Darlene had provided was a block away from the Natty Boh Tower in the middle of a series of row houses, third from the end. I parked diagonally up the street, in the shade of a small maple that allowed a direct line of sight to Bruce's front door. Down the block, but visible above his apartment was the round Natty Boh sign, a one-eyed, mustached, cartoon image perched atop his namesake building. The icon would have been right at home on a Monopoly board.

It was already mid-afternoon, and there was steady foot traffic up and down the block: mothers with strollers, construction workers, men in dress shirts and ties, and men and women in casual pants and tops. No one, however, came in or out of Seth Bruce's row house.

There were multiple possibilities. The address Darlene had on file could have been obsolete. Or he simply wasn't home. In fact, Bruce could be long gone. I wouldn't hang around after breaking into someone's apartment.

After another fifteen minutes, I stepped out of the car and headed across the street.

The row house apartments to my left appeared as if they had been recently renovated. They had a clean, repointed look. Some front doors were of the narrow double-door variety of historic preservation. Bruce's was solid wood, painted a pea green. No window look-through. There was, however, a brass address plate but no name. I stepped up onto the stoop and peered into the double hung front window. No one was home, at least not in the front area, a living room.

The question was, was this even his place? A simple call to the Ivy League-looking detective from last night, telling him about this address, might lead to some answers – if he were willing to share information. Or a call to the FBI, or even to Nate might provide some help.

I stepped down off the front marble steps, and turned my back to the house to mull it over. Actually, I wasn't thinking; I wanted to see if anyone was watching me. I casually looked up and down the block. Nope. I meandered off to the left, away from my car and toward the Natty Boh building. At the end of the block, there was a small side street, more like an alley. I turned left. Another alleyway appeared, and I turned onto it, going behind the line of townhouses.

The alley was wide enough for a medium-sized car, but not much more. On the right was a solid cement wall that gave way to small niches that were parking spaces. To my left, I passed a parking pad, then the rear of the second unit, which had a small open-air wooden deck, and then next up the block, the rear entrance to what I hoped was Bruce's place. There was an empty parking spot with cement walls to either side. It seemed only a Mini Cooper could fit between them. Steps on the left side led up to a new wooden two-story deck. Before I could move onto the property, a construction worker – a man in his thirties in a dirty work shirt, jeans, and construction boots – came out of the opening next up the block. Without breaking stride, I continued walking up the alley. The man, who had short, sandy hair and a five o'clock shadow, pulled out a cell phone, and nodded to me even as he turned his attention to dialing a number. I could hear him talking into the phone as I continued walking forward. In a moment his voice tapered off behind me. I walked a few more feet, then turned around to see the alley I had just traversed was now empty. Either the construction worker had turned the corner or had gone into one of the rear entrances. Hopefully, it wasn't Bruce's.

I backtracked to Seth Bruce's parking pad and turned in off the alley. The first six wooden steps led to the back entrance, and to a rear kitchen door that had multiple glass panes divide by mullions. I looked inside.

The kitchen had been newly renovated. White laminate cabinets lined the right-hand wall, beneath which was a light-colored granite counter, with a glass-front wine refrigerator underneath. Along the left wall was a stainless steel refrigerator and an oven. In the center of the room was a white island that looked immaculate. The floor looked to be hardwood, also immaculate, except for the spot in front of the refrigerator where Seth Bruce was lying on his side, with a pool of blood near his head. There was no movement. His face was partially hidden by the edge of the island. Even though I couldn't clearly see him, I knew it was Bruce.

I tried the door, turning the knob from the back of the handle with only a few fingers. No luck. On the inside was a double cylinder lock with no key; breaking the glass and reaching in wouldn't help.

I sprinted back down the stairs, ran down the alley, and around to the front of the unit. At this point if people saw me, then they saw me. I went up to the pea green door and tried the knob, turning it from the back of the knob just as I had on the back door. It was unlocked. I went in, careful to close the door with my elbow. Seth Bruce had probably opened the door for his visitor or visitors, but they had to open the door on the way out. I darted through the living room, past a staircase on the left, and into the kitchen.

Immediately I saw Bruce on the floor. I walked around, careful not to touch anything. In stepping around the island to see him on his side, there was no doubt how he died. Seth Bruce's throat was cut and he had a gunshot to the side of his head.

9

"I already spoke to your captain. There won't be any obstruction charges against Gidon." Nate, Captain D'Allesandro, was addressing the Ivy League-looking robbery detective from last night, Ed Soper. The two of us had been cordial in Noa's dorm room, but not now.

Soper was pissed. "He turned up evidence in the apartment and kept it to himself," he said, leaning into Nate, about a mere foot from him.

Nate and Soper were with me in Seth Bruce's house. While I had parked myself on the couch out of the way and watched, the two law enforcement men stood at the junction of Bruce's living room and kitchen, trying not to raise their voices at each other. Well, Nate wasn't raising his voice – he rarely did – but Soper was unsuccessfully trying to keep his in check. Behind the two detectives, crime scene people were busy in the kitchen.

"He was waiting for it to pan out," Nate responded calmly. "I'm okay with that."

"Well it panned out, didn't it." Soper looked toward where the victim lay lifeless.

Soper's thought had crossed my mind as I had waited for Nate to arrive. If I had called the young robbery detective right away and told him about the screen capture last night, maybe he would have turned up this address, and maybe Bruce would not be lying on the kitchen floor with a slit throat and a bullet in his head.

"He should be in cuffs." Soper was turning red.

"Major Aronson works with the Israeli Shin Bet and has worked with me. His instincts are usually good."

"I don't fucking care, Captain."

Nate raised his eyebrows at Soper's tone, and whether Soper was aware of it or not, he took a step back after seeing the Captain's expression.

"Detective," I said standing up and approaching Soper, "I apologize. I should have called you, but I was seeing if this address were relevant. Obviously it was. Whether your guys could've prevented the killing, or I could have if I had been smarter, I don't know. I have to live with that."

Soper just looked at me, his face slowly returning to its natural color.

"So, what do you think?" I turned to Nate.

He scratched the side of his almost clean-shaven head for a second. "You've already got this. Bruce was the break-in guy. Whoever hired him, killed him. The *DEATH TO ISRAEL* crap on Miss Biram's wall is misdirection."

"Yeah, this isn't Hamas. If they had wanted something from Noa, they'd have grabbed her and tortured her."

"On the other hand, the kid's throat was cut," Soper set aside being pissed off at least for the moment.

We stepped into the kitchen to look down at the body, which was still being examined by Forensics.

"It does have a certain radical Islamic zeal to it," I looked at the young cop.

"But shot in the head, too?" he wondered aloud.

Nate squatted on his heels and looked more closely at Bruce's head. "It *is* redundant. Makes you wonder which came first, the knife or the bullet? And why both?"

"The knife and then maybe the bullet for mercy?" The robbery detective squatted next to Nate.

"Bullet first," I countered, "and then the knife across the throat as a message."

Nate stood up. "You ever see this before, Gidon?"

"Not like this."

"What did the girl's uncle in Israel say?" he meant Gelvar, the Deputy Director of Mossad.

"About last night? That he didn't know anything was going to happen. Haven't told him about this yet." I shook my head again.

"What?"

"If this *is* about Gelvar, then Hamas or one of their factions might be behind this."

"Gelvar sent something to his niece?" Soper asked. "Something he won't admit, but something someone wants?"

"He said he didn't, but who knows." After another second, "The *DEATH TO ISRAEL* thing may not be misdirection."

"Be nice to know," my friend said calmly.

"Excuse me, Captain." A young African American officer in a blue Crime Scene windbreaker approached Nate. "Two things. First, our victim must've been worried about something, because there are hidden cameras all over the place. I traced the feed to a laptop in the bedroom."

Nate looked at the CSU guy. "Were they live when this happened?"

The young man nodded. "From a quick look, the victim recorded everything. The feed is still open on the laptop. There's even time code."

" 'Just because you're paranoid…'" I began.

Nate turned to the robbery cop. "Work with forensics. Review the video and get me screen captures of whoever was here."

Soper began to say something, but Nate cut him off. "I'll clear it with your captain. There's overlap on our cases."

The robbery detective nodded and looked at me for a brief moment. His expression wasn't warm and fuzzy. But I knew Nate. This was his way of keeping the peace.

"Get it done today," Nate said, and Soper nodded again. My friend turned back to the forensics man, "What else?"

He held up a gloved hand. He was holding a laptop in a sealed forensics bag. "Found this in the trashcan in the victim's office."

Soper turned to us. "Why would the victim throw away—"

"It's not his," I looked from one detective to the other.

The Ivy League cop turned from Nate to me: "Noa Biran's roommate had her laptop stolen yesterday."

"Aminah," I clarified. "It's hers, I'd bet."

Soper nodded, and went on: "Probably taken by our dead guy."

"And he couldn't get in because of Carl's software. That's why it was in the trash. He must have been really frustrated."

"Carl?" Nate asked.

I explained that he was Aminah's boyfriend who had installed lock-out software on the computer.

"These guys are looking for something," Nate said almost to himself. "But why take the roommate's computer?"

Soper's eyes widened ever-so-slightly. "There's a common file."

"A shared email?" Nate continued. "An attachment. Or something embedded. Your college kid may not even know about this." He looked at me.

"Agreed," I said. "The two girls were sent the same file. Maybe one was cc'ed." I let a moment pass. "You're pretty good for an old guy. Very tech savvy."

"I love my iPhone 3S."

"Wait," I looked at the homicide cop. "Aminah's laptop was stolen first. The break-in happened later. Could this all have to do with her and not Noa?"

"Impossible to know at this point."

Soper held up his phone and a photo of Noa's wall, the one with *DEATH TO ISRAEL* and the Hamas flag on it.

"We don't know who Seth Bruce had eyes on, or the real sequence," Nate responded.

"And on whose behalf," Soper put in.

The three of us looked at the body on the kitchen floor.

"We can't ignore the obvious," Nate said.

I turned to my friend. "That this is about Noa?"

"We need to find out." After a moment Nate turned to the forensics man, "If we get you the other computer, can your guys check for common files and emails?"

"Of course."

I looked at Nate: "You'll have to get past Carl's anti-tampering software. Besides, I have a better idea. How would you like to earn some goodwill?"

"The Feds?"

"I feel like I owe them something. We can let them run with this." I pointed to the laptop in the forensics man's hand.

Nate nodded and turned back to the CSU tech: "Leave the laptop. I'll sign for it."

"We're still missing another piece." They looked at me. "There's a third roommate."

Nate turned to Soper who nodded. "She's staying with her boyfriend in Georgetown. That's what Aminah told us last night."

"Talk to her," Nate ordered the robbery detective.

My friend was giving the young cop a lot to do. This was Nate saying to Soper that he had pissed him off by getting in his face.

The young detective just nodded again and looked at me. He knew what was going on, and he knew he had to get off Nate's shit list.

"Find out what the deal is with her," Nate said.

I took another look at the body on the floor. Seth Bruce really was a kid like Noa and Aminah, just a little older.

The Hamas flag and the scrawl on Noa's wall flashed through my head. We needed to keep a closer eye on the girls. I'd ask Jon to help. They had stayed with him last night.

"Maybe your boy Jon can look after the young ladies." Nate had read my thoughts. "My guess is whoever did this won't go after them. They don't want a direct confrontation."

"Not yet."

Nate just shook his head, as if he were running some ideas internally.

"I'm heading back to my place." I moved toward the door. "Jon will be there. I'll talk to him."

Soper called to me: "If something comes up…"

"I'll call. Promise."

I know he didn't believe me, but I meant it at the time.

10

When I entered the office of my karate dojo an hour later, I saw Jon sitting behind my desk, typing on the computer. "Hi, Sifu. Let me finish this and I'll get up."

"No rush." I sat in a chair opposite him, and after a moment of taking in the room, I watched him work. My student was composing an email, but that's not what caught my attention. Jon was dressed in a pink dress shirt, navy and pink tie, and gray pants – a rare business look for him. "I should take your picture and Tweet it to my followers."

"Like you have followers." He smiled without taking his eyes off the screen.

"I'm sure if I were on social media, I'd have friends and followers and stuff."

Jon just smiled some more. "You keep telling yourself that, boss." After a few seconds, he closed the program and turned toward me. "What?"

"It's a nice look, Jon."

"Had an appointment with a historical neighborhood association for one of our properties."

"I'm sure you made a fine impression."

"Didn't matter. All they care about is whether the windows and banisters are historically accurate."

"But you looked really professional when they asked you about it, though." I smiled, and then after another moment, "Tell me how Noa and Aminah did last night after you went home."

He slid the rolling chair out slightly. "They're okay, I guess. I don't think they slept much, but I didn't hear them discuss what happened."

I looked at him. "The girls and I need to talk," I looked at him. "The break-in thing jumped to a new level."

"Why?"

"The screen shot from last night from Noa's computer…I found the guy."

"What did he say? Did he cooperate?" He slid the chair slightly more toward me.

"He's dead. Murdered in his house."

"Whoa." He sat up.

"I called Captain D'Allesandro."

"And? What does he think?"

"Same as me. Somebody's looking for something that either Noa or Aminah has."

"Serious shit."

"Yeah."

"Want me to hang out more with the girls? I have no problem doing that, you know."

I smiled. "I know it'd be tough on you."

"I'll text Noa and Aminah so we can get together when I finish here. They're actually coming to the workout tonight, by the way."

"Don't tell them about the murder. I'll do that when I speak with them."

"Okay." He let a few seconds pass as he thought. "You talk to Katie? You always like discussing stuff with her."

Yesterday I waved him off the Katie subject. "We're not really talking." I briefly explained about Katie wanting space to figure out if we had the right stuff. "To be honest, Jon, I haven't had the time to think about her."

"Bullshit."

I raised my eyebrows.

"I'm sorry. Bullshit, *Sifu*. You'd much rather be with her right now than over here with me."

"Oh, you know me so well."

I looked around the office randomly again, and a stack of three boxes next to the door caught my eye. Two of the three were open, but the third, the size of a shoebox, was not. "What's up with those?"

We went over to the stack. "They came a little while ago," Jon explained. "The bottom two are supplies I ordered: gis, belts, arm and leg pads. The top one, though, came FedEx today, addressed to you."

I hadn't ordered anything. The return address was from a martial art supply house in Manhattan I didn't recognize. I pulled out my Benchmade pocket knife, and flicked open the half serrated/half straight edge combo blade.

"You didn't order this, did you?" he looked at me.

"Nope."

I moved the blade over to the brown packing tape that joined the two top half flaps.

"Wait. Wait!" Jon took a step back.

"Why?"

"It could be a bomb or something from whoever killed the break-in dude you just found."

"The killer doesn't know I exist." I put the point of the blade onto the tape.

"Maybe it's from one of your other million enemies."

"Million enemies?"

I looked at my student, giving him a "Like, really?" expression, and then slit open the tape. Jon took another step back.

I lifted the flaps to see a white inner lining of tissue paper. Beyond that were three items: a business envelope with my name on it in Hebrew, stacks of money, and a cell phone.

"Crap. And I'm trying to convince the FBI I'm not working for the Mossad."

"Say what?"

"Long story."

Gelvar. The Deputy Director of the Mossad was no doubt trying to help me, but it was a dumb move sending me money in an unsecured way. It appeared to be in the thousands of dollars. I had no desire to count it, but I did want to look at the envelope with my name on it. The Hebrew script on the front had a nice, circular flair to it, and toward the top left corner were two Hebrew letters, *dalet* and *aleph*. David Amit's initials. This wasn't from Gelvar; it was from my Shin Bet friend, the man who had introduced me to Gelvar. I opened the envelope to find a letter and a VISA credit card. The letter read: "As promised, the agreed-upon payment for your service this past spring. Glad we met for coffee."

I shook my head. Maybe the box hadn't really been delivered by FedEx. My original thought was correct. It was from Gelvar: the coffee reference…the café on the Tel Aviv promenade before I went to the airport. He was trying to help in case I had expenses, but knew how it'd look if the money had come from him. The enclosed credit card was an interesting touch. Some things cash couldn't cover: rental cars, online plane reservations, and more. The card, if investigated, would trace back to the Shin Bet, not the Mossad. Hopefully.

"What's with the cell?" Jon asked, picking up the phone that had been included in the package.

"It's secure."

"Cool."

I took the phone from my student, put it back in the box, and put the whole thing against the wall next to my desk.

"What now, boss?"

After a second, "I go for a walk."

The students for my post-dinner martial arts class would be filing in within half an hour, and before I began their workout, I wanted to clear my head. "Hold down the fort." I walked past him. "Don't let any strangers in."

There was a lot to consider. There was all this stuff with the break-in last night, and now the murder. We needed to resolve everything as expeditiously as possible.

Once outside, and on my way around the block, I passed a second-hand bookstore on the right and then a small copy-print store. I paused to look in the storefront window of the print shop. A single customer was inside, explaining a paper to a clerk. I shifted focus to the reflections in the pane of glass. No one, at least in the reflection, was looking my way. Bruce's killer or killers were floating around somewhere; reason enough to be cautious. There was also the FBI. The image of the two agents who had interrogated me was never far from the surface.

In resuming my perambulation, instead of continuing down the block to the right, I turned left, visually sweeping the street the way I had come and then to where I'd be walking. As Charles Street was one-way at this point, cars were parked on both sides of the road, facing north. It wasn't difficult spotting the man behind the wheel of a dark green Subaru at the curb, diagonally down from me. He was wearing aviator sunglasses and reading a folded newspaper.

There were dozens of stores and offices on the block, so it was possible he was just waiting for a friend. Or, he could be part of an FBI surveillance crew. Nothing like paranoia.

I continued my walk, turning the corner. By the time I had circled the block, my mind had returned to the dorm room from last night, and then to Seth Bruce lying on the floor of his kitchen. Approaching the steps to my karate studio, I scanned the street again. The parked Subaru was gone, and in its place a medium blue Ford. As before, there was a man in the driver's seat, reading a paper. I frowned for a moment, and then began climbing the cement steps. Halfway up, my cell rang: Nate. "Hey, what's up?" I paused in front of my door. Apparently, I couldn't walk and listen at the same time.

"So what do you think about Soper?"

I turned back to watch the street. "We'll see."

"Yeah. These young guys."

"Thanks for getting him off my ass."

"He's just pissed he doesn't have all the answers."

"Know the feeling. Me, I'm going to beat the shit out of some students."

"Nice to have them pay you for that."

"Yeah. I should be paying them for the therapy."

He laughed, and I hung up and headed inside.

11

Piano Man ran through my head as the regular crowd shuffled in. They were mostly high school and college-age kids, with a few twenty- and thirty-somethings mixed in. I had changed into black gi pants and a red-and-white IDF T-shirt. No belt declaring my rank.

"Hey, Sifu," Jon said, walking over to me. "Nice-looking group, isn't it?" He was clad mostly monochromatically: a pair of black gi pants and a black T-shirt with a red emblazoned dragon over the chest.

I followed his line of sight to a pair of attractive young women who had begun to stretch out: "You're referring to everyone's martial abilities, of course."

"Of course." He kept watching as the lithe students each slid into a full split.

"You built up a nice group while I was gone, grasshopper. I know most everyone, but a few I don't," I nodded to the women.

"It's your reputation, Sifu. I just put the word out."

"Yeah, we can go with that, if you want."

As I continued to scan the class, two more women came in. Both were in their late twenties, I'd guess. They looked like professionals – not really sure what that meant – and they carried themselves well. One was auburn-haired and the other a brunette. The auburn woman was in a purple Ravens T-shirt and cut-offs, and her companion wore gray sweatpants and a blue T-shirt. The latter carried a small green gym bag. They must have been new, prospective students; they stepped into the room and moved over to the side and just watched everyone else. After a few moments they spotted Jon and me.

"Know those two?" I nodded to the ladies.

"No. But I will in a minute." He trotted over to them.

I smiled to myself. He'd have their phone numbers by the end of the conversation. During their few moments of back-and-forth, the auburn-haired woman seemed the more animated of the two. She smiled easily, and was more engaged in the conversation. Her friend stood ramrod straight and maintained a serious face. After a moment, Jon caught my eye, and I headed over.

"Hi. How are you." I held out my hand. "Gidon Aronson."

The auburn-haired woman responded, "Marietta."

"Caroline," the serious friend offered.

"They came to check us out," Jon said.

"Excellent. How'd you hear 'bout us?"

Marietta answered, "Instagram."

I turned to Jon: "Social media at work. My investment in you is paying off."

He just shook his head in mock exasperation.

"Thanks for coming by." I turned from one to the other. "Either of you have martial arts training?"

Caroline, the second woman, nodded: "About six months of Krav Maga."

I looked at Caroline. Physically, she was lean and had an early Katy Perry look, with an oval face and long, dark hair parted in the middle. While she had a big smile when she offered it, her eyes had a serious, penetrating look. Her left hand was still holding the strap of her gym bag, and from what I could see, she was clutching the strap tightly. Her friend, Marietta, had straight, short, feathered hair, but with long bangs falling to the side of her face. Her bright, green eyes were accentuated by black eyeliner, which made them seem even more emerald.

"I'm just here for some good cardio," Marietta offered, "and to learn some cool techniques."

"Outstanding," Jon said enthusiastically. "You came to the right place."

"If you want, you can put the bag in the back of the room," I directed.

"Perfect," Caroline, the brunette responded, and hustled to put the small duffle where I had indicated.

I turned to Jon and asked him to line everyone up. He nodded and then turned slightly, raising his voice: "LINE UP!"

In a matter of seconds everyone in the room fell into ranks: three lines of students, with the second line directly aligned behind the first, and the third aligned behind the second. The higher ranks, the brown and purple belts, began in the upper right of the first row, if you were facing forward, and then the ranks went down the scale until white belts stood in the back row. Jon and I moved to the front and faced everyone.

"Good evening." I started. "Great to see you. I owe each and every one of you an apology for my absence. I'm sure you've been told some wild stories about why I was away." I turned to Jon. "But all I can confirm is that I didn't get as much beach time in Tel Aviv as I would have liked."

The class laughed.

"And as someone before me has said, jumping out of a perfectly good plane is very unnatural. And that's all I'll say about that."

Another laugh.

"Anyway, I promise to make it up to you. Meanwhile, Sensei Jonathan will warm you up." I looked at Jon, who smiled a little too maniacally.

And with that, he began, first spending time on stretches, working from the head and shoulders, down to legs and ankles. He then moved on to push-ups, sit-ups, leg lifts, and more, pushing even the veteran students to more repetitions than they probably had ever done. After twenty minutes of intense, nonstop work, just about everyone was struggling to match the fast, repetitive count. Still, everyone tried to keep up.

Then came the martial techniques: stance work, blocks, punches, and kicks. Over and over. Front kick, side kick, round kick, combinations of blocks, kicks, punches. Up and down the practice hall. Sets of three, sets of six. Back and forth. I circulated up and down the lines.

By the time they were done, sweat was pouring down faces, hair was matted, and T-shirts saturated. Some students were bent over to catch their breath. I looked at the two women I had spoken to earlier. Marietta, the more animated one, was rotating her hips and generally stretching. Her bangs were plastered to her forehead. I could see that she was taking long, deep breaths. Caroline, her friend, was leaning forward slightly so she could bring the bottom of her T-shirt up to wipe the sweat from her face. Her mouth was open as she tried to bring in enough air. I moved to the front of the room.

"It's always helpful to know that despite the pain, the fatigue, the sore muscles, you'll survive." I scanned the room, looking at the bright, red faces and heaving torsos. "So, now that you're warmed up…" I smiled, with just a hint of malice, and worked them an additional fifteen minutes.

Finally, I said, "Go, hydrate."

The group dispersed to various areas of the periphery. Some reached into gym bags to retrieve and guzzle down bottles of water. Others lined up at the two water stations Jon had set up along the back wall.

After five minutes or so, the class began to filter back into their ranks. Faces were still red, and T-shirts were still saturated, but that wasn't stopping anyone. I was about to call "Line up," when Noa and Aminah walked in. Jon said they'd be coming by, and it was good to see them. They both had a slight bounce to their walk, and both were carrying shopping bags from Anthropologie. I had to smile: last night their apartment had been broken into, cops all over the place, potential death threats…and then today, retail therapy. I loved it.

Jon spotted them and hustled over. Each gave him a hug and a kiss, and then the trio turned to me. I pointed to a set of folding chairs off to the side and Jon walked the girls over. Once they were settled out of the way, I got back to work, calling everyone to order.

The class quickly moved back into their positions.

"Now that everyone is finished dripping all over my floor…"There were a few laughs.

"Sensei Jonathan, can I borrow you?"

He sprinted over.

"Anyone here ever been grabbed?"

We moved to the center of the group where Jon and I showed the class a series of grabs and countermoves, with Jon as the aggressor. As soon as he grabbed me, I responded, regardless of whether it was escaping a wrist grab, or a potentially debilitating chokehold. In short order my reactions became more intense, and my lead student ended up on the floor more often than not. I broke down the moves for the various ranks, took questions, and then simply said, "Go, play."

Jonathan and I circulated as the students began to work. Even Marietta and Caroline joined in. As I expected, Caroline, the one who had sixth months of Krav Maga, was the more aggressive. She made Marietta work for her escapes, and when it was her turn to break out of the holds, she moved strongly and assuredly. In the meantime, Jonathan walked over to Noa and Aminah who were still sitting off to the side, and huddled in their own conversation, oblivious to the activity around them. Jon invited them to join the group. Aminah seemed game; Noa shook her head.

He gave up and came back over.

"No luck?"

"Not really."

"Your Jedi powers of persuasion abandon you, Number One?"

"Maybe I should discreetly wave my hand in front of Noa or something."

"If you get one of them to say, 'These aren't the droids you're looking for,' I'll give you twenty—"

There was a *klunk* nearby as Marietta hit the floor fifteen feet from me. Caroline had swept her feet out from under her.

"Ladies," I said to them, "be careful, please, at least until you've signed the waiver." I kept the comment light, but the message was clear.

"Sorry," Caroline said, and helped her friend to her feet.

"Nice sweep, by the way. Just take it easy, and give Marietta a chance."

Caroline nodded, and they got back to work.

For the next fifteen minutes Jon and I wandered around, watching, making corrections, and complimenting the hard-working students.

Once enough practice time had gone by, I lined up the class for the last time, and wished them a goodnight.

As the room began to empty, I headed toward Noa and Aminah. We needed to discuss the plan for later, that they would be staying with Jon again.

Across the dojo, Caroline and Marietta walked over to a water station, along with a group of other students. Noa and Aminah, meanwhile, had grabbed their retail therapy shopping bags and came over. They must have been antsy to leave. Before they had a chance to say anything, though, I spotted a single gym bag against a wall. It belonged to Caroline, the more intense of the two women. She had placed it out of the way before joining the work-out.

"Hang on," I said to the Hopkins girls.

I wanted to be a gentleman and carry the bag to Caroline, so she wouldn't have to come back for it. I jogged over to the gym bag, and lifted it by its molded handle. The weight of the bag's contents caused the handle to pull unexpectedly. I recognized the tug. There could have been ankle weights at the bottom of the gym bag, or even a pair of shoes. Maybe even a few carefully wrapped bottles of wine for an after-workout rendezvous.

But that wasn't it. I was pretty sure what that pull was. The slight tug from the bottom of the bag was caused by a pair of handguns.

12

When you work in security in Israel, you're trained to spot concealed weapons on people and in bags. You're stationed at an entrance of a shopping mall or government building, or at the airport, next to a metal detector and an X-ray machine. When people pass their bags to you, you're taught to discern which ones contain a weapon before that item even gets to the detector. Is there a bulge in a bag that has a handgun shape when you run your hand across the bottom? Does the purse seem particularly weighted? Does the man or woman who handed you the backpack seem ill at ease, sweating, or at the other extreme, too nonchalant?

There are other tricks, too. To keep you sharp, instructors have ringers trying to pass through checkpoints with guns or dummy small bombs in their bags. I spent many hours outside the main entrances to malls in Tiberius, Jerusalem, and Beersheva, profiling patrons, hefting pocketbooks and backpacks, and then rummaging through them to confirm the presence of a firearm.

The gym bag in my hand had such a weight, and as I approached the two women who were standing beside a plastic keg of water, they saw what I was carrying. For a brief moment, Caroline's eyes darted to Marietta. That was all I needed. They were FBI. There was no other explanation. And, considering who looked at whom, while Caroline was the more intense of the two, Marietta was the senior agent.

I passed the duffle to Caroline and she took it, as if it were the most natural thing to be carrying a bag with a pair of guns in it.

"Thanks," she said, and smiled one of the few times that evening.

"My dad always taught me to be a gentleman."

I turned from one woman to the other, but addressed them both. "So, what do you think? The sessions aren't always as intense as this, but we try to keep the pace lively."

"Great workout," Marietta commented.

"Aerobic enough then?"

"Oh, yeah." Her face was still rosy from the exercise.

"And very practical," Caroline added.

"Well, you're welcome back anytime." Along with this back-and-forth, my brain was considering whether they were here to assess me or keep an eye on me. We exchanged another round of "thank you's" and said goodnight.

I moved back to Jon.

"So, what do you think, Sifu. They gonna come back?"

"We'll see. Depends on what they want out of a workout, right?" No need for him to know why they were really here. If they did return, I needed Jon to act completely naturally. Plus, why freak him out?

Noa and Aminah came over. "So, Gidon, what's the plan tonight?" Noa asked. "Can we go back to our apartment?"

"Soon."

"Back to Jonathan's?" Noa turned to my student.

"Yeah, I'd like you to crash there for another few nights. Just want to be sure there're no crazies still looking for you."

"Works for me," Aminah said.

"I loved your shower," Noa looked at Jon.

"Me, too," Jon smiled.

Did she mean *his* shower or *the* shower, and then my mind didn't want to pursue any of that.

"Do you girls have enough clothes?"

They both nodded.

"If it's okay with you, I'd like to meet you at the apartment. We have some things to discuss. I'll be behind you by fifteen minutes."

The three of them agreed, collected their stuff, and headed out.

For a minute or two I gathered up a few items left behind – a lone towel, a pair of forearm pads, a half-filled metal water bottle – and then moved into my office. I sat behind the desk, taking a moment to consider the evening, and then swiveled to face the small box I had placed near the wall. It contained the cash and other items from Idan Gelvar, Noa's uncle, the Deputy Director of the Mossad. It didn't take much to shift my thoughts to Noa and Aminah and to the image of the dead young man who broke into their apartment.

I swiveled back to my desk and opened the bottom-right drawer. My lockbox. Inside was a .40 Glock 23 with a fully loaded magazine beside it. Without another thought, I dialed the combination and took out the semiautomatic and inserted the clip. The holster and permit were in another drawer, and after another second, the gun was attached to my belt near my right back pocket. I slipped on a loose windbreaker and headed out.

The night air had a slight dampness to it, but no rain was in the forecast. Huddled at the foot of the steps to the dojo were a group of my college-age students, both men and women. There was laughter and some general chitchat. I wasn't really listening, but was glad there was camaraderie among them. "Everything good, guys?"

"Yes, Sensei," the chorus of replies came back.

"Goodnight."

They echoed the salutation, and I left them, already setting my mind to the night ahead, which no doubt was going to be a long one.

* * *

Jon lived in the Union Wharf apartments at the foot of Wolfe Street in Fells Point. The complex sat on a small finger of land that jutted out into the harbor, providing a view of gentrified Canton to one side and the newly rediscovered Locust Point to the other. I had to park two blocks away on Thames Street, and considered myself fortunate to find a space.

Jon's street was taken up by his five-story, brick-faced apartment building. It had been constructed with recessed balconies along the building's front, so the vertical plane remained flat. It was a very clean look. My student lived on the third floor and I didn't consider the elevator, taking the nearby steps two at a time. Upstairs, the hallway yielded apartments to either side. Jon's was just twenty feet to the right, past the exposed brick stairwell.

I knocked on his jet black door, and almost instantly Noa pulled it open. "Hi," she smiled.

My forehead furrowed without meaning to.

Last night *DEATH TO ISRAEL* had been scrawled on her apartment wall just above a taped-up Hamas flag. Today, the young man who had done the honors had been executed with a knife across the throat and bullet to the head. Now, Noa just opened the door without a care in the world.

From around a corner I heard Aminah chatting with Jon just a few feet inside. The disbelief at Noa's disconnect to her own safety must have remained on my face longer than I realized.

"Are you okay, Gidon?"

"Yup." I moved in and she closed the door behind me. "You've settled in. No worries, right?"

To my left was a stainless steel and polished white stone kitchen, and Jon and Aminah were working on dinner. Jon was at the stove, adding a white cream sauce to a large pan of penne while Aminah was cutting cucumbers and tomatoes for a salad.

"Hey, Sifu." Jon turned to me, but kept his eye on the pasta. "I thought you'd be longer. Dinner will be ready in a few minutes."

I felt compelled to lecture them on the need to be more careful, but I let it dissipate for now.

Jon picked up a bottle of white wine and poured it over the pasta.

They were all so innocent. I watched Jon stir the penne, observed

Aminah cube a cucumber, and watched Noa pull plates from a cabinet. I saw all that, but also thought of Seth Bruce, the break-in guy from last night, on his own kitchen floor, dead.

"Jon, can you lower the heat on the pasta? Noa, Aminah, can you stop for a moment? I need to talk to you."

The three of them stopped where they were and looked at me. They joined me around a nearby Carrara marble island. "What's up, boss?" Jon said, sliding onto a stool.

"I need all of you to be more paranoid."

"What?" Aminah looked at me.

"I need you to look over your shoulders."

Noa and Aminah caught each other's eyes, not sure where I was going with this.

"Your apartment was broken into last night, there was *DEATH TO ISRAEL* scrawled on the wall above a Hamas flag. The guy who probably broke in was murdered a little while ago, and you," I looked at Noa, "just opened the door without asking who was there. You have to be more careful until all this is settled."

Noa's eyes went a little wide. "The man who broke in was murdered?"

Shit. I had never told them. I was getting mad at them, but they didn't know this piece. "What happened?" This from Aminah.

"Doesn't matter."

"And whoever did it?"

"The police are working on it." After a moment of silence, "You can't just open the apartment door, none of you...unless you know who's on the other side."

"Of course. Whatever you say," Aminah offered.

"We can have a password," Jon offered. "You know, something like," he deepened his voice, " 'The sun is shining...but the ice is slippery.' Or, 'Can I borrow a match?...I use a lighter...' "

I just shook my head and relaxed. "How about whenever someone comes to the door, unless they volunteer who they are, you don't answer."

"We can do that," Jon said, becoming more serious.

"And stand to the side."

Both young ladies looked at me and their eyes held more than a touch of fear in them. That's what I needed to see.

"One more thing. If one of you is using the key to the apartment, I want you to insert it slightly in the lock, then let the key ring fall to the ground. You then say 'Shit' to yourself, but loud enough so it can be heard on the other side."

"Like a password," Aminah said.

I nodded.

"That way if you're home you'll know whoever is opening the door is legit."

Noa looked from Jon to me: "And if not? What if it's somebody trying to break in?"

"There won't be time to call me." I turned to Jon. "You have a baseball bat?"

He nodded.

"Put it right here," I walked over to the opening leading to the kitchen. "That way it'll be handy. Stand just inside the kitchen, and when you see the person's head – not their hands – you swing. Put your body behind it, but don't lose your balance. You'll need the stability if there's a second person. There should be enough room here to get a good swing. Aim for the center of the person's face. Break his nose for sure and whatever else you connect with."

The two young ladies had gone pale. Jon just locked onto my eyes.

"And then once whoever is down, run from the apartment yelling 'Fire!' Call me when you're clear."

A few seconds passed in silence.

"By the way, Jon, nice movie passcodes."

He smiled, but the girls were still shaken.

"Sorry about this bit of reality. Chances are nothing will happen. But like I said—"

"Be a little paranoid," Noa said softly.

"Yup."

"I think the pasta's ready," Jon said, changing the subject, and walked over to the stove.

And with that, everyone got back to work. Aminah went back to her salad-making and Noa returned to taking plates out of the cabinet, though both ladies were moving more slowly than before, my comments surely playing on their minds. I helped set the table, and in a few minutes we were all sitting at the dining room table, eating. Not surprisingly, Noa and Aminah had lost some of their appetite, but Jon was unaffected by my speech. I, too, managed to eat; that was rarely a personal problem. Jon offered some wine, and while Noa and Aminah each had a healthy glass, I waved it off.

It wasn't long before the two college girls excused themselves and headed toward the bedroom.

"I think they'll be sleeping with pepper spray under their pillows," Jonathan said, once they were behind closed doors.

"Not a bad thing. Just don't wake them up in the middle of the night by shaking them."

"Nope." After a moment, "So, you really worried? Think someone will find out the girls are here?"

"Probably not. But I keep that kinda stuff tucked in the back of my mind, you know that."

He nodded.

"I made a mistake today. The girls went shopping. You saw the Anthropologie bags. We weren't keeping an eye on them. They could have easily gone back to their apartment, and if someone were watching to see if they had returned…"

"They could be following them."

I shrugged. "We don't know where else they went or who might have seen them."

"But your Spidey sense isn't tingling or anything?'

I shook my head.

The Student

"But it doesn't hurt to play it safe."

I nodded.

"No disturbance in the Force?"

"There's a disturbance, but not about this."

"See, I don't know if you're kidding or not."

I just smiled, but I was aware of the Glock in its holster near the small of my back.

"What do want to do, Sifu? Camp out on the couch all night? Do you want me to take the first shift or something?

"I'm going to go for a walk."

He smiled. "No, you're not. You're going to park yourself outside in the shadows where you can watch this building."

"I'm going for a walk. It's a beautiful night." And I was going to park myself where I could watch the building.

* * *

The spot I settled on was just interior to the marble stoop of a boutique furniture store called "Off the Beaten Path." The entry alcove was in the shadows diagonally across from the entrance to Jon's building. From this angle there was an unobstructed view of not only the main entrance, but also of a walkway leading to the back. If anyone were to try to access the building, he or she would have to come this way.

I really didn't think whoever executed Seth Bruce knew where Noa and Aminah were this evening, but it was dangerous to assume anything. I also didn't think they would make direct contact, but since they didn't find what they had wanted – thanks to the sophisticated anti-tampering software the girls had – one never knew what frustration might lead to.

Before settling in for my surveillance, I turned off the sounds on my phone and lowered the brightness on the display to an ever-so-slight glow. In other circumstances, I'd turn off the phone entirely. For now, I transferred the dormant cell to a jacket pocket, and then sat on the floor of the alcove, leaning against the wall. Finally, I set up a breathing pattern with long, controlled inhales and exhales: a deep breath in, a measured breath out for both relaxation and an expansion of senses. My eyes stayed fixed on a distant point, yet took everything in. The goal wasn't solely a relaxed mind, but a state where I was half present and half passive: aware of everything around me, but also completely physically and mentally neutral.

The night air grew cool, but it didn't register. I saw a young couple walk past, arm-in-arm, and an older man, unshaven and disheveled, weave along the curb. There was a clean-cut man walking a tan German shepherd, and a lone, young woman with spiked orange air and various piercings in her face stride purposefully down the sidewalk.

From the hidden niche of the darkened alcove my unmoving eyes saw a forty-something couple pause to look at the display in the furniture store window not more than ten feet from me. In another moment, the deep bass from pulsating car speakers reached me before the visual impression of the vehicle did. Gravel crunched up the block and a woman laughed somewhere. The moon appeared briefly, then disappeared from my unblinking field of vision.

Men and women walked into Jon's building, some with determined steps and others more nonchalant; none were suspicious. I saw the lights go out in the residential building one by one until only a few isolated windows remained lit. In my mind, I could see my student and the two girls asleep. There was a baseball bat leaning against a corner just inside the kitchen door.

Back outside, as the early morning hours ebbed on, virtually all foot and vehicle traffic stopped. Not a car, not a bicycle, not a single pedestrian. Finally, barely recognizing that hours had passed, the aroma of freshly baked bread floated past as the sky began to lighten.

I allowed my breathing to change and with that the passivity retreated. For a brief moment I saw myself as a young martial art student in my teacher's class. He had us focus on long, deep breathing while gradually raising our arms. He left us there with our hands above our heads for at least thirty minutes, and when we lowered them, there wasn't the sensation of blood returning to our fingers. The blood had not drained from them in the first place. He said it had to do with the breathing.

With that ancient image in mind, I stood up, recognizing that my muscles and joints weren't stiff – okay, just a little – and I reached for my cell phone. Odds were all was quiet upstairs. As zoned out as I had been, I knew from years of training, along with practical army experience, that no one with malicious intent had slipped past me. There was no concern that someone had spotted the glow of my cell phone and saw me staring out. As luminescent blue continued to brighten the eastern sky, I increased the phone's display brightness and checked messages. One missed call and one message from just after 1AM. I recognized the number: Katie's. I hit play, not sure what I wanted to hear.

"Hi. It's me. I know it's late, but I figured you're still up. I hope you don't mind the call." There was a pause. "I've been thinking. I know that's always dangerous." She laughed. "Give me a call. I'd like to ask you something in person, or at least not in a voicemail." Another pause. "I hope you do call. Take care, Gidon."

I just looked at the display after the message played out. After a moment, I shook my head and pocketed the phone. As the shadows in the alcove receded in its push-pull with the rising sun, I took a long breath and stepped off the stoop and headed for my Jeep.

13

The new day unfolded promisingly enough with a bright, clear sky. But now, in the eastern horizon, streaks of red fingered across the heavens. By ten o'clock the sun was masked by dark layers of clouds. Within the hour it would likely pour across the city, or more realistically, rain in one location, leaving the remainder of Baltimore dry and way too humid. Maybe it would blow over. I didn't have an umbrella in the car, so I knew what that meant.

My Jeep was in a metered spot not far from the Federal Court House near Camden Yards. The main FBI office was outside the Beltway to the west, but Gil Jeffries' office was right here. This is where I was "interviewed" after my escapade with the Federal agents at the airport upon my return from Israel.

"Federal Bureau of Investigation," a pleasant woman's voice came over my phone. "How can I help you?"

Looking out my window, I counted up to the seventh floor, while holding the phone to my ear. "Special Agent in Charge Gil Jeffries, please."

Without missing a beat, the woman said, "Agent Jeffries is out of the building. Can I take a message?"

"Yes, that would be great." I found a tinted window where I imagined her office was. "Please tell her that Gidon Aronson would like to meet her for coffee. That's me, by the way, and fifteen minutes would be good."

"I'm sorry, Mr. Aronson. I don't know if that's possible."

I smiled and let my gaze come back to street level to the main entrance of the cement building. "Well, I hope she can make it, because I'd like to talk to her about what's happening. She'll know what that means. You have my number, so please let me know."

I hung up, and expected that my phone would ring in under a minute. My mind shifted to the voicemail I had received from Katie last night. I don't know why it did, but it did. *I've been thinking...I'd like to ask you something in person.* As I had earlier, all I could do was shake my head.

Meanwhile, no one had stalked Jon or his guests as I had expected, which was good, I suppose. Would have been nice to meet them and ask a few questions. That sounded so polite. I could only picture my demeanor in coming face-to-face with the people who killed Seth Bruce, and who might very well be on the way to doing similar harm to Noa and Aminah.

The phone in my left hand rang. The display simply read "Federal Building."

I let it ring once more and then answered: "Hello."

"Mr. Aronson, it's Special Agent Jeffries. How can I help you?" All business.

"Meet me for coffee. There's a great small café called Betsy's a few blocks away. I'd like to tell you what I've been working on, plus I have a present for you."

"A confession? You want to turn yourself in?"

Nice. A sense of humor. I had to smile. "Not quite, but I know of a situation you'll find interesting."

"Okay. I know Betsy's. Fifteen minutes?"

"Yup. See you there." I paused. "You won't have a hard time recognizing me, will you?"

"No, I don't think so." There was a smile coming through, but maybe it was just my ego thinking I was funny.

After waiting a few minutes, I got out of the SUV and walked to a spot across the street from the Federal Building's main entrance, which was also the door closest to the street toward the café. Two minutes later a group of men and women came out. Most of the men were dressed in suits; other men looked like workmen. The women who had exited were slim, dressed in slacks and matching jackets. All FBI on the way to stake out the café? That was paranoid of me. This was a Federal courthouse building, so many could simply have been attorneys or clients, or just court-related personnel.

After another minute Special Agent Jeffries emerged. She was dressed in a gray business suit with what looked like a black T-shirt underneath. She was walking purposefully, but not rushing. I crossed the street at an angle and at a pace where I could catch up in the next block.

She was walking along a pedestrian-filled Pratt Street toward the Inner Harbor, and I slid even with her just before Charles Street. Betsy's, the café I had suggested, was to the left.

"Mr. Aronson," she nodded, stopping. She didn't smile, though she raised an eyebrow in what may have been amusement.

"Hi. I'm glad I could get you out of the office."

"Always good to get out. What's up?" Gil Jeffries was unfazed by my unexpected appearance.

The sky was continuing to get dark, and the wind had picked up. A small gust blew open her gray suit jacket just enough for me to confirm she had her semiautomatic within easy reach. She probably saw my eyes dart down, but didn't react. A single strand of pearls just above the collar of her black T-shirt caught my attention as well.

She was looking at me when my eyes returned to hers.

"I like the pearls," I said.

"Thanks. What did you want to talk about?" she asked pleasantly.

I smiled. "In a sec."

We continued past Pratt Street where Betsy's was, and turned up Light Street, away from the Inner Harbor.

"What's the difference between a hate crime and an act of

terrorism?" I asked, after crossing an intersection.

She looked at me and paused before speaking. "Not the official definition, but I would say a hate crime is a crime motivated by extreme racial or religious beliefs, and wanting to inflict harm on a particular racial or ethnic person or group."

"They can be anti-black, anti-white, anti-gay, anti-Jewish, anti-Muslim…that sort of thing."

"Of course. You already know this."

"And an act of terrorism?" I asked. I had stopped walking, and people had to suddenly walk around us, but no one seemed to mind. They were too busy in their own conversations or on their phones.

Jeffries looked into my eyes for a moment. "Murder committed usually to promote a political agenda."

"Or a religious one."

"Often the religious agenda is the political agenda."

"Such as with Iran or ISIS."

"What's this all about? What are you involved in?"

"Don't know."

I looked at a store to our right, The Light Street Punt, and turned back to Jeffries. "Do you mind if we make a quick stop here?"

She shrugged and followed me into the liquor store.

The shop was modest, with floor-to-ceiling wine and whiskey racks lining the side and back walls. In general, the general lighting was soft and natural, but spotlights faced down over many of the displays. The register sat on an island in the center of the room. A tall, thin man in his late thirties nodded to us. "Hi, folks. Welcome. Let me know if I can help you."

"Thank you." I smiled back.

The proprietor turned to continue a conversation with another customer, while I scanned the room, quickly finding what I was looking for.

I turned back to Gil Jeffries. "I'm not as ADD as you're probably thinking."

"I'm not profiling you."

Of course she was.

From a whiskey rack, I picked up two bottles of Glenfiddich, a 14-year-old and a 15, and headed to the cashier island. The tall gentleman rang me up. "Would you like gift bags?"

"Please."

He put each in a tall, cardstock gift bag and then both into a heavy plastic bag with cut out handles. I said thanks and we headed out.

"Still want coffee?" I asked Special Agent Jeffries.

"It's your party. You called me."

"This way." I motioned up the street and began walking.

"Betsy's is the other way."

"I know, but there's a great place right here." And with that we stepped into a busy eatery that made sandwiches, pasta dishes, soups, and more. No doubt she knew I was avoiding any prepositioned FBI folk at Betsy's, but if she wanted to hear me out, she didn't have a choice. Besides, she probably felt she could handle any situation that came up.

We stood in line in the upscale cafeteria behind a business-attired couple. In a moment we stepped up to the counter. I ordered a mozzarella sandwich with pesto and mushrooms and an iced coffee. Jeffries ordered just an iced tea, and wouldn't let me pay for it.

In a few minutes we headed with our selections to a table against the back wall. We sat opposite each other. With a slight turn of the head, we both had a clear view of the room.

I took a bite out of my sandwich before she asked the inevitable question. "So, Mr. Aronson, what's up, and what's with the hate crime/terrorism question?" The iced tea remained untouched in front of her.

"First of all, I'm not Mossad, as I already told you in interrogation. I'm not a foreign agent. I'm former military, as you know."

"IDF."

I nodded. "And I've worked with the Shin Bet in the past, not for them. We had common goals, that's all."

"And what goals were those?"

I smiled. I had opened myself to that.

"Without getting specific unless you insist, there were some crimes committed here against people I cared about that led me to persons of interest in Israel. I investigated them in Israel with the Shin Bet's help." Even as I spoke and looked across to Gil Jeffries I could see myself in the night operations that ended with the right people being killed – by me.

"Mr. Aronson?"

I refocused on Special Agent Jeffries' blue eyes and smiled faintly.

"Didn't end well, those investigations?" she asked.

I could still feel the trigger pulls. "There's sometimes a price, even when you win."

She looked at me again, silently.

"Anyway, if I may, I wanted to tell you why you don't have to worry about me. A few days ago, when I was about to leave Israel, David Amit, my contact at the Shin Bet, called and wanted to meet. When we did, Idan Gelvar, the Deputy Director of the Mossad was there, again, as you know."

She nodded.

"He wanted me to look after his niece, Noa Biran, who is a senior at Hopkins. He was worried about her because of all the anti-Israel feeling on U.S. campuses these days. Long story short, soon after I returned, her off-campus apartment was broken into and *DEATH TO ISRAEL* was spray painted on a wall just above a taped-up Hamas flag."

"We know."

"Right. Well, her laptop was messed with, her roommate's was stolen – actually earlier that day – and one of the men responsible was murdered. Throat cut and shot in the head. Or shot in the head and throat cut, depending who you ask."

Both eyebrows went up, furrowing her forehead.

"Captain D'Allesandro and his men are investigating. So, hate crime, terrorism, personal vendetta? Don't know. Which brings me to the present I have for you."

I reached into a pocket and pulled out an empty Baltimore PD plastic evidence bag and gave it to her. This time only a single eyebrow went up.

"Later today you will be receiving a laptop belonging to Noa's roommate, the laptop that had been stolen. I'd have brought the computer myself, but there's the chain of evidence thing, and the fact that I'm not a police officer caused problems."

"Imagine that." She looked at the evidence bag. "What's so important about the laptop?"

"Don't know."

"You're saying that a lot."

"I am. And I want that to change. Someone wants these laptops or the information on them. First they stole the roommate's, and when they couldn't get into it, they broke into Noa's room and tried accessing hers. Since the man who was responsible, or one of them, was subsequently murdered, we need to check the files."

"We?"

"The Baltimore Police and me."

"And you."

"There may be something in the roommate's emails that explains all this, to include the *DEATH TO ISRAEL* scrawl. Is it a terrorist threat or just a smoke screen. We're hoping your computer guys can find out."

"Why didn't D'Allesandro ask me himself?"

"My idea. He wanted BPD to go with it. But Gelvar's niece is my responsibility. If she's at risk, I need to know. We all need to know."

She peered into my eyes once again. It was becoming a habit. "Why would Captain D'Allesandro let a civilian in on this?"

"You know why." Nate had recounted how his daughter had been rescued by my team. "He trusts me and so should you. The *DEATH TO ISRAEL* thing and the Hamas flag may not be smoke, and as

I said, Noa is my responsibility. There's something on that computer worth slitting a man's throat."

"And shooting him."

"And shooting him. It's a pretty strong message. And the people involved need to be stopped, regardless of whether it's terrorism or not."

I turned to the front window. It was pouring. An occasional burst of wind sent the rain diagonally.

"I'll follow up with the Captain on this. If it is terrorism, the FBI will run with it."

"He'll *love* that."

"And all this doesn't prove you're not a foreign intelligence officer."

"You'll have to trust me on that, then."

"So, you were in the right place, right time?"

"Things happen for a reason. I had a teacher who said people are where they're supposed to be at any given time." I pushed the remainder of the mozzarella sandwich to the side. "You know, I was raised here in Baltimore."

She nodded.

"You know I teach martial arts and I also teach American history from time to time at a local private school."

"Yes." Considering she sent agents to check me out at my studio, I would have expected a yes, at least to the martial arts part.

"You know that I was in the Israeli Army. I moved to Israel right after college, by the way, but I've never been interested in the Mossad. I came back to the States a few years ago after my army service, because I wanted to get away and figure my life out."

"But you keep going back."

"Needed to. Things came up."

Before she could pursue that, a low buzzing came from her pocket. She reached into her jacket and took out her cell phone. She answered with her name. After a moment of listening: "Yes. All good. I'm with him now."

Her people were wondering where she was.

She continued: "Guess he didn't want your company." Special Agent in Charge Jeffries gave me a half-smile. It was good to see that. It went right up to her eyes. "About fifteen minutes," she added.

And with that, she hung up.

"Associates worried?"

"They get that way when plans change out of their control."

I nodded. Then, "Well, I hope I've put your mind at ease, about me."

"Telling me what you're involved in and saying trust you, 'I'm not a spy,' doesn't really accomplish that."

"Not even in my suave, honest way?"

She shook her head, again with a slight smile.

"I was a mass communications major in college. Does that help?"

This time I got a full laugh.

"And you, I'd say, were a poli-sci major, or international affairs. Did you always want to be with the FBI?"

She didn't answer. She wasn't revealing anything, but she kept looking at me.

"Another time, perhaps." I stood up and so did Jeffries.

Before either of us moved off, I put the bag from the liquor store, the one with the two bottles of Glenfiddich, on the table. She looked at me.

"They're for your two agents, the two I messed up at the airport. I feel bad about that."

"Why? They fucked up."

"You admit it."

There was that half-smile again. "Everyone knows they fucked up. Especially the agents."

"Well, this will help ease the pain. They'll have to fight over who gets the 14-year and who gets the 15."

"Thanks."

Special Agent Jeffries took a sip of her iced tea, the only sip she took during our exchange, picked up the bag from the liquor store, and paused to look out the restaurant's window. The rain had stopped. There was even the glow of bright sunshine, emanating from above and reflecting off car windows as they drove past. Without turning back to me, Jeffries walked toward the door.

14

By the time I returned to my parking spot the only remnants of the cloudburst were the rivulets of water running down the gutters and the sheen of moisture on the street. In contrast, the sun was out, bright and strong, the kind of brightness that makes you squint.

Was Gil Jeffries still convinced I was a foreign agent? Who knew, but perhaps now there was some doubt, and that was good enough for the moment. I didn't like being thought of badly by good people.

Standing on the sidewalk I leaned against the passenger door of my Grand Cherokee and pulled out my cell phone. I hadn't checked in with Jon after watching his building all night, nor had I returned Katie's call.

What was going on with her, and how was I supposed to react to the renewed contact? Did she want to cut off our relationship or not, and did she want to say it to my face, or give me a big kiss to say she forgave me?

The questions were easily solved, but I wasn't sure I could reach her during the school day.

After two rings, she picked up: "Hi."

I inadvertently paused. "Hi. Didn't really expect you to answer. Thought you'd be teaching or something and I'd leave a message."

"No, not teaching."

"Sorry I couldn't talk last night. I was outside Jonathan's condo, watching for bad guys."

"Oh?"

"It has to do with the Mossad guy's niece I told you about. The one at Hopkins."

"Okay. So, anything?"

"Just the scintillating aroma of freshly baking bread, making me salivate."

"Hmmm."

"Anyway, guess it's a good thing...not seeing the people I'm looking for."

"Means they haven't made the connection from the college girls to Jon."

"Let's hope they never do." I let a moment pass. "So what's up? You said you wanted to ask me something."

"I think we need to talk some more."

"Okay. Where would you like to do that?"

"Would you mind coming by this evening?"

"It'll have to be after class."

"Of course."

I had to smile, because she knew what to expect. I gave her a time, and then before it got weird because we both didn't know what was going on with us, we said goodbye.

Next was Jonathan. What were he and the girls planning to do today? Both Noa and Aminah probably had classes, but I wasn't crazy about them strolling around campus. And unless they were both in the same classes, Jon couldn't keep an eye on the two of them. He could watch one girl and I could take the other. That would work, though we'd both be conspicuous in a classroom of college-age kids, unless there were other adults there. Maybe it would even draw out the two men we were looking for. But I didn't want to put the girls, or Jonathan, at risk. I dialed his number.

"Hi," I said, after getting through.

"Hi, Sifu." He was on speaker; in the car, perhaps.

"How did everything go last night?"

"Excellent. No worries there. What about you? Enjoy your walk?"

Jon knew me. He didn't even consider I was doing anything but watching the entrances of his building. "Yup, no worries." I let a moment pass. "So, what are the plans for today? I don't know if going back to campus is wise, even with you there."

"Well, we're on our way to Gettysburg."

"Gettysburg?"

"Yeah, I need to look at a few properties there and we figured it would be good to get out of town."

"Noa and Aminah aren't worried about missing class?" Before, I wasn't sure going to campus was a good idea, and now I was objecting that they weren't going.

"Both girls have midterms coming up. They each emailed their professors and explained. Apparently, most of what is happening is review at this point, and they have all their textbooks and stuff. Said they can get notes from friends."

"Okay. Just let me know when you head back. How long will you be there?"

"Most of the day. After I check out the properties, I thought we'd go to the battlefield visitor center. Stay late and then do dinner in town."

"Just let me know what's going on."

"Roger that."

We hung up, and I moved around to get into the driver's seat of the Jeep. Just as I started the engine, my phone rang. Nate. "Finished your meeting?"

"A little while ago."

"Good. Meet me at the Maryland 40 Gun Range in thirty minutes."

"Okay."

"Remember where it is?"

"I do."

"See you soon." He hung up.

* * *

The Maryland 40 Gun Range was a gun shop and firing range on the eastern side of town in an industrial park that included a kitchen design company with showrooms, a plumbing supply house, and a furniture distributor. The gun shop was at the far corner end of the warehouse style cinderblock building. Only a few cars were parked in front, either in the open lot or at the curb. The entrance was a simple glass door with the store's logo and name arcing across the center.

It had been a while since I had been there, but the shop hadn't changed very much. It was clean, brightly lit, and with plenty of floorspace, unlike many gun shops. To the left were a few stand-alone display cases with just a few handguns inside, and then offices along the far wall. Straight ahead and to the right were the glass sales counters with various handguns laid out, an easy reach of the sales people standing on the other side.

Nate was leaning on a counter talking with one such young salesman. Further down was middle-aged couple speaking with an older man opposite them, behind the display case. Two handguns were in front of the couple, and the older man was reviewing the features of each.

As I approached Nate, the salesman he was speaking with watched me come over. He was probably in his mid-twenties, tall and lanky. He was in a black Under Armour t-shirt, the bottom of which barely covered a holster and what looked like a 9mm Beretta. He wore Marine Corps desert camouflage pants, and was wearing a tan ballcap emblazoned with the Beretta logo. He just nodded as I stepped over, and I nodded back, "Hi."

Nate straightened. He was in a sky-blue shirt and patterned tie. No jacket. His Glock service weapon was on his right hip next to his belt-clipped badge. I had no idea why he wanted to meet me here.

"So, Nate, need some range time?"

"No, smartass, but I thought you might, and I wanted to talk to you. When was the last time you were on a range?"

"Um, last week."

I looked at the young man behind the counter who was now smiling at us. He had squint lines around his eyes; a guess would say they were from the sun in Iraq, but I may have been wrong. On the other hand, he had a Marine tattoo on his right forearm.

Nate continued: "I bet it was one of those urban setting places, with 'terrorists' hiding out among civilians."

"As a matter of fact…"

"Yeah, yeah. But when was the last time you were at a good old-fashioned range?"

"Been a while."

"Excellent." He paused for a second, then: "You don't by chance have your Glock on you?"

I shook my head. After last night I had returned my .40 semiautomatic to its lockbox in my office desk drawer.

"Of course you don't."

Nate caught the eye of the man behind the counter, who nodded and responded with, "All set for you, Captain. Everything you asked for is in the cabinet." He handed Nate a key ring with a single key on it and two sets of ear protectors.

"Thanks, Tom."

My police friend walked to a break between the counters, and I followed. As I did, I looked over to a side wall and up to a display board of various long guns and carbines to include an Israeli Tavor. Nate led the way to a solid metal door that had a square window set at head height. He paused, there was a buzz of a lock release, and he went through. We walked single file down a short corridor to another door. In a few moments we were standing in the gun range.

There were five lanes with small booth-like setups at the head of each. Every booth included a shelf, partitions to each side, and switches to control the target retrieval system, basically an overhead rail device with a retractable clamp. The range itself was well-lit, with the back wall angled to deflect the fired rounds into a capture pit. The air conditioner was on, not only keeping the room a few degrees cooler than the shop we had just left, but scrubbing most of the acrid propellant from the air. Lanes two and three were already set up, with silhouette targets hanging ten yards out.

Nate walked to lane three, the further lane. "So, Gidon, what's going on with you and Katie?"

I stopped. "Really, that's what you wanted to talk about? You came here in the middle of your day to ask me about my love life?"

He went over to a locked cabinet, and opened it using the key the salesman had given him. Inside were various semiautomatics, plus boxes of ammunition and preloaded clips. Each gun had its slide locked open.

"Here." He handed me a Glock 23 and its magazine. He took out his own weapon.

"If you must know, Dad, I'm meeting her tonight to talk."

I inserted the clip and released the slide. While I slipped on protective glasses and ear protection, Nate did the same. I held the gun in my left hand and looked downrange.

"You really messed up, my friend," my captain buddy commented.

I aimed the weapon and pulled the trigger three times in quick succession. Nate fired multiple times as well.

"I know. It seemed like a good idea at the time to stay the summer and train with my old unit." I fired three more times.

"And she told you it was okay, right?"

"Well, looking back, I don't know if I gave her a choice."

"You have a lot to think about, Gidon." He holstered his weapon and pressed a button on the control panel near his head. I did the same. The overhead rail system pulled our targets forward.

The human silhouettes had white concentric ovals out from center mass with numbers next to each ring. X was dead center, then an unmarked ring, and then nine, eight, and seven. Nate looked at his target. There were .40 holes mostly within the unmarked 10 ring area. The grouping was fairly tight. I didn't fare as well: mine were mostly in the nine area and spread out. One was actually further to the side.

Nate looked at me. "Gidon, really?" He was about to enjoy himself. "What, you're like the Sundance Kid…you have to be moving around to be accurate?"

"Well, I know something you don't know."

"Yeah?"

"I am not left-handed." I moved the Glock into my right hand.

Nate could only shake his head. "*Princess Bride*. That's what you got for me? You're such a child."

"Hey, you knew the reference."

"Laurie's favorite movie." For a brief moment I had an image of his daughter in Israel, the one I had pulled from a basement in Lebanon. Last time I had seen her she'd been working on a therapeutic horse farm not far from Tel Aviv.

I nodded to the target. "Tell you what. I'll shoot with my right hand, you shoot with your weaker one. Then we'll compare."

My cop friend just looked at me, and without taking his eyes off of mine, touched the control panel, moving his target back out to ten yards. I smiled, and did the same. After a few moments we each emptied our clips – Nate shooting left-handed, while I shot with my right. Once "out," we retrieved the targets. As each silhouette approached, I smiled: "Feel like putting money on this?"

"Give me a few more rounds to warm up."

"That'll make a difference?"

He stopped the retrieval system when his target was within reach. There were his six shots from before grouped neatly in the center, and then a new series of holes scattered across the rest of the torso. "Okay, asshole, so it needs work."

My right-handed shots were all center mass, tightly grouped.

We each replaced the targets with fresh ones. "Before you reload, here." Nate turned to the cabinet behind him and pulled out another pistol, which I recognized. It was an HK .45 Tactical. I took the offered gun. It was about an inch longer than my Glock and had an extended, threaded barrel for a suppressor. The frame was tan, but the slide and other moving parts, such as trigger and safety, were all black. *Sweet*, was all I could think.

Nate and I went back to shooting. Every so often we'd stop and analyze. At one point while reloading, I brought up the murdered Seth Bruce. "He really didn't know what he was getting into."

"Obviously." Nate was inserting fresh rounds into his magazine. "The question is who hired him?"

"The killers, the guys on the video from his place?"

My captain friend shook his head. "Someone else. He wasn't just picked from a Hopkins directory."

"Someone who knows the campus."

He nodded. "Maybe."

After another moment, "By the way, and not to cause any problems, I'm still waiting for a screen capture of those guys from the murder scene. Hate to run into the killers and not know it."

"Yeah, Soper is supposed to get it to you. He's chasing down the third roommate who was out with her boyfriend in Georgetown." He pushed the magazine into his Glock. "You told Special Agent Jeffries to expect the laptop we retrieved?"

I nodded.

"The Feds should be able to see if there's something there that will explain any of this."

By now the air was beginning to fill with the distinctive smell from the gunfire, plus brass casings were accumulating at our feet.

"So how was your meeting with Jeffries?"

"Fine. I filled her in on what was going on and how I became involved in all this."

"And you told her your life story, trying to convince her you're not a spy."

"Only got up to sixth grade." I took a moment to switch hands again. I really liked the HK. It was big, but fit my hand well. The initial double action trigger pull was harder than some other guns, but it was smooth.

After another few shots, and still on the subject of Jeffries, I brought up the two undercover FBI agents who came to my workout last night.

"She's just doing her due diligence," Nate said. "You charm them?"

"Hope so." After another two shots, "What's the deal with Jeffries? Know anything about her?"

"Thought you'd ask."

Without breaking the conversation I moved the target out another five yards. The white ring lines were not as clearly visible.

"I have a friend at the Hoover Building," Nate continued. "Word is she was born in L.A., but her dad was asked to work for the State Department, so the family came east while she was still in elementary school. Eventually they were posted overseas."

"She was like a military brat."

He nodded, "But classier. She did high school and college all over: Europe, Asia. Mom was a diplomat's wife. When they came back to DC, Jeffries joined the Bureau. My friend thinks she was fast-tracked."

"She must be bright."

"Just don't piss her off, Gidon."

"Not me."

He turned to me and nodded to the .45 Tactical in my hand. "So what do you think?"

"I like it. A little large. If I were in combat, it'd be perfect, but unless Maryland passes an open carry law, not so practical here."

He nodded and held out his hand for me to give it back. I ejected the clip and cleared the round in the chamber. Nate took the gun, turned to the cabinet, and then handed me another HK. It was the .45C, a compact version of their .45 caliber. He held out a preloaded magazine. "Go, play."

I looked at him like, what was going on, and went back to practicing.

"You could get away with that one, concealed," he commented. "You know, a few years ago, the City Police carried Glock 9s, but there were officers who emptied their clips into big guys but they kept on coming. Some cops wanted to go to .45s, but politicians thought the public would view it as excessive."

"So you compromised and went to the .40s."

He nodded. "Okay, we're done."

And with that, I repeated the procedure to clear the HK, and returned it to Nate. He wrapped his large hand around it, but locked the other guns and the ammo in the cabinet. We exited back out the way we had come.

"So," Nate said, as we walked back through the short corridor toward the front, "what do you think you'll do about Katie?"

"Oh my God, Nate."

"Rachel wants to know." His wife.

"Uh-huh. I'm sure as soon as we figure it out, she'll hear from Katie."

"Yep."

We came through the metal door to the shop and walked over to the lanky salesman in the black T-shirt and camouflage pants. He was virtually where we had left him, at the glass counter. He was just closing a handgun carrying case.

Nate returned the cabinet key and held out HK .45C. "This one."

The man behind the counter smiled, "You called it, Captain." He reached beside him for a stack of forms that were partially filled out. He visually scanned the top one, and then slid them over to me. I looked between the salesman and Nate.

"I'm gifting you the gun," Nate explained. "Just fill in the info Tom has checked off."

I looked at the forms and then up at Nate. "No."

"This isn't a discussion."

"Nate."

"You brought my daughter back. She's alive and rebuilding her life."

"In Israel."

"She's safe. And better there than here, probably."

I pushed the forms away.

"She's alive because of you."

"I was part of a team."

"It was you."

"You don't need to give me anything."

"I do."

"You already bought me the Glock."

"Which you never carry."

"I don't need it."

"I'm gifting you this gun. End of story."

"It's not necessary, and it's too expensive."

"Don't worry about that. Tom knows dealers who know dealers. You don't have a choice in this matter." He stood up straight and put both hands on his hips. His right hand was resting next to his service Glock.

"You going to shoot me?"

"Maybe." He just stared at me.

I took a deep breath, then turned back to Tom, and nodded.

The man in the Beretta cap slid the forms back over to me, "If you have any questions, Major, just ask."

I looked at him. He had used my IDF rank. I turned back to Nate, who didn't say anything.

"The paperwork will clear in four days," Tom offered. The Maryland wait period was seven days, and he read my mind. "The Captain has many friends."

"Who'd have thought?" I looked back at Nate.

"Just promise me you'll carry it, and until then, the Glock. There's bad shit going on with this case."

"You mean because of the Middle East throat-slitting stuff?"

"Just wear the fucking gun."

I nodded.

"You're such a pain in the ass, Gidon."

"Anything else?"

Nate looked at the gun dealer. "Tell him."

The salesman nodded. "I have a friend who's a SEAL. He's back here, and somehow he got the Secretary of the Navy to write him a letter that says that he's permitted to carry a gun across state lines."

"A Get Out of Jail Free letter," I commented, then looked at Nate. "You got me one of those, too, a note from the Secretary of the Navy?"

"Where would I meet the fucking Secretary of the Navy? I'm a cop. I met the head of Homeland Security."

"What?"

"There was a law enforcement conclave in DC a month ago."

"Oooh, 'conclave.' An SAT word."

Nate continued, without paying attention to the comment. "Here." He handed me a folded piece of paper.

It was from the Office of the Secretary of DHS. It read: *Please note that Major Gidon Aronson while serving with the Israeli Defense Forces has saved American lives behind enemy lines. Allow him to carry a concealed firearm -- at your discretion.* It was signed by the current head of Homeland Security.

"Shit." I looked up at Nate.

"Of course," he said, "it's vague about whose army you were in and then there's that line 'at your discretion.' It may be worthless, but it's something. Just in case, keep your Wear and Carry on you."

"Mazel tov," Tom, the man in the Beretta cap, said.

Before I had a chance to respond, Nate's cell phone rang. "D'Allesandro." I watched as Nate listened to the call. His expression revealed nothing, but he did look at me. Finally, he said, "We'll be there in twenty minutes." He hung up.

"What?"

"That was Soper. The Mossad niece's roommate?"

"Aminah?" The girls were supposed to be with Jon in Gettysburg.

He shook his head. "The third roommate who had been in Georgetown with her boyfriend?"

I waited.

"She was walking back to her apartment near Hopkins when some guy assaulted her. She's okay, but the man took her backpack. Guess what was in it."

"Her laptop."

"Yep."

15

The mid-afternoon traffic interfered with Nate's estimate of how long it would take to get to the scene. There was the usual crosstown traffic, but there were also a few street maintenance crews at work that caused extra congestion. So, forty minutes after we left the gun range, we finally pulled onto 33rd Street, three blocks east of Charles. The scene was easy to find: three cop cars and an ambulance were double parked there. I followed Nate and pulled to a stop behind the ambulance. He got out of his sedan and waited for me so we could walk together. We did so without talking, though we did share a look that said, *What will we find?*

Detective Soper and Noa's second roommate were sitting on a bench under a young maple tree. The pair were mostly in shade, but a few blank spots in the leaf cover allowed the sun to come through in isolated, spotty areas. Callie Pierce was tall; even though she was sitting, you could tell from her long arms and legs. Her straight brown hair bordered on red, and she had on a pair of distressed, torn denim pants, a white tank top, and a maroon Georgetown ballcap. Her hands were in her lap, clutching a pair of aviator sunglasses. All in all, she appeared composed and not too shaken. On the other hand, she was physically quite still, with not a lot of emotion on her face. As we approached, I heard her ask Soper, "He'll be all right?"

"His face will be swollen around his eyes for a while and his nose will hurt, but he'll be fine. They'll give him some eye drops, maybe saline, and will probably recommend cold compresses." He saw us approach and stood up. "Miss Pierce, this is Captain D'Allesandro and Mr. Aronson."

We shook her hand.

"What happened?" Nate asked.

Soper turned to Callie. "Let me know if I leave anything out."

She nodded, and kept her hands in her lap.

"Miss Pierce was returning to her apartment after spending the past few days with her boyfriend at Georgetown. She parked here – that's her Sentra near the corner," he indicated a medium blue sedan near us, "and then walked toward the apartment she shares with Noa Biran and Aminah Hadad three blocks away. Just before going into the building, Miss Pierce realized she had forgotten something in her car, and came back here."

"And then what happened?" Nate asked Miss Pierce. He wanted to hear it from her.

"This man came up on my right side," she drifted into a slight faraway look as she brought back the images, "and he moved in front of me. He wouldn't let me go around him. He grabbed my arm. I remember he was wearing a hoodie and had one hand in his pocket. He said he had a gun and that I should give him my backpack."

"And that's where it got interesting," Soper prompted.

Callie continued. "I wasn't going to resist or anything...I had promised my parents I wouldn't, if anything were to happen...so I gave him the backpack. Just as I did, a guy from my building, his name is Ben – who must have been walking by – grabbed him. At some point Ben punched the hoodie guy in the face. The guy takes out this spray, it must have been what was in his pocket, and sprays it into Ben's eyes. Ben screams, and the guy grabs my backpack and runs that way." She indicated down the block.

"Pepper spray," Soper said to us. "Ambulance took him to Union Memorial. There's a uniform with him and she'll get a description when he's up to it."

I spoke for the first time, looking between Soper and the girl. "What about you, can you describe the man?"

Callie answered. "I told Detective Soper…The hoodie was gray and pulled over his head. And he had sunglasses. That's what I saw."

"Hair color?" This from Nate.

"Straight blond. Some of it stuck out from under the hood."

Nate, Soper, and I exchanged looks, each thinking it wasn't much of a description.

"Detective?" she turned to Soper. "I can't be sure because of the hoodie and sunglasses, you know, but I think I may have seen him on campus."

"Why do you say that?" I asked. "You said he was covered up."

"I know, but there's something about the sweatshirt and the sunglasses, and his overall look that I think I've seen before. Maybe on campus."

"We'll see if the young man who rescued her has anything to add. Maybe he can verify the campus possibility," Soper commented.

"And the contents of the backpack?" Nate asked. Soper had already reported this to him when we were at the gun range, but he wanted to hear it from Callie.

"Books, notebooks, some clothes, and my laptop." She paused. "The laptop is insured and everything is backed up, so it wasn't worth fighting over. I can borrow one from my boyfriend for now. I just wished Ben had left the guy alone." Her eyes drifted off again.

"Thank you, Miss Pierce," Nate said, and we stepped away from the roommate. As we did, an EMT from the nearby ambulance came over to her, and started, or continued, a number of health-related questions.

"I figure," Soper put in, "the guy was waiting outside the apartment three blocks away. He was planning to rob her there, but followed her back here when she returned to the car."

"Makes sense," Nate concurred. "And all this took place where? Near this tree?"

"At the intersection."

Nate walked up to the intersection and scanned the area. "Broad daylight. Pretty ballsy, or desperate."

"At least it wasn't the two guys who killed Seth Bruce," I said. "She'd be dead. Her Good Samaritan friend, too."

Soper turned to Nate, "I'm going to the hospital to talk to this Ben kid. I know there's an officer there, but I don't want to miss anything."

Nate nodded, and Soper gave his card to Callie, and then took off.

"Seems like he's settling in." I commented, watching Soper cross the street to his car.

"Yup."

"Yup?"

Nate, distracted, was still looking up and down the block. Finally, he gave me a little smile.

"What?"

"We may have caught a break."

I waited for the explanation.

"Good thing for us Miss Pierce was robbed here and not at her apartment building."

"Oh?"

He pointed up.

On the corner lamppost a metal arm extended over the intersection. Hanging from it was a small cylinder with a hemi-spherical object at the bottom.

"Big Brother?"

He nodded.

"And there's no camera near her apartment?"

He shook his head.

"Do you know where Big Brother lives?"

He nodded again.

* * *

CitiWatch, the camera-based anticrime monitoring division, was located on the seventh floor of police headquarters. I followed Nate, and we parked in an open lot beneath the building. We took an exterior set of concrete steps up one flight and then walked through a narrow corridor to a corner elevator. A few tall, husky uniformed officers nodded to us, as they passed us going the other way.

Up on the seventh floor the elevator opened onto a wider alcove, which in turn led to a narrow, sterile corridor with only a few doors to either side. There were no windows, and only overhead LED lighting for illumination. The hallway was relatively tight. After a right, then a left turn, we came to a fortyish, plain-clothed gentleman sitting at a desk in front of a monitor. He nodded to us, and we continued to an unmarked door at the end of the hall. I looked back to catch a glimpse of the screen the man was watching. It had a view of the corridor near the elevator, meaning he saw us coming before we even rounded the corner to see him. Meanwhile, at the door in front of us, there was an unlocking buzz and we stepped inside.

I had been in situation rooms before, and that's exactly what this space reminded me of. The room was dark-paneled with connected workstations snaking throughout. Computers and personnel were every four feet. Most, but not all, computer stations were occupied, and, interestingly, everyone was in street clothes. No one looked over when we walked in.

Leading the way, Nate cut through the center of the room and over to an aisle near a stretch of windows that yielded a view of East Baltimore. We opened a metal-framed glass door and stepped into another monitor-filled room. Unlike the space we had just left, the front wall held a large screen surrounded by smaller screens. Each held a view of a different intersection. None of the displayed streets were familiar.

The room itself was windowless and dimly lit, cutting down on overhead glare. That plus the dark paneling gave the room a relaxed, quiet feel. A raised area in the center contained several manned computer stations. It was the central hub and command center.

The Student

We walked along a chest-high partition that separated the elevated command area from our outer aisle. A fit, blond-haired man of about fifty looked up from a monitor as we came close. He appeared to be the senior person present, and he was dressed more formally than the others in the room, wearing a light-colored tweed sport coat and a yellow tie. In a way, he was another version of Nate. The senior man came over, a pair of reading glasses laced between the fingers of his left hand. As he moved, the front of his jacket shifted exposing the badge on his belt and his service Glock.

Nate met him as he approached. "Terry, good to see you." They shook hands.

"Always, Nate."

My friend introduced me, "Captain Terry Bell, Director of CitiWatch, this is Gidon Aronson. Gidon is on loan from…" he looked at me for a moment and finished with, "a sister agency."

I smiled, while shaking Bell's strong grip. "More like a distant relative's agency."

"Okay, cousin," he laughed easily, not knowing what to make of Nate's nebulous intro. If it bothered him, it didn't show. "Give me half a second, and I'll pull the recording of your intersection." He walked to back to his workstation, slid on his reading glasses, and checked a spiral notebook. He leaned over a keypad and began typing. Nate must have spoken to him on the way over.

"How many cameras do you have?" I asked as he worked.

"It's not the number of cameras, it's the coverage. We can watch about 75 percent of the city's intersections."

Surrounding the large central screen were probably fifteen monitors, each showing a different location. None of the other personnel, again all in plain clothes, looked up from their own displays.

A cool, air-conditioned breeze brushed past my face, as the A/C cycled on.

"They're not all pulled up here, obviously," I commented.

"We usually watch ten different intersections in the higher crime areas."

"What about the feed from 33rd and Calvert?" I asked referring to the location of the mugging.

The CitiWatch captain responded with a simple, "Nope. Not live. However…" after a few more keystrokes he brought up a new image onto the center screen…"we record everything for 48 hours, in case there's a crime we need to look at. If we don't archive it, it automatically gets erased." He paused for a moment, and then, "Here we go, 33rd and Calvert. Let me pull up the time code…"

The three of us watched the large monitor. Traffic at the intersection came and went. Pedestrians crossed the street, and even a few bicyclists went by. The shot was high angle, as you'd expect from the lamppost vantage point, but the resolution was surprising sharp. Captain Bell had the recording run at twice normal speed, and Noa's roommate hadn't yet appeared.

After another ten seconds, a young lady in a distressed jeans, a white tank top, and a backpack hanging from her shoulders, walked into frame.

"That's our girl," Nate said, and Bell adjusted the recording for normal run.

In a moment, a figure in a gray, zip-up hoodie came up on Callie's right, between the coed and the stores. We watched as he moved in front of her, blocking her way. She tried to go around, but he stepped over, not letting her pass.

"Hang on," Bell said. He tapped a key on the right side of his control panel and the image angle lowered and zoomed in. The camera's flexibility was impressive.

We now had a more clear view of the man in the gray hoodie. As the roommate had recalled, the man's hood covered his head, he was wearing sunglasses, and he had a hand in a pocket.

On the screen, Callie began to unsling her backpack. The three of us were silent as a third figure suddenly appeared and grabbed the mugger. They struggled and then the mugger broke free. The Good

The Student

Samaritan, Ben, punched him on the left side of the face.

"Nice shot," Bell said, mostly to himself, as we kept our eyes on the screen.

The mugger's right hand came out of his pocket with something in his grasp. We couldn't see what it was, but he held it up in front of Ben's face, and then there was a steady stream of liquid spraying into Ben's eyes. The would-be rescuer's hands covered his face, and he fell to the ground. He began to roll from side to side. The mugger looked at him for a split second, grabbed Callie's backpack, and ran out of frame.

"You can't by chance get a clear shot…" Nate began.

"-of the perp's face? Oh, yeah." Bell went back to his control panel and manipulated the recording. He rewound to where Ben had grabbed the mugger. Bell let it play, and then when the mugger broke free, the cop froze the image. He zoomed in, and in the middle of giant screen was the sharp image of the man in the hoodie, clearly showing his sunglasses and a wad of blond hair covering his forehead. "Nate, what's your cell number?"

Nate gave it him, and in a few taps of the keyboard, the image was sent to his phone.

Bell looked at me. "Cousin, you want?"

"You bet," and I gave him my number.

"Okay, Terry," Nate continued, "do your thing."

"Certainly," he said it like Curly from the Three Stooges… *Sointently.*

And with that, Captain Bell's monitors followed the mugger from intersection to intersection as he bolted from one street to another. The cameras stayed with him, until finally he ran out of frame.

"That's it," the CitiWatch captain said. "That's what we got."

"Where was he headed?" Nate asked.

"No way to tell ultimately, of course, but he was running west towards Hopkins."

Nate said it as I thought it: "Sonofabitch."

I looked at Nate. "Callie was right. The guy was from campus."

"Unless he was just passing through."

"Maybe." I turned to Bell. "Any cameras at the other end of campus, along main streets?"

He shook his head. "But we'll get this over to Campus Police." He indicated the headshot still frozen on one of monitors.

"I have a contact from when the break-in happened at Noa's, the roommate of the mugging victim," I explained to the CitiWatch man. "Their apartment was broken into the other night."

"You think they're connected."

Nate nodded. "Plus, the kid who did the honors was murdered."

Terry Bell handed me his business card. "Text me the name and number of the campus officer."

"Will do."

Nate's phone rang, interrupting further conversation. After putting the cell to his ear, he looked at me, but then turned back to the mugger's image on one of the screens, phone still at his ear. Finally, my captain friend told whoever was on the line, "Put it out to Homeland, too." He listened for another moment, and then hung up.

"Soper from Union Memorial," he said to me. "The kid who tried to intercede is okay. The pepper spray did a number on him, but he'll be fine. His description of the mugger matches Miss Pierce's. Nothing more there."

"Did he recognize him from campus?"

"Soper asked. The kid didn't think so."

"Doesn't mean Callie's wrong."

"No. And before you ask, Soper said he'd text that screen shot of Seth Bruce's killers when he gets back to the precinct."

I put on a mock innocent tone: "I wasn't going to ask."

Nate ignored me and turned back to the CitiWatch Commander. "Terry, if our perp pops up on any of your cameras…"

"I'll let you know."

Nate and I both thanked the captain and we walked out the way we had come.

The Student

Not much in the way of conversation happened on the way downstairs – except that he wanted me to promise him something: not, as I'd have expected, that I wouldn't take some stupid action on the case, but that I'd report on tonight's rendezvous with Katie.

My reply was not so polite, and Nate laughed vigorously at irritating me so easily. Without another word on the subject, he headed back to work once we were in the parking lot. As for me, thanks to his remark about Katie, I drove to my martial arts studio, wondering about the get-together tonight.

The time was still relatively early, about 5:30, and I made a conscious decision not to think about the coming evening. I changed into gi pants and a T-shirt, stretched for a workout, and then went through multiple, circular ba gua techniques. I segued into a slower tai chi ch'uan form, and then back to the ba gua.

Finally, I sat down in the center of the room, and attempted to clear my mind – which was more challenging than I'd have liked. The break-in at Noa's passed behind my closed eyelids, as did the *DEATH TO ISRAEL* graffiti, Seth Bruce lying sliced and shot on his kitchen floor, Aminah's stolen laptop, and my meeting with Gil Jeffries. Even Mossad Deputy Director Idan Gelvar floated through.

I set up a breathing pattern and focused on my inhales and exhales. As I relaxed, the images began to dissipate. Then in the last moments before everything melted away, a single thought burst out. *It has to be about emails.* And then emptiness took over.

Fifteen minutes passed. There was no awareness of the time; just at some point my breathing became more active, which in turn brought back awareness. I slowly opened my eyes, and sat there for a few more moments. After another minute, I stood. *It has to be about emails.*

Made complete sense, but the revelation would have to wait. Students would soon be arriving for the evening workout. As was the case yesterday, this was really Jon's class, which really was my class before I had disappeared for the summer. My guilt stimulated a plan for a special, practical session.

The room soon filled, and I found myself looking for the two women I had pegged as FBI agents. They didn't show. Perhaps Special Agent-in-Charge Jeffries called them off after our meeting this morning. Perhaps they didn't want to seem overeager and would show up another night. Perhaps whatever they saw last night convinced them I was a spy, and so they didn't need to come back. Perhaps…no, it didn't matter.

Once everyone assembled we went through the warmup calisthenics, and then the martial routines of blocks, punches, and kicks. While everyone's energy was still up, we continued last night's lesson on breaking out of grabs. Yesterday evening I had left the students to their own designs about what to do once they were free of an opponent's grip. Tonight, I showed them how to respond, based on their individual levels: for the beginners and intermediate students, that included punches and kicks. For the advanced students, takedowns and sweeps. By the end of the evening everyone had learned something new, simple, and effective.

The class ended at 9:00, and I worked with a small group of advanced students for another thirty minutes. After they left, I checked my cell phone. Nothing from Katie, but there was a text from Nate, a screen shot of the two men who had murdered Seth Bruce. Soper had finally gotten to sending the screen capture from the victim's surveillance camera.

I looked at the image of the men. The shot was possibly taken in Bruce's living room, but it was hard to tell because whoever enhanced the image centered on the men's faces. Both were swarthy with dark hair: one had curly hair cut to conform to the curve of his head, while his partner's hair was straight and parted on the left. The curly-haired man had high cheekbones and a triangular jawline. From the angle of the screen capture, his brown eyes seemed flat, emotionless. His partner with the straight hair had dark eyebrows that hovered over the ridges of his eyes. His dark eyes were set, determined. Seth Bruce, if he had any instincts at all, had to have known he was in deep shit the moment the men walked into the room. It was impressive he got as far as the kitchen. Maybe the killers let him get him away from the front window.

After saving the image and compartmentalizing it in my head, I stripped and showered, and then walked next door to the natural foods bistro. The casual, small restaurant still had a few available tables outside, and after ordering a cheese and mushroom panini inside, I grabbed a two-person table where I could watch the comings and goings along the sidewalk. As I waited for the grilled sandwich, I thought about Katie, and how the conversation might go in a short while. I truly had messed up with her. She really understood me. She had become a calm center back when I was trying to find peace after Tamar was killed.

In the months since Katie and I had become exclusive, she was an oasis when recurring nightmares shattered my sleep. She saw me as kind and generous – she once told me that – but had also witnessed my martial side, where I responded violently to personal physical attacks, and guessed that I probably enjoyed it. If that bothered her, she rarely expressed it. She's watched as I taught classes to middle school students on the causes of the Civil War, but also wept on my shoulder after witnessing terrorism up close and personal in Jerusalem.

There was movement in my periphery as a young woman in a maroon apron brought out my panini and salad. I thanked her, and began eating. As I took a bite, my eyes faced either the panini or the street, but neither was what I was seeing.

A little more than four months ago Katie and I had traveled to Israel. She was with me when one bright day when the sky was a deep blue and the air was still, when the downtown Jerusalem traffic flowed and pedestrians both hurried and took their time, and where the day held only potential, a friend of mine went out to her car just after meeting us. She didn't know that a terrorist had left an explosive-filled backpack nearby. Moments after she left us, Katie and I saw her torn apart by the blast.

Ultimately, we dealt with what we had seen in different ways. I finished what I had come to Israel to do, and while I stayed on, Katie returned to the States. I went back to my old army unit to teach and to train, and Katie went home to process what had happened. She said she needed time.

And that's where I screwed up. She said she wanted space, but I should have been close enough to be there if she needed me. I distracted myself with drills of clearing "enemy held" rooms and fast-roping out of helicopters. And so, after a long summer to process that horrific bomb scene no one in a civilized world should witness, Katie had probably had enough.

I looked down at my dinner. I had made little progress on my sandwich; a few bites and that was it. After a deep breath, I looked around. The other tables were now filled with customers, and the woman in the maroon apron was weaving between them, bringing plates of food to a table near me. After she finished her delivery, I motioned to her and asked if I could get a box. She smiled and said sure. Whatever appetite I had was now gone. Maybe I'd eat later. The waitress disappeared and I let my mind replay some of the images I had just run. I wasn't happy with myself.

The server returned with a carry-out box, I transferred my meal, and walked to my Jeep to drive to Katie's.

The ride only took five minutes, but parking on her tree-lined, narrow street was the challenge, with most residents home for the night. I found a spot around the corner, grabbed the carry-out box containing my partially eaten panini, and walked to the older, familiar house that had the Mustang parked in the driveway. I sprinted up the wide wooden steps only to pause at the solid front door. Katie's keys were still in my pocket, but as with my visit the other day, it didn't seem right to walk in. I knocked, and the door opened after a few moments.

"Hi," she smiled, standing next to the half open door. It wasn't the smile that normally lit her whole face. She opened the door wider, and I stepped in. It seemed awkward not to kiss her, so I did…on the cheek. After returning the kiss…on my cheek…she indicated the take-out box in my hand. "For me?"

The Student

"If you want it. It's a cheese and mushroom panini. But I took a bite or two out of it."

"You brought me something to eat and began eating it?"

"I bought it for dinner, but I really wasn't hungry."

"So, you thought you'd give me a partially eaten sandwich?"

"No."

"It's from the bistro next to your place, right? You could have brought me a salad. I love their salads."

I just stood there, not knowing what to say. I *should* have brought her something. I looked at the white box in my hand. "I have no idea why I brought this here. Really."

Katie looked at me for a moment and then smiled her full-face smile, acknowledging she was playfully giving me a hard time. She took the box from me and put it on a nearby table. When she put it down I saw the jewelry box containing the necklace I had brought her the other night was where she had left it. Not a good sign.

She took my hand and led me to the couch where we sat next to each other. She was wearing a sky-blue cotton shirt, a pair of white jeans, and sandals. She looked great. Her face was clearer than the last time we were in this room, like a decision had been reached. She held my hand in her lap. She was letting me down easy, trying to be sensitive.

"I really am sorry for not being here all summer," I apologized, not knowing how else to start the conversation.

"I know," she said quietly, without emotion.

"It was insensitive, and I should have been here. I don't know what else to say."

"There's nothing else to say."

I was hoping for *I forgive you*, but those words didn't come.

The air in the room was motionless. I could hear the hum of the refrigerator coming from the kitchen.

I wasn't going to prolong this. I withdrew my hand from hers, and stood up. Her eyes glistened for a moment. "You're giving up?"

"You wanted time to think. You wanted space. That's what you said." My words were beginning to go in a direction I wasn't expecting.

A moment passed and she stood up, too. "I miss you. I don't know what to do about this."

"That's not what you said the other night."

"I know. I was really hurting over the summer. We both saw the bomb go off on that sidewalk and what happened, and you decided to stay halfway around the world. That was very selfish."

It was…but I didn't say it out loud. Instead, "All I can say is, given those circumstances, with you here, I'd come back, if I had a do-over."

"No, you wouldn't."

My brow furrowed.

"I know you. You cope one of two ways. Either you bury any intensity as best you can, or you do martial stuff, though I'm not sure how that resolves anything. When the opportunity came to be with your old unit, off you went."

"I did."

"And you'd do it again. That's you, Gidon. You also help people unselfishly, because you can. And you do whatever it takes…go where you need to go. And I love that about you."

"But?"

"But I've been asking myself can I be with you under those conditions. You just disappeared for four months without considering me."

"I didn't disappear."

"You did," she paused. "And you will again, if necessary."

It was true. Maybe.

"And I've seen you at work." Her euphemism for seeing me beat the crap out of people.

"You didn't mention my sense of humor."

"Yeah, I'm not sure that goes in the plus column." She smiled.

"So what does all this mean?"

She shrugged. "I don't know."

"You don't know? You still need time to think?"

"I guess. If you're okay with that, unless you just want to call it quits." There was a hesitant look in her eyes.

"What does 'time to think' mean? Do we see each other? Do we not see each other? Do we go out with other people, if we want to?"

"Maybe."

Maybe?"

"I don't know."

"I sense a theme here." I let a moment pass. "So we're not exclusive anymore?"

"I guess."

"Okay."

"Okay?"

I nodded slightly. "It's risky, but if we're…"

"Meant to be, we're meant to be."

Katie took a step toward me and her hands came up and rested on my chest. I could smell her fresh skin.

"Uh, you seem pretty close for wanting space," I said quietly.

"You can back away."

She could probably feel the pounding in my chest. I was surprised my whole body wasn't shaking.

She unbuttoned the button below my open collar. "There's something I've been thinking about."

"Oh?"

"Uh huh."

"Thinking is good." I unbuttoned her top button.

She moved in a little closer, and unbuttoned my next button, and the next.

I closed the space between us and kissed her on the neck. After a moment, I whispered in her ear. "You know what?"

"What?"

"Nate wants a full report on what happens tonight."

"I trust you'll give him something to think about."

All I said was, "Mmm," and we finished unfastening each other's buttons.

16

The text came in about 2 a.m. My eyes had already been open for hours when I heard the single, distinctive buzz.

There were no lights on in Katie's bedroom, but luminescence from streetlamps still washed in. The curtains diffused the light even more, giving the room a monochromatic palette. I was in bed on my back while Katie was sleeping, facing me on her side. We had fallen asleep in each other's arms, but shifted at some point to be more comfortable. For me, though, there was no sleep beyond those first few minutes. I was often wide awake when other people experienced calm and rest and normal REM cycles.

Real sleep was unpredictable. On occasion, when I did sleep, my subconscious usually brought up images of combat. Sometimes they were reruns of actual missions; others were surreal frustration dreams, such as me emptying my clip into a grinning terrorist to no effect. The terrorist would keep walking toward me and smiling. I had gotten used to being jarred awake and my heart racing. Other nights, I'd just lie in bed with my mind running. Tonight was no exception.

Katie's breaths were long and deep, but my eyes were open and staring at the ceiling. I saw my army unit shunting children from a Syrian apartment building so we could deal with a bombmaker in the basement. I was clearing a darkened room when an Islamic terrorist stepped from a doorway holding a little girl at gunpoint. I shot him twice in the head.

The image changed.

I was at a bus stop along a road not far from Tel Aviv. There were young soldiers all around, dressed in their olive uniforms, waiting to return to base. They had their Tavor carbines slung from their shoulders, with their magazines strapped to the sides of the weapons. Cigarettes were handed out and smoked by almost everyone. More than a few of the young soldiers were on cell phones. All were probably just out of high school. A young soldier, about 17, approached a quiet sergeant next to me. The young soldier had a small amount of black stubble on his face and wasn't carrying his weapon. His eyes were fixed on the quiet sergeant. The closer he came, the more something didn't seem right. In a moment he was in front of us. He had that sour smell of old perspiration, and was mumbling something under his breath. Before I could say anything, the quiet sergeant turned toward the approaching man. There was a flash of silver as the young man stabbed the sergeant in the chest. The quiet non-com looked at me in surprise and collapsed in my arms as I reached out for him.

I blinked and saw the ceiling for a brief moment. The image changed.

I was in civilian clothes, running through the streets of Jerusalem toward a blackened storefront that used to be a restaurant. Shattered glass and pieces of brick crunched beneath my shoes. The air was acrid with billowing smoke. I passed a single, lady's black shoe and twisted remnants of a car. I saw bodies, and parts of bodies, scattered on the road like discarded, appendages from a mannequin shop. And then I saw a young blonde-haired girl lying motionless on her back. She could have been eleven or twelve. She had a gaping chest wound. Her head was turned in my direction, and she stared at me with the bluest eyes I had ever seen.

I blinked a few times and for some reason turned to Katie. She was looking at me. I turned to the ceiling.

"Are you okay?"

I looked back at her and smiled weakly. And that's when my cell phone buzzed its single text alert.

The phone was in my pants…on the floor not far from the doorway, next to Katie's pants. Our underwear was somewhere closer to the bed. I looked back at Katie who was still looking at me.

"I need to get that. Could be Jon about the girls or something."

Katie nodded from her horizontal position.

I retrieved the phone and sat on the corner of the bed, pulling up the text.

"What is it?" Katie was up, leaning on an elbow.

"Nate. He's up late. They ran the killers' pictures through Homeland Security." I had to pause as I took in the results. "They're from the Islamic Republic of Iran."

Katie sat up a little more.

After a few breaths, all I could say was, "Shit."

Katie was still looking at me.

I repeated myself. "Shit."

"What does this mean for the girls?"

It has to be about emails. "They have something the Iranians want, and don't even know it."

"How could they have something…?" She didn't finish the question.

I shrugged. "Something to do with her uncle? He's a chief in the Mossad."

She just looked at me.

"I know. Whoever it is tried making it look like a simple theft, stealing Aminah's laptop, but when that didn't work, they broke into their apartment. And when that didn't work, they stole the other roommate's laptop."

"Something in an email or a program or a picture they all share, that someone sent them?"

I nodded again. "And they have no idea."

"And you think it's the uncle who sent them something, what, to hide it?"

"Maybe, but I don't think so. He denied knowing anything about the break-in. Besides, he wouldn't involve family."

"Do you believe that?"

"I do." The statement didn't come out as definitive as I would have liked.

"You have to look at it from another angle."

"Yep."

A few seconds went by, and Katie put her head down on her pillow. "Wouldn't the killers be on a watch list or something?"

"You'd hope so, but apparently not. Just means someone on their side is good at his or her job."

"So what's next?"

"Get some questions answered." I came back to bed and got under the top sheet.

"Like…?"

"The kid they hired to break into Noa's room was a former grad student and a resident advisor. And the kid today who stole the roommate's backpack. She thinks she's seen him on campus. Plus he ran off in that direction."

"How'd the two men from Iran get hold of those kids?"

"That's the question. They must know someone who knows students."

"Professors, maintenance people, men and women in the offices… Hopkins employees?"

"Uh huh."

She looked into my eyes, and the subject reverted to an earlier conversation: "So, are you okay with us getting some space from each other?"

"You mean starting tomorrow?"

"Obviously."

"So this isn't making up." I slid an inch closer.

"No."

"You're a very beautiful, but confused lady."

"Sorry."

"It'll be weird," I acknowledged.

"Definitely. But we have to figure us out."

"I guess we can give each other space starting tomorrow."

We reached for each other and in a few moments began generating heat, literally. I could feel the skin on her back begin to perspire.

A thought flashed through my head. "Crap."

Katie pulled her head back. "What?"

"I have to text Jon. I want to speak to him and the girls about all this and about campus stuff."

Katie looked into my eyes, and then moved on top of me. "Text him in the morning."

17

Four-and-a-half hours later, Katie was in the shower and I needed to get some answers to my earlier thoughts. I was back to sitting on the corner of the bed. First, I called David Amit, my Shin Bet friend. As Israel was seven hours ahead, he was in the middle of his workday – *every* hour was in the middle of his workday for him – but all I got was voicemail. I recorded a message about the Seth Bruce murder and told him we had a screen capture of his killers. I mentioned DHS had identified them as Iranian nationals, and that I'd text him the photo. He'd let me know if any of Israel's security services had intel on them.

Next, I spoke with Nate, who was having coffee at home. I told him I forwarded the pic to my guy in Israel. I also thought about him bringing in the FBI, as this now involved hostile, foreign agents, but he'd have considered that. Until there was more info, Nate wouldn't tell Jeffries; they'd usurp his homicide investigation. His parting question, not half unexpectedly, was about my meeting with Katie.

"You're such a *yenta*."

"Okay, so?"

"Check my Facebook status," I said, and then hung up as he laughed.

Finally, there was Jonathan, Noa, and Aminah. Jon was already up, but he said that the girls were still sleeping. I brought him up to speed on the third roommate's mugging, but he already knew about that.

"Callie texted the girls last night," he said. "I was going to tell you today."

"Thanks. And I meant to tell you last night. I taught and then went to Katie's."

"Oh?"

"Leave it alone, Grasshopper."

He ignored my comment. "So does this mean…"

"It means I'll tell you the next time we spar."

"Oh, good. I'll either be in pain or more pain."

"Perhaps." I had to smile. "So, you back in town?" They had been in Gettysburg yesterday.

"Yeah, my place."

"Keep your eyes open when you go out." I told him about the two Iranians.

"Shit."

"That's what I said. Don't let the girls go back to their apartment. If you need to, go for them, but I'd rather you stay away, too. "

"Got it. We'll stay away."

"Good. If the killers don't find what they want on Callie's laptop, they may come back to Noa and Aminah. They don't know the girls are clueless in all this. And don't tell the girls we've identified the killers. Leave that for me."

"Okay."

"All that being said, can you get Noa's laptop over to Nate? I want his people to go over it. Maybe they can find something."

"Roger that." After a moment: "How do you suppose they found Seth Bruce?"

"And the guy who mugged Callie."

After a moment, "You know, Sifu, there're always protests groups on campus…political, social…Maybe there's a connection."

"There is." Jon had nailed it. "It's the funding." I stood up. The shower in the bathroom was no longer running. "I gotta make a call. Thanks, Jon."

Katie walked out with a towel around her. She picked up a brush on her bureau, and smiled at me. Her wet hair was matted down and her eyes sparkled. I could see beads of water on her neck…and on her calves. I would have moved right over to her to help her dry off, but I was distracted by the need to call to David Amit again in Israel. This time he answered.

"Shalom, Gidon. *Ma ha'inyanim*? I saw that you called before. I was in a meeting. You called back. Important?"

Katie smiled at me and walked back into the bathroom.

After a bit of a sigh, "Maybe. Check your message for an update, but for now, can you find out if Iran funds student anti-Israel protests on the Johns Hopkins campus here?"

"I don't know about specific colleges, just that they fund anti-Israel movements on many American campuses. Hold on. I know someone who might have the answer for you."

No, wait! I wanted to shout, because he was going to call Idan Gelvar of the Mossad. Noa's uncle. I could just see Amit setting up the conference call.

After a brief wait: "Shalom, Gidon."

I was right. Gelvar. I could see his clean-shaven, round face and thinning hair.

"What's up? Something to report?" the Israeli asked.

"In a minute, but first, a question about the anti-Israel movement on college campuses."

"That's why I asked for your help in the first place. To protect Noa from all the craziness." His smooth voice seemed to have some anxiety in it. Not what you'd expect from a man who dealt with terrorism and would send agents into harm's way. Family was different, of course. And it confirmed he wasn't involved in sending Noa something.

"I know. Any idea if Iran sends someone money, specifically for anti-Israel activities here?"

"*Lo*."

"*No*, you have no idea, or *no* about Hopkins students?"

"Both. The BDS movement gets a lot of their money from many

foreign sources." The Boycott, Divest, Sanction movement on the college level. "And Iran is a main sponsor. I can get details. We have people who follow that sort of thing. Why?"

I brought Gelvar and Amit up to speed, essentially restating the voicemail message I left for Amit. After I finished, Gelvar said in a very businesslike voice: "I can send you a few people."

"No. Absolutely not." I could just see Gil Jeffries knocking at my door, because I'm working with Mossad. "I'll follow up on this, but, Idan, you can't send anyone here. The FBI will put me in a Federal prison somewhere."

"*B'seder*," he said. Okay. "But I will if you need help."

I ignored the offer, but maybe I wasn't as convinced as I had thought. "One more thing, Idan, did you send anything to Noa that might be sensitive?"

The reaction in his tenor voice was instant: "No. I would not do that…involve my niece."

"Okay, we'll continue to check her emails and files. There's a connection. She has information the Iranians want. But, nothing indicates terrorism. The two men who killed the young man aren't part of a cell."

"You don't know that." This from Amit.

"And you can't trust Homeland Security," Gelvar jumped in, "or the FBI to share anything, not with you, and not with your police friend."

"Yeah." After another second, despite that lingering last thought, I went back to Gelvar's offer: "Idan, don't send anyone," I repeated.

"I won't," he said.

"If you do, I'm out. You understand?"

"Yes. I promise."

"Okay. I'll keep you updated."

The three of us hung up.

Katie came out of the bathroom, wearing a lacy mauve bra and panties. She was hard not to watch. "You're not making this easy for me, you know."

She just laughed and sashayed over to her closet.

I turned back to the phone and redialed Jonathan, my eyes still on Katie. "Is Noa up yet?"

"No."

"I need you to wake her to answer a question. It's important."

"Okay."

"It's from your idea. Does she know any professor who's actively anti-Israel?

"Hang on. And glad you thought it was a good idea."

I could hear him walking and then a door opening. There were some muffled voices, and then more walking.

"No. She can't be sure."

"Okay. How about this: the night of the break-in, Aminah mentioned "Free Palestine" flyers were being circulated on campus. There have also been anti-Israel speakers. Those speakers may need a faculty sponsor. I don't know. How about that…does she or Aminah know if that's possible, or who a sponsor could be?"

"Hold on." This time, he put the phone down, because there were no sounds of movement or voices.

As he went to ask her, I replayed my logic. Iran was a state sponsor of terrorism world-wide, plus was rabidly anti-Israel. I knew they funded anti-Israel student protests. Gelvar might be able to confirm if someone here received their "financial aid," but his affirmation wasn't necessary. A BDS supporter wouldn't be difficult to entice, so whoever was behind those flyers and speakers was my candidate for either the Seth Bruce connection or to the roommate's mugger.

Katie stepped into my line of sight again. She was wearing a high-necked mauve sheath dress that clung to her curves. That explained the matching bra. She posed with one leg slightly to the side and put a hand on her hip.

"You want this image burned into my memory, don't you, before we cool things off."

"I do," she smiled back.

"Forget me. You teach adolescent boys. They won't remember a thing you say."

"I don't have classes today."

Jon's voice came back on the phone. Katie came over and I asked Jon to hold on a moment.

She looked at me, and smiled a slightly diminished smile. "I have to go. Can you lock up?"

"Of course. Guess we know where the other one lives, if we want to see each other."

"Uh huh."

"See you around."

She smiled, kissed me on the lips, lingered there for a moment, and then turned to the door. I really didn't know how to react, so I didn't. I just watched her leave.

"Hey," the phone in my hand said. "Is that Katie?"

"It was." We got back to our conversation. "What did Noa say?"

"What did *Katie* say?"

"Jon."

"Okay." He paused for a moment. "She doesn't know, but Aminah might. She's right here."

There was a slight ruffling sound and then Aminah came on. Jon had awakened her, and she had that slightly gravelly voice from not having gotten up yet. "Hi, Gidon?"

"Sorry for waking you."

"It's okay. You want to know if there's a faculty sponsor behind the "Free Palestine" flyers and speakers?"

"Yes."

"There is…I think. He may be from the Political Science Department. I don't remember."

"Any way you can check? Would you recognize a name if you saw it?"

"Give me a minute."

There was a pause and Jon came back on. "She's checking the website."

"Great."

A few moments went by as Aminah went off to do her search, and thankfully Jon didn't ask again about Katie. In another minute, Aminah was back.

"Dr. Kenneth Sloane. He's the Department Chair of the poli-sci department. I also checked to see if there's a student Free Palestine website, and there is. It has a listing of dates and events. He's listed there, too."

"Aminah, thank you. Last question, and then you can go back to sleep. You didn't happen to notice where his office is?"

"Ames Hall."

* * *

By 9 a.m. the University had already been up and running for hours, and I had parked myself on a bench beside a walkway that eventually led to the Georgian-style Ames Hall. Above me was a canopy of branches from a nearby oak, and from my shady angle I could see the front and side doors of the building. There was a third out back, but it was a fire exit, so if Dr. Sloane were to come or go, it'd be through one of the first two access points.

I had called Jon a third time to ask Aminah about the professor's teaching schedule and office hours. Both, she said, were on the Hopkins student site, and, bless her, what would have taken me thirty minutes to locate, took Aminah less than five.

While I waited on the bench and took in everyone passing by, I retrieved a few Google images of Dr. Kenneth Sloane. In a photo dated last year, he was fiftyish, with silver hair, parted on the left. There were some strands of black mixed in; the combination gave him a serious look. Additionally, he had a neatly trimmed beard, again mostly silver, cut to follow his jawline. He had black and tan tortoise shell glasses and brown eyes. Based on a group shot of Sloane next to other professors, he seemed on the taller side – unless everyone else was short. His bio declared he was born in Boston, but his family had moved to the United Kingdom when he was in high school. He earned an undergraduate degree from the University of London, and then moved to University of Chicago for a graduate program in political science.

I shifted my weight and looked around the campus. As it had the other day when I was here, the park-like grounds exuded serenity. Brick sidewalks and terra cotta footpaths invited strolls along manicured grass and well-tended shrubbery. Some of the paths led to the various college buildings, while others wove their way through the expansive college grounds.

As the minutes passed, the shade created by the nearby oak slowly shifted, eventually allowing the sun direct access into my eyes. Sunglasses came on, I checked my watch, and headed to where Dr. Sloane would teach his first class of the day. Along the way, I reached into my backpack and donned a Red Sox cap, despite this being an Orioles town.

The brick path led me between buildings, and up and down a flight of cement steps to a prechosen vantage point near a newly repointed Federal-style building. Instead of a bench, this time I sat on the ground and leaned against an old lamppost, pulling out a martial art book; had to look like I was doing something. Since Sloane hadn't stopped off at his office, he must be going directly to his class over here.

In a matter of minutes, Dr. Kenneth Sloane, Professor of Political Science, approached from the far end of the building, a gray laptop messenger bag over his right shoulder. He scooted up the wide steps to the main entrance and disappeared inside. He looked just like his pictures.

According to Aminah's research, the class he was teaching, "An Introduction to Global Studies," would last fifty minutes. He'd have a break, and then after lunch he'd teach "The Politics of the Middle East" for an hour and fifteen minutes. That was a class to sit in on, probably just to stand up and challenge some of his points, assuming they may have been influenced by an Iranian financial inducement. For now, I had fifty minutes to watch the building and see if the dark-haired provocateurs from Iran showed up.

That was the hope. The two foreign agents needed entrée into the university scene and what better access than a professor who may already be on their payroll. Realistically, it was a long shot. Contact had to have been made days ago. No reason for another, but if so, logically, it also didn't have to be in person.

If the Iranians didn't reach out, there were other strategies: I could let Sloane see me watching him, and then stay out of sight to observe his actions. If there were no reaction, I'd revisit my theory about whether he was involved in the first place. The killers needed an in, and if it weren't Sloane, it'd be someone else. I could use Noa and Aminah as bait, but I didn't want to think about that beyond the fleeting thought.

After about twenty minutes, I changed to a third location: the steps of a building, across a grassy patch from Sloane's lecture hall. I also changed into a lightweight, green and blue jacket, and took off my cap.

Student traffic into Sloane's building dwindled, no doubt since classes were underway, but there was the occasional hustling latecomer. As the minutes passed, I watched the foot traffic along the adjacent brick sidewalk. Most of the young men, as they had the other day, wore shorts and either T-shirts or polos, while the women were more dressed up in leggings and short dresses, or short skirts and pastel cotton tops. At some point, two young ladies walked toward the steps I was sitting on. One had shoulder-length blonde hair parted in the middle while the other had long, wavy dark hair. Both turned to me as they climbed the cement stairs and smiled. Naturally, I smiled back, as they continued into the building.

While I watched the building where the poli-sci professor was teaching, I replayed the recent scenes involving Katie. Based on how

The Student

we left things when I returned from Israel, I didn't expect her recent, what…signs of wanting to be together? Katie said she needed time and space to think, but then there was the phone call and of course last night. We really needed to stick to her plan. Maybe we would now.

Across the way, groups of students came down the steps, bringing my mind back to why I was here. I strolled closer to Sloane's building, keeping my angle tangential to the entryway. The political science professor came out after a few moments, messenger bag slung from his shoulder. He descended the steps and moved right. I followed him as he walked purposefully down a brick path.

He passed a building marked Krieger Hall and kept walking, without looking or acting to see if he were being followed. The sun was not yet completely overhead, but the day was definitely becoming warm. A slight breeze teased my face, but I didn't feel any cooler. Sloane stepped off the sidewalk, moving around slower, perambulating students. I did likewise. The professor kept up his steady pace and entered a building marked as a learning center. Despite his determined gait, he didn't check a watch, or appear anxious – as far as I could tell from behind. Maybe he was meeting someone, maybe not.

I stayed with him, and once inside the learning center, realized it was the same building where the campus policeman and I had met the other morning. A cluster of students suddenly crossed Sloane's path, forcing him to almost stop. By the time I weaved through a similar group, the professor was just turning the corner. He walked purposefully down another corridor where I avoided peering at the back of his head, since people sometimes sensed that, and would instinctively turn around.

The professor went up a flight of stairs to a small dining area that had a refrigerated case with prepared salads and plastic-sealed sandwiches. He hovered over a selection of wraps, eventually selecting something. For a moment, the poli-sci man just stood with his back to the cashier, looking out a glass door to a patio, set up with metal chairs and tables. It was the same area where the officer and I had our conversation soon after the break-in.

Sloane turned back, paid for the wrap and a drink, and moved out to the deck. While he chose a seat, I bought a sandwich and found an inside table, allowing for a line of sight through floor-to-ceiling windows.

During the course of his meal, no one approached him – not a student, not an adult, and no one I recognized from a screen capture from a murder scene.

As I watched the silver-haired man, I considered that if indeed Sloane were the killers' contact, he could be a target as well, if they were cleaning house. They killed Seth Bruce. Why not the man who provided him?

Would the professor see them coming? Probably not. Would I see the killers coming for him? Maybe. I leaned back, and felt the presence of the Glock near the small of my back. Nate would be proud of me for carrying it; if I used deadly force, not so much. Nor would any number of FBI agents be very happy. But couldn't worry about them at the moment.

Sloane finished his wrap and took a last pull on his drink. He stood up, tossing his trash into a nearby can. Almost in concert, I wrapped up the remainder of my sandwich, and prepared to follow him. The professor started across the student-filled patio, and walked between round metal tables toward a set of stairs at the far end.

And that's when I saw a man come up the steps to patio level twenty feet in front of him. He was a tall, swarthy man with tight, dark curly hair cut to conform to shape of his head. One of the men from the screen capture was approaching Sloane – no smile, no familiarity, no offered hand. There wouldn't be. This was business. The man who killed Seth Bruce wore a neutral expression.

They were tying up loose ends, just as I thought. The dark-haired man in a black sport reached inside his jacket toward his back. The professor was walking toward him but not really seeing; he was lost in thought, and would be dead in five seconds.

In broad daylight, out in public, the man from the screen capture would shoot Sloane, probably center mass for shock value. Either the Iranians were desperate or confident, or both. The suddenness, the violence unleashed on the professor would likely freeze anyone watching. There were half a dozen college kids at the tables, plus a few older men and women as well. All were potential targets. One wrong look at the killer from any of them, one sudden reaction or move – maybe it'd be from the young man closest to him in the tank top and shorts, or maybe from his companion, a smiling young lady in a flowery sundress – and he'd simply shift his firing arm. It'd be horrific, and over in seconds. He'd walk back to the stairwell and disappear even as the last victim fell to the ground. But all that hadn't happened yet.

I dropped my sandwich and sprang up, knocking my chair backward. I don't remember opening the door to the outside.

I took in the entire patio while simultaneously focusing on the man in the black jacket. Sloane was looking past him.

As the man from the screen shot brought his right hand clear of his jacket, I reached for my Glock. I'd need to bring up the weapon, pull the slide to put a round in the chamber, and fire in one motion. Done it hundreds of times. My left hand began to come up as part of the sequence.

The man's hand cleared his coat. My own hand wrapped around the grip of my gun.

The man with the dark, curly hair saw me. Our eyes locked and he froze. His wallet was half open in his palm. His wallet. Not a SIG, not a Beretta, and not a Russian Makarov.

Instantly, I let all the energy drain from my arms. The man with curly hair cut to conform to shape of his head wasn't who I thought he was. Just some poor guy who had the unfortunate luck to run into a paranoid, wired Gidon.

I completely relaxed. My right hand fell away from the Glock, which I was about to pull from its holster. It remained in place while my arm dropped away, limp. I let both arms go completely passive.

At the same time, I used the energy building up in my body and my lowering arms to pivot my frame 180 degrees. I completely turned my back on Sloane and the man with the wallet, and fluidly walked back into the café. Without looking right or left, I went through the room and exited the way I had originally entered. After rounding a nearby corner, I stopped and leaned against a wall.

No wonder Sloane didn't stop, and I had been too far away for a positive ID. *This is why we train in urban settings*. I said a silent thank you, and allowed my breathing to normalize.

From around the corner, sounds of the café bounced between doorways, off the walls and stone floor, and over to my little niche. No one was shouting *Call the police!* or seemed excited at all. There only sounds were of people talking and chairs being moved around.

After a few additional deep breaths, I went back in, keeping all motions calm and even. I went over to my table – the chair had already been straightened – grabbed my sandwich and backpack, and walked toward the patio. Only a few men and women looked at me, but that might just have been a normal reaction to someone entering the space. No one stared, no one whispered, no one pointed. Maybe the woman behind the cash register gave me an extra second, but then I did shoot up from my chair and knock it over.

Sloane was no longer on the deck. He must have gone down the steps at the other end. As I crossed the patio to follow, I saw the man in the black jacket and black shirt off to the side. He was speaking to friends, motioning like he didn't know what had just happened. I went over to the exterior steps and headed down. Sloane, outside the building, was already on the ground level and walking back in the direction of his lecture hall. Had he seen me? The professor either had his back to me, or I had my back to him, so most likely not. As I fell in a safe distance away, I took off the lightweight jacket I had been wearing, put it in my backpack, and put on a *Ravens* cap, keeping it low over my forehead.

The silver-haired professor headed back to the first building where he had lectured, and based on the timing, was probably preparing for his next class. I parked myself on another bench next to the brick walkway. The fact that no one from the screen capture intersected him en route, didn't negate a meeting could still happen. A rendezvous could have been scheduled inside the Federal-style lecture building. It was also possible that Sloane could be shot, have his throat slit, or be killed any number of ways, and I'd never see it.

Maybe this wasn't such a good plan. Maybe I needed to get eyes on him. Alternatively, the Iranian agents weren't inside, and staying put allowed me to see them coming. And, again, it was possible I had gotten all this wrong and he wasn't the killers' go-between.

I shook my head to myself. Too much second-guessing. Better to see what, if anything, unfolded.

The afternoon proceeded much the same as the morning: the professor stayed inside, I changed vantage points several times, and took off and put on baseball caps and jackets.

Based on his lecture schedule, Sloane was just about finished his afternoon class when my phone rang. It was Gelvar from Israel. His smooth voice simply said, "The Iranians, through a dummy philanthropic fund in Qatar, are indeed funding Islamic Studies at Hopkins, as well as their political science department. They are also throwing money at Columbia, the University of California at Berkeley, and others. We have people watching their accounts." A second passed. "That doesn't automatically mean there are political strings attached to any professors. Remember the money comes from a non-Iranian cover organization."

"I know."

"However," he continued as if I hadn't commented, "substantial sums have also been deposited into the personal account of a Dr. Kenneth Sloane."

"That's what I need to know. *Toda*." I hung up. My sudden disconnect may have been rude, but I didn't want contact with the Mossad man lasting a second longer than necessary.

At least this verified that Sloane was indeed their man, and if he survived the day, I had a number of questions for him. One simply was, what were his sponsors after? They probably hadn't revealed that and, if Sloane were smart, he wouldn't want to know.

By the time his class on the politics of the Middle East was over, I had leafed through the books I had brought, thought about Katie, Jon and the girls, and Gil Jeffries. At some point it'd be necessary to check in to see if the FBI computer people had turned up anything on Aminah's laptop, providing BPD had gotten it over to her. How forthcoming she'd be was a different question.

By the time Sloane came out of his building I had switched up my surveillance technique. I was meandering a few steps from a group of men and women my age when he came down the Ames Hall steps. The professor turned in the direction of his office, so I peeled away from the group to follow him once again.

The Iran-sponsored professor didn't go to his office, though. Instead, he headed to a metal and glass cube-like building, situated on the edge of an oval quad. As earlier, I stayed discretely behind but followed him inside. He continued straight ahead on the ground level, and then almost at the other end of the structure, turned left into a large alcove with a stand-alone coffee bar. I was impressed that the University had so many places to snack and relax. A blond man, probably in his late twenties, was tending the bar along with a slightly younger brown-haired woman with hair pulled back in a ponytail. Both were in white aprons. I sat across the room at a table-for-one, and pulled out one of my books. I was just one of several men and women sitting and reading.

Sloane nodded to the woman barista, but stepped to the side to speak with her male partner. The blond-haired man was partially turned so there was no full view of his face. Their conversation was short. After what seemed to be a few sentences, the man took off his apron, said something to his partner, and turned to leave with Sloane.

As he rotated his body, I got a clear view of his face. A tuft of blond hair had fallen over his forehead, and without having to look too closely, there was a sizeable patch of black and blue on his left cheekbone. The discoloration looked fresh.

As the professor and the barista walked out, my mind flashed to the monitor at CitiWatch. When the captain had played back Callie's mugging yesterday, we zoomed in on the thief's face. He was wearing a gray hoodie and sunglasses, but had blond hair drooping over his forehead.

I flashed to another view on the monitor. In a wide shot of the thief and Callie, a Good Samaritan – she had called him Ben – had stepped in. The image in my head replayed the image on the screen: Ben punched the thief on the left side of his face. The blond man would have developed quite a bruise on his cheek. I got up to trail the barista and the professor and caught sight of them in the first floor corridor.

They were walking briskly. Sloane and the man with the bruised face exited the exterior glass doors, but had paused at the bottom of the entry steps. From inside I could see that a few more sentences were exchanged, and then the pol-sci man walked off solo.

The mugger was the newest player to me, plus he may have had Callie's laptop somewhere, so I stayed with him.

The blond-haired man walked quickly across the oval quad and around multiple, old two-story buildings. Unlike Sloane, he was more nervous as he walked, and looked around constantly, forcing variations to my surveillance: sometimes I'd stay directly rearward, other times further back and to the side. Once, I passed him and followed from in front.

After about ten minutes he sprang up the steps of a curved, glass-fronted building, taking them two-at-a-time. I didn't follow. This building, like most others here, were labyrinthian to an outsider; it wouldn't take much to lose the man who had stolen Callie's backpack. Instead, I leaned against a nearby tree, settling for a view of both front and side doors.

While staring at whatever the facility was in front of me, I mentally replayed Callie's mugging. So, who was this guy, besides being a barista, and how'd Sloane motivate him to steal the backpack? He didn't appear to be a student, but he knew his way around. Most workers on campus would if they'd been here long enough. Simple monetary inducement? Something else?

Once again my thoughts returned to Noa and her roommates. They were a recurring theme…mainly because I had no answers to all this, to include the veracity of the message on Noa's wall. With the Iranian connection exposed, the painted words might not have been just a scare tactic.

And then there was Gelvar. Trust him? And did the Iranians, or Sloane, know Noa was the Mossad chief's niece? A positive response brought up unpleasant possibilities for the future: kidnapping, torture, a prisoner swap of some sort. Hopefully, all this was my worst-case paranoia.

The main entry door to the glass building swung open and a group of five or six students – boys and girls – spilled out, talking loudly enough to clearly hear their interaction. There was some laughter, and one of the boys turned around and walked backward in front of his friends.

There was another movement out the corner of my eye. The side entrance opened and two men emerged. Both were medium height and both were dark-haired. One wore a navy blue sports coat, the other a zip-up black fabric jacket. They moved quickly but didn't seem to hurry; their strides were long and steady. They walked along the brick sidewalk about a hundred feet in front of me, and on occasion turned their heads to scan the vicinity. The one on the left had curly hair cut to the shape of his head and the other had straight hair parted on the left. The straight-haired man looked at me as they went by, and even from this distance I could make out his flat, emotionless eyes. He held my gaze for a second and then moved on.

These were the men who had shot Seth Bruce. No mistaken identity this time. These were the agents who had shot him and slit his throat.

And inside the building was the blond-haired man who had stolen a laptop for them.

I ran for the building's side entrance, the one the two men had just exited, closing the distance in a few seconds. I pulled the door open, noticing that the two Iranians were already fifty yards away. Why weren't there card key locks here or something, restricting access? Shit. Shit.

Inside the side entry alcove, a hallway led straight ahead, plus to the right was a staircase up to the next level. I didn't even know the barista's name to call for him. For no apparent reason except for instinct, I went for the second floor.

I was almost at the next landing when a series of girls' screams reverberated up from below. There was a pause and then multiple, terrified yells for help.

I half jumped down the stairs and ran in the direction of the screams. They had come from the long first floor corridor.

A cluster of students hovered in a doorway a third of the way down the hall. One young woman had her head buried in a male friend's shoulder. Another coed had collapsed to the floor, sobbing. Others had turned toward the wall. A few were staring into the room.

I ran closer. "LET ME THROUGH. LET ME THROUGH!"

They parted enough to allow me in. The room was some sort of small music hall with microphones on stands at one end, and drums and a piano at the other. Angled sound panels dangled from the ceiling.

The blond-haired barista was on his back just inside the doorway. He had been shot multiple times in the chest. Blood had already saturated his pale blue shirt.

I turned to the students looking at him. "Go into the hallway. Now!" They didn't need this burned into their memories, if it weren't too late already. No one argued.

I looked back at the young man on the floor, and lowered my head slightly, anger building. While blood had pooled near the blond man's chest, there was more up near his neck. The two terrorists had also slit his throat.

18

I waited for Dr. Kenneth Sloane in his office. The man who had received money from the Islamic State of Iran had office hours after his last evening class, and I waited for him as the sun set and the sky grew dark. This was no James Bond move, me waiting in a darkened room for my prey. I wasn't going to assassinate him, just ask a few questions. We'd see what would happen along the way.

The professor's office had a single window, looking out onto one of the ubiquitous brick walkways. A tree trunk blocked part of the view, but another university building across the way could easily be seen. Most of its inside lights were on, testifying to a still busy campus. I closed Sloane's venetian blinds and got busy.

I turned on a stylish, gooseneck LED desk lamp, and then moved a table beneath the pair of fluorescent tubes in the ceiling. It was a simple matter to stand on the table and then slightly rotate the tubes so they wouldn't light up. With the blinds closed, the only light in the room now came from the desk lamp. I switched that off to see a narrow strip of light beneath the office door. Perfect. I turned the gooseneck lamp back on and angled its white light on the closed door. Next, I moved the professor's desk chair out in front of the desk, so it was in front of the lamp. The room took on an air of a stark theater set, where a spotlight illuminated only a single, small area of the stage. I left a roll of duct tape on the desk and pulled a bridge chair beside the hinge side of the office door, and waited.

My mind went back to the dead barista in the music room. I had called Nate, of course. After that he made his own calls, and soon came campus cops, BPD uniformed officers, some detectives, and then Nate. Standing not far from the body, I described to my friend what I was doing there. If he were angry or annoyed, he didn't say. He knew I'd have updated him once there was something to tell. There was something to tell.

As I waited for Sloane in the darkened room, two male students walked by in the hallway on the other side of the door. They were talking about an engineering problem involving torque ratios.

A few minutes later I heard a woman on a cell phone. She was going for a run with a friend and she'd study later when she returned.

Mostly, there was no sound at all. The hallway was abandoned, and I was left with my thoughts.

After a few more minutes, someone inserted a key into the lock and opened the door. Professor Sloane stepped in, my candidate for the man who connected the two Iranians with Seth Bruce and with the blond barista who stole Callie's backpack. I silently rose from my chair, invisible beyond the pool of light shining on the door.

The professor took a step into the room, squinted at the desk lamp pointed at him, and flicked the light switch. Nothing happened. No overhead light came on. He looked at his office chair now in front of his desk and illuminated by the desklight. Sloane opened his mouth slightly, then squinting into the bright bulb and tried the light switch again. And that's when I turned him slightly and drove my fist into his stomach.

The professor doubled over, coughing, almost collapsing to the ground. I locked the door. Sloane tried sucking in air, but that wasn't working. I put an arm around him, and led him still bent over toward the desk chair. When he tried to straighten, I pounded him in the gut again and sat him in the seat. In the darkness and in his pain, he never saw my face. In a matter of seconds I had his wrists and forearms duct-taped to the chair's arms. I then waited behind him and to the side, and pulled out my Glock.

It took about two minutes for his breathing to normalize and then one more for him to sit up without wincing. When he was able to, Sloane moved his head, trying to see me, but I was out of his line of sight and behind the lamplight. He attempted to move his arms, but of course, was unsuccessful there, too.

"Who are you?...What do you want?" He was somewhat raspy.

There was no rush to answer. After a very long pause, I spoke calmly and in a voice from behind him: "I've come a long way, and you have two choices. If you give me the answers I want and I believe you, I'll cut you loose and you'll never see me again. If you don't answer me, or if I don't believe you, then…"

I pulled the slide on my Glock, placing a round in the chamber. It was a distinctive sound, and if you've ever heard it, you knew what it was. In case he didn't, I placed the barrel of the gun against the back of his neck just below the curve of his skull. He stopped moving. Then, suddenly, he struggled against the arm restraints. He knew, he felt, the barrel of the gun on his head, but it didn't matter. Panic. Flight reflex. My index finger remained outside the trigger guard so there was no chance of the gun going off, but he didn't know that.

I pressed the Glock into his neck harder, forcing his head forward. He stopped pulling against the duct tape. "No need to panic, Professor. You didn't even hear my first question, and I know you know the answer." I backed off the Glock.

My guess was that Sloane knew the two Hopkins men had been killed. And he had already half-expected someone would come for him. The perfect entrée.

"I sent two men to retrieve a few laptops from some college girls. *College girls!* How complicated could that have been? My men came to you for help." That had been my working hypothesis. "Isn't that right?"

He nodded.

"What did they say when they came to you?"

A heartbeat or two went by.

"They said their government had given me lots of money to teach what they told me, and to run anti-Israel protests. Now they wanted one more thing."

"You gave them Seth Bruce."

He nodded as best he could.

"But he didn't do a very good job, did he? They had to kill him. Do you know that?"

"Yes." His voice had lost most of its volume.

"They shot him and cut his throat." Another few heartbeats passed. "I am not happy. That execution is very distinctive and could lead back to me." For a second or two I let the silence in the room fill his ears. "After that you gave them the blond man, and my two men used him to steal the laptop from another college girl." I said *college* again, like *from a child*. "Do you know what happened to that man today?"

The professor just nodded.

"Once again, I am unhappy." I returned the muzzle of the Glock to just behind his ear.

"They were your men who did that, not me." He had been forced by the gun barrel to look down at his lap.

"I know. Where is that laptop now?"

"I turned it over already…last night. Keith gave it to me yesterday, and I gave it to your men." Keith must have been the barista.

"That's unfortunate."

The man in the chair turned his head slightly to the right, perhaps to get a glimpse of me.

I continued: "The two men I sent have broken contact. They know the killings have made me a bit…discontent." I backed off the muzzle again. "I need to contact them." And with that, I stopped talking, letting the silence and darkness of the room sit on him once more.

In a moment, Sloane slightly turned his head. "I have a phone number," he offered.

"I also have their number, but it doesn't work."

"Maybe they gave me a *different* number. It worked a few hours ago."

I could text them a message from Sloane's phone to set up a meeting.

"What's the number?"

"It's in my cell phone…in my jacket pocket."

"Right or left pocket?"

"Right."

I switched the gun to my left hand, pressed it hard into Sloane's neck again, forcing his head all the way forward, and reached into jacket pocket. All he could see was my arm. I pulled out his cell.

"Where is the number stored?"

He told me, but of course the screen was locked.

"Lock code." There was annoyance in my tone.

He told me. I tried it, and after seeing it worked, I pocketed the phone.

"*Toda rabba.*"

The Hebrew *thank you* was on purpose. I let it sink in. He tried turning in his seat, but I was still in the shadows behind him.

"So you recognize Arabic's sister language. Good. Here's more: *Sheyrut Betachon Kellali.*"

He became very still.

"Some people know us as the Shin Bet or Shabak. I know we're not the Mossad, but I know people who know people."

I pressed my Glock into his neck again.

"I would guess if I were to let you go, you'd waste no time calling your two friends, because I'm pretty sure you know their number by heart."

"I don't, I swear. I don't."

"Or, I can tell the University and the news outlets you have information on both killings, and see how long it takes for the two men to find you."

"I won't talk to them, I swear."

"And I won't mind if they do, because as far as I'm concerned, you're also responsible for the murders. Maybe they'll kill you the same way they killed Seth Bruce, and Keith – that was his name, right?"

He nodded slowly.

"But I have no doubt that before the two men pull a knife across your throat they'll ask who you've spoken to, and you'll tell them, of course. So, I'm going to turn you over to people I trust, and they'll ask you more questions than I did and in greater detail. If you are not forthcoming, I'll let it be known that you gave up your two Iranian friends. Then you can really panic. And one more thing." I moved in close to his ear as I pushed his head forward with my gun one last time. "If you ever find your way back to a college campus anywhere, and you re-start even the smallest anti-Israel activities, I will come back and you'll never see what I'll do to you."

I holstered my automatic, and before Sloane could relax, I wrapped one forearm around the front of his neck and the bar of my other arm behind it. Twisting his head just so, and putting pressure on the main blood vessels in his neck and his windpipe, the circulation to his brain began to ebb. The professor struggled for few long moments, then went limp. Using my folding knife, I cut away the duct tape around his wrists and forearms, and clumped it into a ball, which I pocketed. Finally, I walked to the office door, and opened it. Nate and Gil Jeffries were coming down the hall.

"Perfect timing. He's just sleeping."

19

It seemed I had barely left Nate at Hopkins when he called me hours later at home...at 2:45. But I was still up, sitting at my desk.

"The Feds are raiding a house in Locust Point." That was it, the entire exchange. That and he'd pick me up. At the curb, Nate slowed only enough for me grab the door handle and jump in.

When he accelerated south onto the Jones Fall Expressway, I was pretty sure his right foot was pressed to the floor. There was next to no traffic so there was plenty of room and time to slide around normally-moving vehicles. If we passed any cop cars, I didn't notice, not that it'd have mattered, with his cobalt blue police lights alternating behind the front grill.

The FBI had used Slone's phone – I had turned it over to them – and texted a "Need to meet" message to a number the professor provided. The foreign agents responded with an address not far from Silo Point off of E. Fort Avenue, on the way to Ft. McHenry.

The night around us was calm – as far as I could tell from this velocity – as orange street lights, billboards, and scuffed Jersey walls blew past.

"Who called you?"

"Jeffries," Nate said, coming off of I-83 and onto city streets. He slowed only marginally at intersections. There was virtually no one on the road. "They had a 'no-knock' and were about to breach." A no-knock search warrant. Very controversial.

The *Nice of them to give you a heads-up* was never expressed, but I knew the lack of courtesy irritated my friend.

As Nate took the streets around the Inner Harbor, I could picture an FBI tactical team bursting through the front door of the target home. Would the two Iranian agents be there? Would there be a firefight? They didn't seem to be of the bent to lay down their weapons.

Nate soon turned off the main road onto side streets and into a neighborhood of renovated row houses of varying stories. All were brick-faced, some had new windows, others aging, and a few units had decks just visible on the roofs. In the block off the main drag, all the lights were out behind the windows and no one was on the street. That changed when we turned the last corner. Red and blue lights emanating from Federal vehicles reflected off of cars and scurried across brick facades. A third of the way up the block, dark sedans were angled up to the curb in front of a home with a For Sale sign in the window. Parked up the block, a black SWAT-like vehicle sat idling fifty feet away with an EMS ambulance next to it. In the center of it all, agents in FBI raid jackets clustered near the front entrance of the for sale home. The frame of the clean, new-looking front door had been splintered open.

Residents, young and old, were out on the sidewalks, mainly across the street, watching the locus of activity. You'd never know it was the middle of the night. Nate parked in front of a Crown Vic that blocked the road. Without looking at each other, we got out.

My attention went from the law enforcement people to the residents standing in front of their homes. Most seemed to be in whatever they had on when the commotion started. Some folks were in pajamas, some in sweats. A few women had jackets thrown over their shoulders. Even kids were out. More than a few people, young and old, had cell phones up, filming the goings-on.

We walked around the sedan perpendicular to us, but a tall, thin agent in a suit held up his hand. Nate was ready with his badge and ID.

"Captain D'Allesandro, Baltimore City Police."

The young Fed looked at Nate and didn't seem to know what to do.

After a moment, Nate simply said, "Get Jeffries."

The agent turned away from Nate's unwavering eyes and over to a gaggle of agents in front of the recently broken-into home. Conniker, Jeffries' partner, was holding court, but saw the young agent looking over. The husky FBI man approached us, but addressed the junior agent: "It's okay. I've got them." He turned to us. "Special Agent Jeffries is inside."

There were no further words spoken, and he led us onto the sidewalk and over to the entryway of the home. He remained at the base of the marble steps when we went inside. We didn't have to go far. Jeffries was in the foyer, talking to a forensics woman.

As we looked around, she finished her conversation. The living room was completely bare: nothing on the white walls, no furniture, nothing. It had been cleared out. Just the hardwood floors and empty space. That wasn't entirely true. There was a single, open folding chair near the front window but facing the room. Other than that, just wood and walls.

Jeffries turned to us as the forensics woman went toward the back of the room and into the kitchen. "It's all like this."

"Upstairs, too?" I turned to nearby steps. "Nothing?"

"Empty."

"They were never here," Nate said.

The FBI woman nodded.

Various forensics techs were wandering about. Some were dusting for prints on door knobs and other surfaces. One young man was checking the back of the folding chair near the front window.

Nate said he wanted to look around. He wasn't taking anything for granted. I followed as he went from room to room, poking his head into closets, shower stalls, into alcoves; he even peered into HVAC vents. Finally, he stood in the center of the finished basement and looked around, just moving his eyes. Then he just shook his head and

The Student

we headed upstairs and back outside. The two of us took a moment near the stoop, then began to walk to his car.

Gil Jeffries came over. "Captain…"

We turned.

"I want you to know this wasn't my call." The raid. She knew how Nate felt about being left out.

"D.C.?"

She nodded.

"You called when you could."

Nate knew how things worked, and she didn't have to let him know at all. That was her reaching out.

After a few seconds I commented to Jeffries, "You were lucky."

"I know. They could've rigged the front door."

Nate shook his head. "Would've brought too much heat on them."

"If I were those guys," I nodded toward the gathering of people up and down the sidewalk, "I'd have sent you next door to a family of civilians. Can you imagine with your 'No Knock,' bursting in on a sleeping family?"

She nodded, looking at me, considering. "And if the homeowner came up with a weapon…"

The three of us just watched the scene in front of the for sale house. After a few moments, I turned to the clusters of residents across the street.

Nate followed my line of sight: "They could be here, the two agents, checking to see who turned up."

"I would."

The three of us scanned the crowd for anyone who didn't fit in.

"They're gone," Nate said, and we started back to his car.

Jeffries walked with us. "How did you know about Professor Sloane and the connection to the two agents?" she asked me.

"Sloane not cooperating?" Nate asked with a slight smile. Maybe he wasn't as zen as I thought about being left out of the raid.

"I followed what I knew," I said. "There are anti-Israel protests exploding all over American college campuses. Many of them are funded from outside sources, and one is…"

"Iran," the Jeffries finished my sentence.

"Yup. I know about First Amendment rights, but these groups on campus are often treading on other students' rights. Many are harassing Jewish students in particular and intimidating them. They don't allow the pro-Israel students to peacefully rebut what they're saying. They're rabidly anti-Israel and anti-Semitic. You want a precursor to hate crimes? Here you are."

"And you know Iran is involved here because…" Nate said, moving me back to my point.

"I called my Shabak friend in Israel. The Shin Bet," I looked at the FBI woman, "not Gelvar from the Mossad." I didn't mention that David Amit put Gelvar on the line. "Sloane is receiving sizeable donations from Iran, and since he was already a recipient of their money, the Iranians used him to get someone to steal the girls' laptops. Still don't know why, but regardless, they've been exorcising all connections."

"Seth Bruce and the victim in the music room," Nate said. After another moment: "What's the update on Aminah's computer?" he asked Jeffries.

"Nothing unusual so far. No unusual emails, no embedded files, no unusual search activity or downloads."

"Did Noa turn in her computer?" this from me.

Nate nodded. "Jonathan came by today. I'll get it to you first thing," he nodded to the FBI woman. He looked up at the still dark sky. "Well, in a few hours."

"Can you come by with Noa?" she asked me.

"Just tell me when."

20

We sat in Jeffries' office in two padded armchairs opposite her laminate-topped desk. Behind it, a large window yielded a magnificent view of the Inner Harbor just a few blocks away. The FBI Special Agent in Charge hadn't joined us yet, so Noa and I looked around the room.

The office was clean and crisp – her desk only had a few papers on it. There was no clutter anywhere, not on an end table, not on chairs, nor atop a file cabinet. But it wasn't completely sterile. There were two framed photos on the desk – we only saw their backs – and there were some beautifully composed framed pictures on the walls. One was of a weathered, elderly Catholic priest and an equally weathered parishioner on the steps of a church. Another was of an American soldier holding a young, Middle Eastern-looking child, and a third was of a couple sitting on a beach towel with out-of-focus blue water behind them.

"Interesting mix of subjects," I commented, mostly to myself.

"Gidon," Noa looked right at me, "why are we here…at the FBI?" Behind her anxiety, she had been doing some thinking.

I had never told her about the Iranians' involvement or the murders. "We think there's something on your laptop, or Aminah's, or Callie's that someone wants."

"But why are we *here*?"

"The FBI has the best computer people. Also, someone put up a Hamas flag in your room. The FBI looks into all hate crimes."

She looked at me without saying a word, just trying to read my face.

Before another nebulous explanation came to mind, Jeffries came in, carrying a blue folder. Instead of sitting behind her desk, she pulled up a third chair to sit in front of us, creating a triangle to ease conversation. She held out her hand to Noa: "Hi, Miss Biran. I'm Special Agent Gil Jeffries. I'm in charge of your case." Jeffries turned to me, holding my eyes briefly. "Mr. Aronson and Captain D'Allesandro of the Baltimore Police brought me in on the investigation."

"Okay."

"Since someone seems to want something on your laptop, and since you gave us permission, we went through your files, as you know."

"Yes." Noa looked at the FBI woman, unsure, and just a little of afraid, of what was happening.

"There's really nothing suspicious that we can find, but there are a few emails I wanted to ask you about." Jeffries opened the blue folder and scanned a paper inside. "Along with all your email correspondence, there are a number of letters from your mother and father, of course. That's natural. Recently, though, your father sent you links to several scientific articles, and cc'ed Miss Hadad, your roommate."

"My father would do that sometimes," Noa offered. "Send us stuff."

"He's a scientist?"

"A bioengineer. Whenever he publishes something he sends me a link to the article. I usually read the first few paragraphs and then get lost."

I weighed in: "What sort of work does he do?"

"He's a scientist for an Israeli company involved in desalination. At least, I think so."

"And he lives in Israel?" Jeffries asked.

She shook her head. "Not right now. The company has an office in Seattle. He's been there for about a year, though he travels back and forth to their offices near Tel Aviv. We still have an apartment not far from there."

My mind took off: a desalination scientist from Israel who can turn salt water into drinkable water. What would that be worth to a parched, desert country in the Middle East?

But it didn't make sense. A link to a scientific article wouldn't be worth killing over. Even if it were groundbreaking work, an article could easily be located; you needn't steal the computers the email resided on. Unless there was something embedded in the link.

I turned to Jeffries. "Did you check the link itself?"

"There's nothing there. Just the path to the article."

Another thought popped up: "Noa, do your parents know what's going on, what happened in your apartment…the break-in, the interest in the laptops?"

She shook her head again. "Didn't want to worry them."

"Maybe it's time. And if it's okay, I'd like to speak with your dad to reassure him that you're all right."

Jeffries looked at me, like *What are you thinking?*

A quick plan had formed: a face-to-face with Noa's dad in Seattle. He was a desalination expert from a region where fresh water was scarce. I wanted to find out more about his project – in person – to get a sense of the man. I'd fly to Seattle, but there'd be no point if I were a stranger; he wouldn't open up.

"Noa, can we call your *abba* now? Seattle is three hours behind us, but it should be okay."

"We can do that. You want to speak with my father and not my mother?"

"For now, yes. You can call her, too, later. I'm sure your dad will fill her in. Just tell him about the break-in and that everything is okay. No don't need to mention the Hamas flag stuck on your wall, or the *DEATH TO ISRAEL* crap. I think that would freak out any parent. We can fill them in later, when we know more."

As Noa took out her phone, Jeffries continued to read my face, but my mind was already jumping to how I'd introduce myself. "*I was Sayeret Matkal, but came back to the States after my fiancée was killed in a terrorist bombing. Now I'm looking after your daughter." "I'm an associate of your brother-in-law, the Deputy Director of the Mossad…"* No. Not accurate. I'm not Gelvar's associate.

Gil Jeffries moved off to the side, and I joined her to give Noa a semblance of privacy. Once she got through and got past the initial hello, we heard her matter-of-factly reporting that her apartment had been broken into. No, no one had been home. No, nothing had been taken, though someone tried to mess with her computer. She wrapped up by saying there was someone here who wanted to talk with him. Noa came over and handed me her cell phone.

I paused for a moment, looked at Gil Jeffries, and began: "Shalom, Dr. Biran," I assumed he had a doctorate. "My name is Gidon Aronson, and I know your family in Israel. I live here in Baltimore, and at your family's request, I'm helping the police investigate the break-in."

There was a moment of silence. Then, "Wait. Who are you? And what family in Israel?"

"I'm former Sayeret Matkal and sometimes I work with Shabak. I now live in Baltimore."

"What does that have to do with my daughter and this break-in she just told me about?"

"Your brother-in-law Idan asked if I would keep an eye on Noa… since I live here."

"Idan?" There was a pause as he made connections. "So you work for…ah…his institution?"

I couldn't help but smile. *Mossad*, the name of the Israeli Secret Service, actually meant "institution" in Hebrew.

"No, no. We have a mutual friend, and as a favor, Idan asked that I keep an eye on Noa. He was worried because there's a lot of anti-Israel activities at universities these days."

"So, what's really going on that needs someone like you to investigate?" He didn't refer to me as either Shin Bet or Mossad, but the implication was there.

"I'm just here to make sure that Noa is safe, and to tell you that she's fine. Also, you should know this has nothing to do with Idan's line of work. There have been several thefts of laptops recently on campus." This was a bit of obfuscation here, but essentially true. "That's all."

"Well….okay. Thanks for letting me know."

And with that, Noa's father let the matter drop, though I doubted he believed everything I said. He was going to follow up with Idan. I expected there'd be some transatlantic yelling.

I handed the phone back to Noa, who sent her love to her mom, and then said goodbye.

A split second after she hung up, Noa took a step forward, and looked right at me. "Okay, I didn't have to lie to my dad because I really don't know what's going on, but now you can tell me…What's going on? What's on these laptops? Aminah's and Callie's were stolen, and someone tried accessing mine. This has nothing to do with hate crimes."

"No, it doesn't, and that's what we're trying to find out. That's why we're here." I still wasn't going to mention the murders or the Iranian agents.

And that's when Noa impressed me. She looked from me to Jeffries and then back to me. "You're both full of shit." Before the FBI woman or I could sputter a response, Noa went on: "Tell me about the murders. That guy on campus yesterday and Seth Bruce."

I just looked at her.

"No secrets in this world, Gidon. Not on a college campus. Texts were all over the place. Instagram, Facebook… You guys were there yesterday, taking away Professor Sloane." She paused for a moment. "What did he have to do with the murders?"

"He knows who committed them," I responded.

Gil Jeffries filled in more: "It all may have to do with your father's work. We need to find out what the connection is to your computers."

Noa turned to me and I nodded.

"My father wouldn't do that. He wouldn't send me something secret. It'd be too dangerous."

The Student

"I agree," I said. A father wouldn't do that…I hoped.

"So who'd kill over my father's work?"

I didn't have to reveal it, but I did. "We think Iranian agents."

"Here? In the U.S.? Shit." That seemed to be the common response. Jeffries continued: "But we don't think they're after you."

"Jon know?"

I nodded.

"Iranians," Noa repeated.

"We can put you in protective custody," Jeffries offered. "You and your roommates."

Noa looked right into my eyes. "My Uncle Idan sent you to watch over me, didn't he?"

I nodded.

"Good enough for me. Plus there's what Jon told me about you."

I didn't say anything.

"Just catch the assholes."

21

It was raining in Seattle, but no surprise there. A dreary, dark expanse of clouds hung over the downtown, putting the whole area in slight shadow. The gloom just seemed to hover, like a splotch of deep blue above the skyline.

On the cab ride north from Sea-Tac, my mind was on what I'd say to Noa's father when I caught the driver eyeing me in his rear-view mirror. He seemed to switch between watching the road and watching me. I made that easy, as I had to lean toward the middle of the back seat to get a clear view of where we were going. The angle also gave me a clear view of the man behind the wheel. He was a middle-aged fellow with long, straggly, dirty blond hair and arms covered with tattoos. On his right forearm amidst all the ink I could see a U.S. Navy insignia, with the spread-winged eagle clutching an anchor in its talons.

The ride had started out in silence after my initial direction of where I wanted to go, but it didn't last. After he watched a car peel off from in front of him, the driver looked over his shoulder at me and said, "Not a tourist, right?"

"How can you tell?"

"Tourists use umbrellas." He motioned to the rain on his windshield. "Locals just use raingear." He looked over his shoulder again and nodded at my zip-up slicker. I didn't have the heart to tell him, I just had forgotten the umbrella. He went on: "On the other hand, if you lived here, you wouldn't have asked why."

After a half-nod, I looked off to the left beyond I-5 to Elliot Bay on the other side of the Alaska Way Viaduct. Not many ships in the water, at least not at this point. The sun was still blocked by the dark clouds, so there was no real glare off the bay.

"I'm here on business," I volunteered and stared off to the west.

The cabbie didn't respond at first. Then, "Before you leave, make sure you take the underground tour of Seattle. Even if you're here on business, if you have time, it's worth it."

I smiled and caught his eye in the mirror. "Will do."

About twenty minutes later he skirted the streets of downtown and took me toward the tourist area near the Space Needle and the Chihuly Garden and Glass exhibit. He finally dropped me in front of a gleaming, white tower of a building that was adjacent to another gleaming, white tower of a building. Landscaped between the two was a small park with peripheral and diagonal paths. The entire grouping made up a modest campus. According to Noa, ten stories up on the building that faced the water, her father had a corner office. She didn't know his schedule; just that he was typically there in the afternoon. I hoped he was, otherwise I'd have plenty of time for that underground tour of Seattle.

The line of showers had not reached the small park where the cab had dropped me, so when I sat down on a bench along the grass-lined rectangle, there were no wet surfaces. I looked up at the white building in front of me, unzipped my rain slicker, and took out my phone.

Noa's dad answered on the third ring. "Uri Biran."

"Shalom, Dr. Biran. This is Gidon Aronson. We spoke yesterday."

There was moment of silence, then, "Yes? You have more questions for me, or maybe more information?" He sounded abrupt, maybe annoyed.

"I do...have more questions. Would you mind coming down to the park next to your building?"

"You're here?"

"*Ken.*" Yes.

"I'll be right down."

After he hung up, I pulled up internet images of Dr. Uri Biran. Several were of the same man, but there were others pictures as well: older and younger men who were somehow linked to his name. Another search brought up an article on Dr. Uri Biran, the Israeli desalination expert. The accompanying photo matched one of the Google images. He appeared to be in his forties with dark, curly hair and dark eyes. There was no smile on his face, his brow was taut, and his eyes looked seriously into the camera, as if he were annoyed. I wondered if that were his permanent affect.

As I stared off toward the southwest and to the Space Needle, the unresolved question ran through my mind of how much to tell Dr. Biran about the Iranian involvement, if at all. He was her dad; it would be the right thing to do. On the other hand, he'd want to protect her and insist she leave Baltimore. He might even get in my way if he came to town. There was no reason to think the Iranians wanted to harm Noa and her roommates. If they had wanted to, they could have done that already. Yeah, and the Syrians and the Egyptians weren't going to attack Israel on Yom Kippur in 1973.

A light breeze blew across the small park and a hint of lilac came with it. The break-in, the thefts, the murders all had to do with Dr. Biran's work. Nothing else made sense.

A young man and woman came out of Dr. Biran's building, and casually walked along the pathway parallel to where I sat. They turned onto a diagonal walkway and entered the other white tower. After they disappeared, I looked around. In the midst of a busy Seattle neighborhood of office buildings and tourist attractions, this area was an oasis. Traffic sounds had been masked by the position of the buildings, plus the way they had been oriented, allowed for maximum sun exposure, perfect for the greenery.

In a few minutes a barrel-chested man wearing a black polo shirt and black pants came out of the building closest to me. Dr. Biran spotted me. I nodded in confirmation, and we moved toward each other. As he approached, a lanyard with an attached ID card flapped against his chest.

He stopped a few feet away. For some reason a handshake didn't seem appropriate.

"You flew across the country to see me?" He said it with both curiosity and concern. "Yesterday, Noa said it was just a break-in."

"Everything is okay. Noa's fine. Really, all is *b'seder*." All is all right.

"Why don't I believe you?"

"Because I mentioned Idan's name when we spoke last, and I flew across the country to see you."

Dr. Biran had some gray at each temple and his eyes were more narrow that those in his pictures. Maybe he was just squinting.

"I don't work for him. I'm a friend of a friend, as I related yesterday."

No reaction. His posture didn't relax and his face still held concern. Couldn't fault him for that.

"I think this has something to do with your daughter's laptop, but there's no reason to think someone is after her personally."

"And you flew out here to tell me that."

"I came here to reassure you."

"I'm not reassured, and I don't know who you are."

"You called Idan to check me out."

He nodded. "Idan told me a few things about you. He said you were a good person. But I'm here and Noa's across the U.S. Someone broke into her apartment and now you're here. That doesn't seem like nothing. So what did you come to tell me in person?"

"Really. I came just to talk. Did your wife speak to Idan, too? She's his sister."

"Of course. He told us not to worry. We both wanted to fly to Baltimore, but Idan convinced us not to. But now seeing you, what's really happening?"

"Not much more than Noa told you yesterday. Let me fill in some details."

I recapped the events…the break-in at Noa's apartment that started my involvement, the laptop thefts, even Seth Bruce's murder. That shook him. His shoulders tensed slightly and he clamped down on his lips so they were a straight, thin line. After a second: "Why would anyone want to kill over a laptop?"

"We think it has to do with what you do here."

"Me?"

"You're an expert on desalination, right?"

He nodded.

"You've developed technology that's worth millions, correct?"

"We have a business and we sell our process worldwide."

"Maybe not everyone wants to go that route."

"What are you talking about?"

The Iranian connection. Tell him or not? It would definitely freak him out. It freaked me out, and it wasn't hard to think like a father. If I were him, if I heard Iranians killed someone who broke into my daughter's apartment, I'd be on the next plane to Baltimore to get her out of there.

Dr. Biran made the connection, at least in part. "Industrial espionage? That still doesn't make sense. There's nothing on Noa's computer."

"No proprietary information? You never sent her any encrypted files for safe-keeping, just in case someone came after you?"

"No. Of course not. The only things I've sent were industry articles on what we do."

The couple I had seen earlier, the man and woman who had walked into the adjacent building, came out. Both now had manila envelopes in their hands. They leisurely walked back toward Dr. Biran's building.

The scent of lilac blew across the small park again. For a moment I looked past Noa's father to follow the couple as they continued walking. They were engaged in conversation and never turned toward us.

"What makes you think my business and research have anything to do with Noa's laptop?"

Did he really not send Noa any hidden files for safekeeping? Tell him about the Iranians. Watch his reaction.

"I've been working with a detective in the Baltimore Police Department – he's a friend – and there's evidence to suggest the people who killed the man who broke into Noa's apartment are Iranian."

This time Dr. Biran didn't just tense up; he took a slight step back, the color draining from his face. "What?"

"So, you have to be completely honest with me. Is there anything on Noa's computer that has to do with your research or business?"

He looked at me, hard. A second ago he had blanched, but now his face became red. "No. Absolutely not." The color in his face returned to normal, and then he looked at me once again. "*That's* why you came here. You wanted to see my reaction."

For a moment we locked eyes. Then he turned to leave. "Where are you going?"

"I have to speak with my wife."

"No. Wait."

He turned back.

"Everyone involved – me, the police, even Idan – don't think your daughter is in danger. The Iranians have not contacted her or threatened her. They're not hanging around, they're not watching her…"

"There's never a problem until there's a problem. It's obvious you don't know what's going on. Their agents are ruthless and crazy. I need to get my daughter to a safe place. I'm taking her back to Israel."

"Dr. Biran, no. You need to let me do my job. Noa's safe and I'll find out what they're doing in Baltimore. If I thought Noa were in danger I'd send her away myself. Your brother-in-law, the Deputy Director of the Mossad, would have his men all over the place, don't you think?"

"I don't care. And it's not up to Idan, or you."

"No, it's not. But maybe Noa knows something she doesn't realize. I need her help. There was something on her laptop." I wasn't convinced it wasn't an email or something innocuous appearing.

"Where is she now?"

"With a friend of mine." I had the image of Jon taking Noa and

Aminah out to a bar or something. Hopefully it was out of town. "If you and your wife come to Baltimore, there are more people to worry about. You may even lead the Iranians to her accidentally." I paused. "We're taking care of her, and the Iranians may already have what they need anyway." I told him about the third roommate's laptop being stolen.

"So, you find out what's going on quickly, but I'm not going to let you put Noa in danger." He turned to walk away.

"Dr. Biran…" He stopped, and I continued: "After you talk to your wife, you're going to book a flight to Baltimore, aren't you?"

He didn't say anything.

"Don't do that. It's not going to help." I paused. "If you want to keep your daughter safe, and you need to do something, book a flight to D.C. instead. Stay in a hotel. Bring your wife, if you weren't already planning to. Go to a few museums. The Smithsonian American Art Museum always has great exhibits. Go to restaurants. You won't be able to concentrate, I know, but go anyway. It'll occupy you. If we need you, if Noa needs you, you can come running. You'll be only an hour away. But, do not come to Baltimore unless I clear it. *Hayvanta?*" Do you understand?

He nodded.

"Call me when you get into D.C. My number's in your phone."

He turned to leave again, and again I stopped him.

"Last question. Where did Noa buy her computer? How did she get it?"

"My wife bought it for her. Maybe for Aminah, too. I don't know."

He turned to walk away and this time I let him go.

22

The departure lounge for the 7 p.m. Alaska Air flight to Baltimore fit the mold of a thousand other departure lounges around the world: rows of black vinyl seats facing each other with intermittent table tops on which to rest food, papers, whatever. A single line of seats wrapped the periphery, and these were the premium seats, for every few feet were both USB and power outlets. Additionally, at two locations throughout the waiting area were two islands of standing-height shelves for laptops, again with charging outlets. At the moment all those stations were taken, as were most of the seats that had available power outlets. The flight had a layover in Denver, and the lounge was almost filled to capacity.

With about ten minutes to boarding, I looked down at a copy of Us Weekly that someone had discarded. I didn't recognize any of the celebrities on the cover. As I began to scan the first few pages, my cell phone buzzed with an incoming text.

It was from Nate: *Check the national news.*

I moved to the web browser and pulled up a news site. I scrolled. There was a story on Senate Republicans and Democrats voting for a health care bill along party lines, a story on a U.S. Navy patrol boat firing warning shots at an approaching Iranian Navy fast boat, and a story out of Baltimore: MURDER SUSPECT STABBED OUTSIDE COUTROOM. The article elaborated that Dr. Kenneth Sloane, a Johns Hopkins professor being held on conspiracy to commit

The Student

murder charges, was stabbed and killed as he was being escorted to his arraignment. As sheriffs were bringing Sloane to a courtroom, an unknown man "stumbled" into him and stabbed him. The assailant had moved on before anyone knew what had happened. Sloane collapsed and died before EMTs could arrive. The attacker was able to exit the building before officers realized his involvement.

I called Nate. "Hey," I said when he picked up. "What the hell?"

"Courthouse cameras caught the whole thing, but from behind. It was like Jack Ruby and Lee Harvey Oswald. The sheriffs were bringing Sloane to his arraignment – the last court case of the day – when someone sort of fell into him and stabbed him up under his sternum. In and out. Really knew what he was doing. We figure a ceramic knife to get past the metal detectors. He made a clean exit while everyone was dealing with Sloane, not realizing what had happened. A real fuckup. He should never have gotten that close."

"No angle on the guy?"

"Yeah, as he exited the building. He's one of the guys from Seth Bruce's apartment, the one with the straight hair." The guy I had momentarily locked eyes with outside the building at Hopkins. One of the men who had killed the barista I had been following.

"They had to have someone on the inside."

"Yep. Someone who could tell them the time Sloane was being arraigned. We're checking, but it could be as simple as someone slipping a court officer a couple hundred bucks for the court time."

"I was considering using Sloane as bait."

"Yep," Nate said again. "What time does your flight get in?"

"5 a.m."

"Call me after 7. We'll figure something out. Maybe we'll have more info on who leaked Sloane being arraigned."

"Long shot."

Agreement by silence on the other end. After another moment, "How'd it go with Noa's dad?"

"He's ready to take her back to Israel. Can't blame him. Said there was nothing on Noa's computer from him that'd explain all this. I believe him."

As the boarding notice came up on a digital display behind the gate agents, passengers began forming a line in front of the counter.

"We've got to get these guys within the next 24 hours. They're dialing up the violence. I want the girls safe."

"Forget the call after 7. Just come to my office at 7:30. We'll talk."

"Will do." I hung up, put the phone back in my pocket, and stood in line with the other passengers ready to board.

The line contained a mix of people and of ages; there were business folks in dressy casual attire, others in jeans, shorts, or chinos, and many young women in leggings or casual dresses. More than half the passengers in their twenties or younger wore flipflops.

Out of habit I scanned the people in line behind me, and thought about our dilemma. We needed to draw out the two killers. Sloane had been a safe bet, though the Feds using his cell phone to meet them the other night didn't elicit the intended results. The image of the empty rowhouse in South Baltimore was still fresh. And, I didn't want to use Noa and Aminah, that was for sure, if anyone raised the possibility. Clearly, this had become high risk, and parading them around was not what we should do.

I handed the gate agent my boarding pass. She scanned it, and tore off the stub portion for me to keep. After thanking her, I stepped onto the passenger boarding bridge not knowing what the hell to do.

* * *

"We'll use agents posing as the two young ladies and let them take on the girls' routines."

Agent Edwin Conniker, Gil Jeffries' FBI associate, had made the suggestion. It was 7:45 a.m. Conniker, Jeffries, and Detective Soper had joined Nate and me at BPD's Admin Building not far from City Hall. Nate had his jacket off, with sleeves of his pinstriped blue shirt rolled up to his elbows. He was standing beside his immaculately kept desk.

I didn't say anything, letting someone else voice how stupid the idea was. Soper, thankfully, did the honors: "Really, you don't think two professional, foreign agents who have probably been following these girls for days-"

Hopefully not, I thought...

"...would recognize decoys?"

"Besides," I said, "it's not the girls. It's their laptops."

"The girls are a means to the laptops, as far as they know," Conniker commented.

"And we're not using the girls as bait," I emphasized.

Nate supported my feeling: "No one's suggesting that."

Agent Jeffries went back to the core issue, turning to me. "And you're sure Noa's dad didn't put anything on the device?"

I looked over at her. "That's what he said. And besides, your tech people went over everything, right, and didn't find anything."

She shook her head. She knew the answer. I don't know why she asked.

I stood up and went over to the windows. This was the same building I had visited four days ago to observe the CitiWatch surveillance control center. We were three floors below their situation room.

Conniker tried to save his idea. "So we let the look-alikes walk around campus with the girls' laptops. Make sure they're seen. We stay a safe distance back."

I responded without taking my eyes off the traffic on the Jones Falls Expressway down below and a few blocks away, "The Iranians will spot your coverage."

"What if we funnel them to a location of our choosing?" Nate offered.

We all looked at the police captain.

"Let the look-alikes follow the girls' pattern around campus: go to classes, get something to eat, the typical student stuff, all carrying laptops. We stay back almost as far as we normally would to make sure our coverage is spotted. The look-alikes finally go to a location we can completely cover from afar. Hopefully, the Iranians think there's a gap in our surveillance, and we'll be there."

I looked at Nate who just shrugged, knowing it was a long shot.

Jeffries spoke up this time, repeating the sentiment: "The Iranians will know."

"And one of those guys on an MK-12," Soper mentioned a sniper rifle, "will take care of our decoys, and the partner will scoop up the laptops."

Fifteen seconds of silence was the response from everyone.

"We have to make it worth the risk for them to step into the open," Conniker finally said. "We get the Iranians, maybe we'll find out what's going on."

Probably not. Not those guys.

"Look-alikes won't work," I turned to face the group. "We need another approach."

"We talk to the two college girls," Conniker continued.

"No. Not an option," I said.

The group looked at me.

"Besides, there's still the sniper scenario." Soper again. "No difference… the two college girls or our officers. One Iranian shoots, the other takes the laptops. If we're that far back they'll disappear."

The thought of crosshairs on Noa and Aminah made me sick.

"They won't use a sniper scenario," Gil Jeffries said. "Snipers need a fixed position to set up."

Conniker continued his line of thinking: "We could re-introduce the girls back into their routine. Move them around and don't repeat the pattern one day to the next. The Iranians won't have the opportunity to set up, even if they had the capability. And track the laptops. The girls will be at minimum risk."

"Except for when we lay back," I said, not happy.

A long moment passed as I turned back to the view out the window. I looked down at the traffic. Just below us a red sedan cut off a pick-up truck and another car had to swerve out of the way as the truck reacted.

After another moment of silence I looked back at the group. "They've seen me. The Iranians. I saw them and they saw me. Well, one of them did, outside the Hopkins building after they killed the barista."

"No, Gidon," Nate said.

"If Noa and Aminah are the only option, and I don't think they are, I'll be right there next to them. The agents will come after me first. We funnel them as Nate said. The girls go back to campus, with your people nearby." I looked from Jeffries to Nate. "Later, the girls go strolling or something with no coverage in sight, except for me. I'll be part of the bait, a loose end. Noa and Aminah will be the payoff. They want the girls. I'll be in the way."

"No, Gidon," Nate repeated.

Conniker's eyes lit up just a little. "You could wear body armor."

"He won't." Nate said. "He'll need to be able to move to do all that karate shit." He turned to me. "You know they'll go for a head shot. They'll shoot you between the eyes, grab the laptops while everyone's in shock, and take off."

"I'll be fine as long as they're in my radius."

"No." This time the reaction came from Gil. The senior FBI agent was shaking her head. "You're a civilian. We can't do this."

"So are Noa and Aminah, but that seems to be okay."

I looked at Conniker and Soper. They were just watching us go at it.

After a moment I turned from Jeffries to Nate and back. "I'm not a civilian. I'm an officer of the Shin Bet."

"Christ, Gidon, no you're not."

"I have an ID and everything. Amit drafted me last time I was in Israel."

"That was for one specific operation."

"We can make this a joint Shabak, FBI, BPD operation."

"You're an officer for Israel's General Security Services?" Conniker edged forward.

"No, he's not," Nate responded. "It's bullshit."

I shrugged. "Well, I know people who gave me some authority on my last op."

"You'll still get your brains blown out," Nate's voice was beginning to have an edge to it.

"Not if we have overwatch." Soper voice came from the side. "Position a sniper to cover him. The Iranian agent pulls a gun on Gidon and our guy takes him out."

"What is it with you and snipers?" Nate said curtly.

Gil Jeffries shook her head. "This is great. You and the girls as bait and a sniper overlooking a public street with civilians all over the place."

"What could go wrong?" I asked with a half-smile.

"Overwatch?" Nate turned to Soper who had the idea.

"I know a guy," I suggested. "Baltimore County PD. Former Marine Special Operator. He's done overwatch. Of course it was in Tikrit."

"We've got people, if we do this," Jeffries said. "This isn't Tikrit, or Fallujah, and we're talking two girls and you. I need to make some phone calls." With that, she left the room, followed by Conniker. Soper excused himself too, probably not wanting to be near Nate or me if we started arguing.

Finally, we had the room to ourselves.

"We've got to draw these guys out," was all I said.

After a long moment, where I could have sworn Nate's face colored slightly and then went back to normal, he said, "Your gun is ready."

"What?"

"Your gift. The one you fired the other day at the range. It's in. Go pick it up. Buy yourself a holster and wear the .45 until all this is over. Make sure you've got the damned Wear and Carry on you. This goes badly, everyone is fucked."

I just nodded. *At best.*

* * *

Jonathan, Noa, and Aminah were in Jon's Union Wharf apartment in Fells Point. Though it was just before 10 a.m., the college girls looked like they had just gotten up. Well, Noa did. She was in a pair of boxers and one of Jon's red T-shirts that basically came down to the bottom of the boxers. Everyone else was dressed. They were perched around the kitchen island having a grand time – all had plates and drinks nearby – but I moved the trio onto Jon's couch for the conversation about to come. They walked over in silence, looking at each other.

Once settled, I sat opposite them on the rectangular coffee table, and laid out the latest thinking: the need to catch the Iranians, the plan to march the girls around campus as police stayed close, and then Nate's funnel idea. Jon, standing behind the couch, started to pace slowly.

"Just so you know, you don't have to do this," I said. "In fact, I prefer you don't. We'll find another way."

Jon stopped pacing. "What about officers who look like the girls?"

"Still a possibility."

"But you don't think it'll work," Aminah, sitting to my right, commented. She brushed a few stray strands of blonde hair back behind her ear. Her legs were tucked under her.

"Hard to know."

Noa looked over her shoulder at Jon, but said to me, "Where will Jon be?"

"Maybe across the street."

"And you?" Aminah asked.

"I'll be your escort. I'll be right there if these guys approach. Between you and them."

"Better Sifu than me," Jon said. "But, as Sifu said, you don't have to do this."

Noa again to Jon: "What do you think?"

"I can't make that decision for you." He looked at me.

"I agree." I picked up his thought. "It's dangerous. On the other hand, on campus you'll have police virtually at your side. And when you're off campus, wherever, cops'll be all over the place. You just won't see them. We'll pre-plan all locations to keep it as safe as possible."

What could go wrong? kept resonating even as I spoke.

What I neglected to express was on campus the Iranians could move on them, despite a police presence. They'd simply shoot the cops and then the girls. And off campus, well, the cops would be too far away if something went wrong, except for the sniper on overwatch and me. Hopefully, he'd have a clear shot, which wasn't always possible. As for me, if there were a gun leveled out of reach, there was nothing I could do.

"It's dangerous and risky," I repeated. "Just to be completely clear."

Jon looked at me again. The Iranian agents would have to know the whole thing would be staged. *I'd* suspect that in their position. The question was, would the laptops be worth the risk?

I stood up. "You don't have to decide right now." I knew, though, the FBI and Nate were already setting everything up, picking a location for the girls' off-campus walk, arranging for personnel. Informing higher-ups. The mayor would probably have to sign off, too.

Jon's living room was slowly getting brighter, as the morning sun rose higher in the sky.

"You'll be with us?" Aminah asked me again.

I nodded.

"Okay," Aminah said. "Let's do it."

"And you'll be nearby?" Noa looked at Jon.

"Yes," he caught my eye. *Maybe.*

"Okay." Noa agreed.

"I'll tell the captain, but it still may not be a go. It has to get approval from everyone's boss. This sort of thing makes lots of people nervous, even if you're okay with the risks. Once I know, I'll update you."

I began to head for the door.

There was movement behind me. "You saw my father yesterday," Noa said, now standing not all that far away.

"I did."

"You flew out just to tell him what's going on?"

Dr. Biran had said the same thing. "Yes. I wanted him to hear it all from me and to see who I was." And to see how he reacted when questioned about emailing Noa proprietary information. I didn't say that to her.

"He doesn't trust you."

"I understand that. He doesn't know me. Plus you're his daughter and he wants you to be safe."

"He wants to take me back to Israel, but said he won't. Not yet."

I nodded and turned to Aminah, who had also stood up from the couch. "Have you called your folks in Amman?"

"Haifa. We moved from Amman a few years ago." A moment went by. "No. They're nervous enough as it is. I'm their first child who's gone away to school. This would put them over the edge."

"I understand."

And with that Jon walked me to the door. As we passed the kitchen entrance near the front door, I saw a baseball bat leaning against the frame of the doorway. A little surprise if someone broke in while they were home. He had followed my advice. "Nice bat."

"I always listen to you, Sifu."

"Uh-huh."

"I also put a throwing knife in the freezer. You never know," he shrugged.

"Just make sure your fingers aren't wet when you grab the knife," I smiled.

* * *

Thirty minutes later I was standing in one of the firing lanes at the

Maryland 40 Gun Range. The HK .45C was in my right hand, which was cupped in my left, and pointed downrange. I emptied the eight-round clip into the target with eight successive, quick trigger pulls, and then smiled once the slide locked on empty. It was a great weapon. The recoil reduction system made a difference in the large caliber handgun. I couldn't believe Nate was gifting me the semiautomatic. It was an expensive thank you that was totally unnecessary.

For a brief moment, as I stood there looking at the gun, I was back in a darkened basement outside of Sidon, Lebanon. The building's upper floors had become husks of what was once a fifteen-story apartment tower. Nate's daughter, Laurie, had been kept in a windowless, airless, subterranean cell for almost seven days. For her there was no outside world; only her captors – one of whom I had just shot as he stood watch in the narrow hallway outside her room. It was just after 2 a.m. when I opened the door to Laurie's makeshift prison. Two team members followed me in, suppressed M4s ready, and we instantly shot and killed two men sitting at a table along the far wall. The basement room itself was filthy: the bare floor, the bare walls, even the air felt filthy; dense and hard to inhale. Besides the table at the far end, the sole piece of furniture was a metal armchair, the kind you'd find in an office supply catalog. It was on its side, discarded in the center of the floor. A single, low-watt bulb dangled from a wire coming from the ceiling. It cast a yellow tint onto Laurie who was curled up in a corner. Her dark hair covered her face, and when I brushed it away, I saw purple bruises just below her cheekbones. If that weren't enough, she had a black eye and lips split and swollen from being hit. Her eyes slowly opened. They were glassy.

"Laurie, can you hear me? My name is Gidon. I'm with the Israeli army and I'm here to take you home. You're safe. Can you hear me?"

After a very long moment she nodded slightly.

She blinked a few times and her eyelids squeezed slightly as she tried to focus. I repeated what I had said a moment before but added, "I'm a friend, and no one will hurt you anymore."

Laurie's hands were secured behind her with lampcord. I cut off

The Student

the insulated wire and then looked at her arms and her legs. There were cigarette burns on her right forearm, her bare legs showed no signs of bruising, and her shoeless feet looked dirty but uninjured. I told Laurie I was going to carry her, and again she nodded slightly. I cradled Nate's daughter in my arms, and stood up, reporting into my mic that I had her and we were coming out.

Before I moved to the door, Laurie said something that was just too soft for me to hear. I leaned into her as she said it again, tears rolling down her face. It was less than a whisper. "Thank you." I held her a little tighter and walked out of the room.

The HK .45C was still in my hand as my mind returned to the firing range. I fed a fully loaded magazine into the gun and released the locked slide. The image of Laurie, beaten and burned and nestled in my arms was replaced with Seth Bruce lying on his floor, throat slashed and a bullet hole in his head. I thought of the Hopkins barista who had been killed just as viciously, and I thought of Dr. Sloane, the university professor who was stabbed on his way to his arraignment.

Once again I emptied the semiautomatic into the target. Before, my shots were clustered center mass; now these were all head shots. In a few minutes I was back in the front portion of the store, in the retail section. The tall, lanky man from my visit the other day came over. He was still in Marine camo pants and the same tan Beretta cap, but had on a different Under Armour T-shirt.

"Good to go?" he asked, and I nodded.

Ten minutes later, after final papers were signed and my credit card charged for ammo and a holster, I walked out of the shop with a new gun on my hip. I had promised Nate I would carry it, plus I didn't want the grief.

Tomorrow should bring some answers. A cool breeze drifted across the parking lot and I watched as it rustled some leaves on nearby trees. In my mind Noa and Aminah were sitting on Jon's couch opposite me. They were looking into my eyes for support, like I knew what I was doing. I hoped they were right.

23

There is a law in Einsteinian physics that gravity has an effect on time: a stronger gravitational field has a tighter hold on time than does a weaker gravitational field. From the perspective of an onlooker, a clock on earth's surface moves more slowly, relative to a clock in a plane flying high above the earth. It's also a universal law that when you wait for something to happen, time slows down. Ask any parent anticipating the return of a teenage son or daughter from an evening out with the car. The only exception to the Law of Anticipation seemed to be in Biblical times when the patriarch Jacob waited seven years to marry his beloved Rachel. "Seven years passed as if it were one day," the Bible said.

I was certainly more like a parent than like Jacob when Noa and Aminah went back to classes the next day. They cruised around campus, toting innocuous versions of their laptops, with police bodyguards close by. As an added layer of protection, the girls wore stylish jackets made of Kevlar, plus each backpack held a bulletproof ceramic plate. Both were Gil's ideas. Noa and Aminah just had to remember to position the backpacks in front of them in the event of trouble.

The day went uneventfully, meaning no one suspicious approached them. But that was the plan: let them be spotted but not approached. That would come later, logic had it, when it'd be just the college girls and me, supposedly. The cops would have dropped back, and I'd escort the duo up and down selected streets. Then, the Iranian agents would show up so we could do something about them.

Until that post-school rendezvous occurred, I exercised at my studio, mopped the floor, straightened my office, and went shopping for pants I didn't need at a nearby mall. Mainly, I considered miscellaneous scenarios for when the two foreign agents approached us.

Finally back at home, I changed into a pair of gray Dockers and a navy button-down casual shirt designed to be untucked. I liked the look, but with the new gun and holster, there was a distinctive bulge over my back right pocket.

For a moment my thoughts drifted to Katie and the last time I saw her. She had been wearing a mauve dress that hugged her curves. There was no problem recalling how it felt to be very close to her. Maybe I'd call her later to check in; see how she was doing. I swallowed hard and forced those images away. When my eyes refocused, I was looking in the mirror at the shirt pulled tight over the .45.

I peeled off the dark shirt, rummaged through my closet, and found a similar one in black, but with a wider cut. Once buttoned with shirttails again left untucked, it camouflaged the HK enough not to raise suspicions. I took the gun from the holster, pulled back the slide chambering a round, and set the safety.

* * *

Baltimore has developed a number of trendy areas, such as Fells Point and Canton, Hampden and Locust Point. The area south of the Inner Harbor, Federal Hill, also popular, was my meeting spot with Noa and Aminah. I took Light Street down past the Inner Harbor, and where the Harbor curved east, Light Street continued south into Federal Hill. No longer in the downtown environs, the street here was all of thirty feet wide, with shops and restored row houses bordering each side. If you looked north, you caught a beautiful glimpse of the city skyline, framed by three-story historic buildings. I parked curbside not far from Cross Street Market and walked a few blocks west to

South Charles, which had the same flavor as Light Street but with a few more businesses.

The work day had settled into dinner time, and traffic on the street had thinned out. Men and women, a few with young children, sauntered along the sidewalks, window-shopped or looked for places to eat. As planned, I met Noa and Aminah and their plain-clothed police escort in front of a CVS built with a brick façade to match the historic neighborhood. Noa and Aminah still carried their laptops in their backpacks. Their cop-guardian was in a gray blazer and dark pants and sported aviator sunglasses. That was part of the deal. There was no mistaking he was law enforcement. The cop and I exchanged pleasantries, and then it was just the two college girls and me.

"So, ladies," I said as the cop walked away, "hungry?"

They both nodded, and we walked south, away from Cross Street. We paused at a number of pubs to look at menus, but none intrigued us. We continued past a three-story furniture store, and a comedy club housed in an old theater, complete with overhanging marquee.

"So, tell me about your day."

As both Noa and Aminah described what it was like getting back to classes, I continually scanned approaching pedestrians, as well as people on the other side of the street. No one had curly hair and that recognizable square jawline, or straight, dark hair and dark eyebrows hovering above emotionless eyes. There were screen shots of these faces on my phone, but I didn't need them. I particularly remembered the man with brooding eyes, since we had stared at each other across a strip of grass, outside where he and his partner had murdered the barista. Not only did I not see the two Iranian agents here, I didn't spot any law enforcement either, which meant the cops were doing their job. We continued walking.

When we passed a barber shop with its old fashioned red, white, and blue striped pole beside the door, I paused to look behind us. No one suspicious. We continued on. The girls were now discussing fashion trends. I had no idea when the shift in conversation had occurred.

On the right we passed an optometrist's office, now closed, and then a pub called Uncle Henry's. About half a block beyond the pub, I suggested we go back and look at the menu. We turned around and walked back to Uncle Henry's. As before, no one behind us seemed intent on tracking our little group.

At Uncle Henry's we paused at a three-foot wrought iron fence enclosing a two-table deep outdoor eating area. A podium near the entrance contained several laminated menus, and the girls examined them. After a moment, they both nodded. "Inside or out?" Aminah looked at me.

Inside would have been my choice under normal conditions…out of public view, sit in the rear with a view of the entrance, lift the tail of my shirt for easy access to the HK…but that wasn't the idea. Noa and Aminah needed to be seen. "Outside."

We waited for a hostess, and when she came over I pointed to a table away from the street, near the front wall of the restaurant. When it came to choosing seats, naturally, I went for the one that kept my back to the wall. Noa sat on my right, Aminah on my left. In a few moments we had menus in front of us, as well as glasses of water.

There were seven other tables out front, but only half were occupied. As Noa and Aminah looked at the menus again, I watched the evening crowd. Most were young professionals, some casually dressed, some still in work clothes. A forty-something couple and their preteen son stopped to look at the menu near the podium, and then continued on. As both Noa and Aminah scanned the dinner offerings, I raised my shirt over the .45. The gun probably showed out the back of my chair, but no one would see it, since my seat was almost against the building.

"Okay," Noa closed her menu and looked at me. "I know what I want, but I need to go to the bathroom. Can you order for me, if the waitress comes while I'm gone?"

"Hold on," I said. With Noa inside and Aminah here, one of them would be unprotected, depending on who I covered. I turned to Aminah. "Do you need to use the bathroom?"

She shook her head.

The waitress appeared, and stepped over to our table. "Are you ready to order, or do you need a few more minutes."

"Actually, we all need to use the bathroom. Can you hold the table for us, and we'll order when we come out?"

"Of course. It's straight back and to the right."

Aminah looked at me. "I don't have to go. I could stay here and watch our stuff."

I shook my head. "I don't want to leave either of you alone."

The waitress gave me a quizzical look.

"Big brother," I said. "Very paranoid." Noa, Aminah, and I stood up, the girls slinging their backpacks over their shoulders.

The waitress led us inside. The interior of the restaurant had subdued lighting, plus it had ceiling fans and air conditioning running full blast, putting a chill in the air. To our right was a long bar that had a TV mounted up high. Most of the seats were taken, as were the small square tables on our left. Our waitress pointed to a restroom sign in the back of the room, and moved on to wait on other tables.

The girls turned to me. "Sorry," I said. "I just need to keep you together so I can see what's happening."

Noa shrugged and headed toward the restroom sign. Aminah lasted another moment and then she, too, went back.

I positioned myself so the rear of the restaurant and the front door were both in my line of sight. After another few minutes the three of us were back at our table. Orders were placed: tacos with steak tips for Noa, an Asian kale salad for Aminah, and a salad with grilled salmon for me. Everything was tasty, but that law of waiting for something to happen kicked in and time expanded. While Noa and Aminah talked, I tried to participate while monitoring our surroundings. All was quiet at Uncle Henry's, except when the door to the restaurant opened and the noise from the bar spilled out.

Soon enough – or not soon enough – we were once again walking down South Charles Street. The air had grown cooler, but the sidewalk

The Student

traffic remained constant. Daylight was beginning to fade. We passed a few more pubs, some closed real estate offices, and an open boutique furniture shop. Noa and Aminah stopped to check out the couches, chairs, and tables, while I casually looked around, hopefully appearing to be a bored third wheel. A number of questions occurred to me – primarily, had the Iranians in fact spotted the two college girls sometime today? If not, all this could have been for naught, and we'd have to try the same strategy tomorrow. At least the girls would eat well.

We continued on, approaching an intersection with a row of cars lining up at the red light. None of the drivers looked our way. On the sidewalk, men and women passed by without giving our trio a second glance.

A recurring thought poked through again: if the foreign agents were here, how would they come at us? Point their weapons out of my reach? Shoot before anyone could react? Grab the laptops and keep moving? Personally, I'd wait for more isolation, and shoot from twenty feet out. It all depended on how much one cared about taking a life, and that didn't seem to matter to the two agents.

We crossed the intersection, and two men diagonally on the other side came into my field of view. Both were tall, thin, and in baseball caps. They could have been dark-haired. One could have had straight hair, the other curly. It was impossible to tell. Additionally, they both wore windbreakers, perfect for concealing weapons. What initially had caught my attention was that one of the two nodded in our direction and in unison they crossed towards us. I relaxed, allowing my senses to broaden.

From this distance the pair didn't resemble the men who killed Seth Bruce and the barista. But maybe they didn't need to. Perhaps this was another pair, partners of the killers. No reason to think the Iranian agents were operating solo; they had to have support in this country. Maybe these were those guys: they moved too much in coordination, and there was the way they were dressed in ballcaps and loose windbreakers. The original Iranians could easily have been positioned on another part of the street.

Up until now, I was walking next to Noa and Aminah, putting myself between the buildings and the two girls. Not very chivalrous, but it placed me between anyone hiding in an alcove and the girls. As the two men approached, I stepped in front of the girls and walked toward the men, leaving the girls slightly behind. My right hand began a slow reach toward the .45 near my back right pocket. *Take it easy. Don't kill anyone.* If these were partners to the killers, we needed them for interrogation.

The two men in baseball caps continued crossing the street toward me. They seemed focused. The man on the left was clean-shaven, while the one on the right had a short, dark beard. That didn't negate anything for me. Revolutionary Guards often had beards. I picked out where I'd shoot each to incapacitate, not kill.

For a brief moment the smell of garlic from a nearby restaurant floated past.

The man on the right, the one with the dark beard, locked eyes with me. The distance between us closed another foot. There was something about the man's eyes. Not the color, but something that wasn't there. There was no anger, no concern, no intensity. In fact, they seemed ordinary. Then, as the man broke eye contact with me, there was a slight hesitancy in his stride. He turned to his friend, something unspoken transmitted, and they shifted direction, giving me a wide berth. The man with the beard didn't look at me again.

There was no threat here. These men were friends, perhaps even relatives, out walking the neighborhood, or looking for a bar or a restaurant. Maybe even that comedy club we had passed earlier. The killers, the men I thought these guys were attached to, were still out there, looking for Noa and Aminah, and these fellas weren't with them. Logically, having another pair of Iranian agents in town would have been risky. Too much of a "footprint." Besides, in my "interview" with Professor Sloane, his responses never went to another set of agents. I shook my head at my paranoia.

"I guess we're crossing the street," Noa said from behind me.

"Sorry, yeah," I slowed down so Noa and Aminah could catch up. We stepped onto the sidewalk and paused. I watched the two men in baseball caps move away from us on the other side of the road, up Charles Street.

For a moment, I felt inept. This was the second time I jumped to conclusions, seeing someone who wasn't there. First, on the terrace at Hopkins when I thought a man approaching Professor Sloane was one of the killers, and now these guys. Not good.

"Hey," Aminah said, looking at Noa, "I know a consignment dress shop in this block that has great stuff. And they have evening hours."

They both looked at me and I bowed slightly, waving my hand to proceed.

"So, Gidon," Noa said a second later, "how do you know my uncle Idan? Or can't you say."

I had settled back into my spot, walking between the buildings and the two girls. "Okay, a non sequitur. I don't really know your uncle, just who he is."

Aminah picked up the conversation: "So how did you connect?" Noa must have told her what Idan did for a living.

"We have a mutual associate. He introduced us."

"Oh," Noa said.

A moment passed and I didn't take it any further. There were a silent few steps.

Noa didn't follow up. Instead, "How long have you known Jon?"

"Since he was a puppy."

Both girls laughed.

"He is very loyal," Aminah said.

The foot traffic on the sidewalk had thinned out by now, but there were still plenty of people strolling. Most at this point were dressed casually; if anyone had been in business attire, they had probably changed. I watched everyone. I saw the single men and women walking as if they had a direction in mind, the mixed-gender and single-gender couples holding hands, and more than a few people walking dogs. I also saw the man in the navy blue sports coat approaching from up the block. From this far away it was difficult to tell, but he could have had curly, dark hair. Maybe I wanted this to happen too much.

"It's mutual." My response had lagged a second or two. "The loyalty goes both ways."

We passed a window with a beautiful screen painting of a sailing ship.

The man in the navy blazer was still twenty-five feet in front of us when he leveled a semiautomatic at my head.

There was no warning, just the motion, and I'd never reach the HK over my back pocket in time. He must have drawn the weapon further up the block and had it ready for when he was in range. He'd shoot me, then either fire on Noa and Aminah and take their laptops, or just take their laptops as they stared down at my body that would have a gaping head wound.

A door to a restaurant next to us opened. There was a shift in presence both in noise and in air pressure as the restaurant's air conditioning blew onto the sidewalk.

The only thing I could do was either push the girls out of the way or dive to my right, drawing fire away from the girls. Maybe I could get a shot off before he'd shoot either them or me. Unlikely. All he had to do was squeeze the trigger.

In the split second before I shoved the girls, in the split second before he squeezed the trigger, his eyes darted to Aminah. He looked back at me, and then pink mist erupted from his head as he simultaneously dropped to the ground. Overwatch. Nate's sniper, or Jeffries', up high somewhere.

Before I could move forward, or tell Noa and Aminah to stay put, there was movement behind me. I spun 180 degrees. The agent's partner had his gun aimed at what would have been the back of my head, but was now my face. The pivot caught him by surprise. This was the man who had momentarily locked eyes with me on the Hopkins campus. This was the man with the straight hair and soulless gaze. In the millisecond that he didn't move, I parried his raised automatic moving both my hands, scissors-like. My left hand moved the barrel away from me, while my right hand caught him on his wrist, completely deflecting the gun.

The big caliber semiautomatic clattered to the ground. That was unexpected. Had he held onto the gun, I'd have twisted it from his hand, likely breaking a few of his fingers in the process. Maybe he knew that, and let it go on purpose. If that were the case, he was better – much better – than I anticipated.

He was fast, this killer. He shifted his weight and his right leg shot up to kick me in the gut. I punched straight down with my knuckles into his shin. I felt the impact, but my fist was conditioned and tight, and knew he felt it ten times more than me. As he stumbled back, I drove the heel of my right foot into his solar plexus. He went down. He should have stayed down as the air had been forced from his lungs and as nerves screamed throughout his abdomen. But he rolled as I approached. Somehow, he came back up with a knife, nearly stabbing me with a sharp thrust. I pivoted away from the blade and then stamped diagonally down on the side of his forward knee with my left foot. There was a distinctive crack and he collapsed. My .45 came out and I pointed it at his right thigh, flicking off the safety. His emotionless eyes met my cold, determined look. I stepped slightly to his side so any move he made wouldn't be toward me. He looked at me again, but this time his eyes were filled with hatred.

The next sixty seconds erupted with activity. Cops appeared from every direction…city cops, FBI, plainclothed, uniformed… They must have been positioned in various stores and apartments to either side.

I saw Conniker first who came over with his SIG drawn. When he saw I had the guy covered, he holstered his own weapon, flipped the man onto his front and cuffed him. The foreign agent had to have been in pain. I had probably broken his shin with my punch and I knew I had broken his knee, but he hadn't even winced.

Jonathan appeared on the other side of the street next to Nate and Gil Jeffries, and Noa and Aminah rushed to him. He first hugged Noa and then Aminah. The two law enforcement officers left them and came over.

"Be sure to thank your guy on overwatch." I said as they drew closer. "If he's around, I'd like to see him. Who does he belong to?"

"She's mine," Gil said. "And she's probably already packed up."

"You were pretty lucky there, my friend," Nate commented.

"I know."

For the next several seconds no one said anything. The Iranian agents had planned well, better than expected, coming at me from different directions. The one in front would've had me, too – his gun out of my reach. If it weren't for the FBI sniper, I'd be on the ground lifeless, not him. And his partner should have pulled the trigger as I spun on him. But he didn't. I shook my head. No sense trying to figure that out.

"You, okay?" Gil asked. I nodded.

As various personnel cordoned off the area, others hovered over the first Iranian's body. An ambulance appeared and EMTs dealt with the second assassin.

"So who has jurisdiction?" I looked from one law enforcement office to the other. "Who interviews our guest?"

Nate and Jeffries exchanged a look, but Nate answered, "It's an ongoing discussion."

"Let me know who wins. But you know he won't give up anything …like what they're after."

"Maybe we can find out where his orders came from," Jeffries said. "A name would be nice."

"It may not be in your system. But," Nate said, "I know someone who has a contact with the Shin Bet."

The FBI woman looked at me, smiled, and just walked away.

"She smiled at me," I said, watching her go.

"You're wearing her down."

"Get me these guys' prints and photos, and I'll send them to David Amit in Tel Aviv."

"Just 'cc' me and Jeffries, okay. If it were just you and me, I wouldn't care."

"Got it." A moment went by. "One more thing."

He looked at me.

"The first guy, the one the sniper took out?"

"Uh huh."

"Just before he was about to shoot me, he looked at Aminah."

"Well that's curious."

I nodded. "Yep."

24

An interesting thing occurred just before I ambled over to Jonathan and the girls. Gil Jeffries had already walked away, and Nate had gone to speak with Conniker, when I spotted Jeffries, clad in her FBI raid jacket, looking at me from the other side of the street. She had started to come back over, but then she stopped halfway. She shook her head slightly, and then returned to where she had been. My eyebrows went up inadvertently, wondering what that was about, but since there was no way of knowing, I joined Jonathan and the two college kids.

Perhaps all of ten minutes had gone by since the altercation with the Iranian. South Charles Street was now blocked off by BPD cars, uniformed officers were keeping a growing crowd behind yellow tape, and the Iranian I had dealt with was on a stretcher being loaded into an ambulance.

Dusk had slowly replaced the bright daylight, and while the sky still had streaks of red and blue fingering the western heavens, streetlights on both sides of the road were now illuminated. Storefront marquees had lit up as well, and the combination of fading natural light, the warming streetlights, and the various police lights set an ethereal tone.

Jon and the girls were in front of a store that sold antiques. My student had his arms around both girls: Noa enveloped by his right arm, Aminah by his left. Even in the glow of the store's red and green neon lighting it was clear both girls had gone pale. They had just seen a man killed by a sniper's headshot – with all the gore of that impact

The Student

– and they saw me fight his partner, complete with a bone-snapping kick to his knee.

"Jon, why don't you take the girls over there." I indicated a weathered, wooden bench not far away. "Maybe they want something to drink."

Noa and Aminah both shook their heads. Then from Aminah: "Maybe we can just go home?"

My student looked at me: "I can take them back to my place, get their stuff, and go back to their apartment."

"Maybe you could stay for a while," Noa appealed.

Jon just looked over to me again, not sure if he should. "Whatever you want to do, Jon. Let me ask Nate if he needs any further statements."

Before I had a chance to locate my police friend, he was already coming over. "So, how are you ladies feeling?"

They both shrugged.

"Jonathan, take them home," Nate directed. "We can talk another time if we need to."

"Sifu, you'll be at the dojo tonight?"

"For a couple of hours." There was still adrenalin in my system to work off, plus there were a number of tasks to set in motion: contact the Shin Bet with the Iranians' IDs, get some background on Aminah – not that I thought she was involved – and I just needed to chill.

"Call if you need me."

I smiled at his offer. "I will."

He nodded, and the three of them walked northward toward downtown then turned a corner out of sight.

* * *

By the time I stepped into my martial arts studio, all traces of daylight had long since vanished from the sky. I flipped on the fluorescents as I entered the large practice hall. All was quiet, of course – a stark contrast to what I had just left. Halfway across the room I paused and closed my eyes. I just needed to stop.

No one was here, of course, yet the space seemed both silent and filled with the sounds of men and women kicking and punching. Finally, the sounds retreated, and I let myself be enveloped by the quiet.

A few more minutes passed. Then, not really wanting to, I stepped into my office because things needed to get done. As I crossed the threshold, a text came in from Nate: *Check your email.* I did. There was a quick note from him, with attachments of both Iranian agents' headshots and fingerprints. I forwarded everything to David Amit in Israel.

Would he be up? The time on my phone read 9:04 PM. 4:04 AM in Israel. Without giving it anymore thought, I called him. The cell number Amit had given me some time ago rang with the distinctive Israeli tone that almost sounded like a busy signal. He picked up: "*Ken,*" meaning simply "yes." He didn't sound sleepy.

"*Boker Tov.* It's Gidon in Baltimore. Where'd I catch you?"

"In my kitchen, making coffee. Next time you're here and it's four in the morning, I'll make you some. What's the situation?"

As I locked up my .45, I updated him to include the just-emailed pics and fingerprints.

"So now the FBI trusts you?"

I could hear dishes rattling, and maybe a cup being taken out from a cupboard. There was a television news program running in the background.

"Not entirely. What I sent came from Nate. But the FBI is willing to use me for access to your intel."

"Naturally." More rattling of dishes. "What else?"

"Noa's roommate, Aminah Hadad. Can you see if there's any background on her family?" I told him about the first Iranian looking over at her before he was about to shoot me. "She told me her parents were both educators. They're originally from Lebanon, but now live in Haifa."

"Christian Arabs?"

"Yes. I don't think Aminah is knowingly involved, but it would be nice to have more information on her family."

"Of course. I'll see what I can find out."

"*Toda.*"

With that we hung up. Next, I called Noa's father to let him know we stopped the agents behind the mess here. "They're dead?" He wanted assurance his daughter was safe.

"One dead, one with a broken leg and in police custody."

There was an audible sigh at the other end.

"So, both Noa and Aminah should be back at their apartment in a little while."

"Thank you."

"She's a sweet kid. I'll keep an eye on her over the next few days."

"I appreciate that."

After a moment of dead air, I said goodbye. I dropped my cell onto my desk and scanned the office to realize I hadn't turned on the light. The only illumination came from the wash of light from a window and from the practice hall. It would suffice.

The day had turned out with decent results. The girls were safe and we had one of the killers in custody. There was no doubt he wouldn't cooperate, but hopefully Shabak or the Mossad would have something to share.

I closed my eyes and replayed the events from South Charles Street: the first agent looking from me to Aminah and back. The sniper headshot. The man's partner coming up behind me. Pivoting on him, deflecting his weapon, and my punch to his rising kick. I still felt my kick into his gut that should have put him down, and saw him springing back up with a knife. He was very good.

Without considering turning on the office light, I changed into a gray T-shirt and a pair of basketball shorts, and moved back into the practice hall. For the next forty-five minutes after stretching out, I worked my way through various linear and circular routines. First, some tai chi ch'uan and then ba gua. I picked up a bo, worked on a quarter staff exercise, and then switched it for a broadsword. Finally, I went over to a punching bag and began working different parts of my hands: fists, knife hands, back of the hands, and finally finger stabs straight into the bag. Sweat was freely rolling down from my hair. It also coated my forearms and saturated my T-shirt. After a hydration break, I sat in the center of the floor, closed my eyes, and let my breathing calm my pounding heart.

In a short while, my mind emptied of conscious thought. I could perceive the confines of the room. Soon my mind lost even that...

* * *

Some time had gone by when the sound of a buzzer crept into my consciousness. It paused for a few moments then sounded again. I slowly opened my eyes, allowing the room to come into view. The buzzer was connected to the locked street entrance, and though not really wanting to get up, I slowly stood and walked to the metal-framed glass door. Gil Jeffries was on the other side, brown shopping bag in hand. She waved and I let her in. "Hi. Hope I'm not disturbing you."

"No worries. Come in. Just winding down from a workout."

She stepped into the entryway. She seemed hesitant.

I indicated her clothes: "Almost didn't recognize you without the raid jacket." She was dressed in her usual, professional attire of a tailored blazer and a pair of slacks. A short pendant of small green and red stones sat in the "V" of her open shirt collar.

"Yeah, well, it's hard to be incognito with a yellow 'FBI' emblazoned on your back."

I smiled, and another moment went by.

She lifted the shopping bag. "Brought something for you." She lowered the bag and pulled out a six-pack of Yuengling, handing it to me.

I smiled.

"What?"

"Just picturing you in the FBI jacket walking down the street carrying the six-pack without the paper bag."

"Yeah, not a good image for the Bureau."

"I don't know, could project a more hip look."

"Yeah, that's what the Director wants," she smiled. "Anyway, I was on my way home, thought I'd come by and say thanks for today."

I laughed. "You came by to say thanks?"

"Yeah. It was a tough day."

If Jeffries had picked up I wasn't pleased with my performance earlier, or that the confrontation could have turned out differently, she was very perceptive. Could have been the real reason she came by. Or, perhaps, it was just what she said: a thank you.

"Well, thank you for the thank you. Does this mean I'm not on the FBI's shit list?"

"Not on the shit list but still maybe the foreign intelligence list."

"You're kidding."

"Well, *I* don't think you're a spy."

"In that case, you can come into the inner sanctum." And with that I led her into the main practice hall.

After a moment, I realized I still had a layer of sweat on me, and my hair must have been plastered down. I knew my T-shirt was soaked. "I know this is weird, but do you have five minutes. I want to jump in the shower. I must reek."

"That's not necessary. There's enough air circulation in here," she smiled again.

"Okay, at your own risk." I motioned to the nearest wall. "You okay sitting on the floor? Wouldn't want you to mess up those FBI dress code pants."

"The floor is fine."

She followed me to the nearest wall, and we both sat with our backs against the vertical surface, with me keeping a professional gap between us. I took out two bottles from the six pack and handed her one. I twisted off the cap. "So, Special Agent in Charge Jeffries, why are you being so nice to me?"

"I believe you are who you say you are."

"I appreciate that." I took a swallow or two of the beer, and she did as well. I was tempted to ask what changed her mind. Something must have happened between the last time we spoke and now. Or, maybe she was away from the office and could relax.

Nah. Something changed her mind.

"I also feel like I owe you an apology, particularly after today."

"We all do what we're trained to do. Besides, the girls are my responsibility." I took another pull on the bottle.

"That stuff today, the fighting, was that from the IDF or before? I know you were trained before the army."

I nodded. "The army amplified what I knew."

"Naturally."

"They taught me how to jump out of a plane." I smiled. "And other stuff." Then, "So, you don't think I'm a spy."

She shook her head. "You don't fit the profile."

"Really?"

"Insulted?"

"I don't know how to honestly answer that without getting into trouble."

She smiled. It was getting to be a habit. Again, why was she being so nice?

"So," I said, "you don't seem to share the old government philosophy of loving to dislike Israel."

"I'm not old school."

"Okay." I let a moment go by. "What did you think of today's operation?"

She paused for a few seconds. "We should have anticipated the agent coming up behind you."

"Me, too. They were both very good; well trained. Front and back approach. Very fast and weapon out of my reach. By the way, did you thank your sniper for me?"

"I did. She said you're welcome, and apologized for not taking out the second killer. She didn't have a clean line of fire."

"Not even on my mind."

"So," Jeffries continued, "in retrospect, would you have done anything differently?"

Maybe she *had* sensed I wasn't pleased. "I'll put it in my After Action report."

She only half-smiled this time. "Seriously, what would you do differently next time?"

"On my first day of martial arts class, my teacher said there are three things you can't defend against…"

"A weapon out of your reach, a crazy person, and the person who methodically plans to get you." She knew her stuff. "Two out of three today."

"And the only thing you can do is anticipate as best you can and train so reactions are automatic."

"I've heard that, too. I just think we should have planned better."

I shrugged. Maybe this visit was for her to work through something. For a moment there was a flash of melancholy in her eyes.

The FBI woman checked her watch. "I gotta go," she said, and stood up. She handed me her half-finished bottle of beer and we walked to the door.

"Well, as I said, thank you for the thank you."

"You're welcome." Nothing about talking once they interrogate the Iranian Agent, or anything like that. She wasn't getting that friendly. "Goodnight." And with that she left.

With her halfway finished bottle in one hand and my nearly finished bottle in the other, I walked back to my office. I finished my bottle, and debated about finishing hers. It was an inch from my lips when I saw a notification on my phone for a missed call: Amit in Jerusalem.

"Nothing on the roommate, Aminah Hadad," he said when he picked up. "But we're still checking. On the two Iranians, they're former

Quds Force. Part of a small group that abandoned the ideology of Shia fighting Sunni, and instead have put all their effort into only fighting non-Muslims. They have become mercenaries, hiring out to whoever wants to carry on the fight."

"Wonderful."

"These two are thought to be responsible for the bombings in London and Marseilles this past year, or so our French and British friends believe."

"Lovely. That it?"

"When I have more, I'll call."

"*B'seder.*" Okay.

I hung up, looked up at the ceiling for no reason, and took a few breaths with my eyes closed. After another few moments, I realized my workout clothes were still damp with sweat from the earlier exercise, plus I had that dried, salty sheen clinging to me. I closed my eyes for another few seconds and then headed off to shower.

25

By the time I emerged from my back room somewhat refreshed and in clean clothes, Jonathan had come into the main practice hall and had started working with a pair of broadswords. He stopped practicing as I approached.

"Hi, Sifu."

"Hi. What's up? Thought you were with the girls."

"I was, but we ran into my neighbor Karen in the hall, and she invited us to hang out at her place."

"Okay…"

"They connected right away. Noa and Aminah are still there. Figured it'd be good for them after today. They didn't need me."

I just nodded.

"Thought I'd see how you were doing. That was really intense before." My almost assassination on South Charles Street.

"Yeah," was all I could say.

"I saw that first guy aim at you and then there was the sniper shot. Whoa."

I nodded again.

"Then there was the guy behind you. Holy shit."

"Jon, what can I do for you?"

"I've seen you take down guys, but not under those conditions… gun to the back of your head. Your reaction was awesome."

"Should never have gotten to that point, Number One, really. But 'shots downrange.'"

"What?"

"You plan as best you can, you react, and if something goes wrong, you deal with it and move on. You just do better next time."

He nodded, but I wasn't sure he understood that I should never have allowed the second guy to come up behind me, gun raised. But, shots downrange.

"I need to work out more," was Jon's reaction.

"We both do. But not tonight. Go back to the girls. They still need you and we can talk another time."

"Okay."

We moved toward the front door. "Hang on," I said. "I'll go out with you." I grabbed a jacket and my keys. "Glad you came by, Jon."

We stepped out the door.

"Where're you parked?" I asked, locking up.

Jon pointed to the right, down a Charles Street illuminated by street lamps. "Next block. You?"

I pointed to the left. "See you tomorrow." I gave my best student a hug.

"See you tomorrow," he repeated, and walked down the steps to street level, looked to his left to see who might be approaching him and then turned right, heading down the sidewalk.

I watched him walk off, and then after a moment, scanned the street up and down. No particular reason, just conditioning. The traffic on this part of Charles was all one-way, heading northward, from my right to the left. By now, though it was pushing ten o'clock, there was still a steady flow of cars, and with some eateries having late hours, also a fair amount of foot traffic. A slight breeze blew across my face, and I stepped off the landing and onto the sidewalk.

Movement out of my peripheral vision to the left caught my attention. I nonchalantly turned to see a pair of tall men in open-collared shirts and sport coats walking on the other side of the street. Neither had hands in pockets, nor were they talking to each other. The men were walking quickly in the direction Jon had gone. From where they were, they could easily see my student. Right now, after the last few days, I was suspicious of just about everyone. Paranoia reigned, but, again, just because you're paranoid... I started to head across the street to follow them when they opened the door to a pizza shop and stepped in.

I had to smile to myself, but nevertheless didn't want to relax. The girls were safe ostensibly: one of the two Iranian agents from South Charles Street was dead and the other incapacitated to some degree and in custody. But, nothing had really been resolved. Maybe the FBI or Nate could unravel what I couldn't. Until then *semper vigilans*, always vigilant, was the rule.

Before turning toward my Jeep, I scanned the street one more time. A figure stepped from the driver's side of a dark Buick diagonally across from me. He had parked under a maple and was partially in shadow, but I saw him. The man stepped into the street and moved around to the sidewalk. He began to turn in my direction – his intent may not even have been to look at me – but I avoided locking eyes, just in case. Nevertheless, I had gotten a clear look at him. He was older, balding on top, with gray hair on the side and a neatly trimmed gray beard. The man was on the small side, thin, and dressed in a sharp, dark suit. He could easily have been someone's grandfather or a well-to-do businessman. The suit looked expensive and fit well. He reminded me of an older man in a French film.

It was possible, even likely, he was walking to his apartment around the corner. Maybe he had a rendezvous with a friend at a nearby eatery. Perhaps his office was on the block and he had forgotten something.

I sat down on my cement steps and kept looking forward, following him with my peripheral vision. He was walking down the block in the direction Jon had gone. If I didn't move I'd lose sight of him. He was walking leisurely, but purposefully, like there was intention in his stride. Without standing up, I took out my phone and called my student. "Hey."

"What's up?"

"I need you to humor me."

"Okay."

"Are you still on the street?"

"Yup. About to get into my car."

"Walk back to the dojo. I'm still in front. I'll explain when you get here."

Once the phone was back in my pocket, I casually looked up the block, down the block, at couples on the sidewalk, and at my watch – all as if I were waiting for someone, which I was.

The breeze that had drifted across my face earlier was back. I breathed in the cool air.

After another minute, Jon came toward me from the right.

"Hi. What's up? Everything okay?" Jon faced me but his body was sideways so he could keep an eye on the street. Behind him, diagonally across Charles Street, the well-dressed balding man who could have been someone's grandfather was back. He had slowed his pace and was patting his pockets as if he were trying to locate which one held his keys. He wasn't focused on us.

"Everything's great. Let's go inside."

He dropped his head a little. "Okay," and followed me back inside.

I left the foyer light off, but went down the hall to the main room and to my office. Jon was right behind. I knew he wanted to ask what was going on.

In my office, I flipped on the light. This was probably nuts, but I didn't care.

I sat on the edge of my desk chair and opened the bottom right desk drawer. My lockbox. The .45 HK Compact had gone back in when I had first returned. I unlocked the mini safe, took out the semiautomatic, inserted a loaded magazine, and pulled back the slide putting a round in the chamber. I set the safety.

Jon looked at me.

"I think you're being followed."

"Me, not you?"

I nodded.

"You're going to stay here. Leave the lights just as they are. Lots of dark areas, but light enough in the main room for you to work out in, or to meditate, or to check your phone, or whatever. I'm going out the front and will circle around and come in through the back door. Then I'm going to find a dark spot near the front entrance."

My student looked at me but didn't say anything.

"At some point, walk past the front windows so the guy can see you, but then come back into the main room and wait."

"In the half-lit room."

I nodded.

Another moment went by. "You're using me as bait."

"Yep."

"Cool." Then he lost his smile. "You sure about this, about me being followed?"

"No."

"If there *is* a guy, you think he had something to do with the two men from today?"

"Maybe." He could be an Iranian agent I hadn't considered.

"Guess we'll find out."

"May take a while. He may not come in at all. I may be wrong."

"I can stay all night." Noa and Aminah were at his neighbor's.

"We can't talk to each other. He's got to think you're alone."

"I don't want to talk to you anyway," he smiled.

I smiled back, tucked the .45 into the holster now at the small of my back, covered it with my shirt, and headed toward the front. Just before I walked out the door, I surveyed the place. Dark foyer, dark corridor, semi-lit main room.

Outside, I let the door close, waited a moment, pulled it open as if contemplating something, which I was, but then let it close again. I walked down the stairs and turned left. On the way up the street, from the corner of my vision I saw that the well-dressed gray-haired

The Student

man was sitting behind the wheel of his car and on the phone – or pretending to be. I casually rounded the corner, looking around, as I normally would, and kept going.

The back entrance to my building was off an alley, next to a well-illuminated small parking pad. The back door, locked by a combination lock, led to an inside hallway that was a common corridor leading to a number of upstairs apartments and to my main floor studio. My interior back door had another combination lock. I walked in and moved forward through a darkened rear room to the half-lit main practice hall where Jon sat near a wall, checking his phone. We looked at each other but didn't say anything. I continued toward a dark niche off the front hallway. The front door was straight ahead. The exterior of the door was bathed in light from an overhead fixture, but the wash of luminescence was localized to the outside. I moved into the blackened alcove, and sat down on a ledge used to keep a stack of books, papers, and someone's discarded coat. Before getting too comfortable, I retrieved my phone. As I had a number of nights ago while waiting in the dark entryway to watch Jon's apartment building, I set it to "Do Not Disturb," then tucked it into the folds of the nearby discarded jacket. I closed my eyes for a moment, took a silent, deep breath, then took out the HK.

Time would tell if I were right about the man across the street. He could have been a regular guy going back and forth to his car. He could really have been on the phone. Either he would come in at some point, or he wouldn't. I was okay with either scenario.

There was also another option. If he were after Jon, he wouldn't necessarily come for him now.

More than a few seconds passed. I might have been wrong about all this.

There was movement from the main practice room. Jon came up the corridor past my spot – didn't look for me – and stepped in front of a nearby window. He looked up and down the block just as I had suggested, and then went back to the main room.

Was the man still in his car? Was he just an innocent guy in the wrong place to stimulate my distrust? I had seen more than a few older men, who were somebody's uncle or father or grandfather, who had transported disassembled guns to Hamas cell members in the West Bank, or who had participated in the execution of a young woman for giving Shin Bet information. I had also seen sweet, elderly Palestinians or Israeli Arabs befriend Israelis, and welcome them into their homes. Assumptions were dangerous, but sometimes necessary to stay alive, particularly when hunting very bad people.

DEATH TO ISRAEL. Computers with Lord knows what on them. Two Iranian agents who had killed a Hopkins housing counselor, Seth Bruce; who had killed a young man who worked in a campus café; who tried to kill me on a city street…

Slowly, almost imperceptibly, the front door opened. It was more the change in airflow than movement that alerted me. He had patience, whoever it was. The door continued to open by inches. It was soundless. A figure entered and just as slowly held onto the door as it closed. Once shut, the man turned, and on silent soles moved forward. The man from the Buick. And in his right hand a suppressed Beretta. He had come to interrogate Jon and then kill him.

I clicked off the HK's safety and the man froze.

"You have very good ears," I said softly. He had recognized the sound.

There was no reaction; the man remained completely immobile. Not even a flutter of an eyelid or slight waver of his gun hand.

"Move your finger outside the trigger guard."

His right index finger moved off the trigger and settled on the edge of the guard.

"Now eject the clip."

His thumb shifted and the Beretta's clip dropped, clattering to the floor.

"Point the gun straight up, and extend your arm toward the ceiling."

He raised his gun arm, pointing the pistol upward. His suit jacket came up as he raised his arm.

"Now eject the round in the chamber."

The gray-haired man in the tailored dark suit raised his other hand up to the gun and pulled back the slide. The 9-millimeter cartridge ejected and fell to the ground.

"Just so you know, I'm out of arm's reach," I continued softly. "Now drop the gun."

He opened his right hand and let the Beretta fall. It clunked onto the wood floor.

I raised my voice. "Jon, we're coming in. Move all the way to the left."

"Yes, Sifu," his voice came back.

To the gunman: "Walk straight ahead down the hall."

The man who might have been someone's sweet grandfather walked forward. I let several feet open between us and then followed. He did not say a word. The suppressed 9 mm at my feet said it all.

We stepped into the semidark practice hall. I made sure to stay behind him. Jon was off to my left, but my eyes never left the man in front of me.

"Walk over to the side, and sit on the floor, facing the wall. Fold your feet under you cross-legged, and put your hands under your ass."

He did as I instructed and sat cross-legged, the wall a foot in front of his face.

"If you move, I'll shoot you in your right shoulder at the joint. You're right-handed. You won't bleed to death, but you'll lose complete use of that arm."

A long moment passed.

"You're going to execute me anyway," he said, still facing forward. His voice was low and smooth.

"It's a thought." I saw Jon look at me, but ignored him. "I know who you are."

The man remained quiet.

Jon took a step closer. "Do you want me to go through his pockets?"

"I don't want you anywhere near him."

My student stepped back.

"Is your phone nearby?"

"Yeah."

"You have Nate's number?"

Jon nodded.

"Call him, and tell him we have a third Iranian agent."

The man at the wall turned slightly to the left. "You're the Israeli guardian."

"Keep looking forward."

The gray-haired man in the tailored dark suit who had come to interrogate and then kill Jon turned back to the wall.

And so we waited just like that: the assassin sitting cross-legged facing the wall, and me behind him, with my gun pointed at the center of his back. If I had to shoot him at this range with the .45, he'd probably bleed to death, despite what I had told him. I only slightly cared and would solely lament the opportunity to get more information. The man probably knew that.

No one spoke; not me, not Jon, not the gray-haired man.

Ten minutes later the police came with lights flashing and sirens screaming. While we waited, Jon had turned on more lights, bathing the dojo in bright white. Nate came in first. He had his gun drawn, but held loosely in front of him. Soper was next, more vigilant, followed by Conniker and plenty of uniformed officers. No Gil Jeffries.

"What d'ya got, Gidon?" Nate asked.

"Someone we missed. Someone I missed. Maybe the cell leader."

"I'm surprised he's still alive." He holstered his weapon but the other law enforcement officers kept their guns ready. No one ordered me to lower my semiautomtatic. What had Nate told them about me? That I was an undercover something? Nate and I just exchanged looks.

The officers, guns pointing at the intruder, instructed him to lie flat on his stomach. They zip-tied the killer's hands behind him, then two officers pulled him into a standing position.

"Stop!" Everyone looked at me. I went behind the gray-haired man and kicked out his knees from behind. He collapsed to the ground. "Now you can search him."

I faced the assassin for the first time. His neatly trimmed beard hid some patches of rough skin. His eyebrows were bushy and his forehead creased with lines. None of that was of interest. We locked eyes. "If you try to escape, I *will* put a bullet through your shoulder and then maybe your left knee. These men won't stop me."

He mumbled something in Farsi.

Conniker and Soper were looking at me, as if seeing me for the first time.

Captain D'Allesando turned to his men: "Go...Search him. And maybe one of you guys can pick up the suppressed Beretta near the front door."

Somebody said, "Yes, sir," while others patted down the gray-haired man.

Conniker looked at me. "How did you know?"

"Saw him hunting Jon." I looked over at my student, wondering what he was thinking. We'd have to talk later.

After the officers emptied and bagged the contents of the killer's pockets, they hauled him up, and under careful watch, took him out to a waiting cop car. They weren't wasting time.

I stepped in closer to Conniker: "Where's Jeffries?"

"I'm not at liberty to say."

She was just here. Nate turned to me: "Call her."

I nodded.

Outside, the flashing police lights began to disappear one after the other. In a matter of minutes, the room had emptied. Soon, it was just Jon, Nate, and me, standing in the brightly-lit practice hall.

Nate turned to Jon: "You okay?"

My student nodded.

Then Nate to me: "Later, Gidon."

And with that, my captain friend left.

"You okay?" I repeated the question to Jon. "Not every night someone stalks you and you see all this."

"Yeah," he smiled just a bit. He was still pretty chill, and would for sure use this and what happened on South Charles Street today as great stories. "See you, Sifu. Gonna get back to Noa and Aminah."

We did the manly hug thing again, and he, too, was gone.

With the place now empty, I turned off the lights, locked up, and went out the front door. Standing on the stoop, I pulled out my phone and dialed Gil Jeffries. After several rings, it went to voice mail. I didn't leave a message, not wanting to intrude; she'd see the missed call notification.

I'm not at liberty to say. Conniker's words.

Hmm.

26

When I walked into my bedroom it was just after 3 a.m. I stopped in the open doorway and thought about the scene I had just left: the gray-haired agent I hadn't anticipated, his silent entry into my studio, holding him at gunpoint...

Still in thought, I pulled off my shirt with the intention of getting ready for bed, but all that happened was I'd walk a few feet, stop, think, then amble around some more. South Charles Street started in a loop once again. I was okay with my reaction to the gun at the back of my head, but as I told Jon, I should never have allowed the foreign agent to come up behind me.

There was also the larger picture, the whole scenario of parading Noa and Aminah around. Was there really no other means of drawing those guys out? I shook my head more in my own mind than in reality, only to refocus on a dresser in front of me. My wallet was on top, as well as my cell phone. I had no recollection of emptying my pockets. The wallet had landed next to a framed photo of Katie and me at a picnic table. Her school's annual retreat. We were sitting very close. Without dwelling on it, I opened a drawer to toss in a few items, and spotted another photo, a picture of a young, dark-haired woman standing in well-worn cargo shorts and an Israel Trail T-shirt. Tamar. My fiancée. She was standing beside a pitiful little stream and a low, prickly scrub, and holding up a bottle of water.

It had been mid-August and we were hiking along the canyon

floor at Ein Avdat in the Negev. We had followed a well-worn path, side-stepping small boulders, only occasionally leaving hiking boot imprints in the packed sand. It was just after 10 a.m. and easily in the upper 90s. The sun was high enough to erase any shadows created by the cliff walls, and the unimpeded rays radiated down, baking us and anything out in the open. Most animals in the reserve – ibex, birds, lizards – were resting in niches or in caves away from the direct sun. Only humans were crazy enough to go out now. I had nodded to Tamar and we headed to a cluster of rocks beneath a scraggly tree. As she took a drink from her water bottle, I spotted a line of sweat down the side of her face. Her dark hair had already started to frizz.

"You're sweating," I had said to her.

"I'm *glowing*," she smiled.

"No, you're sweating." And then she playfully threw the water bottle at me.

I closed the drawer, turning off the scene but not the feelings.

The loss three months later on a bright October day when a bomb tore apart a Jerusalem café killing Tamar outside and all the patrons inside, pervaded the soul of Israel. More personally, a part of my being had also been dispatched.

The echoes of that moment evaporated. In their place I saw Tamar's family. There was no conscious logic why thoughts of the present – South Charles Street, the gray-haired older man with the Beretta, Noa and Aminah too – had so easily been supplanted by the past. *Of course there was a reason*, but I didn't care.

I thought about the people who had been part of my life. Her mother was a teacher and her father an expert in cutting-edge agricultural techniques. They were probably retired by now. Tamar had an older sister and a younger brother. They had been my family, but I hadn't been in touch since moving back to the States, or even later during return visits to Israel. It was my fault. Initially, they had reached out, but I couldn't speak to them. And then later, I just couldn't.

Tamar's parents lived in a small community up in the hills of the northern Galilee. Or at least they had. Her older sister, Maayan, was married and lived twenty minutes from them on a kibbutz. The younger brother, last I heard, was in Tel Aviv.

It was time. I didn't know why, but it was time.

I retrieved my cell phone. Late morning in Israel. Though I hadn't called the number in years, it was still anchored in my brain. Where would I catch Maayan? Just contemplating the call accelerated my heart rate.

The ringing pattern cycled three times. Would Tamar's sister let me off the hook for not being in touch? Would she be angry, happy, melancholy because I was a tether to her murdered sister?

On the fourth ring: "Shalom." The connection was clear and sharp, and the voice had the happy lilt I remembered.

"Shalom, Maayan, this is Gidon."

A second went by. The caller ID wouldn't recognize my U.S. number, and I know it wasn't in her contact list.

"Gidon!?" Her voice suddenly had more energy to it. "Gidon, where are you? Oh, my God! Gidon!"

"Hi, Maayan," I repeated. "I'm in the U.S. I just wanted to say hello and see how everyone is doing."

"Two questions before I answer. First, tell me how you are, and second, you'd better have just returned from Mars, because why haven't you been in touch?"

I had to laugh. Maybe it was nerves. "The first isn't a question, but I'll tell you that I'm okay. The second is that I don't know. I have no excuse. No space travel."

"*Ein baya*. It doesn't matter. We miss you. I miss you."

"Likewise. I just wanted to see how everyone is doing. It's been too long and I just wanted to check in. So, what's going on?"

"Everyone's fine. Yakir" – her husband – "works here on the kibbutz. He's in charge of an environmental school they've developed."

"Okay. I don't know what that means," I laughed.

"It has to do with developing green programs for schools and businesses. He does training."

"Okay."

"Gal" – the younger brother – "is about to go into the army. He's computer crazy and wants to go into Intelligence. My parents," she paused, "retired after Tamar was killed. They're okay."

My heart sank slightly. "What does that mean?"

"The life went out of them. They have their friends, us, and they travel around with other parents who have lost children. But they're closed off. They still can't go into Tamar's room." There was a long pause. "They'd love to see you. Are you coming to Israel?"

I didn't have the nerve to say I had just spent a summer there, plus had been back periodically. "I have no plans at the moment."

"Come. Just come."

"I will." I paused. "Now tell me how you are."

And with that we ended up in a twenty-minute conversation. It was so good to hear her voice, and at the same time it filled me with emptiness.

We began to wind it down, and before it became awkward, we said goodbye, along with my promise to call more often.

I sat down – I had been pacing during the phone call – and now a single thought ran through my mind: I needed a personal trip to Israel. No business, no distractions. Just spend time with Tamar's family, people I cared about and who cared about me. It was definitely doable once the current situation with the Iranian agents was resolved and Noa and Aminah were truly out of harm's way. They would have to come first.

The phone in my hand dinged. An incoming text, but not from Nate, Gil Jeffries, or Amit in Israel. The message was from a teacher I sometimes substituted for at a private middle school.

The text read: *knew you'd be up. sub for me at 10? sorry for the last minute request.*

I looked at the time. 5:05. Another night had gone by, lost in my head. Carol, the teacher wanting me to substitute, taught American history to seventh graders. I could do it, but I hesitated. There was a lot going on. Plus Katie would be at school; she worked in student services as a learning specialist. It would be weird, awkward, if I ran into her. Still, the subbing would be a distraction, and it wouldn't take all that long.

I texted Carol back: *sure*. She responded she'd email me lesson plans, with the direction to improvise if I wished. Always good to have flexibility.

I took a deep breath and began to prepare for the day.

* * *

The Sanford Stein Day School was located just outside the Beltway not far from the northwest corner of the city. It sat on a sizeable patch of well-manicured suburban property with ballfields off to the side. The building's main entrance was set right-of-center and sheltered by an overhang. As expected, the parking lot was full, as the school day had already begun. I parked in an open spot not far from a fenced-in basketball court, scooped up a folder of lesson plans, and stepped out.

It took half a minute to thread through the parked sedans, SUVs, and minivans, but long enough to reflect on my last visit. It had been more than a year ago, also to teach a seventh-grade history class. Several adults joked that teaching middle school was truly special forces work, so my training was paying off, apparently. With that thought in my head, I stepped up to an intercom alongside a series of glass entry doors in view of an armed guard sitting at a desk inside. Not only was a monitor perched in front of him, but his desk was positioned sideways to the door, allowing direct views of the lobby and entryway. I pressed the call button, wondering if the glass doors were bulletproof.

He made his query and I responded with my name and purpose for being there. There was a soft click, and soon I was standing in front of the security man's station. As I looked down at him, all I could think was that he'd never get his weapon out in time if I had malicious intent. But, as my only intent was teaching how the North and South couldn't compromise in the decades before the Civil War, he logged me in and gave me a visitor's ID badge. Naturally, I took it off once I cleared the guard's line of sight. I didn't like advertising I was a guest, but part of it was a silent challenge to see if anyone would stop me.

It wasn't difficult remembering where to go: through the administrative wing, up a flight of stairs, down a corridor with student art displayed, then eventually to an intersecting hallway. To the left was the middle school office with classrooms beyond. To the right and down another corridor were more classrooms and Katie's office. I turned right.

I had called Katie earlier to head off any awkward, accidental meetings, but hadn't reached her. I still wasn't sure where we had left our relationship. There was the back-and-forth about her needing space but still being amenable to seeing each other. Very confusing.

As I continued past a set of floor-to-ceiling windows, a boy, perhaps 11, walked past me pulling a rolling backpack. He looked over briefly, expressionless, then continued in the direction of the office. Except for that one student, the halls were empty, at least of kids. All were in class, one would hope. At some point as I continued down the hall, I approached a woman coming from the other direction. She looked to be in her twenties, had on an unbuttoned pink cardigan with the sleeves pushed up, and smiled as we drew closer. I smiled back as we passed each other. She was wearing a lanyard and a staff ID card.

Katie's office was around another corner. I made the turn and came to her closed door. I knocked. No response. There was no one around to ask where she might be. Perhaps teaching, perhaps in a meeting? A chance encounter was still possible; a pre-emptive conversation wouldn't be happening. Meanwhile, I needed to check-in officially, soon I was standing in the middle school office, in front of an attractive, fortyish woman with short, tapered dark hair looking up from her desk.

"Mr. Aronson, hi. How are you?"

"Hi, Diane. About to walk into Mrs. Cayhan's class. Ask me afterwards."

She smiled. "You've done this before."

"I have. I'm not worried."

"Just teach them a few flips or something." With Katie and I dating – or having dated – word about my background had traveled quickly.

"Too many attorney parents. But I'll think of something."

Her phone rang, and that was the end of the conversation. She nodded to me while listening to the person on the other end, meaning she'd talk to me later, so I headed down a mostly empty hallway. The only students to be seen were in front of my destination. At the end of the hall next to Mrs. Cayhan's room, several students had camped out in clusters on the floor, laptops beside them. I heard the name Atticus Finch being discussed.

Mrs. Cayhan's room was pretty much as I remembered it: a whiteboard on front and back walls, a poster of the Preamble to the Constitution on a closet door, and various other posters spread throughout. The student chair-desk combinations were set up in three rows across the width of the room. I went over to the teacher's desk and opened my folder of lesson plans. I posted the homework on the board, per my instructions, and waited.

In a short while an electronic bell rang, the hallway became noisier, and then students came in. They all entered talking; some eyed me, but none missed a beat. They settled down once I got their attention and introduced myself. And then we got started by going around the room so they could introduce themselves. Surprisingly, they were better behaved than I expected: much less chatty. Finally, though, a young girl with long, out-of-control hair – she could have been an escapee from any number of '60s Broadway shows – simply said, "Mr. Aronson, excuse me, but we heard you're a real bad-a--"

She stopped before completing her thought, and everyone cracked up.

"Ah, gossip. Love it," I smiled. "Now stand up. Don't be scared…

stand up."

They all stood, though some hesitatingly. Not unexpectedly, many of the kids were tall – more so the girls.

"Now step away from your desks, leaving space between you and your neighbor."

They complied, shuffling about.

"Now just do as I do."

And with that, I took them through a few basic tai chi movements. Nothing spectacular, just slow, circular movements with controlled breathing. By the time we finished, the energy level in the room had mellowed out. Before it rose again, I got to work.

First, we went over their previous night's reading, covering *Uncle Tom's Cabin*, the Kansas-Nebraska Act, Bleeding Kansas, and the Dred Scott case. I then asked each student to post a fact relating to each of those subjects. That created a white board full of talking points – which the students verbally fleshed out. Mrs. Cayhan had made that suggestion for a review. The next idea was mine: break the class into groups, where each would create a newscast, reporting on the topics from last night's homework. Could they use their laptops? Yes. Could they listen to music as they worked? Yes.

And that took up the rest of the period. By the time the bell rang, the students were solidly into their ideas. They'd continue tomorrow. When they filed out of the classroom, virtually everyone thanked me. That was impressive. Once the room had cleared, I began to scoop up my notes. Almost immediately my cell phone vibrated. Jon.

"Hey, what's up?" I continued gathering my papers.

"They're gone. Noa and Aminah." His voice was slightly higher than what I was used to, and he was talking more quickly. "Noa's father came and took them. Just now."

"Give me more details, Jon." I stopped shuffling photocopies.

"We were sitting in the kitchen having coffee, there was a knock at the door, and it was Noa's father. Noa must have given him my address, because I didn't."

"And?"

"He basically pulled them out of the apartment. Didn't give them a chance to get their stuff or anything. Said something about it not being safe here and he was taking them back to Israel."

"When was this?"

"Just now. They're probably on their way to his car. I can go after them."

And do what? And in terms of me convincing him, by the time I got there they'd be gone. What would I say, anyway, particularly after last night with the unforeseen agent showing up. "No, let them go, Jon. Can't blame him." My energy started to ebb.

"You're gonna call Captain D'Allesandro, right, and track them."

"I don't know, Jon."

"They didn't want to go, Sifu. He didn't give them a choice."

"Maybe they'll be safer in Israel. I don't know if we're any closer to answers here."

"But you'll call Nate and whoever you know in Israel." Like Noa's uncle, the Mossad man, or Amit, my Shin Bet friend.

"Maybe."

"You'll do it. I know you, Sifu." He sounded more upbeat but I was going in the other direction.

"Call you later, Jon." I hung up and looked down at my papers without really seeing them. I finished gathering everything and headed down the hall, weaving between students on their way to their next class. Soon, I found myself in front of Katie's office. The door was open, and she was at her desk, typing on her keyboard.

"Hey," I said, walking in.

She looked over. "Hi. Diane said you were here."

I sat in a nearby chair. "I tried calling this morning." Katie had a single window behind her, at right angles to where she sat, but had the blinds lowered to cut down on glare.

"Sorry." A moment went by. "So how was class?"

"Fine. Went well."

"Good. What's wrong?"

She was always perceptive. "You know I've been looking after these two college kids."

"Uh huh."

"They were staying at Jon's."

"Of course," she smiled.

"Right," I smiled back. "One of the girls is Israeli, and one is Lebanese or Jordanian, I'm not clear on that. Anyway, the Israeli girl's father just pulled them out of Jon's apartment to take them back to Israel."

"Oh?"

"Yeah, and I don't know if it's a good thing or not. I think we've neutralized the threat, but we still don't know what it's all about."

"And with them in Israel, you can't pursue any leads."

I looked over at Katie. She looked fresh and her eyes were bright, but her forehead had furrowed.

"Well we – the FBI or Nate – have two of the Iranian agents who were after them."

"Iranian agents?"

"I didn't tell you?"

"Maybe you did." Katie just looked at me. "You okay?"

"I was supposed to protect those girls, but in my mind haven't been doing a great job. Can't see the whole picture. Been reacting, not a step ahead…"

"Because you can't see the whole picture," she repeated my line.

I looked away, over at Katie's computer screen for no particular reason and saw a partially finished email. "I spoke with Tamar's sister last night."

"Oh?" When I turned back, she was watching me more intensely.

"Felt like it was time. I may pay her a visit."

"In Israel."

I nodded.

"When?"

"I don't know. There're still odds and ends to follow up on here."

"But the girls are gone, right? There's no case."

"There's a case."

"So when you're satisfied."

"Maybe."

"You'll go to Israel. It's what you do."

"I go because that's where I need to take care of things."

Katie stood up and leaned back against a credenza. "I don't know what to do about us."

"I thought we talked about that."

"How long will you be there?"

"I don't know if I'll go, or when."

"The girls will be in Israel, Tamar's family is in Israel."

I nodded.

"You say you'll go for a week or two and then stay longer."

Katie's eyes had gotten wider, and the conversation was echoing a familiar argument. I considering saying, *But you said you wanted to spend time apart*, but didn't think that was wise.

"Maybe you need to let go."

"What?"

"Every time you go to Israel you're back on a mission. It's not healthy. You need to move forward."

"Moving forward is not dependent on my location. What's in my head is in my head. It doesn't depend on where I am."

"You still have nightmares."

"Not all the time."

"You need to have some peace."

"I'm never at peace. The best I can hope for is equilibrium. And I don't have it right now."

Katie's eyes began to glisten.

Several heartbeats went by. "I need to go." I turned and left.

Down the hallways, down the steps, down another hallway, eventually past the guard near the main doors. If I passed someone

The Student

I knew, I didn't notice. I was outside before I could breathe. Halfway across the lot to my car my cell phone rang. Nate.

"Hey," I said.

"Well, you sound terrible." He picked that up from my *Hey*. Wonderful.

"I'm shitty. What's up?"

"The Iranian guy from South Charles Street, the one who almost shot you in the back of the head..."

"'Almost' being the operative word."

"He's dead. The FBI was moving him and he went for an agent's gun. There was a fight, he managed to get the weapon, and another agent shot him. He knew he couldn't escape, so death by cop." A moment passed. "So why are you shitty?"

"Let's go with the two college kids are gone. Noa's father pulled them from Jon's place and is taking them to Israel."

"Wonderful. What are you going to do?"

"Don't know. Right now, I think I'll exercise and then maybe you and I can interview Agent Number 3, the guy from last night – if he's still alive."

"He is, and I was planning to give that a shot today, pending FBI cooperation. Figured you'd want to come along. You can carry my briefcase."

"Thanks, Dad." I reached my Jeep and unlocked the door.

"One more thing."

I stopped.

"Gil Jeffries is in deep shit, or so I'm told."

"Why?"

"Overwatch yesterday on a crowded city street." The sniper.

"She had authorization from higher up."

"Doesn't matter. Someone in DC is pissed and shit rolls downhill."

"Lovely." I opened the door and slid behind the wheel. "I'll call you later."

Nate said, "Right," and I hung up.

27

I retreated to my studio. I locked the door, changed into a pair of black gi pants and a tan IDF T-shirt, and began working out. It was a full-on workout, from stretches and calisthenics to basic movements and advanced techniques. If Jon were here, I'd have invited him to spar with me, but maybe that wouldn't have been smart or safe. I probably wanted to inflict some pain, as a redirection of my own state of mind.

At some point, at the peak of my intensity, I knew I had to go in the other direction. The fluorescents were off in the practice hall once again, allowing only the light flowing in from the windows. As had become habit, I sat down in the center of the workout space and closed my eyes. For a while I just sensed the sweat rolling down my face and dripping down my back. My heart was still pounding from the exercise, almost shaking me, but eventually I regained mental and physical control. The breath, by training, found its way down to the base of my torso and coalesced to form a radiant energy source. I stayed with that image for a while – I had no idea how long – eventually letting the breath expand beyond the lower abdomen to fill my body and then beyond the confines of my skin...

At another point – again, there was no sense of time – various images passed through my mind. The mental reruns were not new: My IDF unit entering a home in Lebanon, sequestering the residents, searching the rooms... uncovering suicide vests in various states of assembly, plastic explosives, nails, rat poison. I saw a block of explosives on a table and a timer counting down…I heard myself shouting orders, rushing out of the room, taking everyone, residents included, out of the house. We had just gotten to the debris-filled street when there was a flash of white light and a surge of heat. For a split second oxygen was pulled from my body, and then a wall of air knocked everyone down as the house blew apart. When we stood up, a young man we had evacuated was aiming a pistol at me. He was perhaps 17, dressed in a green soccer T-shirt, dark jeans, and tennis shoes. I remembered the shoes; they were red. The gun in his hand was a large frame semiautomatic. He was cut down by team members to my left.

The image faded.

I saw myself at point, bursting into a basement room, shooting two terrorists as they were having tea. Their sidearms were on the table, inches from their hands. A captured IDF soldier was on the floor behind them, blindfolded, bound, and beaten. He had been kidnapped almost a year previously, and held as ransom for two hundred terrorists in various Israeli prisons.

The image shifted.

My team was fast roping out of a helicopter on the Syrian side of the Golan Heights, not far from Kuneitra, when an RPG took out the helicopter. Ten of the twelve members of our team were already on the ground. When the firefight with Hezbollah was over, I rejoined fellow soldiers back at the helo that had been shot out of the sky. We found the smoldering bodies of the rest of our team and the four crew members. I had known all of them.

The image shifted again.

There was Benny, who was killed beside me when we stormed a terrorist camp in northern Lebanon; Josh killed by a sniper as we crept through an industrial park… and Natan and Bar and Ofir. I saw all their faces and then their wives, girlfriends, and parents.

I began to sob. The tears came freely.

There were the funerals, flag-draped coffins, and clusters of families and friends hugging each other and shaking uncontrollably.

In another moment I was sitting next to a *Merkava* tank and weeping as the sounds of concussive artillery rolled over me.

I saw faceless men in keffiyehs holding AK-47s…I saw a young girl with long, dark hair, her dirty face partially obscured by her wind-blown tresses. Her eyes, as much as I could see of them, were expressionless as she walked toward us, carrying a grenade.

There were the bodies of a religious Jewish family in their new kibbutz home. It was a Friday night, and the nearby perimeter fence had been cut by terrorists. Everyone inside the house had been stabbed or shot, even the children.

And I sobbed.

And then everything faded to white. Slowly, an image dissolved in. A woman in a tie-dyed dress. She had straight, auburn hair, and was sitting opposite me, eyes closed, in a mirrored posture to my own. I knew her. She was Sammi, my late martial arts teacher's wife who was very much in the present. She lived in Westchester County, New York. She was a friend, a master, and mentor. When you were with Sammi everything was calm.

"Gidon," Sammi was saying, "what are you doing?"

My thoughts spoke: "I'm supposed to protect people and watch over them. Prevent harm from coming to their homes, to their families, to their lives. My comrades…"

"Gidon, stop."

Silence…for a very long moment. "You've forgotten…"

I saw the face of the IDF soldier, the captive, I had saved in that basement…There was the hug and tears from the wife of a wounded soldier I had carried back from a post-midnight mission too far from home…There were the school children in an Arab-Israeli village who came out to give my unit cookies and tea after we had given medical help to a family that had been in an auto collision…There was the rabbi's wife who had been held at gunpoint who I was able to bring back to her family…There was a weathered, gray-haired matriarch in an Arab restaurant who pulled me into the kitchen to thank me for keeping her family safe…There was Nate's daughter working in a kindergarten… And a young girl with a dirty face, partially obscured by her wind-blown tresses. She was walking toward me, carrying a grenade. I had ordered my men not to shoot, to wait. She came up to me to give me a grenade that still had the pin in it…

My breathing re-regulated…and everything faded out. Sammi was gone.

The radiating core in my lower abdomen was back. I was once again conscious of my heartbeat. The confines of the martial studio surrounded me…and I slowly opened my eyes. The room was darker than when I had closed them. The light through the windows seemed more yellow and not as bright. I sat without moving for an unknown period of time and then slowly, unsteadily, stood up. I walked across the dojo and sat in a folding chair. I replayed many of the images to include Sammi's. Was she…there? I had visited her before my last trip to Israel. We had worked out and meditated together.

I allowed my eyes to close. I knew where I was – in a metal folding chair in a darkening room. The echo of Sammi mirroring my posture was still in my head. What did it mean? Whatever it was, it brought me back to center, at least for now.

I took a deep breath.

As I looked around the room, the soft sound of a keyboard being tapped drifted over. Jon was sitting in my office, working on my computer.

"Hey," I said softly, after walking to the doorway.

"Hi. You're back."

I nodded. "How long have you been here?"

"Since three. That was three hours ago, by the way. When did you get to the dojo?"

"I don't know," I smiled. I wondered if he had seen me weeping. If so, he wouldn't say anything. There was probably a puddle on the floor where I had dissolved.

"Nate's called multiple times. First your phone – I heard it ring," he nodded to my street clothes draped over a corner chair; my cell phone still in a pants pocket. "When he didn't reach you, he called me. You were supposed to get together to interview the guy you stopped last night."

"Right. What did you tell him?"

"You were unavailable, and I didn't know when you'd be back."

"*I* didn't know."

Without preamble he changed the subject: "I got a text from Noa a few hours ago."

"Okay."

"They were in Newark, about to board a United flight to Israel."

"She didn't want you to worry."

He looked at me: "That's not going to happen. Not worrying."

With Jon at my desk, I took an adjacent chair, still a little shaken from the meditation. "Of course."

"So?"

"You want me to have her tracked in Israel."

"To be sure she's safe."

"I'll see what can be done."

"Thanks."

A moment passed.

"Call Nate," my student told me, almost like a parent to a forgetful child.

"Right." I dug out my cell phone from my nearby pants. After Nate picked up, my apology came first: "Sorry for this afternoon."

"You okay?"

"Better." A breath, then: "Did you see the agent, the cell leader?"

"No. The Feds weren't cooperating. But I'm not done with them yet. On the positive side, their IT people didn't turn up anything in the programs or email. We knew that. But, turns out the laptops were assembled in Riyad."

"Didn't know they did that over there."

"Apparently so."

"Curious." The conversation I had in Seattle with Noa's father came back. "Noa's dad, the desalination expert, said his wife had bought her the computer. Maybe Aminah's too."

"Why would he lie about that?"

"Maybe he didn't. Assembled there doesn't mean sold there. Noa's mother could have still bought it, with parts assembled in Saudi Arabia."

"Not what I'd bet on. Unlikely the computer came from the mom, and Riyad isn't on the cutting edge of tech. Raises more questions. Something else to think about when you're awake in the middle of the night."

He knew me well. "There's gotta be something on them to explain all this."

"Or it's something else."

"Thank you for the thought we're totally off-base." A moment passed when neither of us said anything.

"So, what're your plans, Sensei?" When he asked, I was looking at Jon looking at me.

"Should be asking you that, Captain."

"I'm going to try the FBI again about interviewing the agent. You?"

"Home."

"Okay. Later." Nate hung up.

I looked at Jon who, of course only heard my half of the conversation. "More questions, you have, Padawan?"

He just looked at me and shrugged. "I don't know what to do about Noa. I want her to be safe. I want to protect her."

"You sound like me."

A long silent moment passed.

"I'm a little messed up right now, Jon." I stared into his eyes.

"You've been messed up before."

"Thanks for that."

He smiled.

"This is different. It's not going away."

"What about 'shots downrange'?"

He had understood what I said after South Charles Street. "It's an ideal I'm still working on. For now I need to find some balance. I'm not seeing all this clearly."

"What can I do?"

"Take the class tonight?"

"Of course."

"I'll come by to teach the lesson, if you could just work them out…"

"Maybe you should stay home and do whatever it is you do when no one is watching." His eyes dropped for a second then came back to mine. "What about Katie? Can you talk to her?"

"No. Not healthy for us right now. She wants me to let all this go."

"That's not going to happen."

"No," I smiled at him. "Meanwhile, I'm thinking of going back to Israel."

"To check on Noa? To follow up?"

"That, and I want to see Tamar's family. Haven't seen them since she was killed. I need to do that."

"How long will you be gone?"

"Don't know." A thought suddenly bloomed, but the idea was usually on my mind whenever I'd leave for Israel.

Jon was quiet.

"Have a proposition for you, and you don't have to answer me now."

He looked at me.

"I keep going back and forth to Israel. It's not fair to you and to the students. You're here more than I am lately."

"Sifu, this is your place. You can do whatever you want."

I shook my head. "I just got back after four months, and I'm going away again. It's not right for anyone." A moment passed. "What if this were really your place. You're doing most of the teaching anyway. I'm like a guest lecturer: I come for a little while and then disappear. Students shouldn't sign up with the expectation that I'll be teaching them all the time, because I'm not."

"No, wait. You're here. *You're* who they want to see. So there've been times you've been away…"

"Too many. Let's make this transition. This will be your place. I'll be the supervising sensei who checks in from time to time to be sure everything's right. We can work out the legalities of ownership. This is your dad's building anyway."

Jon shook his head.

"I'll come by tonight and tell everyone. At this point, they're your students anyway. I just pop in periodically to goose the lessons."

My student looked at me for a long moment. "This conversation isn't over." After a pause, he added a respectful "Sifu."

* * *

Back at my place I found a flight; interestingly, the same one that Noa, her dad, and Aminah had taken, only a day later. Immediately upon booking it, some of the tension I must have been storing dissipated. Maybe it was getting back a sense of control. More likely it was acting on the decision to see Tamar's family. We always had strong, positive feelings for each other. There was also following up on Noa and Aminah, but it wasn't primary. I recognized that it bothered me, so I tucked it away.

I called Nate, told him my intentions, and gave him flight information; someone should have it. He thought the trip was the best thing I had thought of in a while. He'd keep me updated on the case, and told me to say hello to his daughter for him. Nate didn't ask if I planned to see her, but knew I'd try.

Next, there was a specific load of laundry to do. Israelis and many others, some hostile, identified foreigners by their clothing styles. So, last trip I had bought a small wardrobe in local stores. Katie had even bought me underwear. That was part one. Part two was how they smelled; I had also bought Israeli laundry detergent.

As I dug out my Israeli indigenous clothing, I thought about calling Katie. Tell her my plans? No. She had made her feelings clear. What about Gil…see what was going on with her at the Bureau? Maybe there was something I could do. I pulled out my cell phone and dialed the FBI agent.

"Hi, it's Gidon."

"I know." Difficult to tell how she was from that.

"Just wanted to check in. Heard some shit happened."

"Yeah, that." I heard her laugh a little. "It's fine. What's a day without a little something."

A moment went by.

"Can we talk tomorrow?" she asked.

I would be in transit a good part of the day, but reachable until boarding the international flight. "Sure."

"Okay. We'll catch up tomorrow. How was your night?"

"We'll catch up tomorrow," I repeated her line, knowing we probably wouldn't.

28

Given enough time, the check-in and security process at airports really isn't bad. But who gives it enough time? I parked in long-term parking – Jonathan would've been happy to drive me, but I didn't want to do that – waited for the shuttle, and then everyone knows how it goes. There are lines everywhere. I had a suitcase and a backpack, and was happy to send off the suitcase. And once on the other side of TSA Pre-Check, there was time to relax. I grabbed an iced coffee, a newspaper, and was finally able to sit back, at least figuratively, in the United waiting area near the gate.

I had settled in along a row of seats off to the side with a clear view of the gate kiosk and flight monitor, as well as of anyone approaching up the pier. My backpack was next to me on the floor, the newspaper in my lap, and the iced coffee in a holder next to me. But I wasn't in the mood to read.

It would be great to see Maayan, Tamar's sister, and the rest of the family. Of all Tamar's family members, I had the closest relationship with her. Yet, I hadn't called Maayan or been in touch after her sister's death until yesterday. And I didn't know why. I just couldn't.

There was also looking in on Noa and Aminah. That needed to happen too. The cause of their problems was still unresolved, but hopefully, the two girls were safe. There was something going on with Aminah, though she may not even know what it was. Nate and the FBI would work the case from here, and maybe uncover something significant. With the girls secure, I'd follow up with them in Israel, but probably not immediately.

I took a few swallows of my iced coffee and looked down the concourse. The mix of travelers was pretty much the same as it had been when I was at the airport in Seattle: families, singles, and business folk; people dressed in jackets and slacks, as well as jeans, shorts, and T-shirts. More than a few were wearing flip-flops.

And then there was a tallish, slender woman coming up the center of the concourse. She was in a pair of faded, worn jeans, a navy-patterned button-down shirt with shirttails out, and from this distance, possibly sandals. Her hands were free and she had a backpack. Agent Gil Jeffries, still about seventy feet away, was looking directly at me.

I stood as she approached. "Agent Jeffries. You flying to Newark?"

She looked into my eyes. "Ben Gurion."

"Noa and Aminah are in Israel."

She nodded.

"And the laptops came from Riyad."

She nodded again.

"And your boss said you should go?"

"Not really. I'm on modified duty. Seems the Deputy Director didn't like what happened on South Charles Street the other day."

"But you got clearance from your boss, if I recall. And we got the Iranians."

"That's why I still have a job." She paused for a moment and unslung her backpack. "On the other hand, our sniper killed one of the terrorists on a public street."

"The fact he was about to put a round in my chest should count for something," I reflected. It still was easy to visualize the man's gun leveled at me. "And you captured his partner" – the guy I had fought with.

"With your help, but our agents killed him in our own building after he grabbed an agent's weapon."

"Not your doing."

"True. I was being yelled at upstairs when that happened."

"Sorry." Then, in a shift of subjects, "About Noa and Aminah…"

She looked at me.

"You should know that when I was walking around with the girls, and the first guy was about to shoot me…he paused for a second to look at Aminah."

"Did he? That's curious."

"That's what Nate said – who knew about it, by the way."

She just nodded, and her mind seemed to drift for a moment.

"So it's all right for you to leave the country on modified duty?" I went back to the previous topic.

She shook her head. "Personal leave. My boss approved. He's a good guy, despite all the crap coming his way. Said there was too much politics going on anyway, and as long as I could get back to D.C. in 24 hours from wherever I was, he was okay with it. I can get back from Israel in 24 hours," she smiled. "And if we can figure this out, the politics will go away." A second passed. "Aminah, huh?"

"Uh huh." Another second went by. "So, of all the flights in all the airports…"

Gil Jeffries shrugged.

"Nate called you. Gave you my flight number."

"Captain D'Allesandro told me you were following up out of the country. Sounded like a plan."

I just nodded. Nate, I was sure, didn't mention my other, personal reason for going to Israel.

"You can introduce me to your Shin Bet contact."

"I can do that." My intended first stop, however, was not going to be following up on the case but heading north to see Tamar's sister. I looked over at the gate counter. At the kiosk an airline agent had started getting busy, looking at papers and his computer screen. I turned back to Jeffries. "*Yesh lach cheverim b'aretz?*"

The FBI woman looked at me.

I had just asked if she had friends in Israel. "I figure you were at

The Student

IDC in Herzliya while your father was posted in Israel. They have a world-renowned counterterrorism program."

She looked at me, then responded in English to my Hebrew: "I have friends outside Tel Aviv and up on the Carmel in Haifa."

"Me, too. Maybe they know each other." Before she could ask me how I knew she'd been to Israel, I said, "I'm a sensei. I know things."

She paused and shook her head. "By the way, just so you know, I was in the Global Affairs and Conflict Resolution program."

* * *

The flight to Newark, then the change in terminals, more lines, and the long international flight were all-too-familiar. My aisle seat in Economy Plus, compliments of Idan Gelvar's money, made the flight tolerable, but I felt bad for Gil in steerage further aft. She had managed a last-minute aisle seat, but when I went to see her, a nearby crying baby forced us to seek refuge in the back galley. We chatted over plastic cups of water about nothing in particular, from how she was spending time on the flight, to some places we'd been. She was much better travelled than me, thanks to a father in the diplomatic service. My points of interest were mainly Lebanon and Syria, a few European cities, and other places I couldn't discuss.

At some point the cabin lights were dimmed to mimic Israel time, seven hours ahead, with the illusion that passengers would now sleep comfortably. To give that a shot we soon returned to our seats. I did manage a few hours of rest, thanks to noise cancelling headphones.

At about two hours from landing, cabin lights were turned back up, and the energy level among the passengers rose; breakfast was served, lines for the bathrooms got longer, and, generally, travelers prepared for the end of the flight.

When we finally touched the tarmac, passengers applauded. Outside the windows, the sun was already bright, despite the early hour; the sky was cloudless. Cell phones came out, including mine, without waiting for permission from the crew, and soon there were muffled, and not so muffled, phone conversations. After another minute my phone dinged with a WhatsApp message from David Amit: *WELCOME HOME. COME TO JERUSALEM ANNEX. BRING YOUR FBI FRIEND.*

I had told Amit about my trip, but of course not about Gil's, since I hadn't known about it. For the Shin Bet, though, flight manifests and passport information weren't even a challenge. I messaged back we'd see him in a few hours.

The entry process went smoothly. Passport control was a large room with a series of kiosks and inevitable long lines. I used one of the fast-track machines for Israeli citizens, where my passport and features were scanned. Gil queued up in the visitor line and joined me fifteen minutes later. During the baggage wait, I washed my face in a nearby men's room, and changed into an Israeli bought, close-fitting T-shirt with a shallow V-neck. Naturally, Gil Jeffries laughed when she saw me.

As we waited for our luggage to rotate past us, I told Gil about how David Amit of the Shin Bet was waiting for both of us in Jerusalem.

"Of course."

"So," I looked at the FBI woman, "will you be staying in Jerusalem?" I watched a skinny, modestly-clad woman try to wrestle a large Kermit-green suitcase from the carousel. A black-attired religious man came to her rescue.

"I have an Airbnb. You?"

"Hotel room."

"Ah," the corners of her eyes crinkled as she stifled a smile. "Your company expense account."

"Yup, and the company is paying for my rental car, too. I'll need to ditch it, though, and get something that doesn't say 'Hertz,' or 'Sixt' or something along the side."

"Hard to be incognito driving that, even in your Israeli clothes."

This time I had to smile.

The Student

*　*　*

The drive southeast to Jerusalem took about an hour, and we moved fluidly up from the coastal plain into the Judean hills, where the highway became increasingly winding and congested. The slow incline finally peaked as we entered Jerusalem proper and passed the spire-like light rail bridge at the western entrance to the city. We weaved through the midmorning traffic, making our way to the Security Services annex north of the Supreme Court building. Amazingly, we found on-the-street parking.

As we walked to the annex under the still-bright early fall sky, the sidewalk traffic was steady, with business-attired, but casually-dressed men and women walking intently. Virtually none of the men wore ties or jackets, and the women were still in summery, flowing skirts or dresses. Almost all of the women were in sandals.

The building we wanted was along a small north-south side road connecting two main avenues. The quiet street contained both office buildings and low-rise apartment houses, the latter prime real-estate in a tight Jerusalem housing market. At my last visit, the street was newly paved, as the entire area still under construction. But now, the street was even wider, plus lined with thigh-high steel pillars, preventing terrorists, or anyone, from plowing into pedestrians on the sidewalks. Additionally, security cameras had been mounted on poles at varying intervals.

The Security Services annex was nondescript, except that it was set back from the street and behind a fence and a guardhouse. Next to the booth was a card access-only turnstile door and its companion, a magnetically-locked swing door for exiting. Last time, there was no option but to go past the guard.

"Checking in guests before getting to the building," Gil noted. "I like it."

We walked up to the guardhouse.

"Not gonna use your nifty Shin Bet ID on the card access door?"

"If I did, I'd end up in jail."

She looked at me. "Amit gave me a fake one. That way he could disown me if he needed to."

"I like him and haven't even met him."

I smiled and pulled open the guardhouse door. As we stepped in, I moved my sunglasses to the top of my head.

Inside were two guards, both about my height, with short dark hair, and black, square-cut security tunics covering their sidearms. The men, probably on a rotation from one of the elite army units, stood apart: one manned the desk and monitors, the other stood beside a walk-through magnetometer and an X-ray unit for personal items. The moment we stepped onto this block we were already on their screens; these guys didn't like surprises. Gil and I were the only visitors present.

"*Boker tov.*" I looked from one guard to the other.

Both nodded.

"Gidon Aronson and Gil Jeffries to see David Amit."

The guard at the desk looked at his monitor. When he looked back, I noticed he had an olive-colored shoestring-like necklace around his neck with its ends disappearing under the front of his shirt. I had one just like it in my suitcase…for dog tags.

He looked from his monitor to me, then to Gil, and back down to his monitor. He was checking our photos. Amit must have forwarded them; mine could have come from my army identification card, Gil's most likely from her passport.

"Can I see your I.D.s please?"

I handed over my Israeli driver's license and Gil her D.C. one. In exchange, he gave us lanyards with attached visitor badges.

"Third floor?" I asked.

"Yes."

Five minutes later we stepped into a small, but familiar conference room. The door had been left open. Amit was inside, as well as Idan Gelvar, the Deputy Director of the Mossad, the man who started all this at that Tel Aviv promenade café. The two men were sitting at right

The Student

angles to each other at the end of the conference table, a cup of coffee in front of each, and open folders of photos and papers fanned out between them.

Amit saw us in the doorway and stood up. "Gidon, welcome home. Agent Jeffries, Welcome back."

Gil couldn't help but smile at his knowledge. We stepped in and Gelvar rose as well. I introduced everyone: "FBI Special Agent in Charge Jeffries, this is David Amit of the Shabak, Israel's General Security Services," Amit held out his hand. "And this is Idan Gelvar, the Deputy Director of the Mossad."

Gil looked at me, then shook the Israeli spook's hand.

"Careful," I said to her, dipping my voice, "you don't want to be accused of working for a foreign intelligence service."

Gil narrowed her eyes at me, and we all sat down.

The Shin Bet man offered us coffee, which we both declined. I looked at Gil. Her eyes were still bright despite the long flight and little sleep. As for me, I felt somewhat drained. Lord knows how I looked.

Amit, his forehead permanently furrowed, watched us from behind his black wire-rimmed glasses. "Agent Jeffries, how are your parents? Is your father still with the State Department?" Amit's thinning hair seemed slightly grayer than the last time I saw him about a week ago, if that were possible.

"No, he's enjoying his retirement near Annapolis."

"Your parents have a home on the Chesapeake?"

"On the Magothy, a branch of the Chesapeake."

Gil gave me with a questioning look, but I turned from one security agent to the other. "So, what's the latest? How's Noa?"

The Mossad man faced me: "Fine. Her parents took her back to their place in Zichron." Zichron Yaakov, a town between Tel Aviv and Haifa, but closer to Haifa. Nothing in Israel was very far away.

"So, they both brought her from the States?"

Gelvar nodded. I took him in: round face, thinning hair, wrinkle lines branching out from the corners of his eyes. After a moment, Gelvar turned to me, "Thank you for looking after my niece." I wasn't sure whether he was sarcastic or not, considering I potentially got Noa, Aminah, and Jon killed by not watching for more Iranian agents.

"Have you spoken with your sister?" Noa's mom.

The Mossad man shook his head.

Gil: "And what's the story with Aminah?" She was already running with Aminah as our new, possible focus.

"She's home in Haifa," Amit answered.

"And her background?"

"All we have so far is her immigration information and personal family details."

"Which led back to Amman and then to a small town in Lebanon," Gelvar commented. "Obviously, we need more information."

A moment went by.

"So, laptops assembled in Riyad," Amit said. He must have been in touch with Nate. Conniker didn't seem the type to share intel with Israelis. "Don't know what that means."

"Except that someone wants them back very badly," I said.

"Your people are still tearing them apart?" Gelvar to Gil.

"We are."

I half expected the Mossad chief to say, *We have pretty good computer people here*, but glad he didn't.

Gil continued, "Gidon and I will interview Noa."

Personally, I had hoped to see Tamar's family first, but Gil's suggestion was fine. We could speak with Noa, and then Aminah in Haifa. Tamar's sister wasn't far from the port city.

"We need to find out where the girls got the laptops. If Noa's mom *did* buy them, then from where? If not, who provided them?"

"And were they from the same source?" Amit continued.

"Someone put something on them, obviously," Gelvar said. "Aminah's your priority. Start with her."

I shook my head. "I want to first question Noa about Aminah, and

The Student

then we'll see if Aminah's story matches."

Amit continued: "Captain D'Allesandro told me a third roommate also had an incident with her laptop?"

Both Gil and I nodded, but she was the one to respond, "Nothing there. Based on an FBI interview with the roommate, her laptop was purchased before she knew Noa or Aminah."

I hadn't known that. I looked at Gil but turned back to the Shabak man. "Okay, what else?" He was saving something.

"We received information on the older Iranian Agent." The one I had held at gunpoint at my studio. "He is known to us."

Gelvar finished his thought: "He's a Quds Force commander. The British and the Germans have been looking for him for two months. The French for three – all related to terrorist acts on their soil."

The intelligence men let that sink in. This guy wanted to interrogate Jon to get to Aminah and Noa.

Gil looked at both Israelis. Then, after a moment: "Iran has its fingers in Lebanon, Syria, and Gaza. The Intelligence communities know that."

Both Israelis nodded.

"What are the chances of an Iranian cell here in Israel?"

Amit, the Shin Bet man, sighed ever so slightly. "We're already looking into that."

* * *

Standing next to my rental car, I turned to Gil, who had slipped on a pair of Clubmaster Ray-Bans. My sunglasses were back over my eyes as well. "So, freshen up, grab something to eat, and then head up to interview Noa?"

The FBI woman nodded. "Where's your hotel?"

"Ten minutes from here. Prima Kings." I was partial to it, since I had experienced the ground floor being partially destroyed during my last visit. "And your Airbnb?"

"You can drop me outside the Kings. I'll find my way from there."

"Okay." She didn't offer her address.

I unlocked the car doors with my fob, but looked back at the HERTZ logo emblazoned on a wide, yellow rectangular strip rear of the back side window. The rental company's name was on each side of the car.

"That really bothers you."

I shrugged.

The FBI woman looked closely at the logo and then peeled off the magnetic strip with the company's name on it. She held it up and looked at me. She may have had one eyebrow raised.

* * *

The lobby at the Prima Kings had been renovated. Less than six months ago, a bomb detonating outside the ground floor windows precipitated that. The device's compression wave, which I had experienced near the front steps, had blown me back into a metal, cagelike cube for recycling plastic bottles. The blast did more damage to the outside of the building than the inside, basically blowing out windows and taking off chunks of the limestone walls. The lobby took some minor damage; no one was injured, however, much of the large room had to be remodeled; it had been updated with new furniture in the sitting room, new polished stone floors, new counters, different photos on the walls, and fresh paint. After a quick look to see what the owners had done, I went up to my fifth floor room.

Upstairs, my door opened onto an expansive area with a decent-sized bathroom to the left and a closet and dressers to the right. The queen bed was around the bathroom wall on the left. There was an envelope on the left-hand pillow, but I ignored it for the moment, instead going over to the closed, heavy drapes that kept the heat of the sun at bay and the room dark. I opened the curtain and liner to see a panorama that included the Old City off in the distance. If you knew what to look for, you could locate the golden Dome of the Rock and blue-gray domes of the Church of the Holy Sepulchre.

I turned around to scan the room. My eyes settled on the business envelope perched on the pillow. Closer inspection showed no markings on the envelope, save for my first name, hand-written in Hebrew on the front. Inside, a note had been penned by the same hand: "The combination to the safe is the same as your Charles Street address." Only one person would have researched my accommodations to have this put here. I walked to the mirrored closet doors and slid them open to see a white safe the size of a compact microwave sitting at eye level. Its keypad stared back at me, invitingly. I touched the four digits of my dojo's address, red LEDs lit up, there was a whirring sound, and then the word "OPEN" was displayed.

So, what did Amit leave for me? I swung the safe door open only to shake my head at how cliché this was. I pulled out an HK .45C in a holster, several loaded magazines, and Shin Bet credentials. Attached to the ID was a note: "This one will open the front gate." He could have given me all this at the office, unless he didn't want to do it in front of Gil. I put everything back and relocked the safe with a different combination.

Thirty seconds later I was under a medium cold shower. For a moment, I wished Katie were here in Israel. That, however, wouldn't give us time apart, per her request. I still wasn't sure how I felt about all that.

Which brought my thoughts to Gil Jeffries. What was this trip all about for her? Professional validation of her judgment? On the other hand, she had come by after the South Charles Street confrontation to check on me. Was that personal or business? And her being on my flight? She'd have probably come here anyway, independent of me. *Gidon*, I heard myself say, *just be thankful you have an ally.*

After the shower, I got dressed in a pair of black jeans, a gray version of the T-shirt I had on earlier, and a pair of well-worn black Reeboks. The gun and holster went near the small of my back and the

Shin Bet credentials in my pocket. I had to wonder why the official ID this time. Amit must have felt this investigation carried more national security weight than my previous forays. Still, there was no doubt he'd disown me if he had to. I wasn't one of his operatives; I had just been "deputized." Previously, he had said he'd consider my work with him part of my reserve army duty. Without giving any of this further thought, I grabbed my backpack and headed out.

Gil met me outside the hotel's main entrance, looking freshly scrubbed and rejuvenated in a white lace yoke top and faded jeans – not something she'd get away with on the job back home. We grabbed something quick to eat at a nearby café and then headed north to see Noa. We had just left the Jerusalem environs when my cell phone rang. It was Gelvar. I put him on speaker and set the phone on a ledge in the dash.

"Noa will be expecting you this afternoon. Where are you?"

I told him.

"I'll text you her mobile number. You can arrange timing and location when you get closer."

"Okay."

"Expect her parents to be there, too."

"Well, that should be fun for everyone. Thanks for the heads-up." I looked over at Gil. She was watching the scenery, but no doubt listening to the conversation. Back to the phone. "What about Aminah?"

"I'll let you call her. It can be a surprise."

Gil, still looking out the window, commented, "Noa will text her soon as she hears from us."

"*Nachon.*" Correct. Gelvar agreed. "So it won't be a surprise. Still…"

"It'll be interesting. Talk to you later."

Gil turned to me as soon as the connection was broken. "So, not looking forward to seeing Noa's parents?"

"Picked up on that, did you?" My phone pinged with an incoming text – Noa's mobile number from Gelvar. I put the phone in a cup holder. "Her father didn't appreciate my efforts to keep her safe. She was always too exposed…that's his perspective."

"She'd probably be dead, weren't for you. Does he realize that?"

The Judean Hills began to flatten out, giving way to open land on either side of the highway.

"It's not what he sees."

"Well, now she's home. Maybe we'll get some intel since they feel secure here."

"Maybe."

After a while we switched to Highway Six, the main toll road in Israel, and increased our speed, but not so we were passing everyone. As time went on, traffic thinned. To the left was open land with white condo-type buildings in the distance. The Mediterranean coast was about 10 miles off to that side, probably visible from those buildings. To the right, we were close to the Palestinian towns of the West Bank. As such, the security wall, which resembled a noise barrier but more imposing, ran beside us, with the Palestinian populated areas beyond. The housing styles were distinctive: often cement-walled, cube-style houses, flat-roofed, and built very close together. Domed mosques and tall minarets were readily visible.

The remainder of the trip was fairly quiet. We listened to the radio, and at some point I called Noa. I let Gil hold the phone this time, as my holding it was a major traffic offense. Noa, having heard from her uncle, was expecting the call. She wanted to meet on the pedestrian mall in town, not at home. I told her how far out we were and set a time.

Gil put the phone back in the cup holder. "Meeting in public. Her idea or her parents?"

I looked at her, like, *What do you think?* and began to consider what I was going to ask her.

"You know the place?" Gil looked at me.

I nodded. "Came here whenever I was in the neighborhood. Some great places to eat."

Thirty minutes later we began the winding climb up to the town of Zichron Ya'akov. Zichron was at the top of a hill that in some areas afforded a breathtaking view of the coastal plain to the west, as well as up and down the coast. The town dated back to the late 1800s, and was helped by Baron Edmond de Rothschild. In appreciation, it was eventually named in honor of his father, Ya'akov.

Zichron was a bit of an artist's colony, with beautiful, multistoried homes – the expensive ones were on the sides of a hill with a spectacular view – a few galleries, craft workshops, a winery, and a host of restaurants.

Since Noa, or her parents, wanted to meet along the city's popular pedestrian mall, we parked on a residential side street and walked to their location. The upper end of the open-air mall began at the top of a hill and continued at a slight downgrade. Gil and I stayed toward the center of the road, which was paved with tightly-laid gray bricks. Trendy clothing stores and eateries lined both sides; there were ice cream parlors, falafel and shwarma places, as well as boutiques, and arts and crafts shops. Old-fashioned lampposts with dangling, Christmas-style lights strung between them helped separate the middle of the pedestrian pathway from the shops to either side. Despite the workday, there was plenty of foot traffic. Many people sauntered along with small bottles of water, others with ice cream cones. When we were about halfway down the street, we spotted Noa and her parents sitting under a green umbrella at a round table outside a dairy restaurant. We angled over to them. Drinks, but no food, were on the table.

Noa spotted me. "Gidon!!" She sprung from her chair and ran to give me a hug.

We walked over to her parents. I remembered her father from Seattle. Dr. Biran didn't stand as we came over; he just looked up from his seat. The desalination expert had on a pair of reading glasses, though there was nothing in front of him to read, and despite being in the shade, was also wearing a medium blue Israeli-style bucket hat. It was a distinctive Israeli look.

Noa's mom sat to his right. She could have been in her late forties,

The Student

but had an older Audrey Hepburn look about her, with dark hair, pulled back tight to her head. She had smile lines around the corners of her mouth, and clear dark eyes.

I held out my hand. "Gidon Aronson."

"Anat," she said taking my hand, but without a smile.

"And this is Special Agent Gil Jeffries of the FBI."

"Oh?" Anat, looked at Gil.

"Yes, Ma'am. I have my identification if you want to see it," she smiled.

Anat shook her head.

"So, Noa," I turned to their daughter, "how are you?"

"Okay. Basically kidnapped, but okay. Missing classes."

Her parents didn't say anything.

"How's Jon?"

"Concerned."

She nodded. My guess was that she was in touch with him.

Dr. Biran looked at his wife and then turned to me. "Why are you here?"

Gil answered. "We know you had to bring Noa and Aminah home. Safety comes first."

"Yes," Noa's mom answered.

"But we have a few questions. We came all this way to talk to you."

Anat nodded. Nothing from Noa's dad.

Gil continued. "We believe that what happened in Baltimore centers around Noa's and Aminah's laptops for some reason."

"I told you in Seattle," Dr. Biran looked at me, leaning in, "I didn't send Noa anything proprietary."

"We understand," I said. "Something else has come up."

Gil continued, "Mrs. Biran–"

"Doctor," Noa's dad jumped in. "Anat is a medical doctor."

"Sorry. Dr. Biran, we understand that you bought the laptops for the girls."

Before she could respond, a young waitress came over and asked

Gil and me if we wanted anything. We both shook our heads.

When the waitress left, Noa's mom answered. "I was going to, but Aminah's uncle bought them for the kids…as a present."

That was quite a gift. "Do you know where Aminah's uncle is from?"

Noa looked at both of us. "Saudi Arabia."

The mom's posture became slightly more erect. "Why?"

"Do you know his name?"

Dr. Biran, the desalination expert, answered. "Rayyan Omari."

"What he does for a living?"

Both of Noa's parents shook their head, and then Noa did as well. Anat asked again, "Why?"

I gave them the answer many Israelis offer when asked questions about secretive work: "We can't discuss that."

A moment went by, then Noa looked at me. "When can I go back to classes?"

Gil smiled just a bit but her face was still serious. "You're probably better off here for now. Just to be sure."

I had the next question. "When did Aminah's uncle give you the laptops?"

"A few months ago."

That would put it at the beginning of the semester. I had no idea if that was significant.

"So you've met him?" Again from Gil.

All three of them said yes.

"Where? Here, before you left?"

"In London," Noa's dad answered. "He met us there when all of us were spending a few days before going to the States."

My turn again: "Was Aminah's family there as well?"

"Yes."

Noa's mom looked from Gil to me. "You can't tell us what's going on?"

"Sorry." It was an honest answer, because we really didn't know very much. The answers, perhaps, were in a pair of laptops in FBI custody.

Gil looked at Noa. "How do you know Aminah?"

"We met at Bar Ilan University here."

A long moment went by. I felt like something needed to be said, something to put them at ease. "No one here is in trouble, you know. Not here or in the States."

"Good," Noa's dad said. "Because we didn't do anything wrong. And you can tell that to Idan and to the Shin Bet." He looked over at Gil, "and to the FBI."

"We don't think you did. We don't think Aminah did either."

"But there's a reason why people were after the girls," Gil said.

"And we're just trying to get more information," I added.

Another long moment passed as we watched a young couple look at a menu posted nearby.

Noa's mom turned to me. "My brother trusts you."

I nodded.

"The Shabak trusts you."

I nodded again.

"Then I want you to do something for me. Come back and tell us when it's safe."

"Of course."

And with that, Noa's father stood up and motioned for his wife and daughter to follow. They did. Dr. Biran, the father, paid the bill and walked away. Noa looked back at us and despite a sad face, waved. They walked down the promenade away from where Gil and I had come.

"Well," I began, "now we know who bought the laptops."

"Aminah's uncle."

I nodded.

"We still don't know what's on them," Gil observed.

"Something to do with the uncle's work or someone he works for."

"Aminah, or her parents, might know."

"They might."

Gil slipped on her sunglasses. "Our next stop."

29

After leaving the restaurant and the promenade behind, we drove up the coast toward Haifa. On our left the Mediterranean was almost tangible, and we kept the windows down, allowing the fresh scent of the sea to blow through the car.

For the first time in a long time I felt we were getting a handle on all this, or at least moving forward. The girls were out of harm's way as far as we knew, so we could focus on what made the laptops worth sending Iranian Quds Force mercenaries to retrieve them, killing anyone in their way.

Aminah's uncle had those answers. We had questions: Who was he and what could he possibly have on someone that would have instigated all this? Maybe he was a good guy and had stumbled onto something bad? Maybe he was trying to protect himself.

"Maybe he came across something he needed to hide." Gil looked at me, with the wind from the windows whipping her hair. "Or is using it to protect himself."

I didn't want to say I was just thinking that. "Maybe. Or he's not such a nice guy and is blackmailing someone."

"He's got something but can't keep it near him."

"For whatever reason." I turned to her for a moment. "It's all in the ones and zeroes back in Baltimore or DC. Your forensic guys just haven't found it yet."

Our thoughts were moving in the same direction… The first

question really was who was Aminah's uncle? We had already called Amit; the Shin Bet man would find out what he could.

"Maybe he just wanted to get information out."

I shook my head. "If it were just news, there are a million ways to do that." And depending how intense it was, he'd have to be very careful revealing it. Who was he afraid of?

We passed a sign noting Haifa was 20 kilometers away, and my mind drifted to one of the reasons I was here, to reconnect with Tamar's family. Hopefully, I'd see them tonight. They weren't far from where we were headed.

"Don't you think it's weird," Gil interrupted my brief reverie, "that a higher-up in the Security Services and the Deputy Director of the Mossad are letting you, letting us, take lead on this? I'm a foreign national. And you, I don't know what you are."

"Did you just insult us? Me?" I laughed.

"No, that's not what I—"

"Don't feel up to it?"

She had partially turned her torso to face me and had to raise her voice to compete with the air rushing in through the windows. "No. I'm a great investigator," she smiled. "And you're really good at what you do. I just think it's weird that they're letting us take point, that's all. It wouldn't happen in the U.S."

"Different mentality here. Comes from the army, letting soldiers in the field have more independence. Amit and Gelvar know we've been on this all along and have the relationship with the girls. And we're not the only ones investigating, I'm sure of that. We're just one stick poking around the embers of something."

"Maybe we're poking a bear and Amit and Gelvar are waiting for a reaction."

That sounded right, actually.

* * *

Haifa, about 25 miles south of the Lebanese border along the Mediterranean, juts out from the coastline, almost like someone's shoulder. It's a sprawling city, built not only at the base of the Carmel Mountain Range where it meets the sea, but along the side of the mountains and its ridges as well.

Aminah and her family lived in the German Colony not far from the base of the Bahai Gardens. The older sections of the neighborhood were wooded with both duplex homes and garden apartments. Side streets, tucked off busy main roads, provided a mix of urban life and private space. We parked around the corner from Aminah's along a shady side street, the closest spot we could get.

Her house, set back from the road by a small garden, was the left portion of a duplex. We walked past the well-tended flower beds and a pair of men in the yard next door dealing with excavated pipes. A private path led under the branches of a mimosa and up to a covered landing sheltering Aminah's front door. After we noted the plaque marked "Hadad," Gil rang the bell. Aminah was expecting us; we had called ahead, plus Noa had let her know of our visit with her.

Gil turned to me as we waited, "You know, as a fellow law enforcement officer, Amit or Gelvar could've given me a weapon, too."

"You noticed." I could easily feel the .45 at my lower back.

"Of course."

"You're a foreign national. They wouldn't give you a gun," I smiled.

As footsteps approached from inside the house, the workers next door began a lively discussion in Arabic. An older man in a dirt stained, white tanktop and worn khakis was directing a younger man, about 20, who was on his knees, leaning over an exposed water pipe. It seemed there was a difference of opinion about how to do something.

Aminah's front door unlocked and swung open. Her eyes instantly lit up. "Gidon, shalom!" and she gave me a hug and a kiss on the cheek.

"And Special Agent Jeffries," I said.

"Of course." Aminah leaned in and gave Gil a kiss on the cheek as well.

The Student

I looked at Noa's roommate. The last time I had seen her was following our "parade," drawing out the mercenary Quds Force men. Now, Aminah seemed relaxed and rested, and was dressed in charcoal gray leggings and a teal T-shirt. Her short blonde hair looked recently cut, but maybe not, and her eyes were bright and clear.

Before I had a chance to say anything, Aminah leaned inside the doorway, grabbed something, and came back out, hooking a pocketbook over her shoulder.

"I'm really sorry. I know we have to talk, but my parents aren't home and I have to go food shopping." She pulled the door closed and stepped down onto the walk.

"Your parents aren't home?" Gil looked from Aminah to me as we walked past the front garden.

"No, they had to go to London."

My forehead furrowed. "We had hoped to talk to them."

"I'm sorry. My uncle called almost as soon as I got back. He needed to meet my parents there."

"Wait," I turned to face Aminah and the three of us stopped. "This isn't your uncle Rayyan Omari, is it?"

"al-Omari. It is." She looked from me to Gil and back. "Why?"

Behind Gil and Aminah the two workers were both staring down at the exposed pipes. Neither said anything for a moment, then they continued their conversation.

"He's the one who gave you and Noa your laptops, right?"

Aminah didn't move for a moment, and then blanched. "Yes." She looked into my eyes, "Oh my God."

Gil put her hand on Aminah's forearm. "Let's go inside."

She nodded and we followed her into the apartment. Inside, the living room beyond the foyer was a bit dark, with curtains pulled over the windows. Still, there was plenty of sunlight filtering in. Aminah and Gil sat on a nearby couch; I pulled over a chair.

"Tell us about your uncle," I began. "Where does he live? Where does he work, that sort of thing."

Aminah sat with her hands in her lap. "He lives in Riyad. He's about forty, single as far as I know."

Gil followed up. "Do you know what he does for a living and who he works for?"

Aminah shook her head. "I'm not sure. He works with computers. He may be a website engineer or something? I don't know."

"And his employer?"

She shrugged. "The government? That's a guess. Before we saw him in England last month I hadn't seen him in years."

"Don't worry about that," I said. "Would your parents know who his employer is?"

"Probably. But they're—"

"In London," Gil and I said at the same time.

"You have your parents' mobile number?" I continued.

She nodded.

"Your uncle's too?"

Aminah nodded again.

The next question was Gil's: "Do you have a picture of him?"

"In my phone. Who should I send it to?"

"Me." I raised a finger, not sure why. "Along with your parents' numbers and your uncle's."

There was moment or two when no one talked. Aminah shared the photo and the contact information.

"The picture of my uncle is with my parents in London in August."

"And that's when he gave you and Noa the laptops."

She nodded.

"Any idea why he's in London now?" Gil looked at Aminah's hands, which were still in her lap and then up into her eyes. In the background I heard what sounded like a pickaxe smacking a rock. The hammer-on-rock sound continued two more times, then stopped.

"No."

"Or why he wanted your parents to come?" This from me.

Aminah shook her head again.

"Okay, no worries."

Gil and I stood up, and Aminah did as well. We walked toward the door.

"When you speak with your parents…" I stopped.

"Don't mention you were here?"

"No, that's fine. Just don't say we were asking about your uncle. Does that put you in a tough spot?"

"No," she moved some of her blonde hair behind an ear. "If it comes up, I'll just say the checking on me part. But if they ask me directly…"

"Just do what you're comfortable with," Gil said. "Thank you."

We each gave Aminah a hug.

"And you have my mobile number now," I added, "so call day or night, if you need anything."

"I will. Thanks." She gave me a hug and a kiss again.

And Gil and I left. We walked under the mimosa to the front walk, where Gil stopped, sideways to the pair of workers next door. "She's a good kid," Gil said. "Her head is on straight."

I nodded. A moment passed, but we didn't continue walking. "What?" I looked at her.

"Ask Amit to put a car on Aminah."

"Yes, ma'am."

She looked at me. Then, "You were going to ask him."

"Soon as we got back to our car," I smiled.

* * *

Twenty minutes later, I dropped Gil off at her friend's house in the community of Kiryat Tivon, a town not far from Haifa. Outside the car, she slung her backpack over her shoulder and began walking to her friend's front door.

"Special Agent Jeffries," she turned back to me. "You're pretty sharp."

She smiled wryly, turned, and continued up the walk. Gil knocked, a few seconds passed, and the door swung open. A woman about Gil's age and height immediately wrapped her arms around the FBI agent and they disappeared behind the closing front door.

I sat in the car and thought about the day: the briefing with Amit and Gelvar in Jerusalem, the conversations with Noa and her parents, and Aminah's parents being in London with her uncle.

After another moment, and still realizing that Tamar's family was waiting for me, I checked email. Procrastinating? Probably. I also wondered if Jon had checked in. If not, I should probably let him know all was fine.

I looked down at the incoming mail list on my phone. Nothing from Jon, but Katie had written about five hours ago. All the preview line said was something about her being upset. It didn't take much to rerun the two of us in her office, and her telling me I needed to move past my experiences in Israel. The conversation had gotten heated very quickly. I exited the program without opening the correspondence.

After another moment, I grabbed my backpack from the rear seat and pulled out a different phone, a burner bought on my last trip here. It had only been used for a few short calls so there were plenty of minutes left. I looked around for no reason and then dialed a number I had memorized years ago.

The call went right to the voicemail beep. As expected. No outgoing message. No out-of-service recording. Just a beep. As expected.

"Hi," I said. "I'm back. Hopefully more of a pleasure trip than business. I'm staying near Karmiel, at least for tonight." I had named a city in a valley between the Upper and Lower Gallilee. "Talk to you later."

If Ibrahim were still alive, he'd get the message. He'd recognize my voice and would reach out, if he could. He might be in Gaza. He could be in Lebanon or Syria. Or he might be in an unmarked grave somewhere. He could say the same about me.

* * *

The drive to Tamar's sister's kibbutz took three-quarters of an hour. There was a quick stop at a roadside newsstand for flowers, and then it was back to the steady flow of traffic. With the sun low on the horizon behind me, I passed multiple Arab villages on the way eastward in the direction of the Sea of Galilee. I passed Karmiel, the city I had mentioned in my voicemail to Ibrahim, and then exited the east-west road, turning northward onto an inclined, winding road up into the Meron Mountains. Off the wide roadway the valley dropped away sharply, and while the vista begged to be looked at, paint-streaked, scorched concrete barriers warned drivers not to be distracted. Soon, beside a newly paved section of road, a turning lane appeared, leading to Maayan's kibbutz.

Half a minute later, I pulled up to the gate. A security man looked at me from his window in the small guardhouse, and soon the iron fence in front of my bumper retracted on squeaking rollers. Once there was enough space, I drove through.

The communal settlement was familiar. I had been here numerous times with Tamar to visit her sister. It was a great kibbutz with a mix of older, ranch style homes and newly built multilevel houses in what was once undeveloped, peripheral land. Most of the older sections were tree-lined and full of flowering bushes; many houses had gardens in front or to the side.

I soon passed a two-story community center sitting at the junction of two smaller streets, where I took the right-hand turn and followed the curving street for maybe a thousand feet. At that point a modest home appeared atop a small rise, with a wide gravel strip at its foot for parked cars. Two sedans were already there, but there was room for a third. I backed in. Fifteen seconds later I was walking up the small hill, clutching the recently purchased bouquet.

The pounding in my chest increased with each step, but as soon as Maayan opened the door and I saw her familiar, bright smile, any trepidation evaporated. There was a long, long hug, and when we backed away I saw tears had filled her eyes. She wiped them away, just as I began to well up, too. Next to her was her husband, Yakir, and we shook hands and then gave each other a hug as well. "We're glad you're here."

Behind them stood Maayan's parents. They were an older couple, of course. Her dad was a good foot shorter than me but sturdy, had a full head of gray hair, a tanned face, and a big smile. His wife was his height, but rail thin, with stylishly cut short, silver hair. Reading glasses hung on a chain from her neck. More kisses, more hugs. There were two young boys, Tamar's nephews, who remembered me, and they gave me hugs as well. Soon enough we were all ushered into the back yard where we sat around a picnic table filled with bowls of salads, plates of shwarma, pita, hummus, and more. I gathered from the boys that they had been waiting for me, and that they – well, at least the two young men – were starving.

I sat next to the kids, across from Maayan and Yakir, and for most of the meal, felt like a strange visitor from another planet, or at least from another time. After the basic stuff of what I was doing and what they were doing, the conversation turned to politics, naturally, both Israeli and U.S. On more than one occasion I was asked my opinion of the U.S. president, but remained noncommittal. The noise level around the table increased with impassioned opinions expressed by all the adults. As I surveyed the group, I found myself continually looking at Maayan. Her lightly tanned face was framed with long brown hair that had hints of auburn throughout. She smiled effortlessly, and when she did, her entire face lit up, from her white teeth to the corners of her eyes. That's how I remembered Tamar. And when something in the conversation seemed questionable, Maayan would arch her right eyebrow. Tamar had that characteristic, too. On more than one occasion throughout the meal, I'd lock eyes with Maayan for a brief moment. At one point I felt myself getting teary. That took me by surprise. A few blinks, a few deep breaths, and the emotion retreated.

Once the meal was finished and the table cleared, the kids and Maayan's parents went inside. While Yakir remained in the kitchen to straighten up, Maayan and I were shunted back outside. We sat at the table across from each other. There were the inevitable questions of what I had really been doing. I told her about teaching martial arts, the occasional substituting, and about helping friends back in the States. I also admitted to attempting to find some emotional balance. When she said I looked in shape, I had to confess, "Army service."

The famous eyebrow arched. "Here?"

I nodded. "Training with my old unit." A moment passed. "This past summer. I needed to do something intensely physical and to feel I was doing something positive."

She looked at me for a long, few seconds, and the fact I hadn't called prompted what she truly wanted to know: "So, how are you? Really."

I shrugged, "Okay," then had to ask, "How are you? Really."

She shrugged, too.

"Yup."

I asked about her younger brother, who, she reported, was in the throes of a computer project in Tel Aviv, and her parents, who were just trying to get through day to day. And Yakir, her husband? He was keeping busy with his work at the environmental center on the kibbutz.

Tamar's sister turned toward me just a bit. "Are you seeing anyone?"

"You mean like a therapist, or do I have a girlfriend?"

"A girlfriend," she smiled. "I know you're not seeing a therapist."

I looked into the face that shared so many characteristics with Tamar's. "No." A moment, then, "Maybe. I have no idea. Probably not."

Maayan smiled again and left it alone.

Yakir came outside and reported he was going to take Maayan's parents home. He turned to me. "You're spending the night?"

I looked at my almost sister-in-law, who nodded, and that was settled, which was good, because I had no other plans.

I bunked in the spare room but couldn't sleep. What a surprise. I was re-running many of the memories of being with the people I saw tonight – on the weekends, at holidays, hiking trips – and then, not that I asked the recent events to re-visit me, there were the various Iranian agents and their victims back in Baltimore who had their throats slit and had been shot for good measure.

At 3:30, I gave up. I put on a T-shirt and pants, and walked barefoot through the house, out to the back yard. Maayan was sitting in a garden chair, eyes wide open and looking up into the night sky. She turned to me, and we both smiled. I pulled up a chair.

Like Maayan, I turned heavenward. The Big Dipper was right where it should be, in the northern sky.

"So," Maayan looked at me. "How are you?" It was a repeating theme.

She was in a pair of jeans and an emerald green hoodie, zipped up to the base of her neck. Her bare feet were up on another chair.

I told her about the case I was working on, the whole laptop mystery thing, the need to protect the girls, and wondering what it was really all about. I also mentioned I was working with Shabak, using the full acronym for the Shin Bet, which was more common nomenclature with Israelis. "But to answer your question directly," I looked into Maayan's eyes, and once again…shrugged.

30

The text came in on the burner phone at 4:27 a.m. There was a link to a map, and a time – 9:30 a.m. The link opened a page on a Google map, showing a school in an Israeli Arab village half an hour away. At least Ibrahim was still alive. Or, someone had killed him and was using his phone to entrap his friends and contacts. Fun thoughts.

Maayan's house was already full of activity by 7:00 when I headed down to the kitchen to join whoever was there. Both Maayan and Yakir were dealing with the kids, as well as themselves, in getting set for the day. After a few moments, the kids were out the door with Yakir. On his way out he came by and gave me another embrace. He semi-whispered in my ear, "We miss Tamar, but we miss you, too." He looked at me. "Come back soon." And he was off.

Maayan offered me breakfast, but I accepted only coffee. We sat for a few more minutes – basically, we had already said what we needed to say last night – and then it was time to go. Maayan grabbed a petite backpack and we went out the door together. Before we turned to our separate cars, she gave me a tight hug.

I preempted her good-bye with "I'll come back after all this is done."

She nodded a melancholy smile and we both went our separate ways.

As I sat in my car, watching Tamar's sister pull away, I texted Gil that I was heading to see another friend. I'd let her know when I'd pick her up. Then, before leaving the kibbutz, I double-checked Ibrahim's Google map to verify I had the directions correctly visualized.

The Israeli Arab village of Dir el-Asad was off the main east-west road I had driven on yesterday from Haifa. Like Maayan's kibbutz, the village was up in the hills. And that's where the commonalities ceased. It was urban sprawl, at least in this part of town. The curving village roads were narrow, making fluid, two-way traffic barely possible. It was like squeezing through a narrow tube. Vehicles poked out from curbs on both sides, and pedestrians freely stepped off the curb into the street. It was a challenge not to hit something or someone. Commercial and residential buildings were interspersed and were built vertically just off the street, like stacked children's blocks. There were no trees or foliage.

The school Ibrahim had directed me to was up a winding, narrow street on the left, set back from the road, beyond the open gate of a perimeter fence. I parked on the curving road, commercial buildings on my right, with a clear view of any vehicular or foot traffic entering the school's yard. I was 60 minutes early. If the text from Ibrahim were genuine, I'd see him coming. If it weren't, I'd hopefully see the setup. I should have brought a bottle of water.

I relaxed in my seat, and immediately felt the .45 Compact resting near my spine. The semiautomatic didn't have a round in the chamber, and maybe that was a mistake. I could take out the weapon and chamber a round, but there were pedestrians close by, and I didn't need anyone seeing that. If necessary I'd do it, but not until then.

The traffic around me picked up as the morning slowly matured. Cars dropped off students, some vehicles pulled inside the school's fenced area, and a bus even managed to ease its way around a tight corner, missing a parked van by inches.

As the rising sun erased many shadows, I spotted a small convenience store pressed between a bakery and a produce stand. I would have loved a piece of fruit or a drink, but that wasn't going to happen.

While the vehicular activity increased, no one parked in front of me, and no one came up parallel, at least not to purposefully block me in. At one point, there was some sort of stoppage up the hill, and a line of cars, unable to move, snaked down the street. When a late model Honda was trapped in traffic a few feet from my door, the driver – a dark-haired man in his forties with a full head of hair – looked over. I looked at him, then up the hill to the point of congestion, and back. We turned to each other and both held our hands up.

I checked the clock on the dashboard: 9:00. Thirty minutes before Ibrahim said to meet. I wasn't even sure where in the school he wanted to rendezvous – in the front of the building, inside, in an office?

The congestion up the block cleared in another few minutes and traffic began moving.

Across the street, just before the gate to the school, a middle-aged man in an open collar shirt and a sport coat jumped out of the driver side and darted across the road toward my car. Vehicles in both directions slammed on their brakes. Drivers leaned on their horns, but the man ignored them. He took a moment to look at me, and then continued into the fruit stand, disappearing inside.

A minute or two went by, but the man in the open collar and sport coat remained in the shop. If this were an old gangster film, he'd spring out the door, machine gun in hand, and spray my car with lead. I had to smile at the notion, but the front of the store became part of my visual rotation.

A minute passed.

Up ahead, an elderly man slowly emerged from an unidentified entryway and began walking ever-so-slowly on the narrow sidewalk in my direction. He was limping slightly, bent over a cane. My eyes scanned the rest of the sidewalk but came back to him for no other reason than his movement triggered my attention. He was in an old gray suit coat too large for him, and wore a raggedy keffiyeh on his head. No doubt he was a long time resident of the neighborhood.

A younger woman in a loose-fitting, long blue dress passed by on my right and walked assuredly up the hill. She passed the elderly man

The Student

without looking at him. Conversely, the old man didn't look at her.

The traffic on my left, both ascending and descending the inclined street, gridlocked again. Another woman, perhaps in her late twenties and wearing a dark hijab, walked in front of my car, holding hands with a child, and crossed between stopped vehicles to run across to the school.

By now the old man with the cane had walked past me on the right. I kept track of him in my mirrors to see him eventually round a corner and disappear.

My attention shifted.

The woman in the long blue dress had reached the top of the hill and went into what looked like an apartment building.

To my left, the woman in the hijab, holding the hand of the young boy, entered the school parking lot and went in the front door.

The man who had darted into the fruit stand was still inside.

My focus shifted back to the street and sidewalk up ahead of me. Pedestrians were now out and about. Two young men emerged from a café a few shops up, looked around, and settled their gaze on me. They moved down the sidewalk, and as they did so, talked to each other, still watching me.

There was movement to my left.

The old man in the keffiyeh – the man who disappeared around the corner behind me – was leaning over, inches from my driver's side open window. Our heads were a foot apart. I was staring into dark brown eyes that were full of intensity. I took in the rest of the man's face. He was not an old man as I had first thought; he was maybe ten years older than me, with his sun-darkened face covered in a layer of five o'clock shadow. A neatly trimmed mustache lent some length to his round visage. I came back to his eyes. They locked onto mine, seeking to read me.

"And why is a man like you, Shabak maybe, or an undercover IDF soldier, watching us?" His voice was calm, smooth, and in no rush. It was both threatening and not at the same time. "What is there for you here? This is a peaceful village."

"I am neither IDF or Shabak." My Shin Bet and IDF credentials were both in my pocket.

He leaned in a barely discernable amount. "I don't believe you."

There was movement up ahead of my car. A small van had pulled to the curb right in front of me. Our vehicles were nose to nose.

"You're very paranoid," I reflected.

"I am."

"I am neither IDF or Shabak," I repeated.

"I don't believe you," he said again in his calm, steady voice. "And you've made an error. Your motor is off."

It was. I had decided to turn off the engine and not let it idle.

"If you decide to leave, I will reach in and pull you through this window before you've started the car."

The driver of the van in front of me watched me through his windshield. He did not look happy.

"I don't think you will."

Disagreeing, the man at my window nodded ever so slightly.

I shook my head.

We watched each other's eyes for a long moment, and then I dipped my head slightly. The man with the sun darkened face and mustache followed my gesture. Resting in my lap, my .45 was pointed toward my door. The barrel was slightly elevated. At this range the heavy bullet would easily plow through the thin metal of the car door, and rip into the man's lower abdomen. He didn't know the chamber was empty.

The man with the sun darkened face and mustache raised both his eyebrows.

"I am waiting for a friend," I said calmly.

He looked at me again.

I nodded to the driver of the van that had blocked me in. "Perhaps you should send your friend away."

"I can't do that."

The Student

"Well, maybe we should go inside the school. That's where you wanted to meet."

The man in the keffiyeh stood up – he was much taller than he had appeared when ambling down the street – and walked over to the driver's side of the van, no sign of the limp he had earlier. He spoke to the driver, who nodded, but didn't take his eyes off me. The tall man, who was not as old as he had first appeared and who didn't need a cane, took off his keffiyeh, and gave it to driver. He also pulled off the oversized suit jacket. He then came back to me.

"Come, Gidon, let's go inside."

I walked with Ibrahim across the street. "So, still testing me."

Ibrahim smiled. "Have to make sure you've remained sharp."

"Not as sharp as I once was, I think."

Ibrahim let that pass.

"So, who were those guys, the two walking down the street to distract me and the guy in the van?"

"Locals. I paid them to scare an American friend."

"They don't know who you are?"

He shook his head.

We crossed to the school and walked through the parking lot.

"Are you the guest speaker?" I smiled.

"I have no connection to the school. I heard there was an eighth-grade program, so I thought we could be interested guests."

Made sense. We could be strangers to the area and not raise suspicions. We followed a middle-aged couple into the building, past some offices and into a main hallway.

The school was like many of the older Israeli public schools I had been to: wide halls, lockers, classrooms to either side, but this school was more worn. The floors were tiled and dirty. Not all the overhead lights worked. A few broken desks were discarded to the side.

A current of students and parents carried us down the hall. We drifted behind two boisterous boys.

"How are Amira and the kids? Still in England?"

He nodded. "But it's not as I thought it would be. I was hoping to get my kids away from the brainwashing, the *harta* in the PA areas." He used the Arabic for nonsense or bullshit.

"But?"

"England's not the place. Neither is most of Europe. The Middle Eastern communities there are insular and are on the edge of some dangerous things."

"Not everyone in those communities."

He shook his head. "No, of course not, but it's not what I expected when I sent the family there."

"Amira wanted to come back here and live in the north."

"I will if you will."

"Not just yet."

He echoed my thoughts: "Not just yet."

A few moments went by as we passed a classroom that had an open door. The room was filled with students as well as parents. A boy was in front of the classroom, giving a report.

"You're walking well," I looked at his left leg where I had shot him some time ago.

"It's healed. And we're both alive."

We leaned against some old lockers. I waited for a couple to go by. After another few seconds, "I've got something, and I don't know what it is."

Ibrahim looked at me and I told him what was going on, from the *DEATH TO ISRAEL* graffiti on the girls' apartment wall, to the murders to mercenary Iranians, to the mystery of the computers. I brought it back to Aminah and her uncle, Rayyan al-Omari, who possibly worked for someone in the Saudi government.

He thought for a moment. "Amit helping?" It was like saying Shabak, but more personal. He knew of my connection.

I nodded. "He's trying to get intel on the uncle and who his boss is."

"Let me know what he turns up. I'll text you if I hear anything."

The Student

We watched a group of high school-age girls lilt down the hallway. Some were in tight jeans and blouses, others were more modestly dressed and had their hair traditionally covered. It was an encouraging mix of religious and secular kids.

"Mercenary Quds Force soldiers," Ibrahim reflected. He hadn't been distracted by the students. On the other hand, he noticed everything. "I've heard about these zealots. Watch out for them. Very driven."

"What else is new?"

We began walking back in the direction we had come.

"So," I said, looking ahead as we walked, "how are politics in your neck of the woods? You still insulated?"

"For now."

I gave my friend a quick look, just enough for a mental snapshot of his face. He was more worn than I remembered: more gray in his hair and had deeper creases around his eyes. That was one of the innocuous costs of what he did. I took some comfort in knowing Ibrahim had a cadre of very loyal, very dangerous friends who helped him remain safe. I had met some of them. Back when his family lived here, a jihadi leader tried to recruit his younger son. The leader was soon found in Ramallah. And in Gaza City. And in Jenin. And in Tulkarm.

But loyalties change. And there were so many factions. Hezbollah, Hamas, all the splinter groups, and Iran the puppet master, bolder than ever, with an endless supply of money and fanaticism.

I looked at my friend and worried for him.

* * *

Gil and I had just gotten back into Jerusalem and were a block from my hotel when Amit called: "Come to Ophir." He named a base north of Jerusalem. "And come in *madim*." Uniform.

No point asking why.

"And bring Special Agent Jeffries with you, of course."

I hung up and smiled at Gil. She leaned forward a millimeter, "What?"

"You've been called up."

She looked at me as I paused at a stoplight.

"Bring your uniform?"

* * *

After clearing the gate at the Ophir army base, we drove for about thirty seconds over a dusty, barely paved road to a two-story, unmarked rectangular building. Half a minute from the front gate to here – not the scale of bases Americans were used to. This base, like many in Israel, was compact, and an unknowing driver could ride past it without realizing what was here. The high chain link fence was a giveaway though, as were the jeeps and the Zev armored personnel carriers lined up within sight of the road. We parked opposite the desert-colored, boxy structure and walked into the main entrance.

I had been here a few years ago, and not much had changed. Open but partitioned work areas were still to the right and left, with the more private rooms fanning off on the right. We turned toward them. After about twenty feet, narrow corridors intersected, creating a maze feeling. File cabinets now filled the halls, making the narrow passageways even more tight. Since my last visit, the harsh LED lighting had survived, but there was now at least some air movement, which was an improvement. As had been the case several years ago, a radio DJ's voice drifted out from one of the rooms, introducing a song that had started playing in the U.S. six months ago.

Both men and women soldiers passed us usually making eye contact, and I reflected that their faces were so young; most were just out of high school on their mandatory service. I laughed to myself. Must be getting old.

We made a left at a junction and passed a few rooms that were basically empty, except for occupied cots. On each, a young soldier had collapsed face down, dead to the world. All the sleeping soldiers had their boots on.

"Gidon…Special Agent Jeffries," Amit was leaning against a wall outside a nearby, unmarked room, smoking. I had never seen him smoke. He took another drag and showed us into a briefing room.

The conference room turned out to be a small, windowless space with chairs parked around an oversized table. Two soldiers – one my age, one younger – were standing, looking at photos and other papers, while another young soldier, sat at the table engaged in her laptop.

Amit introduced us: "Special Agent Gil Jeffries of the FBI, and Gidon." No other verbal identifier for me. Save for my rank insignia, my uniform was pretty stripped down. The group, no doubt, had already been told who we were.

Amit introduced the soldiers: the men standing and looking over photos were Nir and Alon. Nir was my age, slightly taller than me, solid, with three bars on each shoulder, a company commander. He had blond, buzz-cut hair, and a forehead free of any lines, but he was probably older than he looked. The commander stood with one foot up on a chair and leaned over his thigh as he looked at the pictures in front of him.

His associate was Alon, who was my height, but lanky. He was swarthy, had dark hair, and a three-day beard and was likely Sephardi. Alon also wore a small, crocheted *kippa*. When the soldier shook my hand, I could see the tendons moving in his forearm. Both men carried pistols worn in holsters on the inside of their waistbands, as did I.

The young soldier at the laptop stood up at the introductions. She held out her hand, "Ayelet." She came up to my shoulders, had long, light brown frizzy hair barely contained by a scrunchie. Ayelet had striking blue eyes and what looked like a wry smile, as if she knew some secret about you.

So, Nir, Alon, and Ayelet. The men, I knew, were Duvdevan, soldiers in an elite counter-terrorist unit operating in Judea and Samaria, typically within tight, civilian areas. Sometimes, they'd disguise themselves as locals to blend in with the Arab population to gather intelligence and to prevent terrorist activities. Duvdevan also make arrests of known or suspected terrorists. Ayelet was in Combat Intelligence, intelligence gathered on-site, visually.

"So," I turned to Amit, "*ma matzav?*" What's the situation?

Amit looked at Ayelet, who pulled up a video on her laptop, and sent it to a wall-mounted monitor.

"Courtesy of our friends in London," the Shabak man said.

The clip showed passengers at an airport coming off a boarding ramp. The angle was high, probably from the ceiling. Time code ran in an upper corner along with a camera number.

"Heathrow," Amit clarified. "An Emirates gate."

We watched as men, some in thobes, some in business suits, and some in shirtsleeves, exited the ramp into the waiting area. Women didn't seem part of this group, at least not yet. A queue of passengers stood to the side, waiting to board.

The stream of men continued for fifteen more seconds, and then Ayalet froze the image on a short man in a light-colored dishdasha. "Rayyan al-Omari," she announced.

Aminah's mysterious uncle. Gifter of laptops. Amit must have taken the picture Aminah had sent me and had forwarded it to his contacts at the UK's Security Service. They did the rest.

"This was taken two days ago," Ayelet continued.

"And then al-Omari disappeared," Amit picked up. "Nothing. No sighting, no footprint. London is still looking for him. We all have many questions to ask him." He looked from me to Gil. "On the other hand, we've had more success with Aminah's parents. Our men interviewed them and found out who the uncle works for." He skipped the part about how his men – or more likely Idan Gelvar's Mossad men – located them or where the parents were staying. Amit put his cigarette out in a nearby ashtray. "Marwan al-Rashid, a royal cousin. He's a business man. We're looking into what sort of business."

Ayelet pulled up a stock photo of the man, enlarged from what

The Student

looked like an extended family shot. He was in traditional garb, taller than the men to either side, had a rectangular face beneath his red and white keffiyeh, and had posed with a broad smile. His teeth seemed very white, contrasted with a dark, neatly trimmed beard.

Gil spoke up for the first time since walking in. "Aminah's uncle took something that either belongs to al-Rashid, or has something he doesn't want coming out."

"Yes, I agree." Amit said.

"You haven't heard anything more from the lab on the laptops?" I asked her.

She shook her head.

Amit looked at her seriously, but his tone was matter-of-fact. "Do you think they're not talking to you?"

"No. I have an in." She looked at me. She had told me about her superior, a friend, who had approved and supported this trip.

I looked at the two Duvdevan soldiers. "So, what's going on that you guys are here?" And why was I in uniform? We could have been in Amit's office for the airport video, not on an army base. This had the feel of a pre-op briefing. My gaze ended on Amit.

Amit nodded to Ayelet, who continued to play the image on her laptop. More passengers disembarked. About fifteen passengers later, Ayelet froze the image, and zoomed in on a man in a dark shirt and dark pants. He had his right hand over his face, like he was scratching his forehead. He knew a camera was on him.

"*That* always makes me curious," Amit said. "Our MI5 and MI6 friends, too."

He nodded to Ayelet again, and I watched her eyes became more intense as she looked at the laptop while her fingers tapped on the keys. The image shifted to another view of the man in the dark pants and shirt.

"Their cameras are everywhere," the Shin Bet man said. "You'd have to walk around with a bag over your head 24 hours a day not to be recorded."

Ayelet zoomed in on the new image. The man in black had dark hair and a strong, angular jaw line, barely hidden by the ubiquitous five o'clock shadow. In the enhanced, zoomed-in image, there was some scarring over the man's left eye.

Nir, the solid, taller than me Duvdevan commander spoke. "We know him. He's Riad Kawasme. Lives in Qaltuniya, not far from here. He planned the killing of a number of Israelis along Highway 443 a month ago. He provided the guns and logistical information so one of his recruits could throw rocks at a car while another shot whoever was inside when they swerved to a stop. They killed a family of five."

"The fact that he was on the same Emirates flight from Riyad as al-Omari is an interesting coincidence." Amit continued.

"Following the uncle?" Gil asked.

"And al-Omari has disappeared in London," I looked at Amit. "Be nice to know what Kawasme knows."

Ayelet looked up at us. "This video is two days old. He's back here now, in Qaltuniya."

Alon, the lanky Duvdevan soldier, spoke up. "We're arresting him tonight." He paused for a moment to look from his commander to me. "And we've been asked to invite you along."

31

The general briefing for Alon's Duvdevan team was about to start in an assembly room. Nir and Alon were in front; Amit, Gil, and I were standing in the back. The room was filled with soldiers in olive uniforms sitting in folding chairs. The noise level was fairly high, but it was just the men talking among themselves.

At some point as we stood behind the last row of elite soldiers, I turned to the Shabak man. "You told the commander to invite me?"

"They lost a man last week in an ambush. The target they were after pushed a granite slab out a third-floor window and it smashed onto the soldier's head below. Horrible." He paused. "So I don't want anything happening to Kawasme, because someone is angry."

"They'll be professional, despite that, but no team wants an outsider joining them at the last minute. It's not good. Throws them off."

"I want you there. They know who you are. That will keep them in check, if there's a problem."

"They'll be pissed."

"They'll respect you."

I let it go. There was no choice.

Nir, the solid, tall company commander brought the group to order and began.

"The unit is going out tonight to arrest the man responsible for the murder of the Bregman family last month on Highway 443. He's Riad Kawasme." Kawasme's photo from Heathrow was pulled up on a large screen. "He lives in Qaltuniya. Combat Intelligence has identified his house and we have intel that he will be home tonight. But it's not going to be a simple arrest. It'll be loaded."

Gil, who was standing a few feet away, came over. I leaned in closer to her: "The terrorist has weapons."

The tall company commander continued: "Because we want to keep our presence small so we can get in and out before the entire village knows we're there, I'm reducing the unit size to 15."

There was mumbling among the men at either the reduction of firepower or the fact that some might not be going. More likely the latter.

"In a minute Alon will read the names of the men suiting up, but first..." Nir nodded to Alon, the platoon leader.

The lanky officer who was more fit than he appeared, locked eyes with me. "In the back of the room we have a guest who will be joining us…"

Everyone swiveled to look at me.

"Gidon from Matkal."

I watched the group scrutinize me.

"The Sensei," someone a few rows up called out.

"Yo, Sensei," came another, deeper voice.

"He's here to see a real night op!" someone else shouted.

There was laughter.

Gil said to me, "You have a rep…"

I nodded, then shouted back, "You need the help. A night op for you guys is trying to find your *zubb* in the dark!"

There was even more laughter. I had used Arabic slang for penis.

Details of the night op followed. Alon read the names of the soldiers who would be on the mission. The others were dismissed, and then Nir and Alon continued with the briefing. There were photos of the target's location, a threat assessment, what support we'd have, and many other specifics, such as sniper positions, which team members would take which positions around Kawasme's house, and more.

When the briefing was done, I left Gil in Amit's care, scrounged up equipment, and then went to meet the various team members. We talked additional logistics, we got to know each other – at least beyond just a name and a face – and then I hit the range for both my HK handgun and the M4 I had picked up. There was food, more time to relax, and for me, a walk through the base to be with my own thoughts. In the cool night air, and with the stars looking down, I just stared out at the horizon. I saw Aminah, Noa, and Jon sitting in Jon's apartment. I also replayed the argument I had with Katie in her office, and Gil's kindness in stopping by with beer the evening after my escapade on Charles Street, where I was almost killed.

In my perambulating, I came up to the dark corner of a building. A pair of voices, a man's and a woman's, drifted from around the building's edge. I shuffled my feet so whoever it was wouldn't be surprised to see me. As I passed the corner, I glanced over and smiled at them – an attractive, young *chayelet* with long dark hair and a skinny young man whose body seemed lost in his ill-fitting uniform. The young soldier seemed like a high-school kid by comparison, though he wasn't much older. They were just leaning against the wall of the building, talking. The woman soldier said something about not getting the weekend leave she was hoping for. I continued on.

I mentally reran the briefing from a few hours ago, detailing how the unit would approach Riad Kawasme's home in Qaltuniya. This Duvdevan unit, Nir and Alon's, was the best in the IDF, according to the men under them. I expected no other sentiment from these soldiers. And if anyone had an issue with me being there, they didn't show it. For my part, I wanted to be an asset, and simply not in anyone's way during the operation. I had been on dozens of similar ops, some even with other Duvdevan units. The trick was to be out of the way and part of the team at the same time.

At 0130 the unit began to suit up. I had been given a cubby in the soldiers' quarters to stow the gear I had picked up. I didn't want to think about whose stuff I had or whose cubby I was using. Could

The Student

have been the fellow soldier the unit had just lost. I put a leg up on an unknown soldier's bed corner, retied my boot laces to be certain they were tight and secure, adjusted my knee pads, and checked my vest. I made sure all my M4 magazines were loaded, and then grabbed my radio, headset, and night vision goggles. Finally, I looked in the mirror and peered into my own eyes for a long moment. They were clear and steady. The face around them, though, seemed more creased that I had remembered. They were good creases – experience lines, a friend had once called them. I walked out of someone else's room with a helmet in one hand and vest in the other.

The team assembled near the vehicles for the night: two Zev armored personnel carriers and a SWAT-type vehicle. As we waited I looked up at the post-midnight sky. A few clouds drifted across a crescent moon, and except for the sound of shuffling feet on gravel, there were no other sounds. The base was quiet and the men kept their thoughts to themselves.

I looked at the soldiers. There were 12 besides me. They were tall, short, thin, solid. And their faces were fair-skinned, dark, ruddy; most of the men had beards of some sort. Better for undercover work. There was a *jinji*, a redhead, in the group, with freckles across his nose; that would be tough to go unnoticed in Palestinian towns.

Gil and Amit wandered over as we waited. The FBI agent was now wearing a black Duvdevan sweatshirt. She had made friends with someone. She looked good.

Gil stood next to me but took in the cluster of men. "They all look so young."

"My thoughts, too."

"You're the old man."

I smiled. "I am."

An IDF jeep pulled up next to us, and Alon, the platoon commander, stepped out along with a soldier who had almost white-blond hair, blond eyebrows, and a pale complexion. His eyes were a translucent blue. He was Alon's second-in-command. The group assembled as the jeep pulled away.

"*Chevreh,*" Alon began. "This is an important one tonight. I don't have to remind you that the man we want is responsible for the murder of a young father and mother and their three children: two girls and a boy. The oldest was eleven, the youngest two. And I know we all still feel the loss of Rami, but I expect all of you to do your jobs without emotion, just as you have been trained to do." He paused and looked at his men, including me. "Keep your eyes open."

And with that, Alon, his pale-skinned "second," the medic, and the driver went into the olive-colored SWAT vehicle, parked in the lead. The rest of us separated into two groups, one for each APC.

"Gidon," a squat, solid soldier next to the lead Zev called me over. "Sensei, join us." He held the armored side door for me. I was about to climb in when he said, "I was told you can see behind you, even though you're looking forward."

I looked around as if I couldn't see. "Who said that?"

The young soldier smiled, but he was serious.

I looked into his young eyes. His name was Raz, but his buddies called him Tzav, turtle, probably because of his build.

I smiled at the comment and gave a truthful answer. "It doesn't work all the time, at least not for me. Not something you can rely on." I let a moment go by. "And that's why we're a team where we watch each other's back, right?"

Raz nodded.

The truthful response about my limitations was sobering. I looked over at Gil, took a second to myself, and then climbed into the vehicle.

* * *

The ride to Qaltuniya was quiet. There was no chatter among the soldiers. The vibe in the vehicle, if anything, was tense. Everyone was in his own head, no doubt reviewing scenarios and visualizing the Palestinian town and the target building. Thanks to Combat

The Student

Intelligence and drones, we knew the streets and the buildings. We were already familiar with the twists and turns of the narrow roads. We could picture our unit moving through the village under the night sky. But what we didn't know was whether eyes would be looking down on us from darkened windows. The stillness of those streets belied that a segment of the population was eager and ready to engage us at a moment's notice.

I closed my eyes.

The murder of a young family couldn't go unanswered. Everyone in the APC felt the importance of arresting the man responsible, despite the dangers. And for me, that man may also know why Iranian agents had targeted two young co-eds halfway around the world.

I looked around the Zev. Young, well-trained men about to step into harm's way.

They sat in forward-facing, high-backed, cushioned seats. A center aisle divided left and right sides. With six of us in the vehicle, we only took up half the seating. There was plenty of room for everyone's gear, though each soldier held onto his assault weapon.

My mind drifted to the individuals in the three vehicle procession. There were native Israelis here, of course, but I knew there were also soldiers who had emigrated from Middle Eastern countries, as well as from the U.S., the U.K., and Eastern Europe as well. Israel as a melting pot, reflected in her soldiers.

Thirty minutes after we had left base, word came that we were two minutes out. Balaclavas went on, energy came up. Gear was gathered and weapons were checked. One soldier turned on his helmet-mounted camera. No one spoke.

The Zev APC came to a stop. We exited silently through the side doors. No one used the door in the rear. Its opening was too tight; heads would get dinged.

The team from the SWAT vehicle and the Zevs immediately fell in line and moved toward the village. Qaltuniya was built on a hill and we approached from a ring road. Alon took point, along with a tall, solid man I knew to be from the Ukraine. Our two snipers peeled off to take overwatch positions.

There was no fence, no wall. We just walked right into the still village. All the housing in the community was stacked as it had been in the village where I had met Ibrahim, and our column made its way along narrow streets in from the edge of town. At first, apartment buildings appeared only on the right, but then, shortly, on both sides. Our team of 15 spread out in pairs, except for the last group that had three men, one right behind the other. No one was ever alone. I was in the center with the young soldier who had white-blond hair and eyes of translucent blue. Raz, the squat soldier who had called me Sensei and had asked about my abilities of perception, was behind me.

Street lights dumped circles of luminescence on the ground, but we moved around them, keeping to the shadows. We passed a two-pump gas station that had a light over the office door. Alon took us to the other side of the street.

Moving down the road, we scanned from side to side, as well as up. There were plenty of darkened windows in every building on every floor. Innocent civilians, families, lived here. But there were others, too. Friends of Riad Kawasme, the man we were going to arrest, could be watching, knowing that the IDF would be coming at some point. If we were spotted, word would be broadcast rapidly. And then we'd be the focal point of a crossfire.

A bead of sweat ran down the center of my back.

In our earpieces, Alon ordered a stop. We moved against a concrete wall. Soldiers went into a covering formation of five-man clusters: down on one knee, each man was dedicated to a direction: forward, to the sides, rear, and up. The men were well practiced and experienced. Duvdevan had a reputation for being hard and determined.

I looked at the man taking point. Alon was getting orders in his earpiece from on-site Intelligence. The soldiers around me were unmoving, except for their heads, turning, watching. I locked eyes with the blond soldier not far from my side. We both shrugged

The Student

simultaneously.

In the wash of light from the streetlamps, the buildings around us stood silent. No one was watching that we could tell. The street held no motion. No one was walking, no late-night adolescents coming back from a friend's, no vehicles cruising down the street. It was just empty, with only parked cars along the narrow, barely paved road. But there was more here: the streets, apartment buildings, and stores held many occupants, potentially waiting to grab weapons.

A pair of gray cats, one just behind the other, ran beside us, and then veered off to a trash pile beside a lamppost.

After a long thirty seconds of crouching in the shadows, Alon gave us the go ahead to move forward.

The unit fell back into formation. We cleared the wall next to us and came to a wide patch of sidewalk and a hardware shop set back from the curb. Riad Kawasme's apartment building was in the next block on the other side of a small intersection 100 feet away. It didn't go unnoticed that he lived not far from the edge of town. Easy access for him, in and out.

"Stop," Alon ordered in our earpieces. "Wait further instructions."

We had barely started forward again, but now had to hold motionless in the shadows. Alon, I guessed, was awaiting confirmation that Kawasme was in a particular room. Intelligence must have had someone on the inside. Either that or we were being set up by an informant for an ambush.

I was down on one knee, and while looking forward, consciously relaxed my focus to get a sense of what was around me. Except for the presence of the soldiers, all was quiet. A slight eddy blew across the skin around my eyes, the only area not covered by the balaclava.

A soft voice came through my earpiece: "This is *zayin*." It was one of the snipers who had peeled away from the group. "*Kol b'seder.*" All was okay. He had the target building in his scope.

"This is *chet*." The second sniper. "*Kol b'seder.*"

Alon ordered us forward again.

We passed another cube of apartments and came to a cross street. Kawasme's building was the first on the next block. As we moved down the narrow road, it sloped off toward Kawasme's home. Ground level for the structure was below grade.

Without hesitation, the team took its predetermined positions. Alon and the blond-haired soldier near me went to the front door. I went with Raz, the squat soldier with young eyes, as well as some others to the rear entrance.

In a moment, Alon called for a position check. Various voices came through my earpiece, each saying a number and the words "In position." I was *tet*, nine.

Once everyone checked in, a moment passed. Alon and his blond second-in-command would enter through the front, while simultaneously my group would breach the rear. Other soldiers would hold positions near the windows.

Alon came on the radio again. "I'm going in."

Our teams worked parallel but on opposite sides of the house. A soldier next to me stepped forward and placed a small, rectangular device in the center of the door. Alon's men, I knew, were doing the same thing.

There was a muffled blast and we swarmed through the splintered portal. The blast would certainly have been heard by inhabitants and by neighbors. On borrowed time now, I swung to the right, other soldiers moved left. We passed through a darkened kitchen. No one was there. We moved forward.

The target was either hiding or getting ready to make a stand. He may even try to get past us, somehow.

A center hallway ran through the middle of the house. We were at one end. Straight ahead of us and twenty feet away, Alon and his second-in-command stood just inside the front doorway. Another soldier stepped in from my group and turned on a table lamp. Standard procedure. If there were innocents here, our balaclavas and the weapons in the middle of the night would bring enough fear. This was an arrest, not an assassination.

In front of Alon, to my left, a staircase rose to the second floor. Between the staircase and my position an open door led to a side room. We hadn't cleared it yet, and I could tell someone was inside. I didn't hear anything and didn't see anyone, but I knew. There was something tangible, something about the air being displaced. And whoever was in there was moving.

"In the side room," I called out, raising my M4.

As soon as I had said it, a man in a black T-shirt and loose-fitting camouflage pants emerged. He was clean-shaven but had a mop of dark hair. The man was barefoot. His hands were up like he was surrendering, but in his right hand was a semiautomatic. "Don't shoot!" he pleaded. "I'm armed."

That made no sense.

None of the Duvdevan soldiers relaxed. Alon needed to get to the target. He motioned he was going upstairs, knowing the man with mop head of hair was covered. As my eyes had shifted ever-so-slightly toward our team leader, the man in the doorway took advantage and began pointing his weapon at me.

I shot him in the knee. He collapsed to the floor.

"It's a distraction," I said. "*Lech!*" Go, I yelled to Alon, and he bounded up the stairs with the blond-haired soldier and two others behind.

The medic came forward while my team cleared the room the man had just exited. Two mattresses were on the floor, but no one else was there. When I came back into the hallway, Raz, the soldier who had wanted to know about my perceptual senses, looked at me.

"You knew he was there before he came out."

I nodded slightly, then looked down at the man who had tried to shoot me. He was supine and going pale. The medic began to wrap his shattered knee, while another soldier kept his weapon on the man.

Before anyone could say anything, a voice crackled through my earpiece: "The target is outside. The target is outside. Left side of the house."

With Raz close behind, I sprinted for the back door. As we emerged, I knew the gunshot from my M4 must have been heard beyond the house. If not, the breaching device definitely was heard. We couldn't loiter.

Riad Kawasme had managed to get out a window before Alon and his men made it to him. The terrorist must've climbed out an upper story window.

Was he long gone? Were our soldiers giving chase? We needed Kawasme. Amit needed him. The FBI needed him. And I wanted to put a gun to his head after he gave us what he knew.

As I rounded the corner to the left side of the apartment building, I came to a stop. Our target, the logistician for the highway murders, was facing the concrete wall of the dwelling in the wash of an outdoor flood. His hands were behind him and were zip-tied by a soldier. Alon was already beside him having followed Kawasme out his second-floor window.

Alon turned to me. "He took Option 3." Trying to escape.

"And into our arms," the soldier who had zip-tied his hands added.

Another soldier stepped forward and put a blindfold over Kawasme's eyes.

Several dogs began barking in the distance.

"Time to go," I said.

Raz, next to me, said, "The kids in the village have a WhatsApp group. It's like an activity. 'Kill the soldiers.' They'll be taking up positions."

One of the burlier soldiers draped Kawasme over his shoulders in a fireman's carry. We moved around front. The team from inside was waiting near the stoop. The mop-haired man who had tried to shoot me was already draped over another soldier. The injured gunman was sweating and had trouble focusing. Alon went over to him and shoved a wad of cloth into his mouth. "If you want to live, you'll bite down on this."

There was no response.

Alon picked up the man's chin. "Understand?"

He met Alon's eyes and nodded slightly.

Down the street, lights had come on in various windows.

Another moment passed and there was loud whistling, the kind you get from putting two fingers in your mouth. There was one piercing whistle after another.

"Shit," someone said in my earpiece.

More lights had come on, and down the block men started coming into the street.

In another second the acrid smell of burning tires filled the air.

"*Zayin* and *Chet*," Alon's voice was in my ear, was in everyone's ear, calling the snipers. "Cover our exfil."

"Changing ammo," was the response. They were switching to rubber bullets.

The neighborhood was now fully awake. We looked down the street and saw a mob coalesce. Even from where we stood you could tell the rioters were 14 or 15 years old at most.

We formed up on Alon and headed out, but not the way we had come. We were still in pairs, but now one man looked forward, while his partner covered his back. The mob was 100 feet behind us.

The unit took a turn down a brightly lit side street. We would loop back to our APCs.

We passed an alleyway that had stacked crates at the entrance. On top of them were Molotov cocktails waiting to be lit. The bottles had been prepositioned in the event the IDF would do just what we were doing.

My eyes began to sting from heavy black tire smoke in the air.

Shouts in Arabic got closer.

Raz was covering my rear, and I had to trust him and not look back to see how close the rioters were. *Move forward, Gidon. Look back and you'll be Lot's wife, killed where you stand.*

The soldier carrying Kawasme moved to the front of our column and shifted his cargo, making Kawasme's face more visible. The message to the kids in the village was clear. Shoot us, kill your man.

There was a crash next to us as a Molotov cocktail hit the ground. There was a pair of young high school-age kids heaving the flaming bottles.

Where were our snipers?

There was another bottle crash next to our column, inches from the feet of the blond soldier, Alon's second-in-command. He was sprayed by flaming gasoline across a leg, arm, and side.

As he dropped to the ground rolling, the soldiers next to him fired automatically toward the two young men who had thrown the crude incendiary devices. They purposefully missed, and the young men scattered. Command's rules of engagement stated that these boys, now empty-handed, were no longer active threats. No deadly force was allowed, unless there was a weapon in the attackers' hands.

The blond soldier was back on his feet. We couldn't tell if he'd been burned – his uniform was smoking but there were no flames. We had to keep moving.

The team hit another intersection. Off to the side was a second Molotov cocktail station.

"On the right!" I called.

Alon's voice yelled in my ear, "*Negev!*" The word typically referred to the southern region of Israel, but not in this case. A light machine gun let loose behind me on the setup, and a group of five kids broke off, running in opposite directions.

We continued another half-block and then, from the space between two buildings, a kid with a round face emerged, a lit bottle in his hands. He stopped, and looked directly at me, across the rubble-strewn street. He couldn't have been more than 15.

Don't do it. How'd he think this was going to end?

The kid rotated his torso, pulling back his arm to launch the Molotov. My M4 came up.

He's just a boy. A boy with a flaming weapon.

The Student

Head shot?...Center mass?...Shoulder?
He's someone's son. Someone's son trying to kill me.
I shot him once in the lower gut, just off center to miss his spine.

The supersonic round went through him, and the kid collapsed to the ground. He'd live if he got to a hospital soon. He'd live and hate me.

Another boy appeared from the space between the two buildings and pulled his friend away.

We continued forward, Alon still at point. We passed two more apartment buildings, cut across a narrow street near an open field, and onto the ring road. I didn't know what was going through Alon's mind, but as we headed out of the village, I had to wonder why we hadn't been better covered by the snipers.

Two support vehicles pulled next to our APCs just as we came up on them. The new group of soldiers took covering positions.

The injured mop-haired man, the one I had shot in the knee, went into the SWAT vehicle with Alon and the medic. Kawasme, still blindfolded and zip-tied, was dumped in the aisle of my Zev, between left and right rows of seats. Doors were pulled shut and we drove away from the village.

For a long moment, no one spoke. We were all safe. No casualties, except maybe some burns on the blond soldier, but he seemed okay. And we had Riad Kawasme, the man who planned the death of Israelis who were simply driving down a highway; in this case, a young family of five. He may also have been responsible for the disappearance of Aminah's uncle in London.

I removed my helmet and pulled off my balaclava. My hair was matted down with sweat.

As I looked around the Zev, the other soldiers had removed their headgear as well. Some of the men were leaning back in their seats. There was still a lot of adrenalin, but relief was evident on each face.

I looked across the aisle to see Raz watching me. We nodded to each other, then we both leaned back. The armored vehicle's diesel engine was quiet, and there was a slight sway as we drove around a curve, but that could have been just the driver. The Zev went over a series of bumps.

I visually reran the mission, remembering every detail… moving through the village, the buildings to either side, avoiding the pools of light… entering Kawasme's house, shooting the man in the knee as he lowered his gun toward me…the exfil…and looking the boy in the eye as he paused to throw his Molotov cocktail. In the replay, the boy's eyes reflected the flame of the lit rag. I also felt the kick of the M4 and saw the kid fall.

A low, smooth voice near me said, "It's Friday night." Shabbat for some, for many.

I had no idea or hadn't thought about it, being lost in the mission. I wondered if Alon our team leader realized it. He was religious.

A moment passed and I closed my eyes.

Thank You for bringing us home safely.

* * *

When we pulled into base, darkness still covered everything, the predawn light several long hours away. As earlier, the white and orange floodlights bathed the parking lot in sepia. The moment we exited the vehicles, army doctors hovered over the wounded man and the blond soldier. The former was now unconscious and being positioned on a stretcher. Kawasme was handed over to two husky soldiers who escorted him away, still blindfolded and bound.

Amit and Gil came over.

"How was it?" Amit asked.

"You heard. You saw." Some of the soldiers had worn cameras.

Amit nodded.

Gil was looking at me. She had probably seen me on someone's camera shoot the boy. Off to the side, loud voices erupted. One of the soldiers from the other Zev had gotten in the face of one of the

The Student

snipers. The soldier was yelling about them being out of position. There was some shoving and other team members stepped in.

"Come." Amit motioned for us to step away. Gil and I walked with him back along the row of buildings.

"So, you'll let me know what Kawasme has to say about Aminah's uncle, if he knows anything," I said. "That was the point of all this – at least for us."

Amit stopped walking and turned to me. "I have some news." Gil was next to him and quiet.

I looked from the Shin Bet man to Gil and back.

"We identified who Marwan al-Rashid is." The Royal Saudi Arabian cousin who Aminah's uncle worked for…the guy we believed the uncle had something on.

"Okay."

"He's Minister of Culture for the Kingdom. Supposed to be very forward thinking. But maybe not, if he's behind all this."

I looked at Gil. There was something more. He could have told me this later, after the mission debrief. "What else?"

"Aminah has left the country."

I stopped walking.

"Sometime this afternoon," Gil added.

"We had a man on her, as you suggested," Amit continued.

Raz and one of the other soldiers walked passed, our eyes met briefly, but I wasn't really looking at him.

The Shin Bet man went on: "She came out of her house in Haifa with a backpack, got into a friend's car, and rode to the airport." He paused. "There was no order to stop her."

I didn't know what to say. Aminah had become the focus of all this. It was her laptop that the Iranians were interested in…the one given to her by her Saudi uncle. Noa was just her friend, and they had to cover their bases. It was Aminah the Quds Force agent had looked at on Charles Street. And it was Aminah whose uncle had suddenly called her parents to leave Israel for reasons unknown.

Gil was looking at me to see how I'd react.

"Where'd she go?" I asked Amit calmly.

"She flew to Athens, and then boarded a Qatar Airways flight to Amman." A moment went by. "She's in Jordan."

I looked at Gil, whose eyes held mine, but said nothing. I turned back to Amit. "Tell me what you know."

A second went by.

"Not much. She received a call from her mother who was still in London. She said for Aminah to meet them at the Kempinski Hotel in Amman, and not to ask her questions. They already had a room booked there. She reassured Aminah that everything was okay." Meaning it wasn't.

Amit had known about this before the mission. We'd talk about that later. "What else?"

A military ambulance went by, no doubt with the unconscious mop-haired man.

"Idan had his men watch for her at Arrivals."

"Do you know where she is?"

"The team followed her taxi out of the airport but lost her in downtown traffic."

I didn't like where this was going. "Idan had a team waiting at the Kempinski, right?"

"They did." He looked in the distance over my shoulder then back at me. "She never arrived."

There was silence between the three of us.

Finally, Gil said, "There's more."

I looked at the Shin Bet man and tried to keep my slow boil suppressed.

"The Royal cousin, al-Rashid, left Riyad," Amit let out a breath. "He's in Amman, too."

32

Gil sat across from me and didn't say anything. Thirty long hours had passed since the conversation with Amit, and we were sitting in a quiet nook in the Dan VIP Lounge at Ben Gurion airport. In less than an hour I'd board a flight to Athens and connect to a Qatar Airways flight to Amman, the same route Aminah had taken two days ago. Once in the Jordanian capital, I'd settle in, find Aminah, and get her the hell out…provided I could locate her, provided I wasn't arrested for being a spy, provided Marwan al-Rashid, the uncle's Royal boss, didn't get a hold of me first for interfering in whatever he was trying to achieve.

I looked over at Gil who was just staring at me. She thought my rescue plan was a bad idea, conceived to assuage my guilt about not seeing all this sooner and for not protecting Aminah better. She thought it was unrealistic, incredibly risky, and I'd get myself killed.

I wasn't so sure she was wrong. There'd be no contact with Idan's Mossad men; I'd be on my own. I didn't know the language that well, though I had a rudimentary knowledge of Arabic and some choice Arabic curses. I did know my way around Amman, thanks to some forays with Sayeret Matkal, but, again, I wouldn't have the benefit of a team or backup. And number one on the Hit Parade was that possibility of being arrested as a spy since I was now working alongside the FBI as well as Shabak. There was even the fact I was officially still in the IDF. While Jordan technically had a peace treaty with Israel, and intel did go back and forth, it was still a hostile country with

The Student

radicalized elements throughout its society. As soon as I showed my passport at passport control, I could be flagged.

Maybe this wasn't such a good idea.

Gil and I sat opposite each other in upholstered chairs, with floor-to-ceiling windows on one side providing a clear view of the tarmac and runways. To the other side, chairs were positioned around small, round tables, as well as simply at right angles to each other. Not far from where we sat, a small buffet of croissants, cereals, and coffee had been laid out. French toast and scrambled eggs were in their own chafing dishes next to them. Neither Gil nor I felt like eating, but I had a small bottle of water within reach. I hadn't opened it.

The priority lounge was relatively quiet for midmorning. Maybe fifteen travelers were there at most, and the majority of them, men and women, were dressed in button-down shirts or blouses, and pants or skirts. No kids, no one dressed in shorts or T-shirts. This was a business group.

Gil lowered her eyes for a moment, and then stared out at a Lufthansa Airbus taxing across our field of view. She had voiced her opinion only once when we discussed it in Amit's conference room, and then basically hadn't said anything since.

Amit thought this was a bad idea as well.

* * *

"Don't go. Not yet." We were in the same Shin Bet conference room in the Jerusalem annex where we had met Amit three days ago. The Shabak man was speaking. "Wait until Idan's men have done their surveillance in Amman. Or in London. They'll watch Aminah's parents and try to find the uncle. He'll give us al-Rashid who will lead us to Aminah."

"He's not going to wait." Gil said to Amit but looked into my eyes.

"She's my responsibility..."

The three of us had traveled back to Jerusalem from the army base, leaving the interrogation of the men we had picked up to Amit's people.

"You're not one of Idan's men," the Shin Bet officer reasoned.

That was ironic, as that was exactly what the FBI accused me of... being an agent for Mossad.

"You're not trained like them. You're a natural investigator, but you don't know their tradecraft."

"I know Amman. I've been there. More than once."

"Let the men investigate, narrow where to look, then go in."

"al-Rashid's already there. There isn't time."

"What are you going to do?" Gil asked.

I looked over at the woman who had seemed to become my partner. I didn't like the frown that had become embedded in her forehead.

I turned to Amit. "You said a taxi picked her up at the airport."

He nodded.

And the Mossad team lost her in traffic. "Get me the name of the taxi company that picked her up. And Aminah's parents' names. I'll go from there."

A moment went by in silence. The room was like a dead zone.

"Look," I turned from Amit to Gil and back, "worse case, I'll be in place when we have something to go on."

"That's not the worse case."

"So if I get caught, Idan's men will have to get me out. Or call my old unit."

A moment went by and Amit shook his head ever so slightly, "I don't think you should go." Then his voice lowered; there could have been a slight sigh with it. "How are you planning to go in?"

"Not crossing the border in the middle of the night. And not with an Israeli passport." I looked down at the desk where photos of Aminah, her uncle, and the Royal cousin were spread out. "I'll fly to Athens and switch planes. I'll enter the country on my U.S. passport."

Amit was shaking his head again.

"I'll just be a guy looking for a missing student. And I don't want to know anything about the Mossad agents in Amman. No names, no

The Student

photos, no contact info." I paused for a moment and had to smile. "In case I'm asked."

Gil looked at me. "This is a bad idea."

* * *

We went back to the hotel in the early evening. Prior to that, though, while still in the conference room, Amit and some of his men had given me a quick refresher on the layout of Amman – major streets, neighborhoods, political climate, and more. The last things we discussed were ways to get out of the capital city, and, as I preferred, without relying on Idan Gelvar's men or assets. I became familiar with the location of the American Embassy in Amman, in case, as an innocent American citizen, I needed their resources. If Aminah were in tow, she could always seek asylum.

Gil and I parted company outside the hotel, opposite the fountain in Paris Square, as we had before. She went off to her mysterious Airbnb basically without saying anything, and I went upstairs to my room.

I immediately turned on the air conditioning and opened the curtains a maid must have closed earlier. The evening view of the Old City was ethereal, with the darkening blue sky blending with the steadily blossoming city lights. The result was a radiant glow emanating from the ancient walls and buildings.

All I wanted to do was collapse onto the bed; there hadn't been much rest after the raid last night, along with the update from Amit and the follow-up discussions. Instead of heading into the shower, though, or just falling face down onto the covers, I took out my cell phone.

Katie. The call was overdue.

I didn't know how I felt about her, honestly, having tucked the relationship in a corner somewhere. If I didn't want to think about her, a voice intoned, that was telling me something.

There was no way of knowing when the next opportunity would be to speak to her, not with Jordan happening tomorrow. I owed her a call, if only to say hi; I didn't want to talk about the relationship or where we stood. In my head there was an echo of telling my men to write to loved ones prior to a big mission. Was that what this was? A just-in-case call?

I checked my watch – early afternoon in Baltimore – and dialed her cell.

As the number rang, my breathing became more shallow. The number rang two more times.

She should have been at school. Maybe she was in a class. Maybe she didn't recognize the number. Maybe she did.

Just say hi and simply talk to her.

Her voicemail message came on, and for a moment I felt robbed. The beep sounded.

"Hi, It's Gidon. Sorry for not responding sooner. Hope you're doing okay. Thinking about you." I didn't say what I was thinking, or not thinking. "Just wanted to hear your voice. I'll be out of touch for a little while, and wanted you to know that."

A few heartbeats went by.

"Also, about this summer when I stayed here longer than I said I would, that wasn't right. It was something we should've talked about. Anyway, I am sorry about that, and I wanted you to know."

A few more heartbeats.

"Anyway, that's it for now. I'll be in touch when I can. Bye."

I tapped the disconnect icon, and tossed the phone onto the bed, probably with a little more emotion than I expected.

A call to Jon was also in order, but instead, I went over to my backpack and pulled out the burner phone I had used to call Ibrahim the other day. After powering it on, a text popped up:

Person you're looking for is marwan al-rashid, a royal cousin. will get more information and contact you.

I should've told my friend we had uncovered that. May have saved him some time and favors. There was always a fear of putting Ibrahim in danger, though knowing him, it was other people who needed to be afraid. It amazed me how he came and went unscathed in the labyrinthian paths of that world.

I dialed Ibrahim's number. As it had a few days ago, the phone rang and went immediately to the voicemail beep.

"Hi. Thanks. Got your message. Just wanted you to know that I will be taking a side trip to Amman to see the student I had mentioned to you. She apparently has gone to the capital for unknown reasons. Anyway, I'll be in touch when I return." And may Allah continue to watch over you.

* * *

The Dan Lounge at Ben Gurion began to empty as boarding announcements for multiple flights came up on the monitor. Gil and I headed out.

We walked to the gate without saying much of anything. We had already gone over my strategy to find Aminah and even talked about how to get her out. Besides, we wouldn't casually go over operational details in public. As we walked past a smokers' cubicle off to the side, what she did mention was that the computer forensics team back in the States was re-examining the hardware from both Aminah's and Noa's laptops. Maybe they had missed something. It seemed like old news.

We came to my gate. An agent had started processing boarding passes, and passengers were filing past him, heading to the jetbridge. It was time to go.

Gil stepped in a little closer.

I was conscious of people moving past us.

The FBI woman looked directly at me. "I still think this is insane, but if anyone can bring Aminah back, it's you."

"Thanks."

I hoisted my backpack onto a shoulder and turned toward the gate.

"Hang on," she said.

Gil put her hand on my arm, leaned in and whispered, "Watch your back, Aronson," and then turned and left.

33

The drive northward from Queen Alia International Airport to Amman was mostly fluid, with fewer cars on the road than I'd have expected. It was midafternoon, and the sky was a solid ceiling of bright blue except for a few high altitude clouds toward the eastern horizon. To my left was a north-south line of mountains, just east of the Jordan River Valley and the Syrian-African Rift. There was a companion line of mountains on the western side of the valley in Israel.

My arrival at the airport and the subsequent processing at passport control had gone smoothly, with barely a look up from the expressionless middle-aged man examining my American passport. As he ploddingly scanned the document, there were a few moments of unease as I watched him stare at the screen. In front of him stood an American who had citizenship in Israel, was an officer in the IDF, worked with the FBI as well as the Shin Bet, and was probably also unofficially associated with the Mossad, courtesy of Noa's uncle, Idan.

Maybe the man seated in the booth in front of me wasn't as bored as he looked. Perhaps there were alerts he adroitly noted but didn't convey in his expression. When asked, I responded that I was here on pleasure and staying in Amman at the Kempinski Hotel. After a few moments of silence while he tapped on the keyboard, he finally looked up blank-faced, and said simply, "Enjoy your stay in Jordan."

Forty minutes later, despite the disinterest from passport control, I drove my Optima rental onto Abdoun keeping a lookout for possible

The Student

tails. I played the slow-down-speed up maneuver, and even pulled off the road into the parking lot of a nearby restaurant– I drove the Kia completely around the single-floor eatery to be certain no one was following me, and then continued the drive to Amman.

Twenty minutes later, I drove up to the entrance to the Kempinski, past a sky-blue Toyota Land Cruiser, and parked in a loading/unloading space. In a matter of minutes, I was standing in front of white marble counter, chatting with a smiling, dark-haired reception agent. Her name tag read Tala. Yes, she had my reservation, and yes, I would be staying for six nights. That was a guess on my part. Hopefully, it wouldn't be the better part of a week, but realistically there was no way of telling how long it would take to locate Aminah. Tala ran my credit card – David Amit's actually – and then handed me an envelope with a card-key. She mentioned a dedicated parking lot around the corner and also handed me a tag to put on dashboard in view of the windshield.

After another ten minutes – I had moved the car to the hotel lot – I opened the door to my fifth-floor room. The room was dark, so I slipped the card key into a small receptacle on the nearby wall, and the lights and air conditioning came on. Beyond the short alcove was a queen-sized bed nestled in a niche along the wall and made up with an immaculate cream-colored bedspread and white pillows. The headboard was dark walnut and ran across the length of the alcove. End tables were on each side of the bed, matching the headboard. Opposite the bed and across the gray carpet were a pair of white upholstered armchairs and a glass coffee table. I dropped my small suitcase onto the bed and my backpack onto one of the armchairs. Without even looking out through the curtains, I picked up the phone on the left-hand nightstand.

To find Aminah there were a few leads. Well, there was one: Aminah had taken a taxi from the airport, so there was the taxi service to check out. Before doing that, however, there was something obvious, something that shouldn't be overlooked.

"Reception." It could have been Tala, the receptionist who had checked me in.

"Hi. Can you connect me to Yamin Hadad's room, please."

"One moment."

Yamin was Aminah's father. When I had returned from the night raid, Amit reported that Aminah's mom had booked a room for her daughter here. Or so she said. We figured it was a ploy.

The receptionist came back on the line. "I'll ring it for you, Mr. Aronson, but you can dial it yourself. Dial two and then 623."

So they did have a room. Actually one flight up from me and down the hall. What were the chances Aminah was there?

In the receiver, there was pause, dead air, and then ringing. I looked about the room, at the paintings, at the bureau, at the flat screen television on the wall opposite the foot of the bed.

After the fifth ring, the call went to a standard hotel voicemail, and I hung up.

No surprise that Aminah wasn't here. I went over to my backpack and pulled out a sheet of paper on which I had written a list of Amman taxi companies, created with the help of one of Idan's researchers. The taxi service I needed was halfway down, with the ones above it already crossed out; crossed out, in fact, in Jerusalem. I also opened my small suitcase, dug toward the bottom, and pulled out my folding Benchmade knife, the three-and-a-half inch combo blade, half-serrated, half-straight edge. While the knife had a pocket clip, I didn't use it. Instead, I slipped the knife fully into my pocket. No one needed to see it. Finally, I looked around the room and left.

* * *

The Jewel of Jordan Taxi Service was about two kilometers away, on the other side of Queen Noor Street, around the corner from the JETT Central Bus Station. Except for the main streets, most of the roads were narrow and crowded with cars and small delivery vans, with drivers weaving around slower or double-parked vehicles. In a way, it wasn't much different than areas of Jerusalem, or Rome, or any Old World city.

The taxi office was along a narrow strip of a road, almost an alley that had the feel of an industrial zone, even though it was just off a main thoroughfare. On the left side of the street was a warehouse for plumbing supplies with angled parking slots in front. Opposite it and across the barely paved road was a supermarket with placards taped to a smudged picture window, then a mechanic's shop with oil patches staining the driveway, a bicycle store, and then the taxi office. The ribbon of a street was two-way, but it was impossible for cars to pass each other in opposite directions, without one giving way. Customers and workers walked in the street, and cars in the road spent more time on their brakes and horns than on the accelerator. In front of the bicycle shop, boys were test riding their bikes in between gridlocked vehicles.

The taxi office to the left of the bicycle shop was perhaps two car widths wide with a driveway blocked off by two metal trashcans. I drove up to the trashcans, threw the Kia into park, moved the cans, and pulled into the space I had opened. My front bumper came to a stop a few feet from a balding, middle-aged man sitting on an inverted crate in front of a raised garage door. He was essentially blocking any car wanting to pull in. The man was dressed in an open collar white shirt and tan slacks. He had watched without expression as I had moved the trashcans and pulled up, basically, to his shoes. I stepped out of the Optima, conscious of the Sixt car rental logo on the side near the back panel, and approached the man.

"Hi. Do you speak English?"

He looked me over. "Yes. Of course."

"Fine. Great."

He didn't get up. "What can I do for you?"

"I'm looking for the manager or the owner of the cab company." I nodded to a sign next to the open garage door that read *Juel of Jordan*

Taxi in English next to Arabic characters. I wasn't surprised at the phonetic spelling of "Jewel." Before the man asked, I offered, "I need help looking for someone who may have used your cab."

"The owner's inside."

The man stood up. He was my height and had broad shoulders, but his upper arms weren't as muscular as they once must have been. No doubt he was still pretty strong, though, if he had worked in this shop for a good number of years.

The man led me inside, past a taxi with its hood raised and a cluster of men peering at the engine. One of them was poking a water hose. They turned to me as we walked by. I smiled and nodded. Most nodded back. The man in the open-collared shirt walked me into an office that was more storage space than anything else.

Boxes were everywhere. Cartons had been stacked floor to ceiling so not even the walls behind them were visible. A battered Coke machine in a corner hummed loudly enough to be irritating after a few minutes. To the right of the door a desk sat beneath a partition window overlooking the inside of the garage. We could clearly see the men peering under the hood of the cab we had ambled past. The desk was remarkably clear of papers.

"The boss usually sits there," the man explained, pointing a rolling chair at the edge of the desk.

After a moment, he pulled out the chair and sat down.

"You're looking for someone who may have used one of my cabs?"

I smiled and nodded. "All I know is she came to Amman and told me that she was going to get a cab at the airport to take her to her hotel…but she never got there." For a second or two my eyes wandered over his workspace. There was a picture of the middle-aged man on a licensing form taped to the wall just above his desk.

"Who are you?"

"I'm her teacher from her school in the U.S. She's maybe 19 and I teach her at a university."

"You came all the way here to find her?"

The Student

I shrugged. "She disappeared, and I'm worried."

One of the men who had been poking around the cab engine in the entryway, came into the office and just watched us. He was tall, mustached, and wearing a blue T-shirt and jeans.

The owner, still seated, looked at me for a long moment with his dark eyes, and then his face broke into a grin. "Ah, I understand, she's your *student*." He looked over at the man who had just walked in and said something in Arabic. From what I could gather, he said I lost my sweet, young girlfriend, though he wasn't that polite in the description.

"No, really," I said quickly, reacting to the sarcasm. "She's my student. Nothing like you're thinking."

"And she came to Amman and now she's missing."

I nodded.

"We have a good police department."

"Of course. I'll go there next, but this is personal, and I wanted to be here to do what I can. Her parents are friends."

The man in the doorway said, "She rich?"

"No. She's just a kid. Her parents are just regular people."

"There are many cab companies in Amman," the owner stated. He reached across his desk for a stained ceramic cup of coffee. He took a sip. "What makes you think she's used one of my cabs?"

"I don't." I pulled out the list of Amman cab companies that I had made back in Israel with the help of a Mossad man. I showed him the list with his company's name halfway down. "I'm checking all the cab companies and showing them her picture until I find out where she went."

"Go to the police," the owner stated.

The man in the doorway nodded. "Police."

"Have you ever been here before?" The man in the chair asked. "Amman can be a confusing city."

I had a quick flashback to my sayeret team driving through a neighborhood not too far from here at three in the morning. Five of us, all dressed like locals, some in keffiyehs, had been crammed into a small Peugeot. Each of us carried a pistol. We were looking for a very particular apartment in a very particular building.

"No. I've never been here."

"Go to the police," the man at the door repeated.

"Do you have a picture of the girl?" The owner looked from me to the other man and shrugged, *It couldn't hurt.*

I pulled up a picture of Aminah on my phone that I had from my first meeting with Idan and Amit in the Tel Aviv. It was the group shot of Noa at a party. Jon had his arm around her. Aminah was next to them. I spread my fingers on the image, zooming in on Aminah.

"This is her." I showed him the picture.

The owner of the cab company took my phone. "She's pretty." And then as he looked at the picture for another moment, his expression changed. It was just a flash of a change. One moment the smile was there, then his cheeks dropped, and then the grin was back. If I had looked away for a second, I would've missed it. He showed the picture to the other man who didn't say anything. The owner handed me back the phone.

"I've not seen her," the owner said, "but I don't drive the cabs very much anymore and never to or from the airport." He paused for a moment. "Come back at 9:00 tonight. That's when my airport man should be here."

"And you think he might know something?"

He shrugged. "It's possible."

I put the phone in my pocket. "Okay. I really appreciate it." I looked from the owner to his friend in the doorway, "I don't know what to say. Thank you, thank you." I shook the owner's hand and then his friend's. "I'll be back at nine." I looked again at the two men and walked out of the cab owner's office.

There was no way I was setting foot in this office at nine tonight.

* * *

Four-and-a-half hours later the sun was just below the horizon and Amman was sliding into evening. Ambient daylight was quickly giving way to streetlights, while busy evening traffic was morphing into a more leisurely flow along the boulevards and smaller streets. Almost all commercial vehicles by this time were back at their businesses. Busses and cabs still moved along the streets, but their proportional numbers had decreased.

At 8:15 I pulled into a spot along the small road that led to the Juel of Jordan Taxi company. The plumbing supply warehouse up from the entrance was on my left, the now closed food store on my right. The mechanic and the bike shop were closed as well; basically, the entire block was deserted. Due to the paltry municipal lighting, my car, parked near a dumpster, would seem like a vehicle left for the night. Or so I hoped. The rental, in fact, was one of several cars parked in various spots along the road, one directly under the universal icon of a red circle and diagonal line over blue field.

A thought occurred to me, and I got out of the Kia, and peeled off the magnetic SIXT logos, just as Gil had done to my rented Hertz in Jerusalem. In under thirty seconds I was back in the car watching the entrance to the taxi company.

The garage door I had walked through earlier today was now closed, shuttered by a steel rolldown door. Next to the closed vehicular entrance, however, was a regular entry door. Light was bleeding out along the bottom edge. No doubt the broad-shouldered owner was inside along with a few of his men, waiting to ask me a few questions. Maybe Idan's Amman team really didn't need to be kept in the dark. At least I could have gotten a gun from them.

I shook my head, responding to my own thought.

Twenty minutes later, at 8:45, a well-polished, black Audi Q7 SUV pulled up to the taxi office. Two men, both taller and huskier than me, stepped out and walked to the entry door. Without hesitating, they made their way inside. No doubt they'd wait out of sight until I came in. Then, at some point during my conversation with the owner, they'd appear and would ask why I cared about Aminah. They would try to be persuasive.

But that's if I went in.

I looked at the spotless Q7.

Their license plate was too far away and at the wrong angle to get a view of it. They, too, like others on the street, were parked under a no parking sign.

How long would they wait? Their patience would be limited, and they'd get surlier as time passed. I was glad I wasn't the cab owner.

8:50 came and went. I stayed in the car.

8:55.

9:00. The time expected for my office visit.

I scanned the length of the street in front of me and used the mirrors for the portions behind. No one was outside. No one walking, no one driving. It was as if word had gone out to stay away from this block. Not even dogs or cats seemed to venture out.

So where was Aminah? Not here. Was she even still in Amman? She could already be the guest of Marwan al-Rashid to leverage her uncle, the uncle who most likely sent her something on al-Rashid for safekeeping.

DEATH TO ISRAEL and the Hamas flag on Noa and Aminah's wall. This was crazy, but not to the Royal. Misdirection, maybe. Fear certainly.

9:15. The men inside continued to wait. The door to the office stayed closed, and the line of light at the bottom remained on.

Were there other means of egress? I hadn't checked.

I turned my car on in anticipation of something happening, not wanting to wait for someone to emerge, in case the sound traveled.

The lines on the car's digital clock reconfigured as another minute passed.

On the other side of the Jordan Valley to the west, would Gil have gone back to Jerusalem from the airport after seeing me off? Would she and Amit be waiting by the phone? Would Gil have gone back to DC?

9:30.

What about the terrorist we had brought in from the night raid? Did he have relevant intel? No way of knowing, and I wasn't going to check for a text.

9:38.

The office door opened and the two husky men came out and walked back to their Q7. They didn't look at each other or talk to one another. They just got into the SUV and pulled away. They were not happy.

Five minutes later, the balding cab owner, the man I had spoken to earlier, came out with the fellow who had been in the office with us this afternoon. The owner left the lights on inside but locked up. Standing in front of the door, they both looked around, said something to one another, and then the associate walked off. The owner stepped into a well-worn, light-colored Mercedes and pulled away. I followed.

He drove down a series of dimly lit side streets, which soon fed into the wider Zahran Street, which was helpful because the steady traffic camouflaged my trailing car. He continued west on Zahran, passing the Fifth Circle. Traffic had clustered at the roundabout, but I weaved in between a sputtering Saab and a late model Hyundai to keep the aging Mercedes in sight. At the Sixth Circle the cab owner headed south. I followed, staying far enough behind to put a handful of vehicles between us. As we passed a mall, I checked my mirrors to see if anyone was on my tail – not that I was paranoid. I swerved, slipping between a city bus and a produce truck, and checked the mirrors again. All looked calm.

Up ahead, the cab owner in his Mercedes turned right. I followed twenty seconds later. No one behind me made the same turn.

We were now off the main drag. Traffic became much lighter, as the neighborhood turned into a mixture of apartment buildings and houses. Residences lined both sides of the quiet street but tucked between the buildings on the right were a few cafes. Most were closed, but one or two were still open, with tables set up outside. As I drove past, I could see couples sitting across from each other, with what looked like cups of coffee in front of them. Further up the block, old trees draped the sidewalks, casting deep shadows.

The Mercedes, almost a full block ahead of me, made another right turn. I followed to see that the taxi owner had pulled to a stop at the end of a strip of stores, and into an available parking space. I parked on the opposite side of the street.

The only shop open in the strip was a small convenience-hardware store. In the window, laundry detergent was on display, as well as a desktop fan and a few pots and pans. The man got out of his car and walked back to the still-lit store. Once he was off the street and in the shop, I moved the Kia into a spot on the next block. This was no longer about surveillance; the cab owner and I needed to have another conversation. I walked back toward the taxi owner's worn Mercedes.

The man I had been following, the man who said he didn't know Aminah but did, had parked his car out of a pool of light, mostly in the shadows. Fortunate for me, not so much for him. I moved deeper into the blackness against the doorway of a closed flower shop not far from his car, and waited.

No one was on the sidewalk, not on this side, nor across the road. The only traffic was a single, badly muffled pickup that rumbled past and disappeared somewhere to my right.

The owner of Juel of Jordan came out of the hardware store five minutes later, a stuffed white plastic bag in each hand. He walked over to the right rear door of his Mercedes, the side closest to me, and fumbled to lift the door handle with a hand weighed down by the heavy shopping bag. Finally, he managed to get the door open. The man dropped the packages onto the back seat.

From my position in the shadows, I looked up and down the block, confirmed we were alone, and silently moved forward.

The taxi owner had straightened up from leaning inside. He closed the door, which made a less-than-solid *thunk*, and then began to take a step toward the front of the car. I put my hand on his shoulder and spun him to face me. The middle-aged man, the owner of the taxi service and probably the man who had picked up Aminah at the airport, saw my face for a millisecond before I drove a fist deep into his solar plexus.

He doubled over and heaved whatever was in his stomach onto the ground. It was impressive he remained on his feet. After a few seconds I leaned over next to his ear.

"You set me up, Karam." I had seen his name and photo on an official document near his desk earlier today.

He tried to shake his head but started heaving again.

"I understand Arabic, Karam."

Another moment passed as just enough pain had cleared his body to completely understand what was happening.

"You—" He squeezed his eyes shut.

I took out my folding knife and flicked it open with the snap of my wrist. The blade clicked, locking into place. His eyes opened suddenly.

"You're…" he was hoarse… "Mossad," he rasped.

"You should be so lucky."

I brought the edge of the blade up to his neck with my right hand, while simultaneously pushing my left fist into his lower spine, forcing him to arch over backward. The taxi owner was now on the verge of losing his balance, rocking onto the back of his heels. His arms flailed out, trying to help him regain equilibrium. With the high-low pressure – knife high at his neck and fist low into his back – I kept him just shy of falling straight back. I walked him deeper into the shadows of the buildings.

My voice was calm, not far from his ear. "Tell me about Aminah Hadad."

"I…don't know her."

I pressed the knife into his neck and he pulled away in reaction. He began to fall backward, but I didn't let him go all the way over.

"You now have blood running down your neck onto your shirt." An educated guess and an image he needed to have. "If you don't tell me what I want to know, the owners of these stores will find your body in the morning. When they look more closely they'll see a dried pool of blood from the slice across your neck – unless dogs get to you first and tear at your face to drag your body away."

I let a moment pass on that image and pressed the knife a millimeter more into his neck. "Aminah Hadad got into your cab at the airport. Then what happened?"

He tried to step backward both to get his feet under his backward-arched body and to lean away from the blade. I pressed into his skin not far from the edge of his trachea.

"Tell me now. Maybe, if I let you go, you'll have enough time to get to a hospital before you bleed to death."

"Okay, stop!"

A second passed.

"I gave her an envelope. A policeman gave me an envelope… to give her once we got downtown."

"A policeman?"

"That's who he said he was. It's the truth."

I doubted it, but the envelope part may have been accurate. "Go on, Karam." How Aminah got into his cab of all cabs was unimportant. He probably had just held up a sign with her name on it at the airport. "I'm waiting, and you're losing blood. I feel it on my hand."

"Stop! I'll tell you. I'll tell you."

The blade was still against his throat, but I had no idea if he were bleeding.

"I was instructed to tell her it was from her parents. She read the letter, then told me to pull over. She got out and ran away. I swear. I never saw her again."

"You're lying." I pushed my fist into his lower spine and he fell backward another inch. A little further he'd fall over backward to the ground.

"No, NO! I swear. That's exactly what happened."

"Who were the men waiting for me tonight at your office?"

The Student

He didn't say anything.

"C'mon, you can tell me."

He was silent.

"You're going to end up in a puddle of your own blood right here. Right now."

He didn't say anything. Just gurgled a little bit. I had an idea who the men were, who they worked for: Marwan al-Rashid, the Royal cousin. Amit had said he was in Amman.

This taxi owner was a go-between. Aminah had disappeared and might be having a less-than-pleasant conversation right now with a man who was likely behind the killing of a young dorm counselor in Baltimore, who had also ordered the death of the barista at Hopkins who had stolen the roommate's backpack. A man who had agents try to kill me, and now probably had Aminah kidnapped. All for what was on her laptop. I needed an avenue to al-Rashid.

"Let's try this another way, Karam." As I held him at the breaking point of his balance, I was conscious that we were still in a public area. All I needed was someone to stroll past us.

I walked the taxi man backward into a small alleyway. His eyes were no doubt shifting from side to side, as he realized he was being moved further away from any potential help.

"After I left your office this afternoon you called the two men. I want that phone number, the one you called."

"I can't. I can't." He almost began to sob. "Please."

Two very long seconds passed in silence.

"Put your hand in your pockets."

He didn't.

"Do it now."

Another second went by and he slowly complied, putting each hand in the side pocket of his pants. "Please, please…"

I released some of the pressure on the knife at his throat, allowing him to regain tentative balance. He probably felt a small measure of hope. It wouldn't last.

I stepped slightly away and then kicked out the back of his right knee. Karam collapsed straight to the ground, his torso still upright. I leaned in from behind, reached over the top of his head, fingers spread wide, and locked them onto the ridges just below his eyebrows. I pulled his head back. There was nothing he could do. He was forced to stare up at the dark heavens, his throat completely exposed like an offering.

I moved the knife back to the side of his windpipe. "If you don't answer me, I will do to you what the radicals do to Western nonbelievers. So, think, Karam. What is the phone number you called?"

A long moment passed, and in a small voice gave me a seven-digit phone number with an Amman area code.

"You know it by heart, Karam? If you're lying to me…"

"No, no, this is it, I swear," he said to the sky. I could feel the voice vibrations in his larynx with my knife hand. "They made me memorize it so there'd be no record."

A long second passed as I held his head back with one hand while keeping the edge of my knife at his throat. He began to say a prayer.

I let him say a sentence or two and then stepped away as silently as I had approached.

It took the cab owner fifteen seconds to realize I was no longer holding him. He straightened his head and looked around. The bald, middle-aged man who had driven Aminah from the airport, and who had delivered a message probably from al-Rashid, tried to stand up, but collapsed on weak legs. I watched from deep in the shadows as he managed to stand upright on his next attempt. He stumbled back to his car, and got in. It took another second or two as he located his keys and started the engine. He pulled out of his space, and swerving slightly, accelerated down the dark street.

My heart rate had picked up slightly, now that it was over. Not that I needed to justify what I had just done to the taxi man, but he was the only lead. Karam would have nightmares. Welcome to the club. Maybe he'd stay away from those other guys.

I walked back to my rented Optima, thinking there was no way for

The Student

me to track the phone number, no way to set up a team surveillance on the owner of the phone, no way to mount any op on my own. My ability to move forward was limited. Logically, the enforcers who came to Karam's shop tonight would be the next step. Find them, get one alone, have a "conversation." But I couldn't do that. I had no resources to locate them, other than following the cab owner. There was seeing where al-Rashid was staying; he shouldn't be hard to find, stake out their vehicles, see who gets in. Maybe someone in his entourage had a black Audi Q7 SUV, the vehicle the enforcers had pulled up in.

As I drove back to the hotel my mind ran through the options: stay here, poke around some more, or ask Amit and Idan for help. Every passing minute put Aminah further at risk. There was also the cab owner who might mention our encounter to someone. Doubtful, for if word got back to al-Rashid, well, it wouldn't help the cab owner's future. I'd have to text Amit, and let Idan and his men put together a plan. I'd stay here to be part of any operation. That was non-negotiable.

Twenty minutes later I pulled into the Kempinski parking lot. It was almost midnight, and the parking lot appeared filled, but had a few empty spots on the far end. Tall lamp posts lit the area, virtually wiping out any shadows. Pretty good coverage. Not surprisingly, closed-circuit cameras had been mounted below the floodlights, and looked down on the cars and any pedestrians.

The night air had become cool. Across the street a young couple walked holding hands. I wondered if they'd do that in daylight hours in this city where radical Islam was taking an increasingly strong hold. Perhaps. The city, while ancient, still had its modern, cosmopolitan areas and vibrant nightlife.

As I walked across the lot to the hotel, I pivoted 360 degrees for a sweep of the area. No doubt anyone watching the security feed would have found it unusual, but in today's world, maybe not. The sky-blue Land Cruiser was still parked near the entrance, and a uniformed doorman had taken up a position near the sliding front door. Tala, the receptionist who had checked me in, was no longer at the desk, as her shift had probably ended. I wouldn't have minded a smile from her. Instead, a distinguished man with a trimmed black mustache was speaking with a tall, dark-haired guest. There was some French going back and forth.

Before I could even begin to test my high-school French, movement off to my left caught my attention. I turned to see the back of a slim, young blonde woman as she disappeared around a corner to the bank of elevators. For whatever reason, I picked up my pace, hustling past the reception clerk who had lifted his eyebrows as I passed.

Soft piano music filled the air. There was a lounge not too far away. Maybe there was live music.

I rounded the corner. The elevators were straight ahead. The young blonde woman had already stepped into a waiting elevator and was out of sight to the side. The image of the woman, that split-second glimpse, had left an imprint: she was shorter than me, and wearing a loose maroon top and dark jeans. Her blonde hair was cut short, and she was carrying a navy North Face backpack over her shoulder. Along the top front of the backpack above the curving zipper someone had affixed a yellow, smiling emoji patch. The smiley face was winking and had its tongue out.

As the doors began to close, the young woman stepped back into view. She was staring down at her phone, scrolling. She didn't see me looking at her.

Aminah.

34

I called her name. Aminah looked up at me, blankly. Nothing. No, "Gidon!" No recognition. Nothing. She just stared at me.

I sprinted forward to shove my hand between the closing door and the edge, but didn't make it. The walnut laminate door slid shut just as I had reached it.

"Shit."

I pressed the call button. The elevator was already on its way up. Her room was on 6. A quick look at the neighboring elevator's floor indicator – it was on 4 – left no option. I ran into the nearby stairwell.

What the hell? My guess was that in the split second Aminah saw me she didn't process it was me in front of her. She certainly wasn't expecting to see me in Jordan, let alone in her hotel.

I took the steps two at a time. The handrail on my right was gunmetal-toned, and the stairwell itself was cement block. Overhead lighting was bright and the floor-level entry doors were clearly marked in Arabic and English. Why had I noticed those things?

I rounded the third-floor landing.

If Aminah truly didn't recognize me she'd head to her room. If she did, she might just have hit the lobby button and gone back down. If she were trying to avoid me, she might go right back outside and disappear. I rounded the fifth-floor landing.

Aminah had looked fine. What was she doing here? I knew her parents had called and told her to meet them at this hotel. They had to have been coerced. They could have met Aminah back in Haifa. Aminah needed to get out before it was too late. I pulled open the door to the sixth floor and ran into the hallway.

Her room was to the right. A quick look up the hallway. No one in the corridor. With my heart racing from sprinting up six flights, I looked to the left. Aminah was standing in front of the pair of elevators. She came running over.

"Gidon!" She wrapped her arms around me, then stepped back. "What are you doing here?"

I came to get you the hell out. "Are your parents here?"

"No. They said they'd come tomorrow afternoon." She looked into my eyes. "Is everything okay?"

They're probably being forced to get you here by Marwan al-Rashid's men.

"I think so, but we need to talk."

"My room's just down the hall."

I wanted to take her downstairs, walk out the door, and right to my car. We'd have to find a safe place until we could board a flight out, or Amit could direct us back to Israel. But she wouldn't leave, expecting her parents to meet her later on.

"Let's go down to the lounge." Closer to the front door.

"Sure," Aminah shifted her navy backpack, slipping both arms through the straps and moving it onto her back. I watched her eyes. Her brow tightened in concern.

The elevator opened – she had already pushed the button – and we went in. The door closed and we starting heading down.

"How did you know I was here?"

"I didn't." Which was the truth. "I just knew you had left Israel for Amman. I have a friend who has been keeping an eye on your passport."

"Your FBI friend?"

I nodded. Close enough. "I still feel responsible for you."

"I'm fine." She touched my arm. "Really. My parents called me in

Haifa and told me to meet them…that they had a room here. They'd join me, and my uncle would come and explain everything."

I just nodded. The elevator door opened and we stepped out.

"Have you spoken with your uncle?" The uncle who had given her the laptop.

She shook her head. "No."

We walked past the front desk and the reception clerk with the neatly trimmed mustache. He looked up from a list he was reading and then back down, paying no attention to us.

"Let's sit over here." I directed her to a set of upholstered armchairs in an alcove not far from the front door. Soft piano music was still drifting in from somewhere down the hall.

Aminah let her backpack slide off her shoulders and she eased it to the floor next to the chair. We sat at 90 degrees to each other. I had a clear view of the lobby and the corridors to either side. With a slight turn of my head I could see the driveway through the large plate-glass windows. The downside was that we could be seen from the street. Maybe this wasn't a great spot.

"So, what's going on?" She looked at me.

"You tell me. Run through what you've been doing since you arrived here." The cab driver said that after reading a letter he had given her, she took off. Where'd she go?

A moment passed. "Nothing exciting. I arrived yesterday, got a cab at the airport, and went to a hotel. Today, I went shopping. That's it. I ate out. Really. Nothing special."

I shook my head. "Back up. Coming in from the airport. In the cab. What happened?"

"You know about that? How do you know about that?"

"I came here to look for you. I spoke with the cab driver, figuring you'd pick up a cab at the airport." An image ran through my head of me pulling the balding, middle-aged man into the shadows, and taking him back off-balance with my knife at his throat.

"We were on our way here, and the driver handed me an envelope.

Said it was from my parents. I opened it. It was from my mom."

"That didn't seem weird, that he would have a note from your mother?"

"It did, but he said my father had contacted him, and when I opened it, he was right. I recognized my mother's handwriting."

"Still odd, though." Timing was off. Conceivably, how would the cab driver had gotten the letter so quickly if her parents were in London? Unless they weren't.

"Yeah." She watched me watch her. "But it was from her."

Aminah had always struck me as being level-headed. Of the two college girls, Aminah was the first to go along with my idea to lure out the Iranian agents by walking out in the open with me on South Charles Street. She was the logical one. Until now. The fact that this seemingly random cab driver had a letter from her mom would not have made sense. Handwriting can be faked.

"What'd it say?"

"To leave the cab immediately, to not go here, but to the Crowne Plaza. Just for the night. I could come here today."

"You didn't think that was strange?"

"It was to be sure no one was following me. That's what the note said." She leaned in slightly. "What's going on?" she repeated.

"I don't know." It was both a lie and the truth. "I'm still concerned, that's all."

"You and the police caught those men in Baltimore."

I nodded. And the man who hired them was in this city. Probably nearby.

"I've been thinking about going back to Hopkins," she continued. "My parents might even come in for QuadFest."

This was crazy. Aminah was here as if nothing has happened since that night of her apartment break-in, and she was planning to go back for some sort of festival?

I looked over at the reception clerk who was busy typing on a keyboard. After a moment, he stopped, then went into a back room.

I returned my attention to Aminah. "This whole thing, the business with the laptops, is still unresolved. We don't know what's on them that started all of this, but it's connected to your uncle." A few seconds passed. "I'd just feel a lot more comfortable if we weren't waiting where people were expecting you to be, even your parents – and it's not that I don't trust them." Another partially true statement.

"So you want me to go somewhere else for the night?"

I nodded.

She looked down at her hands and then up at me. "Okay." After another second or two, "What do you have in mind?"

"We'll find another hotel. And your parents will still be able to reach you on your cell, right?"

"Of course."

"Don't call or text them that you've moved. We have no idea if someone is listening in somehow."

"Got it."

"You can stay in touch. Just don't say anything about where you are."

"Okay."

A few seconds passed. I looked around. There was a partially eaten piece of baklava on a plate not far away. Outside, on the other side of the window, a solid-looking man with a shaved head was walking up the driveway. He was dressed in a black polo and black pants. His biceps, chest, and shoulders were well muscled. He moved fluidly, assuredly.

"You want to leave now?" Aminah asked as I was still watching the man.

"I do."

"Can I go up to my room and get some clothes?"

"Of course."

Aminah began to get up, but I put a hand on her leg to stop her. "Hang on."

The glass doors to the lobby slid open, and the solid-looking man with the shaved head walked in. We both watched as he paused halfway between the entryway and the reception desk. He looked around to include a glance in our direction, and then walked off to the left, down a corridor leading to where the piano music was coming from.

"Okay."

We both stood up and walked past the reception desk which was still unmanned. The man with the muscular arms had made a turn at the end of the corridor on the left. He was nowhere in sight. In fact, no one was in sight. The lobby was empty. The polished floor, the brightly-lit reception area, and the empty lounge all highlighted we were alone. Even the nearby abandoned plate of baklava signaled stillness. While it was just after midnight, I'd have expected more guests down here. I missed the .45 HK sitting in the small of my back.

We turned the corner to the bank of elevators. The neatly uniformed reception clerk with the trim mustache stood in front of a lit call button, carrying a small parcel. As we approached, I could see the box had someone's name on the label, and a room number. It looked like it had been opened. The clerk and I exchanged nods. He smelled of cologne.

The elevator door on the right slid open. Aminah stepped in first. I went in next. The clerk carrying the parcel came in last. The walls of the elevator car had framed advertisements for upscale restaurants.

Before I had a chance to turn to face the clerk, two things occurred a millisecond apart: slight pressure on my back and a crack of a spark. I was still looking at a photo of a restaurant.

Stupid. I should've let the clerk go in first. I knew what had happened. He had reached into the small parcel.

Aminah was on my left in my peripheral vision, which had begun to constrict.

A surge of electricity shot up my back and over my head. And then there was…

* * *

...the sound of a conversation. Not nearby, not far away. It was in Arabic. I couldn't make out what was being said. It could have been two voices. Or more. Hard to tell with the pounding in my head.

There was no transition between the electric shock and now. No sense of time going by. Nothing in between. Just the surge up my back and then the conversation in front of me somewhere. There was also a cool breeze on my face. Air conditioning perhaps.

My eyes were still closed. *Run a systems check before alerting anyone that I was conscious.*

My neck and shoulders ached, as well as my lower back, no doubt from the sudden contraction of the muscles. Without moving, there was no way of telling if my arms and legs were functional. All seemed well, otherwise. No other pain, except for the sore muscles and the headache. What I could discern was that I was lying on my side, slightly curled, on a carpeted floor. The nap was pressed against my cheek. I was not bound in any way. In the back of my head I heard the voice of an Israeli soldier, the one who had spoken to me just before we climbed into the armored personnel carrier for our raid on Qaltuniya. He had said something about me being able to see behind me. Considering the desk clerk had zapped me from behind, I would have smiled if I could have.

It was time to see what was going on. I moved my head slowly and let a moan cross my lips.

There was movement nearby, I was grabbed around each bicep, and lifted. My feet came off the ground. As I opened my eyes I was dropped into an armchair. I moaned again and my vision cleared.

Straight ahead, and sitting in another armchair facing me was Marwan al-Rashid, the Royal cousin. He was in a white thobe and a red and white keffiyeh. He looked the same as he had in the photo we had been shown in the briefing back on the base: square jaw, neatly trimmed black beard, piercing dark eyes. He sat nonchalantly, with his legs crossed, reading *The Guardian*. Next to him was a man who, based on his features, could have been a younger brother. The senior al-Rashid was my Ace of Spades, the man behind threats to Noa and Aminah, and who no doubt had brought in Iranian Quds Force mercenaries to retrieve the laptops and extract whatever information they could from the girls and whoever else they could.

I looked around. The room appeared to be a luxury suite. Was I still at the Kempinski? Beside me stood two men, the same two men who had paid the cab owner a visit earlier this evening in a black Audi SUV. Both men were facing me, unmoving and expressionless.

"The Mossad has gotten very good at copying these," the Royal cousin said. He put down the newspaper and picked up a U.S. passport. "This is yours." He thumbed through it. "Really, a very good copy."

"It's the real thing," I responded a little weaker than I expected. "Why does everyone think I'm Mossad?"

al-Rashid looked over and raised an eyebrow.

"The FBI thinks so, too. I'm not."

al-Rashid turned to the younger version of himself, then back to me. "Mr. Aronson, you are responsible for the death of my men. And I am surprised you are here. Not unexpected, but surprised. If that makes sense."

His voice was almost like an NPR host, soft and slightly deep. He enunciated well, in polished diction. Expensive schooling. There was also the trace of an accent. Maybe French, or Dutch. Maybe Swiss. I really didn't know.

"I'm not Mossad. I came looking for Aminah. And whatever happened to your men, they brought it on themselves." I had flashes of the confrontation on South Charles Street and of the gray-haired man in my studio with the suppressed Beretta. While looking at the Royal brothers in front of me, I took in the entire suite….the furniture, the paintings, doorways, the large men to either side of me. After another moment, I turned my head and made it obvious I was looking around. "Where's Aminah?"

"Getting reacquainted with her uncle" – the man who had stolen something from al-Rashid and had hidden it in her laptop. "And you're here to rescue her. How did Mossad know she was here?"

"I'm not Mossad."

The younger brother reached for a piece of paper on a nearby coffee table and approached me. He stopped a few feet away and held up an 8x10 photo. I had seen it before, in the FBI conference room in Baltimore, just after I had my run-in with two agents at the airport at the start of all this. It was a photo, taken with a long lens, and was a shot of David Amit, Idan Gelvar, and me sitting at that outdoor café on the Tel Aviv promenade just before I had left for Ben Gurion to come back to the States.

"It's not what it seems."

"When Aminah came in from the airport, I had the cab driver give her a letter from her parents, or so she thought." The Royal cousin seemed almost bored. "She was to leave the cab, so we could see who was following her. And look who turned up shortly after that."

"That was a coincidence. That meeting," I nodded to the picture, "was Gelvar asking me to look after his niece who is a student in Baltimore."

"You're not very convincing." He looked at me with his hard, dark eyes, and then smiled ever-so-slightly. "You never asked me who I am."

The room went completely silent.

I never asked because I already knew. Because David Amit of the Shin Bet had told me.

The man on my left put his hand on my shoulder.

"I'm not who you think I am," I said to al-Rashid.

It was time to get out of here.

I stood, simultaneously rotated my left arm to shrug off the hand of the man to my left. Once fully upright, and brushing off the guard's hand reaching for me, I horizontally rammed my right elbow square into the man's sternum. No matter how much muscle someone builds up in the chest, the breastbone still only had a thin covering over it. In fact, weight-lifting exposed the bone. My elbow had the full power of my rotating hips, augmented both by my opposite arm pulling back

The Student

and my coordinated, focused breath. I knew what that elbow strike could do to a piece of concrete because I had practiced it. I also knew that I not only cracked his breastbone, but the energy of the blow continued below the surface to his heart. Without even thinking about it, I continued the motion of the elbow, scooping the same arm around his head. Bringing my other hand into play, I violently twisted the guard's head. There were grinding sounds, and the burly man collapsed to the floor.

I turned to the other guard who was reaching inside his jacket. He was tying himself up with his cross-body motion. I closed the distance and stamped out into his knee joint. He fell straight down onto his shattered leg. On his way down I planted the heel of my other foot just behind his ear, breaking his mastoid process. His eyes rolled up slightly as he fell over.

Before I turned to the al-Rashids, there was a crack of a spark and then a surge of electricity up my back and over my head.

* * *

This time when consciousness returned, in addition to the headache and muscle aches, my hands and feet were bound. I was also being held up by my upper arms. As before, I tried to get a sense of the room while my eyes were still closed. There was no air conditioning, and there was a sense of a tighter enclosed space.

Someone slapped me, hard. My cheek went numb and it felt like it had exploded at the same time. I opened my eyes.

The elegant hotel suite was gone. We were in a basement workshop of sorts. There were benches, miscellaneous tools, and a few chairs. No windows, but overhead LED floods filled the room with stark, bright light. Straight ahead of me and leaning against a far wall, was the senior Royal cousin. He was just looking at me with his dark eyes. His younger brother, dressed the way his older sibling was in the red and white keffiyeh, stood but a few feet in front of me. He had been the one who had struck me. When he spoke his voice wasn't as smooth as his brother's. It was slightly higher and had more of an edge to it.

"Majid is on the floor turning blue," he looked at me, eyes wide. "And Radwan is probably dead by now."

He punched me across the other cheek and then, rotating his arms, drove the other fist into my gut. I saw that coming and exhaled as the fist plowed into my abdomen. It took much of the force out of it, but I still involuntarily doubled over. Powerful arms held me up. My head, from the repeated electric shocks, was cloudy, one cheek was now throbbing, the other going numb, and it was hard to inhale; taking in small amounts of air was the only thing possible.

The senior al-Rashid spoke from the back of the room. "If you're not Mossad, they should have hired you."

With my eyes closed, I said, "They…tried."

"So, you're not Mossad. Doesn't matter… American, FBI, CIA–" al-Rashid approached from the back wall. "My guess is IDF. An American who joined the IDF. One of their Special Forces units."

I tried to smile, but my cheeks wouldn't let me. "I'm just a guy looking after the girls."

The older Royal cousin stopped beside his brother, whose face was now flushed from the effort of pounding me. "I do know one thing," the elder said, stepping closer to fill my entire line of sight. "You don't know what's on the laptop."

I lifted my head and looked at him. "Account information."

al-Rashid's expression changed for a moment, like the taxi driver's back in his office when I had shown him Aminah's picture. That conclusion was something I had been thinking of. What else could it be that Aminah's uncle had on him? He wouldn't care about compromising photos. Money to fund terrorism was my guess.

He recovered quickly. "If that's all you have, then there is nothing for me to worry about. Thank you."

My head dropped. It was fogged but still clear enough to work the logic. A cold sweat suddenly covered me. If it weren't about money,

The Student

there was only one thing left. Operational plans of some sort. Terrorist operational plans.

"So now, my IDF friend, my brother Saleh will work on you, because that's what he does. We'll go about our business, and at some point we will trade you, if you survive. The Israelis say they don't negotiate with terrorists, but they do. So do the Americans. So whoever you work for, they'll pay an outrageous price for you. If you survive," he repeated.

Saleh al-Rashid took off his keffiyeh to reveal a full head of closely cut dark hair. There was a thin layer of sweat on his forehead. He motioned to the men holding me up, and they lifted me so I was completely upright. The brother set his feet on the floor a shoulder-width apart, and then pounded me with a tight fist on the left side of my abdomen, and then on the right side with his other fist. He was getting into a rhythm. My vision began to narrow. The brother hit me with a left hook across the side of my face.

While I still could, I gathered my thoughts and directed them down to the lower third of my torso. My breath, though it wasn't really my breath, began to coalesce there like a ball or a small sun. It knew what to do out of habit. I did it all the time. My breath that really wasn't just breath, began to expand within me, and I willed it to pack every fiber, every tissue.

The brother hit me in the ribs.

Once my body was permeated with radiant light, I let my mind go, slipping not into unconsciousness, but retreating from the pain that had been filling my trunk and searing through my head. Before he hit me again, I closed my eyes. I breathed as best I could and tried to relax on the exhale. Another blow from younger brother caught me on the other side of my face.

From somewhere behind me, the older brother, the man who had manipulated everything, leaned in. "In case you're wondering, you don't exist outside these walls. You've disappeared. Your car has been returned to the airport. There's no record of your rental. There was no hotel stay at the Kempinski. The owner of the cab company doesn't know you. No one has seen you in Amman. We're the only ones who know where you are." A second passed. "Not even Mossad will find you."

I re-opened my eyes and saw the entire room, all 360 degrees. I reached out to the periphery, to see all four walls at once.

And Saleh al-Rashid hit me in the gut again.

35

I had to stay detached. There was no choice. My body was being battered. That I knew, but I couldn't allow my mind to connect to all the nerve endings that must have been screaming.

There was no sense of time, and barely any visual recognition of what was occurring. My mind was imprinting, but I wasn't aware of it. I was completely passive. Limp.

At some point I was on the floor. Then I was upright. Then I was in a chair. A black hood went over my head.

I was in a damp room with little light.

I was stripped to the waist and spread out on my front across a board. Something repeatedly hit me across my back…

The black hood. Movement. On the floor. Cold, wet concrete against my cheek.

I was picked up, dragged. Head submerged in a container of water, pulled out. Submerged again. If I coughed or choked, I wasn't aware of it.

I was back on the floor. And then picked up by strong arms again.

I let my consciousness resurface ever so slightly. I saw a workbench, and retreated into myself as voices approached. I had no idea what they were saying or even what language they were speaking in. I couldn't allow that much mental presence.

There was the face of the younger al-Rashid in front of me. Then another face. And a flashlight in my eyes.

The Student

I was back on the floor. And then picked up again.

There was a red and white keffiyeh in my line of sight. My passive mind recorded the older al-Rashid looking at me. Over his shoulder was the workbench. It was filled with varied items: a table lamp, a faucet fixture, a doorknob, tools, a small windowpane. The glass had been broken. There was a large pot of some sort, and a few cloth shopping bags, bulging with whatever filled them. A chair was off to the side, upside down and with a strap around its legs. All this made an impression, and part of my brain said, "You're in the maintenance room of the hotel."

The younger brother began punching me in the ribs. I felt nothing. They tossed me into a wall, and I fell to the floor.

Sometime later they hoisted me vertical again. As they held me up, the workbench was once more in my line of sight.

Again, it made an impression. It was calmly distracting – something else to look at. Before they turned me around, I saw a cell phone on the bench. al-Rashid, or one of his men must have taken it out of a pocket, so it wouldn't bother them while they dealt with me.

The black hood was shoved over my head and I was carried over someone's shoulder. Then they laid me out in the back of a vehicle of some sort. As the vehicle made turns and swerved, the motion rolled me slightly from side to side.

I was thrown over someone's shoulder as before, and carried down a flight of stairs.

I was on a cement floor again. There was the body of a man next to me. His face was covered in dried blood from cuts in his forehead. His cheeks had patches of faded black and blue. One eye was swollen shut. The other was fixed off in the distance and lifeless.

* * *

Some time had gone by…maybe. For some reason there was a feeling of daylight somewhere; other times there was a sense of night.

Movement in front of me played on an endless loop: men coming and going…I was carried again… placed in a chair…other times held up and my head turned from side to side…

At one point two men in red and white keffiyehs were arguing. One pointed to me and shouted at the other…

More time passed – or maybe it didn't – and another man walked into the room and looked into my eyes and shone a flashlight in them. I think that happened once before. He took out a stethoscope and approached me…

* * *

My mind was both recording and playing back; it was like a program running in the background. It played images of Baltimore… of a dorm room…of two college girls…a firing range, a detective next to me…laptops …looking up at the night sky in a friend's backyard …walking, clad in battle gear, through a village in the middle of the night…seeing a young blonde woman in an elevator looking up from her phone at me…

"Gidon…"

The visuals changed. I was with a group of soldiers, bursting into a basement to find a beaten, disheveled young woman curled up in a corner. We shot two men standing nearby. I scooped up the woman who looked into my eyes with tears running down her face…

The next video played: I was sitting in a restaurant, across from a blue-eyed woman wearing a black T-shirt and a gray suit. She had a badge and a gun on her hip. The image shifted. The same woman was standing over a car and peeled off a magnetic rental car label near the back window.

"Gidon."

I was hiking along the floor of canyon with a young woman dressed in cargo shorts. She was holding a water bottle. Her face…it was a face I hadn't seen in a long time and I knew I missed it.

"Gidon…" The voice seemed familiar.

The woman's face dissolved away. It was replaced by a man's with sun-darkened skin and a mustache. I was sitting in the driver's seat of a car and he was leaning toward me at the open window.

Another shift. Now there was a woman in a tie-dyed dress. She had straight, auburn hair, and was watching me. I knew I had seen her in a meditation not long ago. There was a sense of calm about her. Now, she was looking right at me. Her lips moved. *Hang on.*

"Gidon." The voice was a man's, coming from outside my head. "Breathe, my friend. Breathe."

The voice grew more clear, and the face of the man with the mustache was back, pushing out the woman who had been looking at me. I knew who that woman was…Sammi, my teacher's wife, a friend.

"Gidon, breathe. Come back."

The program in my head stopped. A blank wall was in front of me.

There was no way of telling how far away it was. My eyes weren't focusing.

The room behind me was soundless, filled with dead air. Then, "Gidon…"

I moved slowly to see who had been talking. Pain radiated from my ribs and abdomen. I stopped moving my torso but turned my head just enough to see Ibrahim. My vision cleared. Ibrahim, the friend I had seen in an Arab village playing the part of an old man, and then later walking with me through the hallways of a school.

"Can you stand?" His voice was steady and not very loud, as if he didn't want to be heard too far away.

I blinked a few times. "Let's…find out."

My voice had come out much softer than I had intended, but apparently it was loud enough for him. Ibrahim reached under my arms and helped me up, taking most of my weight. After a few seconds, he gingerly allowed me to put more pressure on my feet.

"I'm okay. It's not my feet that hurt." I looked at him. "But don't let go."

He began to walk me out toward the door, taking the majority of the pressure from me. After a few steps, I slowly turned to see a man on the floor. I didn't recognize him, but he obviously had been in the room when Ibrahim had entered. The center of his chest was covered in blood.

With one arm still around me, Ibrahim opened the basement door with his free hand. On the other side was a dark, low-ceilinged hallway, lit by a few bare bulbs. To the side of the door was another man on the ground. This one had been shot in the head.

I slowly looked at my friend. "Any trouble getting in? Get hurt?"

"No."

He was still half-carrying me. There wasn't enough strength in me for a smile, but still I had to say it, though it didn't have much volume: "I got shot rescuing you."

We walked past the body on the floor.

"You didn't get shot, my dear friend. You were scratched."

"I got shot. You…still…owe me."

We climbed the stairs – actually Ibrahim took the steps; I was lifted – and we stepped outside. It was dark. It could have been midnight, or three in the morning. I couldn't look up to scan the heavens. There was enough ambient glow, though, to see we were behind a cement-walled building. Two more bodies were on the ground near the door, lifeless.

"My car is around the corner."

I nodded, or thought that I did. I could feel the blood draining from my head and my vision beginning to go.

At some point Ibrahim placed me in the back seat of his car. In a few moments, streetlights went by. We made some turns, but mostly drove straight. It was impossible to tell how long he drove. Ibrahim didn't seem to be in a rush, but maybe he was. I faded in and out.

We finally came to a stop. His door opened, and then mine. Again, Ibrahim lifted me. I looked around to see where we were. We were in a residential neighborhood, toward the end of a block of houses. Each home was separated by a low cement wall, and late-model cars were in

The Student

driveways and on the street.

The night was still dark – there was no moonlight or streetlights – and the block was silent. Ahead of us was a concrete walkway up to the front of a two-story stucco house. There was no foliage in the yard, and the cement work looked fairly clean. Of the nearby houses, the one in front of us had lights on behind curtains in the first-floor windows.

With Ibrahim's prompting we started up the path. I was able to walk a little better than before, but then maybe he was doing all the work. About halfway I had to stop. Ibrahim held me steady. I looked at the dark, front door ahead of us. There were no house numbers or other identifying information on the door or the facade. "Where are we? Who's here?"

"A Mossad safe house."

In my semi-lucid mind I managed a smile. My Arab friend knew the location of the Mossad safe house.

He saw the grin and just shrugged. We continued up the walk.

The front door opened as we approached. In the entryway stood a tall, slender, dark complexioned man. His right hand was out of sight, holding something. Another man stood behind him, to the side.

Ibrahim helped me forward, and before the man in front could say anything, my friend spoke softly but loud enough for the men to hear, "This is the one you've been looking for."

Ibrahim began to hand me over to the Mossad agent. As the dark-complexioned man in the doorway reached out for me, Ibrahim, added, "Be careful. He's broken on the inside."

I looked over at my friend, the man who had found me in some basement in some building in Amman, and wanted to say something. But I couldn't because I passed out.

36

As consciousness returned, the first sensation I had was that I hurt, really hurt. My chest, sides, and back. There was also a blanket of pain along the surface of my abdomen, but that was duller. What else? The right side of my face throbbed, up along the cheek.

I didn't know if I could move. Didn't know what worked and what didn't…what was broken and what was not. The assessment would have to wait. The only other thing I could concretely tell was that I was on my back.

I wanted a sense of the room before opening my eyes, same as after being shocked, though that seemed a long time ago. My breath stayed slow and even, and I reached out, sort of with my skin, to check the confines of this space. This room seemed smaller than the basement I had been in – that's what I could feel – and there were people speaking nearby. In Russian. A man and a woman…not too far from me. Their voices were calm and unrushed. Definitely Russian.

I kept my eyes closed.

Ibrahim had taken me from the basement; that I remembered. I knew that he half-carried me to his car. There was an image of a house, a long walkway, and the door opening ahead of us. The rest was fuzzy.

Russian? Why would people around me be speaking Russian? Was I still in Amman? The language should have been Arabic. It made no sense.

The air shifted around me as someone approached. In fact, the

The Student

person came very close, in front of my face close.

I opened my eyes to see a man with short, dark hair and a trimmed beard reaching for my head. I parried his incoming arm with my left hand, and then sat upright. With no break in motion, my left hand continued to grab the back of his head while the right went for his throat. His neck was now locked between my two hands. My fingers reached into the hollow between his neck muscles and his trachea, and began squeezing his windpipe. There was a clatter of something falling to the floor to my left. And then,

"Gidon!"

I looked over to see Gil Jeffries standing beside my hospital bed. Her cell phone was in her right hand, its position frozen in front of her. I turned back at the man standing over me. He was in blue scrubs and his face beginning to turn red. I looked back at Gil.

"You're in a hospital."

I returned to the man in front of me. His mouth was open slightly, pulled back in pain. I let go, and collapsed backward into the bed.

"Sorry," I said softly, suddenly exhausted.

The man backed away, a hand to his neck, as he began cursing in Russian, Hebrew, and Arabic. I was definitely in Israel.

"Sorry," I repeated.

The man – I didn't know if he were a doctor, a nurse, an aide – walked out of the room, still mumbling, followed by the woman he had been speaking with.

"Nice to know you haven't lost your edge," Gil said, lifting the IV pole I had yanked over. It was connected to the back of my hand by an intravenous line. Hanging at the other end was a bag of clear fluid.

"Not blood. That's good."

Gil nodded. "No internal hemorrhaging. That's a miracle. You do look like shit, though."

"Don't sugarcoat it for me, Sundance. Tell me what you think." I closed my eyes for a moment and then reopened them.

"You're in Hadassah Hospital on Mt. Scopus."

"The Trauma Center," I mumbled. I had visited soldiers here. Never had the pleasure as a patient, though. Until now. "How long have I been here?"

"This is your second day." Gil stepped a little closer. "You were missing for three. The Mossad officers you found got you across the border to a waiting helo."

"I wasn't the one who had found them." I pushed my hands and forearms down into the mattress to try raising myself, but didn't get far. I fell back into the bed.

"Take it easy."

"Not a chance. Gotta see what works." Again I pushed my forearms into the bed, but as before, wasn't able to lift myself very much. Pain swept over my entire torso. "Okay, I'll rest for a moment."

"Smart." A moment passed. "You may have noticed, you're in a private room."

"I notice everything." My eyes were closed to get a handle on the pain.

"Just saying, it's uncommon for regular folk to get a private room here. You must rate."

With my eyes closed, I began the ball of energy visualization again and tried to relax. "Not really," I spoke, breathing as deeply as I could, which was challenging because of the radiating pain. "VIPs get private rooms, as do intelligence officers who need to be debriefed securely."

"Well, good for you. Meanwhile, rest. I'll come back later."

"No." I opened my eyes.

Gil looked at me.

"Help me up. Please."

She continued to look into my eyes.

"You give me strength. Help me up."

She hesitated for a few seconds, then moved the IV pole, lowered the side rail, and reached for me. Gil put an arm around my shoulders, simultaneously dropping her center of gravity. "Ready?"

I nodded.

Between Gil providing stability and lift, and whatever energy I had, I managed to push myself into a sitting position. Blood shifted down from my head, causing passing dizziness. It took a moment to acclimate.

Gil didn't react to the wavering...maybe she didn't see it. Instead, "Amit is on his way, incidentally."

"Oh, good." I didn't know if I meant it sarcastically or not. The throbbing all over my torso had evened out. Half my focus was there. "Any sign of Aminah?"

"She's back in the U.S. I put her on a watch list."

I looked over at the FBI woman. "It's not good that she's back in the States."

"Why?"

"I don't know." After a second, "Help me off the bed," I swung my feet over the side of the bed. "We're going for a walk."

"You're crazy, but wait a second." She darted out of the room and came back with a walker.

With Gil within grabbing distance, I slid off the bed, stood up, and reached for the walker. I took a step. And then one more. Gil stood beside me, holding the IV pole.

"How are you even able to walk?"

"No casts or braces. No breaks." I took a breath. "As long as my legs aren't broken, I can walk...and disassociate the pain – to a point. And there's having been beaten regularly in training. Builds a high pain threshold." I took another step, but winced. That sort of undid the line about how much control I had. I breathed some more. "al-Rashid was interested in pounding on me, not breaking anything. That wouldn't have been as much fun, apparently."

"al-Rashid?"

"Not the royal cousin we're looking for. His brother, Saleh. Must be the enforcer in the family." I slid the walker forward and took another step. "I'd like to remake his acquaintance, in the not too distant future."

After a few more steps, I had to stop.

"Do me a favor, call Amit and tell him to come tomorrow."

"Okay??"

"There are a lot of images in my head to sort through before we talk."

She nodded, then while I waited texted Amit. "Done."

"What time is it?"

She held out her cell phone. 9:11PM.

We headed back to my room, passing an older, gray-haired man in a bathrobe. His face was familiar. A politician, perhaps. He looked like Shimon Peres, but that wasn't possible, as Peres was dead. We nodded to each other. He continued on, and so did I, with the walker: step, slide the walker, step until we were back in the room.

As we moved over to the bed, I half-turned to Gil. "I have this distinct image of Aminah saying she wanted to go back to the U.S. There's also the fact that she had no hesitancy to go to Amman. She wasn't afraid."

"Something's going on."

"More than before. You have her under surveillance?"

Gil nodded. "She's with relatives in Philadelphia. We're running a check on them."

I shuffled back into bed. "You've been here since they brought me in?"

"Pretty much." A moment went by as she looked at me. "In case you talked in your sleep, you know." She smiled.

"Did I?"

"Not a word."

I smiled and lay back in bed. "I'm going to close my eyes and sort through all the images from when I had the pleasure of al-Rashid's company. I know he said some things, and I must've seen stuff, too."

"You do your thing, Sensei. I'm going downstairs to get something to eat." I nodded. "I'll bring you back something good."

I wasn't hungry. "Thanks."

After Gil left, I closed my eyes to bring back the mental images of

The Student

the time with the Royal cousins. I lasted only a few seconds and then promptly fell asleep.

* * *

I opened my eyes sometime later to see bright sunlight pouring through the windows. I scanned the room: the door to the hallway… mostly closed, overhead lights off, bathroom door half open. A few chairs. High up on the wall facing me was an analog clock with large numbers. Hadn't noticed it before. Great powers of observation. It read 9:40. I had been out for 12 hours.

Slowly, I sat up. The pain was still radiating throughout my torso, and it would be for a while, but it was manageable. I needed to move around. I slid out of the bed, and as I stood – conscious of the lack of dizziness – noticed the IV had been disconnected from the back of my hand. The port was still there, but the tubing was gone, draped over the box-like control unit on the pole. Something else had changed in the room. A cafeteria tray with some covered food had been placed on a tray table, and there was a green shopping bag on a nearby armchair. I shuffled over. The bag held my clothes, with my cell phone on top. Gil's doing. Her visit while I was sleeping didn't bother me, but hospital personnel coming and going was different. It was disconcerting that I was so out of it, that I didn't feel the IV being removed. A finely-tuned sense of awareness. Right.

Taking my time, I changed out of the hospital gown and into my street clothing. I then sat in the chair, making sure my feet were flat on the ground with my back straight. The pain that wrapped my torso was constant, so it had become more of a steady background hum. I closed my eyes and retreated to a few days ago…

My questioning the taxi owner…Seeing Aminah in the Amman hotel. Her not seeing me from the elevator…then the conversation in the lobby. She was innocently oblivious. Said she was going back to Baltimore. I had a clear image of her sitting in the chair at right angles to me.

…Marwan al-Rashid's face in front of me, smiling. He held an 8x10 photo I had seen before, a three-shot of Amit, Noa's uncle, and me…

Being held by two men and Saleh al-Rashid taking off his keffiyeh before working me over…

Marwan, the Royal cousin looking at me after I told him what I thought was on the laptops… *If that's all you have, then there is nothing for me to worry about.*

The scene faded….to a field of white. After an unknown amount of time, the door to the hallway all but silently swung open, and the ambient sound in the room changed. I opened my eyes to see Gil walking in with Amit.

"Shalom, Gidon," the Israeli nodded at me. "Looks like you're ready to leave."

"I need to check out." I stood, not letting the background pain rise to the surface. "Can you get that done, please."

"The doctors want you to stay another day," Gil said.

"So you know more about me than I do."

"You are in my charge," Amit said.

"No, I'm not."

"Stay another day," Gil Jeffries said. "Let them be sure there's no internal bleeding."

"There's no internal bleeding."

A moment passed in silence.

"There's a place around the corner where we can talk," Amit said, a little somberly, and walked out. Gil and I looked at each other and followed him, though my pace was slower than hers. Amit led us to a secluded alcove with several cushioned armchairs.

"I need to leave here," I said, after sitting down.

"Stay another day," Amit responded. "It's quiet on this floor. Do your meditation thing. Recall what you can. Do you have all the answers?"

"More than I did." They looked at me, but I turned to Gil. "You have a leak. You know the picture you had when you first interrogated me, the shot of my meeting with Amit and Idan Gelvar on the promenade in Tel Aviv?"

She nodded.

"al-Rashid had it. Showed it to me to demonstrate he thought I was Mossad."

"You sure?"

I nodded.

"Shit."

"There's more. The laptops?...We can eliminate one thing that might be on them. It's not about money."

"Well, that's good and bad." Gil again.

"Why?"

"While you were getting your massage in Jordan, the computer folks at home pulled chips from both laptops that weren't part of the operating system. They were purely storage, camouflaged as part of the RAM. That's why they were so difficult to find. The tech people think they contain an algorithm that generates passwords for bank accounts."

Amit turned back to me. "What makes you think this isn't about someone stealing al-Rashid's passwords? He would kill over that... Someone could drain his bank accounts."

"Maybe that was his concern originally. Not anymore. Just as my massage was getting started," I looked at Gil who had used the *massage* phrase, "I said to al-Rashid that this was all about account information. He smiled and said something like, 'If that's all we have, then he doesn't need to worry.'"

"So what is it?" Gil looked at the Shin Bet man then back to me.

"Something with Aminah. Always has been. Maybe it started out about the bank passwords, but now it's changed. I don't know. And Aminah's back in the U.S.?"

She nodded, and added. "I'll call DC and update them about her possible relevance. Not that we know any more."

"Get surveillance footage from the airport where she arrived," Amit suggested. "Maybe there'll be someone else on the flight we'll recognize."

Gil nodded.

"And I'll call MI5," Amit went on. "Her parents are supposed to be in London. I want their security services to do some checking on them."

"Anything from the man we brought in from Qaltuniya raid?" – the post-midnight raid I had gone on.

"Yes." He suddenly did not look very happy. "We have an Iranian cell in the West Bank. Our new guest is slowly giving us details about their operations. They're stockpiling some weapons, planning something." The Shin Bet man paused, as if he didn't want to discuss it further, then pulled out his phone. "Now something for you." He touched an icon and then turned his phone around. On the display was a photo of Ibrahim. I couldn't tell where it had been taken. The Shin Bet man looked at me. "Who is he?"

The debate in my head didn't last a second. "He's my friend."

"He pulled you from al-Rashid's men. He took you to a Mossad safehouse in Amman. This is from their front door."

That brought back some images, the ones of a long walkway up to a house and the door opening as we approached.

"Who is he?" Amit repeated. His voice had gotten softer. "He knew where you were kept, and he knew the location of our safehouse."

"He's a friend."

"He's not in our records."

I just nodded.

The Shin Bet man continued: "We heard from a Jordanian source that an IDF team rescued a kidnapped Mossad agent in the capital six days ago." After a second, "They mean you, and that was your friend... He got in, killed the guards, and got you out."

I nodded again. "You need to delete his picture. From all records.

He won't be safe otherwise."
Amit stared at me in silence. Then, "*B'seder.*" Okay.
"*All* records."
He understood, but I didn't believe he would do as I asked.

* * *

Gil and Amit left me in the alcove. They wanted me to get back to recalling what I had seen and heard. *I* wanted to get back to recalling what I had seen and heard. Maybe it was good forcing me to stay here. I had no place else to go, except a hotel room. I could try to figure this out here.

I cleared some space in the alcove and began a tai chi form. The effort of moving the furniture made me dizzy again, and the pain in my torso came up a notch, but neither stopped me. I needed the space to work on my balance, my pain tolerance, and I needed to clear my mind. With a clear mind, ideas and images might come to the surface.

For the next thirty minutes I worked on my forms. At some point a few patients wandered by, watched for a moment or two, and then left. I didn't see their faces, nor did I wish to…didn't want to actively look at them.

The form had three sections. I breathed evenly, was conscious of my footing and weight shifting, and of trying not to think of anything; to just feel the moves. At the end of the three sections, I re-did them, going through the same form but its mirror image.

Finally, I sat down in a nearby armchair, and let my mind wander. I lost sight of the room around me.

Instead, there was the al-Rashids in the hotel room…the photo of my meeting at the Tel Aviv café…Saleh al-Rashid taking off his keffiyeh…his sweating forehead…

Black hood over my head…my body being thrown against a wall. On the floor. There was someone else on the floor. A man. Unmoving….

There was a flashlight in my eyes…a face in front of me…and in the background a workbench filled with items needing repair.

My mind examined the scene from all angles. I moved around the face that was close by…zoomed in on the workbench behind the man, pulled back to look at the entire work area. Zoomed in again on the table, but this time focusing on each item: the table lamp, the faucet fixture, doorknob, tools, the windowpane with the broken glass. The large pot, the upside-down chair off to the side, and the cell phone.

I opened my eyes, and for a very long moment just stared ahead. My breathing, which had slowed down, came back up. I was conscious of my heartbeat. There was a clock on an adjacent wall. Three hours had gone by.

Back in my room, I went over to the bag Gil had brought that had contained my clothes. My cell phone was still inside. The first call went to Gil; the second to Amit. The first part of each conversation was straightforward: Aminah's uncle, the man who had worked for Marwan al-Rashid and the one who stole whatever it was from his boss, was dead. He had been beaten until he was lifeless.

The second part of the call made my throat go dry. I told each agent what I had seen in the basement where al-Rashid had held me. The image had become more and more clear. Among all the items on the workbench was a large steel-type pot that could have been a pressure cooker. Next to it was a cell phone. Gil, Amit, and I and a lot of other people all knew the same fact: a pressure cooker and a cell phone were basic components of an explosive device.

37

Once the private jet belonging to the American Embassy finished its climb, I unbuckled my seat belt and stood up. The pains in my chest and back were still there, of course, and the bruised muscles across my stomach continued to be a presence. Joining the list was a steady headache. The roar of the engines through the fuselage wasn't helping, but the noise wasn't as intrusive as it would have been on a commercial flight. I looked around the aircraft's interior. Up front, emblazoned on a partition near the cockpit door was the seal of the United States. Amazing what the words "credible threat" could muster.

I walked up and down the aisle, and at some point put my palms against a bulkhead for a runner's stretch, first one leg, then the other. I rotated my arms and shoulders as well. When I moved my head in a circle, the headache became more intense, but then settled into its constant annoyance.

Gil and Amit were already huddled over a table in the back of the plane, discussing strategies and what was going to happen once we landed. Six hours ago, we were in Amit's conference room.

* * *

"A workman could just be repairing it," Amit had said, referencing the pot I had seen on the workman's bench.

"Okay, now that someone has said that, can we move on?" I was grumpy. The thought of Aminah being involved in terrorism didn't fit.

The Student

"She's a well-adjusted, stable, college kid."

"We'll see," Gil commented.

Both the FBI Special Agent and Amit had turned their people loose on Aminah's social media footprint.

"She's not a jihadi. She's an innocent college kid."

Both law enforcement agents looked at me.

"I know, BDS on campus, 'Oh, the Israeli occupiers.' Impressionable kid. Not her. Doesn't fit."

"She could be a courier," Amit said. "Or have been coerced."

"Any word from London?" The British Security Services were supposed to check on her parents.

Amit shook his head.

"Why did she go to Amman where al-Rashid happen to be?" Gil asked.

"Because she got a call from her parents who told her to go."

Gil looked at me with one eyebrow raised.

"I don't know. I do know she's a good kid. You've met her."

Gil nodded, but didn't say anything.

Amit sighed, and then, "We have the video of her coming off the plane at the Philadelphia airport. Maybe we'll recognize someone else." He turned to a fourth person in the room, a young woman I had seen on the IDF base before the night operation. Her name was Ayelet. Her dark blonde, frizzy hair was again pulled back and was still barely contained by a scrunchie. Amit nodded to her, and the young analyst typed on her laptop. A surveillance video came up on a large, nearby screen.

The angle was on a jetway door leading down to a plane. It was a familiar perspective. It was the same angle we had seen on the Heathrow video not all that long ago. In a moment, passengers filed up the boarding ramp, cleared the jetway's entry door, and into the terminal proper. One after another, the passengers emerged. Most looked tired, some were disheveled, others looked refreshed. All moved purposefully. Amit, Gil, and I focused on their faces. No one seemed familiar.

As we watched, Ayelet offered, "We ran each of the passengers and crew through facial recognition. Nothing."

We continued to observe everyone who had gotten off the plane. No one turned away to hide a face.

"There she is," I nodded.

Aminah came off the jetway, moving fluidly, following the person a step in front of her. She was wearing a pair of dark leggings and a sweatshirt that had "London" across the front. Her short blonde hair was all but covered by a ball cap. The four of us watched as the remaining complement exited the ramp. Ayelet froze the image just after the final person cleared the frame, and looked at me. I turned to Amit and Gil.

No one said anything, then Amit offered, "She looked calm, not ill at ease..."

"Back it up to the beginning, please." Gil stepped over to Ayelet.

She did, and we watched the procession again.

First, a tall man in a T-shirt and shorts came off, followed by a few couples with young children in hand, then everyone else. The column of passengers continued. Once in the lounge area in front of the entry doors, a few people sidestepped the slower-moving passengers. As we had seen on the first pass, no one had looked away from the camera or covered their faces.

"Okay, stop," Gil said.

The screen froze on Aminah. The image was crystal clear.

"She's a college kid, right?" Gil said to no one in particular. "She's been home in Israel, then overseas, traveling. Shopping for sure. Twelve-hour flight maybe. She's flown internationally before. She knows what to expect: boredom, fluctuating cabin temperatures, long times between meals..." She looked at us again. "What doesn't she have?"

We turned to the still image again. Aminah was mid-frame in her leggings, sweatshirt, and carrying a medium-sized purse over her shoulder.

I smiled. "No carry-on. She had a backpack when I saw her in Amman." I could visualize the navy backpack and the smiley emoji along the top.

Gil continued, "Maybe someone else has the backpack? You know to put something inside?"

al-Rashid?

"Maybe it was checked." This from Amit. "Let's be certain."

Before we asked, Ayelet pulled up an exterior view of the baggage area. She had anticipated the request and had it cued. We watched as Aminah pulled a single, medium-sized suitcase off the carousel and headed for the exit doors. No backpack.

Amit: "So much for that."

"Why now?" Gil asked. "Why go back to the States now?"

A few seconds passed. I turned to the Shin Bet man. "Where's Marwan al-Rashid? Still in Amman?"

Amit nodded to Ayelet who got to work on her laptop.

"And check his brother, Saleh, too," I added.

In my head I revisited my conversation with Aminah from the Kempinski lobby. "She wanted to go back to Hopkins. She thought it'd be safe because we got the Iranian agents in Baltimore. Also, something called QuadFest was coming up, and her parents might be coming in."

Gil went over to another laptop. In a few moments she pulled up the Hopkins University home page. "QuadFest is an arts festival held on the various quads at the Homewood Campus." She paused and then, "Starts tomorrow night."

"Of course it does."

Ayelet interrupted. "Marwan al-Rashid is back in Riyad. And Saleh, based on the U.S. Homeland Security, entered the U.S. yesterday." Shared intelligence. Ayelet scrolled. "He entered on a diplomatic passport along with two other men."

There was a long silence in the room.

Gil looked from Amit to me. "The explosive devices used in

the Boston Marathon bombings were pressure cooker bombs left in backpacks."

"In 2002," Amit said softly, "terrorists placed a bomb at Hebrew University, in the cafeteria. Nine people were killed, and a hundred were injured. Five of the dead were Americans. The terrorists didn't wait for a QuadFest."

The room went silent. Out of my peripheral vision I could see Ayelet looking at us.

Amit turned to Gil. "You call your people. I'll call mine."

* * *

The air route to the U.S. from Tel Aviv arced north, skirting the southwest corner of England, peaked about midway across the Atlantic and then curved southwest past Nova Scotia, Massachusetts, Connecticut, and finally down to Maryland. As the diplomatic jet was crossing Upper Chesapeake Bay, Amit stood up from a hunched-over conversation with Gil, and came forward to sit next to me. His forehead was taut.

"Just spoke with the British Security Service," he looked at me with humorless eyes. "Aminah's parents were taken from their London hotel room a week and a half ago. Turns out MI5 was already watching the people who had abducted them…they were *dmuyot ha'shudot*." Persons of Interest.

I listened in silence, and then glanced back to Gil. She was still at the table in the rear of the cabin, but was now on the phone.

"The parents were taken to a house in a working-class suburb of Manchester. British Intelligence was listening in and heard the captors forcing them to call Aminah. My call to MI5 put everything in perspective and gave them a sense of urgency."

"They're going to raid the house."

"In under an hour, once everything is in place."

I just nodded and he went back to the rear of the cabin.

The Student

Aminah had been in Amman because her parents told her to go. They had no choice, and Aminah was almost certainly being watched the entire time. Now, she probably had no choice in taking her backpack to Hopkins once it would be given back to her. al-Rashid – either one – had found a way to get the device into the country. Would Aminah know what would be inside?

Twenty minutes later we landed at a small, private airfield on the periphery of Baltimore-Washington Airport. As we taxied, the sun had touched the western horizon, throwing beautiful streaks of red and blue into the sky. Military fields were too far from Baltimore, and we needed to get moving; the arts festival was starting in under two hours. Even the pilot had pushed it, making the typical westbound twelve-hour flight in ten.

The plane had barely rolled to a stop when flight attendants opened the cabin door and quickly moved out of the way. We hustled down the steps and into a waiting gunmetal Tahoe. Its driver took off before all doors were closed.

Conniker, Gil Jeffries' FBI partner, and the driver were in front; Amit, Gil, and I were in back.

"Mr. Amit," Conniker said, shifting around to talk to us, "Welcome to the United States. Mr. Aronson, glad you're okay."

"Thanks." It was the first pleasant thing the FBI man had said to me.

Conniker handed us Federal ID badges. Gil took a holstered automatic from her partner, and then slipped on an FBI raid jacket. I wasn't going to ask for a weapon. Instead, I looked at my FBI ID and then up at Conniker, eyebrows raised.

"If anything goes south, I'll deny giving it to you." Conniker was straight-faced.

"That's the agent I know," I smiled.

As we sped northward on 295, the Baltimore-Washington Parkway, Conniker took out a tablet that had a Hopkins University campus map pulled up. He then reviewed where law enforcement would be. The

Homewood campus was basically an immense, 140-acre rectangle, with lecture halls, offices, libraries, dorms, administrative buildings, and more, populating the entire property. The graphic made the buildings look almost like Monopoly hotels. In between the structures, and really all over the place, were walkways, roads, and four quads and multiple other, large grassy areas. QuadFest was set up on all the quads, and of course, they were not contiguous to make surveillance easy, but separated by all those buildings, roads, and walkways. He sent the map to Amit's and my cell phones.

No one questioned Hopkins as the target. Aminah coming back for the festival was all anyone needed.

Gil asked about bomb disposal units.

"We have three of ours and three from local law enforcement. We can be anywhere on campus within ten minutes."

The Shin Bet man and I exchanged looks. Too long. A lifetime for people in a blast radius.

The Parkway dumped us onto city streets, and we blew through intersections and red lights, weaving between cars and pedestrians.

"Should've brought my motion sickness pills," Amit said without humor, and half to himself.

The Tahoe's tinted windows kept us anonymous; there was more than one angry look from drivers and people trying to cross a street.

As we moved onto North Charles Street, not all that far from my martial art studio, Amit's cell phone audibly vibrated. He pulled it out, and spoke to the caller in English. After only fifteen seconds, he said, "Thank you," and disconnected the call.

Gil and I eyed him.

"The raid in England. Aminah's parents are fine. They were in a back room. al-Rashid's men – there were four – are all dead. No casualties in the assault team."

"We need to get to Aminah," Gil said.

Eight minutes later we pulled up to the half-circle campus road on the southern end of the University's rectangle. BPD patrol cars,

The Student

unmarked Federal vehicles, and a large, black mobile command post were parked all around the South Gate entrance.

When we emerged from the Tahoe, a tall, dark-haired agent handed us earpieces and mics. Almost immediately the cell phones around us all pinged.

"Those are texts," the agent said, "with photos of Aminah Hadad, Saleh al-Rashid, and his two men."

At the mention of Aminah being grouped with al-Rashid and his men, my mouth went dry. Overhead, I could hear the high-pitched percussion of a helicopter.

I pulled on a black IDF sweatshirt.

"Hey there, Major."

I turned to see Nate D'Allesandro, my Captain friend. "Hey."

We gave each other a quick hug. He set off a number of nerve endings.

"You look like shit," he observed. "How was the Amman Hilton?" Nate referenced the "Hanoi Hilton," the infamous Vietnamese prison.

"Basement was interesting. I'll go back one day with some of my army friends," I smiled. After a second, "Glad you're here."

"It's my homicide case." He then nodded to Ed Soper, the detective he had assigned to the case all that time ago. We exchanged half smiles.

I introduced Nate to Amit, who shook his hand. Then, after the pleasantries, my captain friend pulled me aside.

"You up for this?"

"What do you think?"

Nate reached into a shopping bag he had been holding, pulled out an HK .45 C in a holster, and handed it to me. "Full clip. Chamber's empty."

I pulled back the slide and set the safety.

As I attached it near the small of my back under my sweatshirt, he asked, "Do you have your Wear and Carry?"

Nate knew the answer, but I played along with the tease. "And a letter from the Director of Homeland Security. Both are at home."

"Too bad."

Conniker gathered everyone, gave the group last-minute instructions, and then the law enforcement crew dispersed up the nearby walk and onto campus – all the agents, but Conniker and Gil. Conniker came in close. "You're still a civilian. Keep that in mind."

"That's right, Gidon," Nate said, patting the automatic under the back of my sweatshirt, with a wry grin.

Conniker walked up the grass-lined path between lecture halls. Gil came over and had to shake her head, but didn't say anything.

"He's back in character," I looked at her. "Don't you outrank him? This is your show."

"He was on the ground to set it up."

"You helped put two and two together."

"And if we're wrong about Aminah, her backpack, and everything, this'll be an anti-terrorism drill no one will forget…ever."

Amit watched the group move off, but lightly grabbed me by the upper arm. "I need to stay back. Expecting a call from Jerusalem."

"Okay." I looked at him, but didn't say anything further. If he had wanted to tell me more, he would have.

Gil and I headed up the walkway, side by side, but didn't say anything. The sounds of a band tuning up filtered through the spaces between various buildings. Once we passed between the admissions building and Malone Hall, we came to a T – one quad was to the left and one to the right. Gil nodded to me: *You go that way, I'll go this way.*

"Talk to you soon," I said, and she went left and I right.

Signs for QuadFest were all over the place – oversized arrows with event names printed on them, pointing the way to various happenings and exhibits. To the left was an oval quad, to the right, where I was walking, was the bigger, rectangular Wyman Quad.

By now daylight was gone, and regular campus lighting had been augmented by floods, mounted high up on telescoping poles. Nearby generators sounded like small lawnmower engines. Students had already started arriving, and soon enough, the area was filled with

The Student

people.

I entered the expansive, rectangular grassy area and had to pause to take it all in. The quad was framed on all sides by walkways. On the outside of the frame were side by side Georgian-style buildings, separated only by narrow sidewalks. I didn't know what all the buildings were, but could guess: lecture halls, offices, auditoriums, perhaps. I had an idea, since I was here not that long ago, but the familiarity was camouflaged by rows of booths, lining all the walkways. In each booth, artists and crafts people were still laying out their wares.

The stands were assembled of aluminum poles, with either green or blue fabric for walls. I started up the eastern leg of the quad, only superficially looking at the vendors. My focus was on the crowd.

The attendees were predominantly students, but there was a mix of older adults as well. Regardless of age, people congregated at almost every kiosk. The glass artists, metal artists, painters, leatherworkers, and more, drew people in. I scanned faces and looked for a navy backpack with a smiley emoji along the top.

The helicopter continued to circle above the campus in the night sky, its running lights clearly visible. After a moment, I looked back at the crowd in general. I was amazed at a few things. The first was how there were no security stations at the campus entrances. In Israel, barriers would have been set up to funnel people through a guard station, and security people would check bags and ask questions. They'd *look* at you. The United States was still fortunate and naïve.

One of Conniker's men approached from the opposite direction. We nodded to each other and kept moving. I continued to scan faces.

There was some chatter in my earpiece…a possible Aminah sighting that turned out to be someone else. There were so many college kids, so many similar builds and features.

I passed more jewelry makers, metal artists, cloth painters. At the top of the quad's rectangle and midway across, curved steps led up to a small plaza and more buildings. I passed the stairs and crossed to the western side of the rectangle, looking up at the rooftops. They were all in shadow, thanks to the lighting coming off the buildings, pointing outward and down. Great locations for snipers, behind lights and invisible to anyone looking for them. Maybe my guardian angel from South Charles Street was up there. It'd be a tricky shot, though, considering the density of the crowd. An FBI sniper would need major authorization for a "take the shot."

My headache returned, if it ever left. My sides hurt, and my back still ached. I continued forward.

The crowd became thicker – and then I smelled roasting meat. The food tent. In another few feet, forward motion slowed, as visitors looked at placards to see what nourishment was available. If Aminah were here, she'd easily blend in with all these kids. I pushed my way through the group. Faces went past to my right and left. No one familiar.

Maybe Aminah wasn't here at the festival. It was possible we misread the whole thing, that I made assumptions about what was on the worktable in that basement. My earpiece was silent as well, adding to the uncertain feeling. No sightings of Aminah, al-Rashid, or his men. As for kids with backpacks, there were plenty…large, small, blue, black, green…

After a complete circuit, I moved to the center of the quad to scan the area again. All I could do, all anyone of us could do, was keep looking. I started to walk back, moving counter-clockwise, when a uniformed university security man waved at me and approached.

"Officer Richburg," I said as the campus cop came over. Richburg was the university officer on the scene when Noa and Aminah had the break-in, plus we had chatted about possible leads.

"Mr. Aronson, how are you?" He paused as his eyes took in the bruises healing on my cheek.

"I'm good, really. You're up to speed on all this?"

"Looking for the three individuals? Yeah. And I remember the kid from the break-in at her apartment. Know what's going on?"

"Not really."

"Virtually all my men are here. Those were the orders." He paused and then looked around. "I've never seen so many Feds."

We both smiled and we both kept walking.

I made another circuit and then headed over to Gil's area. Decker Quad, an oval, grassy expanse, toward the southwest end of campus, was a short walk between a few buildings and along another walkway. As I approached, I could see booths set up along its periphery as well. At one end, a band was playing rock and roll classics. There were probably twenty people sitting in chairs at the front of the stage. I made a slow circuit, just as I had done at the other field. In the course of the walk-around, I didn't see Gil, but did spot three other Feds. I headed back.

Conniker's voice in my ear asked all the agents to check in. One by one they did. Nothing. No one had seen Aminah, or al-Rashid, or his men.

If Aminah were here, I'd love to see her walking hand in hand with some guy. I'd be content being wrong about her. We would chat, and she could prove us all misguided about an explosive device. I took a deep breath, conscious of my ailing ribs. At the Boston Marathon, three people were killed, and hundreds injured. At Hebrew University, what did Amit say…nine dead, a hundred injured?

I walked to the northern end of the quad and climbed the semicircular stairs I had skirted earlier. Eight steps up. Hopefully, there'd be a decent vantage point. I sprinted to the top of the marble steps and turned around. It wasn't much of an elevation, but it was something. At least the entire area was in front of me: the parallel rows of kiosks to the right and left, the flow of visitors, lights, footpaths slicing across the field, people everywhere.

This whole thing with Aminah didn't make sense. She seemed to not know what was going on.

The food booth. That's where I'd place a device for the most casualties.

I walked down the steps and headed toward the line of booths on my right. I weaved in between clusters of college kids and individuals, always looking at their backs and watching the approaching faces. And then, up ahead, about fifteen feet, a navy backpack with a smiley emoji.

The smiley face was winking and had its tongue out. From the back, I could see that Aminah was wearing the ball cap she had on in the airport surveillance video. It still covered her short hair. I closed the distance, calmly calling my location into my mic. I quickened my pace.

"Aminah."

What were the odds of another navy backpack with the same emoji, being worn by a woman of Aminah's build and wearing the same type of ball cap?

The young woman I had last seen in the elevator of an Amman hotel didn't turn around. Maybe she hadn't heard me. There was a lot of ambient noise. One of the floodlight generators hummed nearby. That had to be it.

"Aminah!"

My mind flashed to the cell phone on the workbench in that basement. All someone had to do right now was place a call to that phone. When it clicked through, at this distance, those around Aminah – myself included – would be shredded by a wall of ball bearings, nails, and screws. There'd be a hundred bodies on the ground, bleeding and dying. Booths would be torn apart. Windows in the surrounding buildings would be shattered. And then there'd be staggering silence.

How could al-Rashid have turned her? Her family had left Lebanon, moved to Jordan, and then to Haifa. She was Christian, if that made any difference.

Aminah kept walking forward, toward the mass of students in front of the food booth.

Her visit to Amman a week ago couldn't have been a coincidence. Everything I had known about her must have been carefully planned: her stay here as a student, her life in Haifa, the trip to Jordan. She hadn't been turned. Her trip was for final instructions. She was a sleeper.

I closed the distance, and reached behind me for the gun Nate had handed me earlier. Without removing it from the holster, I clicked off the safety. I knew exactly how long it'd take me to draw and fire.

"Shut them down," I said into my mic. "Now."

"Roger that," some voice responded.

I left my weapon where it was. If I took it out, someone would see it. There'd be screams, panic, and if there were a button in Aminah's hand, she might push it. There might be a dead-man's switch. I wasn't going to shoot her in the back of the head, regardless. I kept my hand behind me, though, close to the .45.

Aminah stopped walking. As she turned, I continued forward. In another second I saw her face.

Tears were running down Noa's cheeks.

Noa. Not Aminah.

I looked at her hands. Both were gripping the backpack's support straps running down her front. No dead-man's switch, no button.

"Noa," that's all I said.

She was sobbing. "They're going to kill my parents and my brother."

"You need to stop moving."

"They're going to kill them if I don't leave this bag where they told me." The tears came faster, and she started walking again.

"Noa, stop." I stepped in front of her.

I had no idea if the bag were wired to her, though she said she was instructed to leave it. They could've lied, and removing it would detonate the device.

"Your family is safe." I had no idea where her parents and brother were, let alone if they were safe. "Is the backpack connected to you in any way besides the carry straps?"

She looked at me for a second, confused, then shook her head.

"Put the bag down."

She shook her head again, still crying.

"Everyone's safe, I promise."

"Let me speak to them."

If the device in the backpack had a back-up timer, seconds were going by.

"I can't. We shut down all the cell towers in the area."

"What?"

"The phones don't work."

"What?" she repeated.

A thought flashed by. "Noa, what's in the backpack?"

"Drugs. Drugs," she repeated. "I was told to leave the backpack on the side of the food booth. Someone was going to pick it up. If I didn't do it, or looked inside, they'd kill…"

A bomb set off by an Israeli student at an American university… the niece of the Deputy Director of the Mossad. It was brilliant.

"Please put the bag down." I repeated the request in Hebrew.

"No."

"Noa." She wasn't going to get past me, and she knew it.

"You promise about my parents and brother."

I nodded. God, I hoped her family was okay.

Noa lowered Aminah's backpack.

"Step away from it, please."

She did.

As we moved back, a cluster of Feds ran over to us. Gil was in the lead.

"Noa," she asked. "You okay?"

She nodded.

"Back away some more."

As Noa stepped back, Gil turned to face the people around us. She raised her voice and took out her ID. "Ladies and Gentlemen, I'm FBI Special Agent in Charge Gil Jeffries." She held her ID up high. "Please calmly move to either end of the quad. Do not run. Walk calmly, but quickly." She repeated the instructions two more times, each time indicating with her free hand to move back. The other FBI agents nearby repeated her instructions and moved everyone back. None of the Feds had given an explanation, just the command to move away. Slowly, the area cleared. Some people ran; most just walked rapidly.

Gil and I were fifty feet from the backpack when she said, "EOD is on its way. Cell service will stay off until they give us the all clear."

I nodded and watched as the agents continued to move the visitors back. On the edge of a group of students, at the eastern end of the rectangle, three men had remained behind. They were watching us. The man in the middle was shorter than his companions. His face, even at this distance was completely recognizable. It resembled his older brother, Marwan, and the last time I had seen him clearly his forehead was glistening with sweat, just a foot in front of me. The men beside him – one tall and slender, the other husky – may have been two of the men who held me up while al-Rashid pounded me. It didn't matter if they were or not. The man in the center was definitely Saleh. He saw my recognition, said something to his men, and they sprinted up the line of booths toward the northern end of the quad.

"al-Rashid," was all I said to Gil and took off.

The trio ran past clusters of students, past blue booths and green booths. They jumped over people sitting on the grass. The tall, slender bodyguard was in the lead, and he shoved kids out of his way. al-Rashid was just behind him. The third man looked back at me. There were screams. I heard the helicopter overhead, and my chest began to erupt in pain. I hadn't run for a while, not since the man in front of me had hammered my ribcage and abdomen.

They were heading toward the curved circular staircase I had stood on not ten minutes before. I pulled the .45 from its holster.

The distance between us closed. They had the disadvantage of clearing people out of their path. I was twenty feet behind. The faces of young men and women whisked past on either side. It was just a matter of time before one of Saleh's men took out a gun.

I knew how to fire a weapon while running. The steadiness came mostly from the knees. Don't lock your legs as you run.

Some kid, a young man, I think, cut in front of me.

"Get down!"

He dropped to the grass and I jumped over him. The tall, slender bodyguard had reached the curved steps and began to race up them. al-Rashid was right behind. At the base of the eight marble steps the third man turned and brought his gun up. I shot him three times in the chest.

I ran past him and up the stairs without even a glance at the body.

The small, circular plaza at the top had a tree or a bush or something in the center. Beyond it, at the far end, staircases on either end led to a colonnade.

The tall, slender bodyguard and al-Rashid took the right-hand steps two at a time. al-Rashid stumbled, recovered, and continued up to the colonnade. Once at the top they pushed a group of students aside and ran forward.

I climbed the steps, the pulsing in my head steadily increasing with every step. My ribcage was already filling my torso with sharp, stabbing pain.

At the top of the stairs I had to stop. It wasn't the pain. The covered passageway was filled with students who had sought refuge far from the commotion in front of the food booth. Many were fiddling with their phones, no doubt trying to get a signal. Some students screamed, seeing the gun in my hand and probably the intensity in my eyes. They backed away.

The colonnade I was now inside led to buildings to my right and left. Straight ahead, though, was an open quad. al-Rashid was fifty feet away, running toward the other end.

Before I had a chance to move, a fist caught me in my side. Pain shot through my chest and enveloped me. For a moment I couldn't see, and without meaning to, took a step back. My eyes opened. The tall, slender man was beside me. He had known exactly where to hit me. He knew because he had been there, in the basement, holding me up as his boss hammered my chest, sides, and abdomen.

He tore the gun from my hand and rotated it, effortlessly, and began pointing toward me.

The safety was off, and there was a round in the chamber. I might just see the muzzle flash in the split-second before the bullet mushroomed through my heart or my head.

With its own reaction, my right foot shot up, whipping into the slender man's wrist. Involuntarily, his hand opened, and the .45 was knocked clear.

His response was instantaneous. His right foot lashed out at my chest. I managed a partial turn. The deflected impact still sent waves of pain across my ribcage.

I breathed through it, because I knew what his next move was going to be.

He was a tall man. Long legs. He was going to kick.

I backed up as he fired out another kick. I rotated just enough for him to miss me. He put the foot down and his other foot began to rise. By the way he lifted his knee, he was going for my head. I pushed my legs down into the ground, and sprang forward, stifling the rising kick while capturing it in the crook of my arm. I swept out his supporting leg.

He fell to the ground, catching the impact on shoulders, and rolled out.

As he came up I closed the distance again. Now there wasn't room for him to kick. I was right on him, and I liked working in close.

He began to punch me with his right hand, but I blocked the incoming fist with my left arm while simultaneously stepping to his side. We were now hip-to-hip, almost like in a tango. My right hand was already up, fingers spread, curved and stiff. They went to his face. My index and middle fingers found his eyes, the rest of my hand locked onto the mask of his face. I still had forward momentum. I yanked his head straight back and arced it violently down to the brick and concrete walkway. There was no mistaking the crack of his skull.

I stood up as the pounding in my head went from temple to temple. My chest muscles spasmed with every inhale.

Now conscious of people around me, I retrieved my .45, set the safety, and looked out at the quad where I had last seen al-Rashid running. He wasn't there. The quad was still filled with people, but I could tell. Saleh al-Rashid was gone.

My eyes narrowed as the headache moved down my forehead.

I looked at the motionless, slender man on the ground. And that's when they told me I collapsed.

38

This time when consciousness returned I didn't first assess my surroundings with my hearing. I just opened my eyes. The sights, sounds, and smells were too recent and familiar. Drab walls, antiseptic, doctors being paged.

Gil was in a chair opposite the foot of my bed.

"You're in my hospital room again," I said.

She put down a stack of papers and came over. "Well, you're in the hospital again."

The overhead light had been turned off, and the blinds were down partway. There was still plenty of daylight coming in. I looked up at the ceiling for no reason and then over at Gil. After a moment, and after gathering some mental strength, "Everyone okay?"

"Yes."

"The backpack?"

"More than twice the explosives than Boston."

"Secured?"

She nodded.

"Good."

I lifted my head and tried to sit up. The bed had been raised to a 45 degree angle, but it didn't help. I got as far as pulling my head forward when throbbing rushed to the top of my skull and nausea came up in my stomach. I let my head fall back into the pillow.

"You're in Union Memorial, in case you're keeping a tally.

Concussion. Probably had it since your vacation in Amman."

"And that's how I'll always remember my time there." I tried to smile, but wasn't sure my facial muscles managed it.

"If you need to puke, there's one of those curved spittoons right over here," she pointed to a nearby rolling tray.

"Thanks. I'll see if I can save it for later."

"You've been out for twelve hours."

I nodded and wished I hadn't.

"Aminah and Noa?"

"Aminah's in London with her parents, talking to the British Security Services. They still have questions about her involvement with the al-Rashids. I may need to fly over."

MI5 wanted everything neat and locked away. I was okay with what we knew. "And Noa?"

"In Federal custody. Amit's in DC on her behalf. He'll be by later and explain all that."

"What about her parents?"

"Amit will explain," she repeated.

I tried to sit up again. I took it inch by inch and managed to sit up without either passing out or throwing up.

"Bravo. You gonna heave?"

"Maybe."

I looked at Gil. She was back in her traditional FBI office attire: Navy blue blazer and matching slacks.

"Back on the job?"

"Of course."

"And your work status?"… thinking about how some people had been unhappy with her.

"All is well." After another moment. "By the way, in case some nurses swoon over you, it's because you're famous. You were caught on cell phone video taking out that tall guy."

"Oh, God."

"Bad angle, though, and your face isn't too clear. Have to know it was you. Maybe you can still use it to get some new students." She smiled.

"I was wearing your security ID."

"Uh-huh. 'We're not at liberty to discuss who you are,' though we leaked that you're an undercover agent, and any attempt to reveal your name is a felony."

"Thank you."

"So, Mr. Kent, your secret is safe."

Gil walked back to where she had been sitting and picked up her phone and the papers from a table. "Gotta go. Be back later, if I can."

"Thanks."

She headed for the door, but then turned back. "Who's Sammi?"

"What?"

"Sammi. You said the name at some point while you were out."

"I don't talk in my sleep or when I'm unconscious."

"Yeah, you do. And you said the name very clearly."

"I don't believe you." I took a breath, then, "Sammi was my teacher's wife."

"You had a thing for your teacher's wife?"

"No, NO. My teacher died."

"And you hit on his widow?"

"No. Not all. Sammi's a friend. Always has been…just a friend."

"Uh-huh." She smiled.

How do I explain that Sammi, or at least my projection of her in recent meditations, had pulled me from despair, plus helped me keep it together in that Amman basement.

"Later." Gil headed out of the room.

The moment she was gone I leaned back into the bed.

* * *

As the day progressed I had three more visitors. First, Katie. She told me that Nate had called her, because he thought she should know

I was here. He was trying to fix what was broken. As soon as she told me that, I made a mental note to have a conversation with my friend. On the other hand, I did call her before going to Jordan, and perhaps that sent a message other than I was apologizing for any insensitive behavior on my part.

Katie stayed for half an hour, and didn't ask anything about what had happened, just if I were all right. She told me about school, and other innocuous stuff. On the way out of the room, though, she wanted to know if we could go to dinner once I was back in my routine. My response: "Let me get out of here and we'll talk about it."

Jon came next. Said that Katie had called him. He was his enthusiastic self, and wanted to know everything that had happened, which I couldn't tell him. He wanted to know what was going on with Noa and Aminah, and I couldn't tell him that either. I placated my number one student with a promise to teach him how to apply meditative techniques to pain control. That intrigued him. He already had some ideas.

The last visitor of the day was Amit. After walking in, he closed the door, and sat in the seat where Gil had been.

"We don't know where Saleh al-Rashid is. Neither does the FBI. Likely on a Saudi jet over the Atlantic."

"You'll find him."

"Yes, we will."

"Tell me about Noa and Aminah."

"Aminah, you know the story. Her parents were forced to call her. Later she was instructed to give Noa the backpack. It's why you couldn't find Aminah at the arts festival. She wasn't there."

"Noa was."

He nodded.

"And your calls from Israel?"

He took a deep breath – he probably didn't mean to – and let it out. "The man you brought back from Qaltuniya told us about an Iranian cell in the West Bank."

I nodded.

"The man also told us about an operation to take three Israelis hostage."

"Noa's parents and brother." My mouth went dry.

"They took them to a house outside of Tulkarm. My men and a Duvdevan unit – same unit you had gone with – executed a hostage rescue. That's the call I was waiting for when you and Agent Jeffries went onto the university campus."

He paused and I wished he hadn't. Rescues in a hostile setting were always risky. So many factors. You plan, you practice, drill repeatedly, and pray.

"Noa's mother and brother are fine. Her father…her father was shot in the lower right abdomen by one of the Iranian mercenaries. The *abba* was trying to help our men. He's still in recovery. Hasn't regained consciousness, but the doctors are hopeful."

I pictured Noa's father outside his office building in Seattle, and then wearing the Israeli-style bucket hat, and giving us a hard time when we met them outside a restaurant in Israel.

"Two Palestinians and two former Quds Force soldiers were shot and killed in the raid," Amit continued. "Our men returned safely."

A few seconds passed.

"You'll let me know about Noa's father."

"Of course."

"What about Noa? Gil said she's in Federal custody."

"With some diplomatic interventions, I hope we can get charges dropped. She didn't know what she was doing and was being manipulated. Worse case, maybe, she'll have to leave the U.S. for a period of time."

All I could think about was how distraught Noa must be. "You have to talk to the FBI about letting her go home to see her father."

The Shin Bet man took off his rectangular glasses and rubbed his eyes. "Conversations are happening. We'll see."

More than a few seconds went by. I stood up, and then shuffled

The Student

over to a nearby wall to lean against it. In about a second, the headache forced me to sit down again. After a few long breaths, "From worrying about stolen account passwords to bombing a university."

He nodded.

"Why not build the bomb here?"

"*Ani lo yode'ah*. I don't know. That part has the feel of something rushed. Maybe it would be easier to implicate Noa, Idan, and the Mossad that way. And less risk of exposure before they were ready." Another few seconds passed. "There's something else for Homeland Security to worry about: how the al-Rashids got the bomb here. Many people on upper floors of Federal buildings are quite upset."

"I'm sure you'll hear about it."

He nodded. We chatted about other operational details, and then he headed out. He had more face-to-face visits in DC, and then he was going home in the morning. I knew he'd be in touch.

* * *

I was released the following afternoon, and spent most of the next several days lightly working out, teaching lessons, and just trying to get my head around everything that had happened. At night, sleeping for any length of time was still a challenge. I was only able to manage two consecutive hours of sleep at best. Katie came by every few days, and she never raised the subject of going out again, though I expected that conversation was still in our future.

Gil stopped by occasionally after work. She hadn't gone to London as expected. Instead, she came by when she could, usually catching me toward the end of a teaching session or a workout. We'd grab a quick snack and then she'd head home. I was waiting for my worlds of Katie and Gil to collide.

Nate and I met at the firing range, where I filled him in on what the FBI hadn't already revealed. I also apologized for not seeing his daughter who was in Israel, the one I had rescued some time ago. He was understanding. He knew I was preoccupied, either on a mission or getting the crap knocked out of me. I told him I *let* them beat the crap out of me. The retort caught him in the middle of emptying his clip at the target, and he laughed so hard, he missed the entire silhouette.

After our conversation about the investigation and all that occurred in Israel, I felt like I needed to go back and just walk the streets and paths of that land. Take some trips up north. See Maayan again. Perhaps Nate and his wife would come with me, and make a personal stop of their own.

As time went on, I found myself in a post-mission funk. It would pass as my mind cleared; that I knew. One bright spot was a call from Amit, reporting Noa's father was recovering and out of danger. Noa was also able to return to Israel without any restrictions, and come back to the U.S., if she wanted. Charges had been dropped. There must have been some interesting phone calls crossing the Atlantic. Maybe someone figured she was already so full of intense anguish that was sufficient punishment.

The Amman Hilton, as Nate had called it, plus the fight at Hopkins continued their residence in my mind.

The al-Rashids had retreated to the safe havens of Saudi Arabia or who knows where.

At some point, after I had consistently returned to my studio, Jon came into my office while I was working on my laptop. He sat himself in the chair beside the desk. "So, Sifu, have a thought for you."

I looked over.

"You know how all this started because Noa's uncle, the Mossad guy, asked you to look after Noa?"

I nodded.

"Think he knew about any of this stuff…that any of this was going to happen?"

I leaned back in the chair. "Maybe."

"Maybe?"

"I ran through all this before in my head. Could be coincidence that soon after he asked me to check on Noa that something happened. Or maybe he knew something was going on, but didn't know what it was, and couldn't officially check it out."

"So he used you to poke around."

"Maybe."

"Doesn't that make you angry?"

I shook my head. "It's pointless. Could still be a coincidence. There's no way of knowing. However Idan would respond to that question, not sure I'd believe him. And besides, the girls really did need help." I looked at my senior student. "Also, I'm too tired to put more energy into that avenue."

Jon sort of smiled, paused, and then went back to whatever he had been doing.

And the days continued on.

Two weeks after the events at the university, I was getting back to some mindless chores, such as straightening my office. While I was going through a stack of mail, I let a news program run on my laptop, giving me something to listen to. The segment included a piece on colleges increasing security at public events. There had to be a balance, a university president expounded, between not restricting access to the courses, programs, and facilities while still maintaining everyone's safety.

Welcome to today's world, genius.

At that point, I needed to not listen anymore, and turned to my emails. There was a new letter from Amit, posted with an empty subject line. A click and a scroll revealed a single word in the text space, "Damascus," and an attached video. I clicked on it.

The video began as a long shot down a busy, urban street. No audio. The camera zoomed in on a black Mercedes SUV. From the angle of the shadows, the time of day looked to be either about 10:00 AM or 2:00 PM. The camera shifted to a storefront as Saleh al-Rashid emerged, carrying what looked like a large gift bag. The video followed al-Rashid as he slid into the passenger side of the SUV, while a taller man in a sport coat got behind the wheel.

The view cut to another shot of the vehicle driving down the street of a suburban neighborhood. The shadows, extending from trees and parked vehicles, were longer. Again, al-Rashid could be seen in the passenger side.

The perspective had just switched to another long shot, when the air in my office shifted. It was a very slight change, barely there, but it definitely happened. Someone had opened and then closed the front door. There was also a change in presence in the room.

I froze the image on my laptop and lowered the screen. I didn't need to watch it to know what was about to happen. The black Mercedes SUV would drive past a small car – a Fiat or a Peugeot – filled with just the right amount of explosives and armor-piercing projectiles. An observer nearby would push a button and that would be that. Hopefully, the assassination team had been careful about collateral damage.

But my mind wasn't on al-Rashid or whether he met his end in an explosion or by seven bullets fired into his center mass. It was on the person who had just walked in the front door.

The studio was completely silent. I took a slow, deep breath.

In the bottom right drawer of the desk was my lockbox. The HK and a loaded clip. I walked around the desk, not even considering it, and paused at a quarterstaff leaning in a corner. No. Not this weapon either. I walked out of the office and into the practice hall.

Standing in the middle of the large room was a woman, about ten years older than me. She had straight, auburn hair, and a radiant face. She was wearing a muted, flower-patterned top and jeans, and had a messenger-type pocketbook bag hanging diagonally across her torso.

I looked into her dark eyes, the softest I had ever seen, and my mood instantly improved.

"Hi," she said and smiled. "I came to see how you are."

"I'm good, Sammi. I'm good. Come in. I have a few questions for you."

ACKNOWLEDGMENTS

As the disclaimer states, *The Student* is a work of fiction. Locations and people have either been created or used fictitiously for the purposes of story. In some cases, real-life locales have been altered to meet the needs of the narrative.

In creating *The Student*, I leaned on a number of people who were invaluable sources of information, whether for their foreign language expertise, location knowledge, or military details. Thank you, then, to Gabi Gordon, Adin Rodman, and Elisha L. (all three in Israel), as well as to Larry Aronhime and Ian Lever. Please forgive any site alterations I made for the sake of the story. I would also like to express my appreciation to the staff at FreeState Gun Range in Middle River, Maryland, just outside of Baltimore. They educated me and helped me pick out a personal weapon for Gidon.

To AJ and Jeff, thanks for your thoughtful perspectives and well-considered advice.

For editing expertise and recommendations, Bonnie Gordon was my go-to expert, as well as my wife Becky. Any structural or syntactic errors that made it through to the final manuscript are my own oversights.

Finally, a special thank you to Kevin Atticks and his very capable crew at Apprentice House. You wouldn't be reading this without them!

ABOUT THE AUTHOR

Steve Gordon, the author of the Gidon Aronson series, was born and raised in Baltimore. For many years he taught American History and ancient world cultures in a local middle school. His writing credits also include a memoir for *Good Housekeeping* and television series work for Maryland Public Television.

Apprentice House Press
Loyola University Maryland

Apprentice House is the country's only campus-based, student-staffed book publishing company. Directed by professors and industry professionals, it is a nonprofit activity of the Communication Department at Loyola University Maryland.

Using state-of-the-art technology and an experiential learning model of education, Apprentice House publishes books in untraditional ways. This dual responsibility as publishers and educators creates an unprecedented collaborative environment among faculty and students, while teaching tomorrow's editors, designers, and marketers.

Outside of class, progress on book projects is carried forth by the AH Book Publishing Club, a co-curricular campus organization supported by Loyola University Maryland's Office of Student Activities.

Eclectic and provocative, Apprentice House titles intend to entertain as well as spark dialogue on a variety of topics. Financial contributions to sustain the press's work are welcomed. Contributions are tax deductible to the fullest extent allowed by the IRS.

To learn more about Apprentice House books or to obtain submission guidelines, please visit www.apprenticehouse.com.

Apprentice House
Communication Department
Loyola University Maryland
4501 N. Charles Street
Baltimore, MD 21210
Ph: 410-617-5265 • Fax: 410-617-2198
info@apprenticehouse.com
www.apprenticehouse.com